J. Margot Critch currently lives in St John's, Newfoundland, with her husband Brian and their two little buddies Simon and Chibs. She spends equal amounts of time writing, listening to Jimmy Buffett's music and looking out at the ocean—all the while trying to decide if she wants coffee or a margarita...

Award-winning author of sensual, emotional adventures of the heart, **Rebecca Hunter** writes sexy stories about alpha men and spirited women set in Australia for Mills & Boon Dare. She lives with her family in the San Francisco Bay Area.

If you liked *Taming Reid* and *Pure Temptation* why not try

Bad Boss by Jackie Ashenden
Driving Him Wild by Zara Cox

Also by J. Margot Critch

Sin City Brotherhood

Boardroom Sins
Sins of the Flesh
Sweet as Sin
Forbidden Sins
A Sinful Little Christmas

Also by Rebecca Hunter

Blackmore, Inc.

Best Laid Plans
Playing with Fire
Baring it All
Hotter on Ice

Discover more at millsandboon.co.uk

TAMING REID

J. MARGOT CRITCH

PURE TEMPTATION

REBECCA HUNTER

MILLS & BOON

First Published in Great Britain 2020
by Mills & Boon, an imprint of HarperCollins*Publishers*
1 London Bridge Street, London, SE1 9GF

ISBN: 978-0-263-27758-6

MIX
Paper from
responsible sources
FSC™ C007454

This book is produced from independently certified FSC™ paper
to ensure responsible forest management.
For more information visit www.harpercollins.co.uk/green.

Printed and bound in Spain
by CPI, Barcelona

TAMING REID

J. MARGOT CRITCH

MILLS & BOON

For my author besties, Janice and Candace.

Thank you for all your love, support, advice, plotting sessions and late-night conversations over wine.

You're the best!

CHAPTER ONE

REID REXFORD RAISED the glass to his lips and tasted the amber liquid it held. Up until that moment, the *tres leches* cake had been the best thing he'd tasted that night, but his cleaned plate lay forgotten on the table next to the unlabeled bottle of rum that Gemma had brought. They were preferred customers at the Cuban restaurant owned by his close friend, Arlo. And for a good deal on Rexford Rum for his restaurant, Arlo gave them a great table every time they came in and allowed them to do such things as open their own bottle of Gemma's newest concoction at their table.

Reid took another small sip, and this time held it in his mouth, rolling the rum around, savoring the intricacies and the layers of the flavor on his tongue. It was smooth, delicious. He tasted it again, as his brother Quin did the same, this time taking a moment to inhale over the rim of the glass, pulling the scent into his lungs—it was dark, sweet, but spicy, with notes of cardamom, cinnamon, and something else he couldn't yet place. It was absolutely exquisite. He winked at his sister. She had really outdone herself this time.

"Well?" Gemma asked, her eyes wide with anticipation for their opinions. "How does it taste?"

He shrugged casually. "It's pretty good," he said, putting the glass down. A clatter from the kitchen briefly muted their conversation.

Reid looked at Quin, who drank from his glass again and also put on a casual demeanor in an attempt to needle their younger sister.

Gemma's smile dropped. And Reid knew her well enough to tell that their nonchalance clearly annoyed her. "Come on, guys," she said. "This is one of the best batches I've ever made, and you both know it. What do you mean, it's just *good*?"

Reid laughed, and put a hand on her shoulder, shaking her lightly. He knew how important the quality of her rum—and his opinion of it—was to her as she'd meticulously worked on the recipe for months, perfecting the proper blend of spices, making sure it would be just right before it had even been mixed, distilled and barrel-aged. The bottle they were tasting was a product of her love and dedication that had been more than five years in the making. "We're messing with you, Gem. It's delicious! You're right—one of your best yet."

She smacked his shoulder, took the glass from his fingers and sipped it herself. His sister's satisfied smile spoke volumes to Reid. Gemma, a perfectionist, who was rarely fully satisfied with the finished product, was proud of her newest rum.

"How'd you make it?" Quin asked, pouring a little more from the bottle into his glass.

"The short answer is I cut the cane sugar with honey and then added more later in the process, and I used those cognac barrels I picked up in France last year. Plus a few more special touches here and there." She winked.

"Honey?" Reid started calculating cost per bottle formulas in his head as he swirled the glass in his hand, watching as the legs of the liquid—thick and rich—trailed down the sides. "Sounds expensive," he noted with a frown, recalling the recent high price of honey.

"Probably," she said, with a shrug. "But you're the numbers guy, I'm just the cook." She wasn't just the cook; she was their master distiller. She'd trained for years—since before she was even legally allowed to drink rum—to be as good as she was, and Reid was more than proud of her. It might have been his business savvy that had elevated Rexford Rum Distillery, and Quin's marketing expertise and networking that had had made the exclusive luxury brand popular and well-known, but it was Gemma's rum that had put them on the map, making them a premium spirit to be found in the collection of every rich and powerful man and woman in the country. "But, if it helps," she continued, "it's specialized enough, given the fact we only had six cognac barrels, that it's a very small batch. We can raise the price even more. Put it in a funky bottle, make it a luxury item. Drive up demand. You know our customers; they'll want it if they think the next guy can't get it. Quin will put the perfect spin on it in marketing, and we'll make oodles of money."

"Solid plan," Quin said, draining his own glass in celebration with a smile on his face.

Reid knew they were both correct. "All right, email me the ingredients and quantities you used, and I'll start crunching some numbers tomorrow."

"I'm taking tomorrow off, so I'll get it to you first thing on Monday morning." When he looked at her, she raised her hands. "Dude, I work enough hours during the week that I can take a Friday off every once in a while. You should do the same."

"Fine." He turned to Quin, always in business mode, even when they were supposed to be having a quiet, leisurely dinner together. "We'll get started on a marketing plan, and we can launch in the summer."

"On Monday," Quin clarified.

"So, you're all taking Friday off, then?"

"Yup. Thursday night is the new Friday night."

"Fine. On Monday," Reid agreed, knowing he wouldn't win the battle.

He turned back to Gemma, already formulating a game plan. "How will the batch have aged by summer?"

"It'll be perfect." She plucked her phone from her small purse and smiled when she looked at the screen. "I'll send you that list first thing in the morning, but for now, I'm out of here."

"You have plans?" Reid asked.

"Yeah, I have a date. Unlike you, I do have a life outside of rum, you know. I haven't given up on all of my wild ways," she said with a wink.

The allusion to their past lives made Reid cringe. In their younger years, the three of them had spent a lot of time at nightclubs, at parties, while their parents worked at making Rexford Rum, the business that had been in their family for generations, a well-known brand. But overnight, their lives had changed with the death of their mother, and their father had stepped back from business. It was then that Reid and his siblings had realized it was up to them to keep the business going if they wanted Rexford Rum to stay alive. He'd had the most complete turnaround, abandoning his raucous lifestyle, settling down, getting married—as well as that had worked out for him—while his brother and sister, as devoted to the business as they were, still managed to find lots of time to have some fun.

"And you know what, I'm wondering why you guys don't have anything lined up for yourselves tonight."

"Who says I don't?" Quin shrugged a shoulder. "The night is still pretty young for me, lots of time to round up some female company."

"You're such a romantic," Gemma said, rolling her eyes.

Reid felt his sister's gaze settle on him. "How about you, big brother? Any hot plans tonight?"

"Gemma—" He'd planned on crashing on the couch with a drink and watching the game, but the unlabeled bottle of rum on the table had changed that. The thought of heading down to the office and planning the new release and cost calculations had his fingers tapping on the table. When it came to passion, the distillery had replaced everything else in his life.

"I know, *you're busy*," she countered, using the words he'd said many times against her. She pursed her lips as she studied him and tilted her head to the side. "When was the last time you were on a date?"

When the urge struck him, which, honestly, wasn't often, Reid had no problem finding women, those who, like him, weren't interested in a drawn-out affair, but an actual *date*? Where he sat across from a woman, and they talked and got to know each other? He poured another finger of rum into the short glass and brought it to his lips. "You know when," he said, grimacing behind his glass, before he took a large swallow.

He could feel his sister's exasperation at him. "That was over two years ago," Gemma told him—like he didn't know—shaking her head. "Carolina did a number on you. But you can't be alone your entire life because of one mistake."

He looked at her. "That *one mistake* almost cost

us everything. I'm not going to let it happen again. So could you just get off my back already?"

"That doesn't mean you shouldn't see any women ever again," she told him. When he said nothing, she kept going. "Two years, Reid. What happened wasn't your fault. Since that whole thing with Carolina, we're all a lot more careful with our information. She's the one who got into our databases. She's the one who turned the information over to our competitors. You made a mistake in trusting the wrong person. We all did. It's time to move on."

"I'm not interested," he insisted. "I've got enough going on with the business. I've completely ruled out any type of relationship. Where would I find the time to devote to another person?"

Gemma's sigh was one of impatience. He knew because he often heard it in his direction when they argued about that very subject. "Fine," she said, standing. "I'm out of here. I'm busy, too, Reid, but I find a little time for a social life."

"Have a good night," Reid told her, dismissing her, not wanting to discuss his social life—or lack thereof—any further. "Be safe."

"You know I will."

"Don't forget, we have a party to prepare for next week," Reid told her. "There's still lots to do." Every year, they threw a party for their employees, industry insiders, and preferred customers. This year, however, they'd decided to go bigger. They'd spent the entire year planning a huge party at a hip beachside rooftop bar in South Beach. They'd shelled out huge cash for one of the country's most popular DJs, and in addition to their regular guest list, they invited celebrities and members of the press. More Quin and Gemma's doing, the party wasn't his kind of scene, but he was hoping to make some serious connections and it would help put Rexford Rum on the map.

"I haven't forgotten, *Dad*," she said, rolling her eyes, earning herself a glare from Reid. She raised her hands in surrender. "Believe me, no one is forgetting about work, or the party." She kissed him on the cheek. "Love you guys. Bye."

"Make good choices," Quin called out to her, and that earned him a middle finger over her shoulder as she made her way outside. When she was gone, Quin pointed a finger at him. "Speaking of the party, we've been meaning to talk to you about this—at least try to look like you're having fun. You don't want to be mistaken for one of the bouncers with that serious look you normally have on your face."

"Fine, I'll smile more. Will that make you happy? But sorry, I won't have time to schmooze with celebrities. Some of us will have to make sure things are running smoothly."

"That's why we hired a very capable event planning company," he told him. "Who we're paying very well to make sure everything is okay. I know it isn't normally your scene but promise me you'll have fun. It's going to be great for us."

"Fine, I'll have fun at the party. I just hope the cost will be worth it to the business."

Quin sighed and poured himself some more rum. "It will be. We went through the projections ourselves. With the press coverage and the online buzz we've already created…dude, it's going to be amazing."

Despite his reservations, Reid smiled at his brother. He'd been a hard sell when it came to the party. He thought the it was an egregious expense, one that could put the distillery at risk—not only financially, but its failure could hurt their brand. They had some of the best event planners in Miami working on it, but he wasn't sure he could put the faith in it like Quin and Gemma did. "I hope so. I hate to think we bankrupted the company for an excuse to invite a certain professional wrestler-turned-actor to our party."

"Already RSVP'd," Quin said with a wink, reminding Reid that despite his opinion of the event, the Rexford party was looking like the hottest ticket in Miami. He knocked back the remainder of the rum. "And on that note, I'm out of here, too."

"Yeah?"

"A friend of mine has Heat tickets. Courtside."

Reid nodded in approval. "Nice. Close enough you can yell at the coach again?"

"If only he'd listen to me." Quin shook his head.

"Have fun. Don't get arrested. We have too much to do in the next couple of days and I don't have time to bail you out."

"You can count on me, bro." They bumped fists, and then Quin was gone as well, leaving Reid alone at the table with a mostly full rum bottle and the bill. "Typical," he said to the closed folio, which held the bill. But it didn't matter to him. What good was money if he couldn't use it to treat his siblings at their favorite restaurant?

He nodded to the server, who quickly came over to collect his credit card, and she smiled as she leaned over the table, giving him a peek at her ample cleavage. They made eye contact, and she said, "Thank you, Mr. Rexford," in a sultry, breathy whisper. He sat back, away from her—his body language putting a barrier between them. She picked up on his cues and straightened, immediately reverting back to being his waitress. He handed her the rum bottle. "Can you see that Arlo gets the rest of this?"

"Of course, I'll put it in his office."

"Thank you."

He watched closely as she walked away. While the waitress was gorgeous, and they would definitely have a great night together, it wouldn't do. She was his regular server at his favorite restaurant, and even though Reid could barely remember her name, she was much too close to him, and knew exactly who he was. But as his eyes followed the sway of the server's hips, his attention caught on the cloud of red hair of the woman sitting at the bar.

The curve of the woman's spine and her smooth skin tempted him, as did the completely open back of her black dress, cut just above what looked to be an ample ass. The woman laughed at something the bartender said. Her laugh was loud and vivacious, and rang out in the quiet, dark space of the restaurant. But neither her volume nor the looks it garnered from the other patrons seemed to embarrass her. He could feel the energy emanating off her, bouncing against the cellar walls, hitting him square in the chest. It sounded stupid, corny, but the small restaurant felt brighter with her in it.

He couldn't help but watch her as she brought her glass to her lips and sipped. Her eyes closed, and her full lips turned upward in a delicate smile and she said something else to the bartender. She was easily the sexiest woman in the room.

He smiled and stood. Checked his watch. He could go talk to her and still get home early enough to put together a plan for the newest rum. Maybe the night wouldn't be such a bust, after all.

Lila Campbell really liked the small, underground cellar vibe of the restaurant. She'd gotten word that the Cuban restaurant was one of Miami's best-kept secrets, and the somewhat hard-to-find restaurant hadn't disappointed. Her dinner had been delicious, and the follow-up cocktail was divine. She was now working on a dessert of in-house-made vanilla bean ice cream drizzled with a thick spiced rum sauce that was so decadent, she'd have to spend extra time at the gym working it off.

Holding her phone above her, she took a picture of herself bringing a spoonful to her mouth. She checked it—*definitely cute*—and it was good to post. Some people hated selfies, thought they were shallow, but Lila didn't care. She thought back to when she was younger. Maybe she would have been one of those women who judged others like that, but she knew it would have been her own insecurities at play. Taking a picture that she felt was good enough to post was hard for her, but it was getting easier. Sure, she still saw the nasty comments some trolls left on her posts, but she just had to shrug and move on.

"I gotta ask you." The pretty bartender, Amanda, leaned closer. "Are you that girl from Instagram?"

"Which one?" she asked. "There are a few girls on Instagram."

"Lila, is it?"

"Well, my name is Lila."

"I knew it." Amanda nodded at her drink. "That one's on the house. Yours is one of my favorite accounts."

"I'm glad to hear it. Come here," she crooked her finger at her, and when she leaned in, Lila snapped a picture of both of them. "I'll post that one later. Thanks for everything."

Arlo's would get a stellar review on her blog, and she knew that her word would ensure they had month-long waiting lists for at least a year. It had happened before, and she took a moment to revel in the online power she had. The staff was friendly, and the drinks and food were delicious. As she sipped her rum and Coke, she again hummed appreciatively at the flavor of—she checked the label on the bottle behind the bar—Rexford Rum, which was not cheap, but a local favorite, the bartender had told her.

Tilting her head to the side, she thought something about the name was familiar. And then she remembered. She'd managed to secure an invitation to their upcoming party next Saturday when their marketing manager had reached out to her about attending in exchange for a few posts. The buzz was that it would be attended by athletes and celebrities. The address she'd been given was for the rooftop of a swanky beachside hotel, and it promised to be a good time. She was looking forward to the party but being seen there would also boost her own reputation. Which would help her gain more negotiating clout for when she met with the GO! Channel.

She'd been in talks with the network for months, to take her well-known online persona and translate it to television. She could imagine it now, traveling around the world, the steady paycheck that would give her more stability, and let her put down some roots in Los Angeles. She never thought she wanted to settle in one place, but as she got older, she saw the value in having a home to call her own.

As she brought her spoon to her lips again, she froze, feeling someone come up behind her. Lila straightened her spine, turning on her best thousand-yard stare, which she used whenever men approached her when she traveled alone. She was ready for every cheesy pickup line. She'd heard them all. With her cocktail in hand, Lila turned, took a sip, hoping to look cool and indifferent, but instead her eyes roamed up the man's body to his face, and she gulped down her drink in one mouthful. He put his hand on the back of the empty stool beside her. She watched, transfixed by his long, strong fingers as they flexed on the wooden frame of the back. "Is anybody sitting here?"

She shook her head, unable to speak. It had been a long, *long* time since a man's looks—his presence—had left her so completely dumbfounded.

"Good," he said with a smile.

"Your usual, sir?" the bartender asked him.

"Please," he answered, without taking his dark brown eyes from her. "And get another one for the lady."

Usually, the presumption of a man buying her a drink would have driven Lila insane. She hated overbearing men, and normally, she would have asked him to leave, but there was something about the man next to her that intrigued her. Whether it was his extreme confidence, his impeccable looks, or the scent of his cologne, she was rooted in place. And it had been so, so long since she'd been in the company of a gorgeous man. Amanda looked at her in confirmation and she nodded, willing to get to know the stranger.

He took the seat next to her, and in a short time,

the bartender put a tumbler with a couple of fingers of dark liquor next to her new drink.

He picked up his glass with long, confident fingers and used it to gesture to her own glass. "What did I just order for you?"

"Cuba Libre."

He drank from his glass and nodded. "Good drink."

"Yeah," she agreed. "I'm told it's Rexford Rum, based here in Miami. I have to say, it's pretty good."

"Just pretty good?" He smiled. "I've heard it's the best."

"Well, I don't know about that," she teased, sipping from her glass, not taking her eyes from his as he did the same. She felt a spark that sizzled between them and stuck out her hand. "Hi, I'm Lila."

"Lila," he repeated, letting the last syllable roll off his tongue. She wanted to keep hearing him say her name. "That's a pretty name."

"Thanks, I've had it all my life." He smiled at her joke, and drank from his glass, but said nothing. "Do you have a name there, hun?"

He seemed to hesitate, but then change his mind. "Reid."

"What can I do for you, Reid?"

"I was just at my table, but then I saw you sitting here. And I'm curious why a gorgeous woman like yourself is sitting here all by herself," he told her.

She bristled at his comment. "What's wrong with me sitting alone? We're well into the twenty-first century." Reid opened his mouth to speak, but Lila didn't give him a chance. "Maybe I just like my own company. Maybe I *choose* to be here alone. Isn't that a good enough reason?"

He blinked quickly, probably not used to having women speak to him like that. "Do you want me to leave? If you're enjoying your own company, I don't want to intrude."

Lila thought of telling him to leave, thought of leaving herself. Lila didn't normally like to invite male attention, especially when she was on assignment, because it was hard enough for women traveling alone, without bringing men into the mix. But there was something about Reid—and she couldn't back away. "No," she said, putting her fingers on his wrist. "You can stay."

"Good."

She wasn't sure why she'd touched him, but it had proven to be a mistake, as Reid took her hand in his, turned it over, and brought it to his mouth. He placed his lips to the inside of her wrist. His warm, dry lips on her almost caused her to stop breathing. Who was this man—this stranger she'd found in a small South Beach restaurant—lighting a trail of desire from her pulse point all the way to her own South Beach?

It was stupid, risky. This guy was a complete stranger. He could be anyone. But when the tip of his tongue flicked against her skin, she realized that it didn't matter who he was.

Reid's lips closed over her skin again and his dark

eyes connected with hers. Lila was transfixed by him, as the rest of the small restaurant fell away. Just the two of them existed in that moment—and she didn't even know his last name. Maybe privacy and anonymity were for the better. She had built up her blog and her reputation to where they were, and she knew that one public misstep could ruin her, especially with everything she had coming up. She had to be on her best behavior. Any rumor or scandal could end her. But none of that seemed to matter when Reid looked at her.

But thankfully, her sanity won out. "Wait," she said, her words more sighed than spoken.

He backed away immediately, releasing her from his touch. "What is it?"

She took a deep breath and gulped down the rest of her drink. "I don't even know who you are. Who are you? What's your last name?" He didn't say anything. "No last name, Reid? Or do you just go by your first—like Sting or Bono?"

"Oh, I have a last name—I'm just not keen on sharing it."

Lila shook her head, and then laughed at the seriousness of his voice. The fact that the man wouldn't give her his last name was a real red flag for her. "You sound so fucking dramatic. What, are you in the mob or witness protection, or a serial killer, or something?"

"That did sound dramatic, didn't it?" he asked with a lopsided smile. She nodded. "I'm just a private person. I promise, I'm not in the mob or witness protection, or a serial killer."

"You know, if you were any of those things, wouldn't you insist that you weren't?"

"That's a good point. I guess you'll have to trust me." He looked around and waved to the bartender. "Amanda, can you come here for a second?"

She stopped wiping down the counter and joined them.

"Amanda, you can vouch for me, right? I'm a good guy?"

The bartender smiled. "He's a preferred regular customer, close friends with the boss, and a good tipper."

"Thanks Amanda."

"No problem, Mr. Rexford," she said and went back to her task behind the bar."

Lila and Reid both shared a laugh at his name having been revealed. "So, I guess you have a name, after all."

"I guess I do."

"I always consider service staff to be the best judges of character." She leaned in closer to him. "And I have to say hearing a guy is a good tipper is a major turn-on for me."

"That's the first time a woman has ever told me that."

"You should date more socially conscious women, I guess."

"Yeah, I guess so," he said with a smile.

Amanda came back and nodded at their now-empty glasses. "Another round?"

Reid looked at her. She wasn't sure what to say. Another round would keep them talking at the bar. But refusing another drink would free up the rest of their evening, whatever they hoped to do with it. Reid took her hand again. "Tell me, beautiful, do you want another drink?" he asked, his thumb tracing light but red-hot circles over the inside of her wrist. There was no way he could miss her thundering pulse beneath her skin. "What do you want?"

Lila tried to find her voice, but it was nearly impossible. *What do I want?* "I want you to keep touching me."

"Do you want to get out of here?"

Lila's mind raced through the lusty fog he'd created in her brain. She felt a connection with the man sitting next to her, but she wasn't sure if she was ready to go somewhere with a complete stranger—no matter how good of a time she knew they would have together. Never in her life had she had a one-night stand with a strange man. She may have possessed a sense of adventure, but she wasn't reckless. With as much as she traveled, Lila knew the world could be a dangerous place. As a woman, and a solo traveler, she had to look after herself—another reason she was glad to have the legitimacy of a potential network deal ahead of her. But as the stranger's deep brown eyes bored into hers, she could barely think straight. The promise that was held in the strange man's touch, his rich scent and his deep voice, were almost too much to bear. "What do you have in mind?"

Amanda backed away discreetly, giving them some much-needed privacy.

Reid leaned in next to her, pushed her hair away from her ear and got closer so that his lips brushed the outer shell of her ear. She shivered at the contact. "I'm not going to pretend here. You're gorgeous, and I'm interested," he whispered. "We have a connection, and I want you underneath me, on top of me, bent over a table. I know we could have fun together, at least for one night. So, yeah, we could put off the inevitable for a couple of hours, get another drink or two, talk, get to know each other, but I don't see why we should."

"Especially since we already know enough about each other?" She teased, trying to lighten the mood. Part of her—the reasonable part—wanted to say no to him. Every ounce of self-preservation begged her to refuse him. But instead, she put her hand on his rock-hard thigh.

He put his hand over hers and it was then she saw the way his pants were tented, showing her that he did indeed want her as much as she wanted him.

"I think we know enough about each other," he told her. "Don't you?"

She nodded. This was it. She was going to do something she had never done before—a one-night stand with a strange man. "My hotel is near here."

Reid signaled Amanda, and before she could stop

him, he'd taken out his wallet and laid down several bills to pay for her meal and drinks. More than enough to cover the total and still have enough left over for a sizable tip—just as she'd expected. Soon they were out the door, and in the alley where the restaurant entrance was located.

They walked up the street and she inhaled. There was normally something so sweet and sensual about the smell of Miami—the scent of midnight jasmine, the sand, the sea, the smell of the food and coffee. Glamorous people wearing expensive perfume and cologne. Even at night, this close to the beach, she could almost smell the suntan lotion, coconut and shea, and the fruit-flavored cocktails. Citrus. Rum. Reid. It might have all been in her head, but walking next to Reid, his hand at her lower back, his fingertips curling over the skin exposed by the risqué cut of her backless dress, she knew she wasn't imagining it—there was something else in the air. The night, the city itself, breathed sex. It filled the air and covered them like a blanket.

She looked up at Reid. He hadn't said a word since leaving the restaurant.

"Where are you staying?" he asked.

When the small white stone boutique hotel came into view, she said a quick prayer to the nookie gods, thanking them for the short walk. "Right here," she told him.

"Thank God," Reid murmured in a little prayer of his own. It shocked her when his arm snaked around hers and he whipped her around and pushed her against the outer wall of the building. His head lowered, and before she could catch her breath, his lips crashed onto hers. Reid's kiss was hard, demanding, and it was exactly what she wanted. Correction: what she needed. Her lips parted and he took full advantage, his tongue was warm, wet and searching, stroking against her own.

Her arms encircled Reid's neck and she pulled him closer. He moaned and pressed her into the exterior wall of the hotel. One of his thighs found its way between her legs, and he pressed it against her already wet panties. His touch was almost enough to make her fall to the sidewalk, but thankfully, he was the one holding her up.

With a groan, he pulled away from her, his eyes smoldered. "I'd better get you inside, before I fuck you right here." He took her hand, and all but dragged her through the hotel lobby to the elevator. When the doors closed on them, he pulled her to him. Kissing her again. The man had a devilish mouth. And she had no choice but to submit to his sinful lips. He smoothed his hands down her arms, and found her breasts, squeezing them. She thrust her chest toward him, leaning into his touch, willing Reid's fingers to go further. His fingertips curled underneath the thin material of the low neckline of her dress. She wanted Reid to never stop touching her. But the elevator came to a halt, and she barely noticed when the doors slid open in front of them.

"Lead the way." His whisper was gruff in her ear, and she pulled him down the hall. At her door, her hands trembled so that she could barely use her key card. He chuckled, took the card from her fingers, and slid it easily into the door. It was slightly embarrassing that she was far more aroused than he was. Men rarely affected her in such a way. But there was something about Reid. He made her brain so foggy with need that she couldn't think straight.

They walked into her room. But instead of stripping the clothes from her body like she wanted Reid to, he took a step back, deliberately putting several feet between them. "Do you want this?"

"I wouldn't have brought you here if I didn't."

He took a step forward. Closer, but still out of her reach. "Lila, I want to hear you say the words. That you want this."

Lila looked over the man in front of her. She didn't have to look at the large bulge of his cock to see how much he wanted her. His strong body was rigid, tense. His shoulders heaved with heavy, desperate breaths. His whole body demonstrated his desire. But he still stood before her, seeking explicit consent from her, and she smiled, charmed by it.

It was her call. Despite his powerful presence, and the effect he had on her, she was in complete control. Lila took a step toward him, bringing her breasts flush with his broad chest. She wasn't wearing a bra—as if the low cut of the back of her dress would have allowed it—and her sensitized nipples sent shocks of electricity throughout her body, as they brushed against his chest. He reached down and grazed her fingertips along the ridge of the bulge. He shuddered underneath her touch, and she grinned.

Lifting up on her toes, she leaned over and brought her lips to the edge of his ear. She snaked her tongue out and traced the outside. “Reid, I want you. And I want this.” She paused. “I want you to fuck me.”

He let go of the breath he was holding. He put his fingers on her jaw and drew her face upward to his. The hunger in his eyes was unmistakable. “This can only be one night. You know that, right?”

“Sounds good to me.” She was in Miami for a little over a week, and she already had a full itinerary. Where would she fit in more time with Reid, even if she wanted to? And plus, if she already felt like falling completely apart at his touch after only a few minutes, how would she survive another encounter? “I know. That’s what’s best for both of us. I don’t expect anything else from you, as long as you do the same.”

His smile was easy and charming. And she was struck again with how attractive he was. The chiseled jaw, high cheek bones, straight nose and dark brown eyes all joined forces to create one irresistible man. And while she knew nothing about him except his name, he was everything she would have asked for in a one-night stand. “It’s a deal,” he said, putting out his hand.

Lila let out a laugh that was more like a breath

at his formal gesture, and she took his hand in hers. When their palms clasped together, Lila felt as if they shared one pulse as electricity traveled between them, strong enough to power the entire city.

In the quiet room, they looked at each other, neither's eyes wavering. But Reid's friendly smile then turned wolfish, as if he knew that she was his, and he would spend his night feasting on her.

Without releasing her, he pulled on her hand, causing her to crash against his firm chest.

"Now, where were we?" he murmured.

"I think, outside the hotel, you promised to fuck me," she reminded him.

"Oh yeah, that's right," he said, his fingers curling over her waist and venturing lower. He kissed her, and just the feeling of his lips against her made her moan.

Already she was growing accustomed to Reid's touch, and she knew that until her dying day, she would crave his fingers and lips. Through the anticipation that clouded her brain as his hands roamed underneath her dress, she reminded herself of their agreement.

Just for one night.

CHAPTER TWO

REID DROPPED TO his knees in front of Lila, and with his hands on her round, lush ass, he pressed his face to the lower part of her abdomen and inhaled her scent, opening his mouth against her, and the silky material of her dress, pulling her essence more deeply into his lungs. He wasn't sure what had possessed him to go home with her. He didn't even know why he approached her or why he came on so strong. It wasn't like him; he normally didn't lose control over women. But despite himself, something about Lila had drawn him in. She was vivacious, gorgeous, and when he kissed her—tasting his own rum on her tongue—it did something to him. He didn't have a chance when it came to her. He was a goner.

He should be at home, or at the office, making sure the last-minute things for the party were finalized and that no crises were about to occur, but that didn't seem to matter to him when he was about to bury himself fully within a woman he needed more than he did his next breath. He looked up at her and saw she was watching him, her green eyes not leaving his, her chest heaving. "What are you waiting for?" she breathed, pushing her fingers through his hair.

"Just taking a moment to enjoy it," he told her.

"There will be lots of moments to enjoy tonight, won't there?"

"You know there will."

"Well, get to it then," she told him.

"Yes, ma'am." He smoothed his hands up her thighs, underneath her dress, his palms gliding over some of the smoothest, silkiest skin he'd ever touched. His journey paused when his reached the lace edge of her panties. Stopping just short of ripping the delicate undergarment in two pieces, he instead hooked his fingers underneath the fabric and pulled the peach lace down her thighs, dropping it to the floor. She stepped out of her panties gingerly and he pushed up her dress so that the tight skirt sat above her hips, exposing her center to him fully.

Lila was delectable, a masterpiece, a treat to be admired and enjoyed by every sense. His mouth watered with a hunger for her, his appetite voracious like he'd never experienced before, and he needed to taste her.

He slid his hand down the entire length of her leg, exploring, lightly tickling the back of her knee, squeezing her well-formed calf, wrapping his fingers around her ankle and draping her leg over his shoulder. He leaned forward, burying his face between her creamy thighs. He gripped her ass, bringing her closer to him. His fingers dug into the firm flesh of her behind, as his tongue spread her lips and he flicked the sweet little bud of her clit with the tip. She moaned, arching into his mouth, and twisted her fingers in his hair, and pulled. Hard. But with Lila surrounding him, unable to hear or feel anything but her, the pain barely registered.

Lila was so responsive, so delicious, and with every stroke of his tongue, pinch of his lips, every slide of his fingers, her moans grew louder, and he could feel the tension build in her body. Her thigh muscles clenched against the side of his head, muffling her cries. She was perfect and he could listen to her desperate sounds forever. His own body ached with the need to be inside her. But he stayed his course. Even though his dick threatened to burst through the material of his pants, he wouldn't stop until he made her come first.

When he hit the right spot, the tremor of her body became a full-fledged earthquake that made her shake. With his lips surrounding her clit, he sucked, prodded with his tongue, bringing her down from her climax, and riding out every aftershock of pleasure with her.

When her grip on his head loosened, Reid stood while unbuckling his pants. But her own fingers joined his, and she beat him in withdrawing his dick. She stroked his length. But he was so goddamn close to erupting that even though he hated to, he had to push her away.

He was so far gone that he almost forgot his golden rule. “Condoms?” he asked her, his tongue thick with passion. Of course, he didn’t carry one with him. He wasn’t his brother. He couldn’t remember the last time he’d had the need, as he wasn’t usually one for spontaneous encounters.

“Right.” On wobbly legs she walked over to the bed and dug into the cosmetic case that sat at the foot. She pulled out a small foil square and he nearly shuddered with relief.

He crossed the room in a matter of seconds and instead of laying her on the bed, he picked her up and sat her on the small desk next to her laptop. He stood between her parted thighs as she ripped open the packet and rolled the condom over him. Her touch was torture, but he would soon find his sweet relief. He didn’t even have time for either of them to undress. He needed to be buried deep inside her. He lifted Lila, tilting her hips to the right angle. When she wrapped her legs around his ass, he held her against the wall as he entered her.

She was hot, wet. *Heaven.* And as he pumped his hips, thrusting into her, he brought both of them higher and higher. If he thought eating from her was amazing, being buried deep inside of her sweet heat was pure bliss.

Lila, her arms wrapped tightly around his shoulders, sought out his mouth with her own. He kissed her lips, and the flavor of her that coated his tongue mingled with the taste of her mouth. He swallowed the moan that came from her throat as it met his own.

Sliding against her slickness, Reid knew he wouldn't last much longer. He broke away from her mouth, and trailed his lips in a line across her jaw and down her throat. And judging by her moans and sighs in his ear, he knew she wouldn't either. Reid gritted his teeth and vowed to hang on until she came again. Her body tightened against him, and her breaths became pants. He increased the speed of his thrusts, and she clenched around him. That was all he needed. He let go, his toes curled in his shoes, and he came with a groan and buried his face in the crook of her neck. The comedown was blissful, and as his balls emptied, she milked him of everything he had.

Taking a breath, he released her, helping her get her footing on the floor. As she straightened her dress, Reid pulled off the condom and tossed it in a nearby trash can. He caught his breath as she reached into the small fridge in the bar area, pulling out two bottles of water. He finally looked around and saw that they were in a huge, luxuriously appointed hotel room. Large windows with panoramic views of the famed South Beach and Atlantic Ocean.

"Sparkling or still?" she asked, holding the two bottles aloft.

"Still's good." He took the bottle from her. "Nice room."

"Yeah." She took a swallow of the water. The red flush still colored her cheeks. "I travel a lot for work. I normally stay at more modest places, but what the hell? I'm in Miami. I got a great deal. I might as well treat myself, right?"

He didn't know a lot about treating himself lately, but he nodded. "What do you do?"

Her lips pursed. "I thought we weren't exchanging information?"

"You're right," he said, taking another drink. He needed to hydrate but with every swallow, her taste vanished from his mouth, and he craved it, wanting nothing more than to get it back. Asking her the question had been a mistake, since they'd agreed on anonymity. If he asked her about who she was, then it would lead to her asking about him. No matter what, his privacy was the most important thing to him, and he was committed to not putting himself out there ever again.

"You know, I don't ever do this," she said, her back to him, as she used her fingers to brush through her red hair, checking out her reflection in the mirror. He could see the small red marks he'd made on her neck, and the rash from his five o'clock shadow marred her creamy skin.

He caught her eyes in her reflection in the mirror as he straightened his own clothing. The finality of them straightening up disappointed him. Despite their agreement for it to be one night only, he wanted more time with her. "Do what?" he asked.

"Meet strangers, immediately have sex with them."

Reid shrugged. "You don't have to explain yourself. I don't care what you do—or have done—with anyone else." He went to her, cupped her jaw and trailed his fingers down her delicate throat, soothing the redness he'd caused. "The only thing that matters is that we're here together. And I've got you tonight."

Lila was quiet. She stood back from him, pulling her jaw away from his fingers. "Well, Reid. This has been a lot of fun. Thanks."

He frowned. "Are you kicking me out?"

"No, but you said it would just be once."

"I didn't say that."

"But you said—"

"I said it was one *night*." He looked casually at his watch. It was only nine thirty, and he made a dramatic show of removing his watch from his wrist, laying it on the nearby nightstand. "The night isn't over yet."

CHAPTER THREE

THE SUN WAS higher in the sky than usual when Reid woke the next morning. He sat on the edge of his bed and wiped his palm over his face. He was exhausted, worn, and could barely find the energy to stand. *That's what you get for not staying on schedule.* He was thirty-five years old. Too old to be out so late with strange women. As tired as he was, he couldn't regret spending the night with Lila, no matter how out of character it was for him.

Eventually he mustered the strength to stand and pulled on a pair of gray sweatpants. After only managing to get a couple hours of sleep, he was tired, irritable, and even though he'd been with Lila until the early morning hours, he was nowhere near physically sated. He wanted her again. Lila's image took up real estate front and center of his mind, and he didn't know if he'd ever be able to forget her. Every time he closed his eyes, she was there. He could hear her voice, smell her on his skin, taste her on his lips, and when his head finally hit his pillow a few hours ago, he realized just how empty his California king bed was. Jesus, he was in trouble. His determination to stick to his plan of having just a one-night stand was wavering. No matter how much he tried to forget her, Lila had completely consumed him. And the next morning, she still did.

In his bathroom, he propped himself up by placing his hands on the bathroom counter, and in the mirror, he caught sight of the day-old stubble that colored his jaw and the dark, tired circles under his red-rimmed eyes. Thank God his siblings had decided to take the day off. Now he could just hide out in his office. And no one would see him in his current condition, and know he'd been up for most of the night.

The need for coffee was strong. So strong that when he inhaled, he could already smell the aroma of it already brewing in the kitchen. He sighed. One—or both—of his siblings had apparently let themselves into his house and made coffee. Even though they had their own homes, both Quin and Gemma had keys to his and often let themselves in. But because he normally woke up before either of them, it was the first time he hadn't already been dressed and ready for their visit. He would undoubtedly face some sort of inquisition this morning about why he wasn't yet awake.

He straightened and groaned with the movement. He was in shape, but his body was sore from the previous night's exertion. His night with Lila had left him seriously discombobulated and had already completely thrown off his morning routine. He had to get back to what he knew—his office, work, his family. He started to mentally tick through his to-do list for the day, and he blanked, not able to remember a fucking thing. He wondered how he could possibly have clarity when all he could think about was the red-haired woman with whom he'd spent the night.

Still wearing only his sweatpants, Reid walked into the large kitchen of his house, and as always, it was made bright and warm by the morning sun through the windows and glass door. He squinted against the harsh light and saw Gemma and Quin getting breakfast ready. Both sets of eyes looked at him, and it was as if they'd known what he'd done the night before.

"Well, if it isn't Sleeping Beauty," Gemma said over her shoulder, standing at the stove over a pan of sizzling bacon. Quin was sitting at the table, drinking coffee, scrolling through the tablet in his hand.

Reid grunted in response and made a beeline for the coffee maker. He poured himself a mug and looked in the frying pans on the stove, which his sister would no doubt leave dirty in the sink for him to take care of. Egg white omelet, bacon and sliced fruit, most likely from the trees in Gemma's garden. Snagging a strawberry from the cutting board, he ignored their curious stares.

"How was your date?" Reid asked his sister, sitting on a barstool at the kitchen island and hoping to take their attention off him and his rumpled state.

"Not bad. He was nice, but boring. Cute, but no real connection there, you know?" She shrugged, not too broken up about it.

"Sorry, Gem."

"It's fine. I'm still young and pretty." She plated bacon and eggs, and brought them over to the table, putting one in front of him. She looked over his rumpled, tired appearance. "Which is more than I can say for you. Here's the real question, though. What did you get up to last night?"

"Nothing. I stayed at the restaurant for another drink and then I left." He averted his eyes, pretending to be interested in the swaying palm trees that surrounded the pool and Jacuzzi that made his backyard a personal tropical oasis.

"Does it feel like Reid isn't telling us something?" Quin asked Gemma, dragging Reid's attention back to his siblings.

"Yeah, I think so. You slept in, too."

He put up his hands. "So, I slept late. A guy can't sleep in?" He briefly considered taking their keys back. He couldn't put up with his siblings before his coffee had a chance to work.

"He can, but it isn't common. Especially on a workday. What time did you get home last night?"

Reid sipped his coffee. He wasn't about to reveal to his brother and sister that it had been sometime after four a.m. before he'd left Lila, retrieved his car and made it home. "Not too late. I'm a grown man—older than both of you. Why do I have to answer for myself?"

"Defensive," Quin noted.

"You look like hell," she pointed out. "Did you get any sleep?"

"What are you guys doing here, anyway?" he asked.

"Way to thank me for making you a delicious breakfast." She took a bite of her bacon.

"Sorry. It's just that you both said you were taking today off."

"We talked about that. And believe it or not, we felt bad about it. You must be rubbing off on us."

"And we thought we'd make breakfast, and all go in together. Just like old times," Quin told him.

"So far, *I'm* making breakfast and Quin is reading the sports scores," Gemma added.

"And I'm keeping up-to-date on current events."

"Plus, you were right. With the party coming up, and launching the new rum, it's not a great time to be taking days off." "Yeah, sounds good. Just let me shower and we can all ride in together." As he ate and drank his coffee, Reid began to feel more awake. Thinking about the distillery helped him focus his mind. "Don't forget to send me the recipe listing for the honey batches."

"That was the plan."

"You know I don't mind you guys coming over, but you could think about calling first."

"Why? In case you have a woman here?" Quin scoffed. "Like you'd let anyone near your house."

Reid considered flipping off his younger brother, but Quin was right. That was exactly why he met women at their homes…or hotels. Again, the image of Lila was enough to make his temperature spike.

"I tried calling you before we came over," Gemma told him. "Twice. It went right to voice mail."

Behind his coffee mug, Reid frowned, trying to remember when he'd last seen his phone. He'd been in Lila's bed, his face again buried between the creamy smooth skin of her thighs when it had rung—it had been a European distributor who had no concept of time zones. For the first time since taking the reins at the distillery, he'd ignored his phone, but when it rang again, he'd disengaged from Lila, frustrated, he plucked the device from his pants, turned it off and put it on her hotel nightstand.

Where it probably still sat. "Shit," he muttered.

"What's wrong?" Quin asked.

He shook his head. "Nothing, my phone must have died. I guess I forgot to charge it." He had to figure out some way to get in touch with Lila to retrieve his phone. The only way he could think was to go back to her hotel room and hope she was still there. He looked up from his plate and realized that his brother and sister were watching him. "What?" he asked.

"Everything okay?" Gemma asked.

"I'm fine. I'm just tired. I didn't get a lot of sleep."

"Maybe that'll teach you to stop screwing around and focus on your job," Quin joked as he raised his coffee mug to his lips. Gemma snorted into her own coffee. Both of them knew that Reid was the most serious of the three of them. It wasn't often he was the one to miss work or be anything other than in complete control.

Reid gave in to his earlier impulse and flipped his brother off and finished up his breakfast. He tried to put his missing phone out of his mind and appear to be invested in the conversation. "All right, I'm focused. You guys want to talk work, let's do it. Are all of the press invites ready for the party next week?"

"The press invites and more," Quin said. "All the usual suspects." He rattled off some local and national news sources. "Everyone wants an invite to a liquor launch party. I've also extended some invites to bloggers and online influencers, some local, some further out."

Reid rolled his eyes. Everyone was a celebrity in today's shallow influencer culture. And that was not the sort of image that he wanted to portray with Rexford Rum. "Why?"

"Because everyone uses the internet, grandpa. If influencers are talking about us, it'll only increase sales and open us up to new markets."

He couldn't argue with that. But he wasn't sure if it was the right way to go about it. Reid had had this argument with Quin before. His younger brother wanted to make Rexford mainstream and more accessible, while Reid wanted to focus on boosting its luxury brand status. "We discussed keeping Rexford a luxury brand. Not a party one." Reid recalled their wilder days, and he wasn't interested in revisiting them, or being known as the brand chosen by those young adults who partied hard on spring break.

Quin shrugged. "Can't it be both? You don't know the disposable income or the follower counts that some of these young people have, and if they're on Instagram sipping our rum, we could go global. That's what we want, isn't it?"

Reid knew he wasn't going to win the argument, and he knew it wouldn't be the end of the discussion. But shirtless in his kitchen, with Lila's scent clinging to his skin, he wasn't about to try. "Fine. We'll discuss it later. I'm going to go shower."

"So, we're all driving in together?" Gemma asked, clearing the plates from the table.

"No," Reid said too quickly, earning him strange looks from his siblings. He'd left his cell phone with a complete stranger. That meant if Lila had the know-how, she could break into his phone and be privy to all sorts of information about him and the company. He had to catch up with her before that could happen. But that would mean seeing her again, and he now knew he couldn't trust himself around the woman, as his body heated in response to the idea of seeing her.

Even as his heart thundered in his chest, and his

blood rushed south, he had to hurry. "I changed my mind. I'll take my own car. I've got something to do before I head in. I'll see you at the distillery."

Lila turned off the water and walked out of the glass shower stall, drying herself with the fluffy white hotel towel. She towel-dried her hair and glanced at her reflection in the mirror, noting her clear skin, her bright eyes and the indulgent smile that perched on her lips. A night of spectacular sex could certainly do that to a girl.

Brushing her teeth, she thought about her night with Reid. It had been incredible. She never hooked up with men when she was working. But she was glad she'd made an exception for Reid. Shivering with the memories of how he'd kissed and touched her, she pulled on the hotel bathrobe and let the thick terry cloth cover her body before she walked out into her luxury suite. It was time to get to work and write her review for the restaurant she'd visited the night before. Where she'd met Reid. She hadn't gotten a chance to make any notes after eating and would have to write her review from memory. But when she racked her brain, trying to remember anything about her dinner and drinks, or the atmosphere of the restaurant, all she could remember was Reid.

She sat in front of her laptop for a while, the blank page of her Word document waiting for her to begin. Lila sighed. She lacked inspiration. The blog post she'd agreed to write eluded her, but she was certain she could write a thirty-thousand-word thesis on the way Reid had made her feel the night before.

Bored and suddenly lacking motivation, she pulled up her blog and looked through her old posts. Parties, adventures and cultural events filled her archives. From Oktoberfest, to Coachella, to Carnival, to that unfortunate day she'd spent on Grand Exuma for the Fyre Festival, she had attended some of the best parties and most amazing events and festivals on the planet. She looked around her hotel room and sighed again. On paper, her life was incredible, full of fun. She was lucky to live the life she did. But as she looked around her room, Lila couldn't help but note the sameness. She may have treated herself to a beachfront luxury hotel in Miami, but when you looked closely, every hotel was the same. The same beds, the same mass-produced art, the same TVs, the same desks, the same citrus-scented shampoo in the bathroom.

That was why she needed to secure that deal with the GO! Channel, one of the world's most prominent travel networks. For months, she'd been pitching her own television show to air weekly with added online content, website access, the whole nine yards.

She loved to travel, but without an actual home to call her own, she was beginning to tire of life on the road. The television deal would give her the best of both worlds. She could travel, but she could also put down some roots in LA and give her a home base. It would give her a schedule, and the fame and financial stability so that her day-to-day life wouldn't be such a grind of posting for likes and clicks, and searching for new income streams.

"All right Lila, get to work, or get a real job," she chided herself. She turned back to her blank document, but the white space continued to taunt her. When she tried to remember anything about Arlo's, she could only see Reid. But she had to focus. She had to finish that one review before she moved on to her next Miami experience—she checked her open appointment book: a scooter tour, a couple of beachside food trucks, parasailing, and then Saturday night, the Rexford party. She had a lot of fun lined up for the next couple of days, and she couldn't seem to motivate herself to do any of it. At least there would be rum at the party. Maybe she'd get another Cuba Libre. Her mouth watered, remembering the taste of the cocktail she'd had the night before. But first, she had work to do. *Write the words; drink the rum.* Unable to focus, though, her eyes shifted to the bed, with the sheets that she and Reid had rumpled. She'd readily agreed to just one night with him. But now she wished that she'd asked for more, or given him her number, or something. Even though it was unlikely he'd call or anything—he'd made it perfectly clear that he was not interested in more than one night. But having had that night with him, there was no doubt she wanted another.

And that was when she saw a cell phone on the nightstand. It was black, whereas hers was pink. It must have been Reid's. She picked it up and turned it on, wondering how she would ever get it back to him. There was no emergency contact number on the lock screen, but the picture displayed was of Reid, with a man and a woman who both shared similar facial features—the same brown eyes and high cheekbones. Probably his siblings. They were standing, smiling proudly, next to a sign that said Rexford Rum Distillery.

Lila blinked and tilted her head as she took in the image. It all clicked into place. Reid. Rexford. She'd spent the night with one of the men who owned the facility she'd been set to tour? She returned to her computer and searched his name, and there he was, a picture of Reid in all his handsome, sexy glory. That second round she'd craved with him was now entirely possible. She would see him at the party.

She was still gripping the phone when a knock on the door startled her. She hadn't ordered room service and she couldn't imagine why anyone would be coming to her room. She put the phone on the bedside table. She walked to the door, checked the peephole, and saw the familiar profile of Reid Rexford. Pulling open the door, she gave him her sultriest smile. "Reid," she purred in a way she'd never done before. He'd apparently turned her into some kind of wanton sex kitten. "What brings you by?"

She raised her arm and leaned against the door in what she imagined—hoped—was a seductive pose.

She saw his eyes roam up and down her body. The robe concealed most of it but thankfully hung loosely at her chest, gaping to give him a peek at her cleavage. His eyes flickered with a flash of heat that she recognized as desire. But a muscle in his cheek ticked as he set his sensual lips in a frown. "I think you have my cell phone," he told her in a no-nonsense baritone.

Rejected. Putting on her best sex kitten impression had barely affected him. Had she played her cards right, he should have ripped the robe from her body and carried her to the bed for another round. But instead he only wanted his cell phone?

"I do," she said over her shoulder, turning away. "Come on in."

He started to take a step forward, but instead remained in the doorway. "I'd better not."

Lila turned her head and struggled not to grin when she saw that his eyes were fixed on the king-size bed, and the sheets he'd helped rumple. Lila sauntered to where his cell phone lay on her nightstand and held it up to him. She shifted so that the loosely tied robe slid off her shoulder, still cinched at her waist, but gaping even further, showing off the rest of her chest and the tops of her breasts. She looked at him from across the room. "You going to come and get it?"

Reid stood and watched her for several beats, not

moving from the door. He huffed out a breath and stretched his neck, not taking his eyes from her. She thought he might leave outright without his phone, that she'd pushed him, but her fears proved to be unfounded when he took a step inside the room. He shut the door behind him and turned the lock. "I'm going to get it."

CHAPTER FOUR

LILA'S BREATH STOPPED short as Reid stalked toward her. His gait was sure and his gaze unwavering. She'd prodded him, poked him, and now Reid was delivering. He stopped in front of her, but he didn't reach for his phone like she thought he might. Instead he pushed the fluffy robe from her chest. The cool air of the hotel room hit her skin, causing small goose bumps to rise, and pebbling her nipples. She felt her pulse pounding in her throat as he stared at her bared breasts.

"What happened to one night only?" she reminded him.

He stepped even closer, so that the tips of her breasts skated against the material of his shirt. She knew that underneath that was the dark curly hair she'd slid her hands over. Her palms itched to do it again. "If you don't want me here, I'll just take my phone and leave."

She shook her head. "That was your rule, remember? Not mine."

She heard what might have been a growl emanate from deep within his chest and his mouth captured hers in a kiss that bordered on ravenous. She attempted to breathe through her nose but was only able to take in his spicy cologne, and as his tongue swept in between her parted lips, she got a taste of his minty toothpaste.

She kissed him back, hopefully matching his intensity, but she wasn't sure that was possible. He made her feel wanted, desired. The way his fingers curled over her body, she could tell that he needed her, craved her. And to be wanted by a powerful, sensual man like Reid…

She shuddered against his chest and her arms encircled his neck to draw him closer. He lifted her, and she wrapped her legs around his waist. He walked her to the edge of the bed, dropped her so she landed on the mattress flat on her back and spread her legs. Taking her by the ankles, he brought her legs to his shoulders. He placed a hot kiss on her ankle and unbuckled his pants with one hand.

Thankfully the box of condoms was still on the nightstand from the night before, and he reached over and grabbed one as he pushed his pants down his thighs, rolling the latex over himself. "Sorry if this is a little quick," he grumbled, as he lined himself up with her center. "I've got to get to work."

She moaned when he rubbed his length against her. "Fine by me," she told him, her eyes flutter closed at the luxurious contact. "I've got stuff to do today, too."

"Not yet, you don't," he told her, sliding inside her in one long, hard stroke.

She arched off the bed and met him thrust for thrust. The angle of his movements made his cock glide against her clit, hitting her in just the right spot, bringing her closer to orgasm with every stroke. He leaned over her as his hips thrust, capturing one nipple between his lips. With his teeth and tongue, he plucked at the strings of desire within her, playing her body like an instrument until she came with a crescendo, crying out Reid's name as he buried his face in her chest, his breath hot on her skin, and he played out his own release.

He hovered over her for a moment. Then pushed himself off her body, and tossed the condom in a nearby trash can, while she straightened her robe.

"Nice trick, Reid," she said.

"What's that?" he asked, using his fingers to comb back the black hair that had fallen over his forehead.

She shrugged. "Leaving your cell phone, just so you'd have to come back to get it?"

He picked the phone up from the table, and immediately his thumbs moved over the screen. "Is that what you think happened?"

"Isn't it?"

He didn't look up from the screen. "Did you access anything on this?" he asked, studying the screen.

That caught her off guard. "No, I just saw it on

the nightstand before you showed up. Are you accusing me of something?" she asked, instinctively tightening the robe around her waist.

He looked at her, his eyes roaming up and down her body, as if appraising her, gauging her reaction to his accusation. "No."

"What, did you think I'd hacked your phone and stolen all of your secrets?"

"No, I'm sorry," he told her, crossing the room to stand in front of her. He cupped her jaw in his long, strong fingers, and she couldn't help but lean into his touch. "I guess I'm a little paranoid. I have reasons to be cautious." She looked up at him and saw a certain vulnerability in his eyes.

"Why?"

He didn't respond, but she saw him look down at his watch.

"Time to go?" she teased.

"Yeah, I have to get to work. And if I recall, you have things to do, too."

"That's right. This is it, I guess?"

"Yeah, I guess so." He looked away. "It's probably for the best, don't you think, parting like this?" It looked like he didn't think that. Her pride stopped her from disagreeing. But she remembered that he was one of the owners of the Rexford Rum Distillery. Where she was headed later that afternoon. Maybe she would see him there. "Well, it was fun, Reid."

He turned around to smile. "Yeah, it was, Lila. I guess this is goodbye."

"I like to think of it as an 'until next time.'"

He laughed. "Next time." With that he was gone. And despite wishing he'd stayed, Lila smiled. Reid might not know it, but *next time* would come sooner than he could have imagined.

When Lila saw her agent's number on the screen of her ringing cell phone, she answered more quickly than she normally would. "James, do you have good news?" she asked by way of greeting him, hoping he would have a GO! Channel contract to offer her.

"Not yet. I was chatting with the execs and they have concerns."

"What kind of concerns?"

"They're afraid that people won't know who you are. You aren't a mainstream celebrity, and you've never carried a national campaign. They don't know if your face—as gorgeous as it is," he added, "will be able to carry a television show."

Lila closed her eyes and took in the news. "They should just look at my follower numbers, the analytical information I provided to show that I know what I'm doing. People know me, and my word on a product or place means a lot."

"I know that, and so do many others. But you need to prove it to these guys. Let's come up with something big," he suggested. "Get into business with a brand. Why don't we get together and brainstorm a way to convince these suits that you've got the juice?"

Lila frowned. "Fine. Listen, I've got work to do. Can we talk another time?"

"Yeah, sure thing. And we will find something for you. It might just take a little while."

"Thanks," she said without much enthusiasm. "I'll talk to you later. Bye." She leaned back on the bed. She needed the GO! Channel offer. It would be her way to settle down, find an apartment in LA—establish a home base, a place to call her own. She made a good life on the road. But she was starting to tire of it. A reduced travel schedule would be a good thing for her before she suffered burnout.

Again, Lila thought of Reid. Her body tingled in anticipation of seeing him again. They'd shared a definite connection and with her plans to visit the distillery later, while she didn't think he would bend her over his desk, she wished he would. But she wondered if maybe she could propose some sort of arrangement. Hopefully he'd be interested in a business relationship, as well as their sexual one.

CHAPTER FIVE

HAVING MET WITH Gemma and Quin to go over next week's work plans, Reid was now alone in his office. His laptop was open to his full calendar and a quarterly earnings spreadsheet, but he'd be damned if he could find an ounce of focus to actually do anything with either of them. It was thoughts of Lila that still sat at the forefront of his mind. She consumed him, even more than she had before he saw her earlier that morning.

There was a knock on his closed door. He knew it was impossible, but wouldn't it be something if it was Lila knocking? His heartbeat sped up—just a little—at the improbable idea and he shook his head. "Foolish," he scolded himself right before he called out, "Come in."

The door opened and Gemma poked her head inside. Reid felt like an idiot for even thinking it could have been Lila, even for a second. "Hey Reid, you busy?"

He looked at his open laptop. "No, what's up?"

"I have the ingredients and cost lists for the honey batch for you." She handed over a scrap of paper where she'd jotted down the ingredients.

"Thanks." At least it would give him something to train his brain on. He clearly wasn't getting anything else done. "And I only had to ask you half a dozen times."

"Yeah, I wanted you in a good mood for the favor I'm about to ask you," she said, sitting on the corner of his desk.

He narrowed his eyes at her. "What is it?"

"Remember the guy I went out with last night?"

"Okay, but no connection?" he repeated her earlier words.

"You forgot cute. Yeah, well, he called and wants to get together for happy hour. I've decided to give him another chance."

"And what's that have to do with me?"

"Welllll," she said sweetly. "Remember when we were talking about travel bloggers and influencers earlier? I set up a tour with one today. But if I'm at a bar, I can't be here."

"Still doesn't sound like my problem," he told her.

"Reid. Please. It's just an hour of your time."

"Gemma—" With the lack of sleep from the night before, he'd planned for once on having a relaxing evening, finishing up his work, crashing on the couch with a drink and watching TV. But who was he kidding? More likely, he would end up staying at the distillery until after dark, and then using his home office to finish up whatever tasks seemed necessary on a Friday night—if only to distract him from going back to Lila's hotel room. "I don't give tours."

"But you know your way around the distillery. It's nothing in-depth. You know enough to give her a basic tour and let her try a few things."

"You should know I'm too busy to show around someone who thinks she's too good for a group tour. Especially one of those Instagram influencers. Those people are all style, no substance."

"Listen to yourself. Those *influencers* have more reach than many large marketing firms. They know how to spread the word. If she likes us, Reid, she could make us huge. She's doing us a favor here. I arranged it with her weeks ago. It'll take an hour out of your oh-so-busy afternoon, and then you can get back to working on the financials for this batch."

"How did you know—"

"Because you're my brother and I know you. I could see the gears turning in your head the minute I put that bottle down in front of you last night."

"I can't do the tour."

"Can't or won't?"

"Both. Get one of your workers to do it."

"They're all gone for the day."

"I'm—"

"I know, you're *busy*," she finished for him.

"No, I'm uninterested," he told her flatly.

"No, you're impossible. And I'm out of here," she said with finality, heading to the door.

"I don't give tours," he said again.

Gemma huffed out a breath. "You're such an asshole. You know, maybe you need to get laid, Reid. It might put you in a better mood."

"Drop it." To the contrary, it had been just a few hours since he'd left Lila's hotel. He could still feel her on him, the need for her clawing its way up his back. Lack of great sex wasn't his problem, but he wasn't about to share that with Gemma. It would give her too much ammunition, and he would never hear the end of it if his sister knew he'd gone back to the woman's room that morning.

"I've got work to do," he tried again feebly, knowing full well that there was no doubt he'd stick around the distillery while his sister went on her date. "But fine, I'll do your tour. She gets an hour of my time, and that's it."

Gemma smiled, knowing that, as always, she'd gotten her way with her older brother. "You're the best. And I'll forgive you being such a grumpy bitch, if you promise to do something fun today," Gemma called out to him.

Alone again, he snorted. He'd had plenty of fun already. But there was still work to be done. He had to make sure the distillery was poised for massive success, and if that meant entertaining some blogger for an hour to ensure a positive review, then so be it. Inexplicably, Lila kept making her way to front and center of his brain. And it surprised him how much he'd rather spend another hour with her than with anything having to do with rum.

When the cab stopped outside of the Rexford Rum Distillery, Lila was surprised the small, two-story building—gray concrete, unassuming—was her destination. The only thing marking it as the right place was the old wooden sign—the one she recognized from the picture of Reid and his siblings—bearing the Rexford name along with Established 1809.

She paid the driver and got out of the car. She walked up to the wooden door and pulled on the large iron handle. The door didn't budge. Locked. Her driver pulled away from the curb, and she was left standing in the empty parking lot.

"Just great."

Looking in through the small windows, she saw the equipment of the distillery, but the room appeared dark and empty. Gemma had told her that they would be closed to the public by the time she got there, but that she would be out front to meet her. Lila looked around for any sign of life, but the place was completely vacant.

She'd confirmed with Gemma the day before and double-checked the time in the email. She was on time, at the right place. She didn't have a phone number for her, besides that of the distillery, and she dialed. Several rings went in before the voice mail started, so she hung up. She knocked on the door before feebly trying the iron handle again. Still no movement. From a look around at her surroundings, she knew she wasn't in the safest area of Miami, and the sooner she could gain access to the building, the better.

Alone in the empty parking lot, she figured she'd walk around the side to see if she could find somebody, or another way in. She came to a side door. She pulled the handle, surprised when it opened. She walked inside, and was greeted by a stony silence, a sterile concrete staircase that led upstairs to the second floor. Lila took to the stairs, hoping she would find someone there. *Or I'll be kidnapped in this creepy-ass building and never seen again...*

So, doing what was almost instinctive to her, she turned on her cell phone camera and started a livestream of herself, lost and trying to find another person in the Rexford distillery.

"Hey, guys, it's Lila," she said into the lens as she climbed the stairs, "and as you know, I'm in Miami right now. I should be touring the Rexford Rum Distillery, and sampling some amazing rum, but instead I'm lost in a horribly boring hallway. There's no one around, and I have no idea where I'm going. Hopefully I find someone to help me, and not be doomed to walk these lonely hallways forever." She opened the door on the second floor, turned a corner and breathed out a sigh of relief, grateful to be in a carpeted reception area, with some furniture and uninteresting art prints. She turned back to the video recorder on her phone. "Still no signs of life, but at least I'm not in some concrete dungeon. If I don't make it out alive, avenge me." She saw that there were already hundreds of people watching her video, asking questions, leaving comments. There was a hallway past the reception desk that seemed to lead to some offices, and she walked further. Maybe she'd find someone down there.

Reid, alone in the office, cocked an eyebrow at the click of high heels and a female voice that reverberated throughout the empty hallway outside. "Oh shit," he muttered, looking at his watch. He'd missed his appointment with the travel blogger. He'd meant to go downstairs earlier to let her in, but he'd lost track of time going over the costs for Gemma's new batch of rum.

He got up from his desk and walked out into the hallway and didn't see anyone. But he could hear her down in the reception area, around the corner out of his sight. He tilted his head and listened to the far-off voice. The laughter in it was familiar. He knew that voice. He started down the hallway in the direction of the sound, turned the corner to where his receptionist's desk was located, and smacked into a small, warm body, sending the woman crashing to the floor.

The first thing he noticed was the flash of red hair. He was frozen in place. A buzz of electricity shot throughout his body as she looked up at him from the floor. "What are you doing here?" he asked.

He shook his head and, remembering his manners, reached down, extending his hand to help her to her feet.

"Well, it was either find a way in, or stand outside."

Reid frowned. "That's not what I meant. How did you find me here?"

"How self-obsessed are you?" she asked him, brushing off her skirt. "Reid, not everything is about you, you know? I'm here for a tour."

"You're the travel blogger Gemma invited?" he asked, incredulous, unable to believe that this was just a huge coincidence.

One of her perfectly shaped eyebrows arched upward. "You know, I'm sensing a lot of attitude from the person who didn't keep an appointment, leaving me stranded in the parking lot."

He relented. "I'm sorry. I was supposed to meet you outside, but I lost track of time." For several beats, he stood in dumbfounded shock. He couldn't believe that she was there. In his office.

"Why don't we start over." She extended her hand, officially introducing herself. "Lila Campbell."

Even though he knew touching her would prove to be a mistake, Reid shook her hand. "Reid Rexford." He couldn't take his eyes off her. "You know, I didn't expect to see you again, but I'm not upset about it."

She picked up her phone and looked into the camera, ignoring him. "And, ladies and gentlemen, I successfully found another human being. Everyone say hi to Reid." She turned the camera on him, and he saw himself in the screen.

Reid gave a humorless wave, and she put away her phone. "You were recording?" He couldn't stop the rigid tension that straightened his spine at the thought of her recording on premises, in an area where she shouldn't have been.

"I just went live for my audience. They like those little slices of life."

He was still tense from being on her camera, and he worried that she'd explored other parts of the distillery without supervision. Neither of them spoke until she looked around. "So, is Gemma here? She's supposed to show me the place."

He shook his head. "No, she got called away and had to leave unexpectedly, so I'll be showing you around if that's all right."

A quiet moment passed between them, and Reid knew they were both thinking about the night—and morning—they'd spent together. There was an inkling of doubt in his mind, though. He flashed back to how they'd met. Had she known who he was the entire time? Was hooking up with him part of her plan? Seducing him to get inside information? He'd been burned in the past, and he wondered if, like his ex-wife, Lila had set him up. And she had had access to his phone. He'd been hacked, manipulated before. But as he looked at Lila, he didn't think so. He hoped that it was his intuition, not his libido, telling him to trust her.

She raised one eyebrow. "You and me alone in the building, you think that's a good idea?"

It was as if she'd read his mind. He led her down the stairs to the distillery. "I think I can behave myself if you do."

Reid couldn't help but watch the sway of her short, flowy dress as she walked. He was entranced by it, filled with the familiar pulses of desire. He could still feel her. *Taste* her.

"So, where do we start?" Lila asked him, glancing at him over her shoulder, catching him in the act of checking her out.

"Start?" he asked, his eyes snapping up to meet hers.

"The tour?" she reminded him. "That's why I'm here, remember."

Right. "Yeah." He tried to recover. "We start right here. If you'll follow me, I'll show you all the ins and outs of Rexford." He hadn't intended any innuendo in his words, but as soon as they were out of his mouth, he realized exactly what he'd said. He hoped she hadn't caught it, but when Lila spoke next, he realized that he'd met his match.

"You promise?"

Lila attempted to keep her eyes off Reid's ass as she followed him around the distillery, trying her best to listen as he told her about the business and the process of making rum. She looked up at the man beside her as he walked her past copper vats, dodging hoses and other equipment as he talked. Despite its popularity, Rexford Rum was still a small family operation. "So how did you guys come to start up a distillery?"

"Rum is in our blood," he explained. He stopped in front of an old hand-drawn portrait of a man. Reid pointed at it. "Joseph Rexford was our ancestor, and also a thief and a vagrant," he said with a smile. "Generations ago, he fled Scotland evading arrest, and he somehow made his way across the Atlantic Ocean and landed in the Bahamas. He began his new life as a rumrunner, illicitly bringing Bahamian rum to the Florida coast. He was one of the first notorious distillers and bootleggers—a profession he passed on to his sons, who passed it on to their children, and so on. The Rexford clan was also responsible for sneaking rum into the US during prohibition in the 1920s. Since the 1700s, the Rexford name has been synonymous with rum.

"Rexford Rum operated on a small scale through the generations. After prohibition, our great-grandfather legitimized the business for the first time. By the time it was my father's turn to take the helm here, through bad luck and worse investments, there wasn't much left, but Mom and Dad turned it around. They made the distillery successful, but when Gemma, Quin and I took over, we made our rum the best."

Lila was certain he had just given her the speech given to most tour groups. But she wanted to know more about Reid and the Rexfords. "Was rum always your calling? Did you want to follow in the family business?"

"I was always intrigued by the lore of Joseph Rexford. I liked the idea of a family history filled with pirates and bootleggers, but when my mother passed away, my dad gave up the business and moved out west. Between myself, Gemma and Quin, we didn't want it to die on our watch." He looked around thoughtfully, as if he was recalling the memories and experiences he'd had in the room. "We all grew up in this building. It's been in the family for more than one hundred years. Our grandfather and father taught us everything we needed to know. Gemma was distilling long before she could legally drink—but that's strictly off the record," he said with a sly wink. "And now she's the master distiller. It's been about ten years now since we officially took it over, and we've acquired the neighboring buildings and expanded operations significantly."

Lila looked around the distillery. While the equipment was gleaming and kept in pristine shape, the signs of age and wear of the building itself were apparent. But she could tell Reid truly loved the place. "And even though you could work out of a new facility, you still run it out of the same small building."

"Yeah." He reached out and patted the stone wall. "This place is the heart of the business. There's a lot of history inside these walls. I couldn't imagine going anywhere else every day."

"You're a traditional guy," Lila noted.

He nodded. "I wasn't always, but yeah, I guess I am now. My brother and sister think I'm old-fashioned, but the Rexford name, my family, the rum, that's all there is, right?"

For several seconds, Lila considered her own family. Her parents who didn't support her; the ex-husband who didn't believe her capable of anything. She blinked their images from her mind, and saw that Reid was watching her. Their eyes met for a moment, before the intensity in his stare made her avert her eyes.

"Yeah, I guess." Desperate to change the topic, she brought her attention back to their surroundings. She had to get to the job at hand. Learning about the distillery, and the man himself. "Tell me more about all this—where the magic happens," she said with a sweep of her hand.

He looked relieved to again be talking about rum. "This is normally Gemma's domain, and she rarely lets us in here without supervision."

"Well, I guess we'll have to try our best to be good."

Lila noticed the way Reid's body momentarily stiffened before he went back into tour mode, leading her over to two large boilers. "Forgive me. Gemma and her guys are a lot better at this tour than I am. I rarely get the chance to come down here anymore."

"It's fine." She subtly gave Reid a once-over. "I know she's left me in good hands."

She wasn't sure he'd caught her intentionally

innuendo-laced comment, but when his eyes traveled down over her body, leaving a trail of fire in their wake, she knew he did. His hands clenched into fists at his sides, and as he pushed them into the pockets of his sensible pants, she remembered just how talented those hands were.

They regarded one another for several tension-filled beats before she forced herself to look away. She cleared her throat. “So, Gemma’s the master distiller? That’s impressive.”

“Yeah, like I said, she’s been working here since she was a teenager, but since then, she’s studied all over the world, practicing with some of the greatest rum makers there are, including our grandfather. Quin and I might keep the place running, but she’s the lifeblood of the business.”

“And what is your job?”

“As my brother and sister like to keep reminding me, I’m the boring numbers guy. Quin is head of marketing and PR. He’s the fun, charismatic one, but I handle the business side of things. It’s just the three of us running it with a few small teams. We might sell internationally, but it’s still the same family-run place it always has been.”

She smiled. Once again, she could see how devoted he was to his family. It was commendable. He was responsible, sensible, but passionate. Sure, she’d seen that passion the night before, but responsible and sensible wasn’t the impression she’d had of the man who’d seduced her in a restaurant and took her quickly, fiercely in her hotel that morning. He wasn't at all what she went for when it came to men—she liked them more adventurous and carefree—but she might be tempted to make an exception for another go-around with Reid Rexford…

Lila mentally slapped herself. *Down, girl. You're here for work!* She had to think about her future and see if Reid would be open to some sort of partnership. That was one thing that could secure her the GO! Channel deal. But she wouldn't be able to do that if she couldn't keep her hormones in check. Straightening, she tried to tamp down her attraction to him. She tried to separate herself as the woman who'd slept with him from the blogger who was there for information. "That doesn't sound boring. You keep the lights on, and keep the place running. You can be as charismatic, or make as much fabulous rum as you please, but without the boring numbers guy, there isn't a business."

Another beat of silence passed between them. And Lila was sure at that point they would never get to finish the tour. Not that that would be the worst thing… "So, why don't you tell me about making rum? What's the step-by-step process?"

"All right," Reid said, rubbing his hands together, and pointed to the drums. "It all starts with sugar cane…"

Even though the distillery was Gemma's domain, and he'd argued the opposite, Reid still knew the place inside out. Thankfully, back in control of the situation, he started the tour. He went over the process with Lila, giving her a spiel that he remembered from his days of running the tours. But he'd never had an audience like Lila.

She was a stunning woman, all generous curves and red hair. But it wasn't just her looks that drew him to her. She was vibrant, vivacious, and her energy filled the distillery as she hung on his every word. He could feel her attention so acutely that he had to concentrate to keep the words coming from his mouth. Reid gave her the chance the check out one of the giant stills, and as she walked around it, taking notes and asking questions, even the intricacies of her movements intrigued him. The way her pen went between her lips as her sharp eyes took in the process, the way she restlessly drummed her fingers against her thigh, not out of boredom, he knew, but to expel the excess energy that coursed through her.

They moved over to the charred oak barrels where they aged the rum. He saw the cognac barrels from Gemma's new batch in one corner. Her notebook—which contained her recipes—lay open on top. Rolling his eyes at Gemma's carelessness, he snatched it up before Lila could sneak a peek at the words scribbled on the pages. But all it earned him was a curious look from her. Smooth. "And that's the end of the tour," Reid said, sliding the small coil notebook into his pocket. "Now's the fun part—the tasting."

"The rest of the tour was pretty interesting. That does sounds like it's more fun, though." She smiled, laying her fingertips on his forearm. "But I know a more fun thing we could do together."

"I thought we promised to behave ourselves?"

She walked past him, and her smile was daring—and sexy. "That was you. I never promised any such thing."

Reid clenched his fists and counted to ten in his head. It was barely enough to bring down his libido. He was barely hanging on. He had to remind himself that there was something strange going on with Lila's reappearance into his life. She had called it a coincidence. But he didn't believe in coincidence. While his dick might be happy to have Lila in his presence, he had to consider the other possibilities.

On one hand, she might be a spy, sent by a rival distillery. On the other hand, she could be out to get the inside scoop into his personal life, to air his dirty laundry. Wouldn't be the first time those things happened when he wasn't careful about who he trusted.

He ground his teeth, but still couldn't stop himself from putting his hand on the small of her back to guide her into the tasting room. Immediately, he regretted the lapse in judgment. He should have kept his hands to himself; he would never have touched another distillery guest in such an intimate manner.

He was so attuned to her that he could feel Lila stiffen underneath his fingers. Her head turned in his direction, not surprised by his touch, and she gave him that same devastatingly slick grin. He knew he was done. She didn't move away from his touch, and instead settled back against his hand and continued walking with him.

He turned on the overhead lights to the tasting area—the large room was designed and lit for intimacy despite its size. Edison bulbs on strings and in sconces lit the stone walls of the room, which held several long old wooden tables, big enough to accommodate larger tour groups. He gestured to a spot on the center of the bench that ran along one of the tables. "Take a seat. I'll be right back," he told her.

He let his gaze linger on Lila for a second before he went into the next room to prepare the tasting. As he pulled out a couple of flat boards and the small glasses that went with them, he thought about the woman waiting for him. It had been a long time since he'd let any sort of need or desire rise to the surface. But since she'd come into his life the night before, she'd completely turned him upside down. He shook his head. If he wasn't careful, he would find himself in a vulnerable situation with the woman. He poured himself a shot of rum and downed it in a fortifying gulp.

But first. He had to think about the distillery. He had to put the business, his family ahead of his own goddamn sex life. Gemma and Quin were counting on him to make sure Lila left with a good impression of the Rexford distillery. He had to forget the effect that Lila had on him. He had to be on his best behavior. He had to think about the business.

"Pull it together, Reid," he muttered, giving himself a mental shake. As per the standard they'd set for the tours, Reid finished preparing the tasting boards with the selection of rum, giving visitors a range of what the distillery had to offer. And even though he would rather be laying Lila out on top of the old oak table in the next room, and burying himself deep inside her, he had to be professional.

Professionalism had never been a problem for him before. As Gemma and Quin were quick to remind him, he was the serious, boring one—the one who never let anything get in the way of work. Why Lila was such a temptation him, he didn't know, but he normally didn't have any trouble separating the business from his dick.

But that didn't mean he could stop thinking about the woman waiting for him in the main room. He'd had an incredible night—and following morning—with Lila. When they'd been completely anonymous. But now she knew who he was, and that made him feel more vulnerable than he liked.

He frowned and poured himself another shot of rum. It had been a while since he'd done the tasting spiel, but he knew the qualities of each type of rum and could explain it in detail. He wanted to give Lila the authentic, typical experience, but his desire for the woman was anything but typical.

With Reid in the other room, Lila was able to finally take a deep breath, but it did little to settle her. Reid

Rexford was as formidable as a brick wall, and seemingly unflappable despite her giving him her sexiest looks. She, however, was completely shaken. His inquisitive, even skeptical, eyes had bored through her. She'd enjoyed the tour of the distillery, but she was glad she'd recorded it because after seeing Reid, she found it difficult to remember anything he'd said to her.

Given the passion he'd exhibited the night before, she'd been surprised by how stiff and serious he looked in the distillery. It was difficult to reconcile the businessman him with the passionate lover he'd been. They could have been two different men, but when he put his hand on her, low on her back, she'd nearly sighed with pent-up pleasure.

Using the reversed camera on her phone as a mirror, she checked out her reflection, and smoothed her hair. *Still cute.* When she looked up, he came back into the room and laid down two wooden board platters that contained four small glasses each. The whole time, he kept a noticeable distance from her.

"What do we have here?" she asked, eyeing each of the glasses.

"Here's a sample of our regular rums—" he pointed to each glass "—white, amber, spiced, and we finish it off with a cream rum."

He went into a speech about each of the products, about the differences in production, laced with humorous tales of Joseph Rexford. Reid knew the family lore, but she was more interested in learning about him. “And we start with the white rum.” He picked up the small glass that held the clear liquid.

They both held up their glasses of white rum, clinked them together in salute, and took a sip. The clear rum was smooth, some of the best she’d ever had. Normally her rum came mixed with fruit juice and topped with little umbrellas. But without the decoration and overpowering fruit, she was able to taste the clarity of the rum. She drank again, and their eyes connected over their glasses. When his glass was empty, he put it back on the table. His posture was rigid, his serious face set with hard features.

“Can I ask you a question?” he said after a beat of silence.

“Shoot.”

“Why are you here?” he asked, surprising her.

Her mouth dropped open in shock at the almost accusatory tone he used. “What does it look like I’m doing here? I’m taking a tour of your business.”

“Why though? I’ve got to know. Did you know who I was when we met at Arlo’s? And then you show up here. It’s all a little too coincidental for my liking.”

“If you remember, last night, you approached me. The only thing I knew about you until today was that your name was Reid, and that you’re good in bed. I’ve been in touch with Gemma, and she’s the one who invited me for a tour. You know, I really don’t like having to explain myself to you.” She narrowed her eyes at him and saw that he was still suspicious.

"Whether you like it or not, it's just a coincidence. Are you accusing me of something, Reid? What's with the inquisition?"

"I don't believe in coincidence, fate or happenstance. I don't understand how we meet in a restaurant, sleep together and then you randomly show up at my business. Is this a way to get extra information, an inside scoop for your blog?"

"What, *In Bed with the Rum Baron*? You think that's a traffic booster? Please." When he didn't say anything in response, and just looked at her critically, anger quickly replaced any other feelings she might have had for Reid. "Are you fucking kidding me?" she asked, indignant, standing from the table. "I don't need a salacious story to sell people on my brand. I wanted to take a tour of the distillery because I like your sister, and maybe I wanted to see you again. Jeeze, you're so freaking hot and cold. I don't understand you."

He shook his head. "You're right. I shouldn't have said that. It seemed… Never mind."

"You can't just accuse me of what—trying to gain your information, and then say forget it. I'm just going to leave." Like that, she saw her dreams of them working together burst into flames. Without a brand partnership, she could kiss her television career goodbye. But her integrity was worth more than that. "Thanks for the tour."

"Lila." Reid's voice remained even. "Please don't go. Believe me, I'm very sorry for what I've implied. It didn't come out the way I meant." He exhaled. "I've… I've been burned before. And I don't normally see women more than once. So, my reaction to seeing you this morning, and then seeing you here—it's all too incredible for me."

Even though she knew she should be halfway out the door, she briefly forgot how insulted she'd been by him. She could see the mix of emotions on his face. He looked uncomfortable, troubled, confused, frustrated, vulnerable, and Lila was intrigued. She sat back down and watched him. "What happened? Who burned you?"

He shook his head. "It's nothing I'm eager to talk about, especially to a stranger."

A stranger. That stung.

"It's a story best left for another time," he continued. "Or never. But I'm a little more careful now than I used to be. And seeing you here today confused me." He picked up the next rum, the amber. "Shall we carry on? Forget that I even said anything?"

There was a story there, a reason for his sudden shift in attitude, and despite feeling a little hurt, instead of telling him to go fuck himself and walking away, Lila was eager to dig a little deeper to hear it. The man in front of her was intriguing. But he was also kind of a jerk. Good thing he was sexy as hell on top of it. "Sure." She picked up the next small glass, still mad at Reid, but willing to drink his rum.

He cleared his throat. "This is the amber," he told her, back in business mode. He held the small glass aloft, and Lila did the same, the light shining through a liquid gold. "It's medium-bodied, aged three years, and caramel and spicy in flavor."

He brought it to his lips, and she drank hers, as well. It was just as good as the first. It didn't have the same burn that most straight liquor had, a testament to its quality. The only burn she felt came from the infuriatingly complicated man who sat across the table.

"What do you think?" he asked.

"About the rum?" she countered, shrugging. "It's good." She looked at the two shots still in front of her. "I'm glad I had lunch, though."

"We can skip the rest if you want to leave."

"And let it go down the drain?" She laughed. "Never. I'll just carb-load later to soak it up." She picked up the next. "What's this one?"

"Our signature spiced rum. Flavored with a combination of spices. The recipe is one of Gemma's most tightly held secrets. I'll be honest, Quin and I don't even know how she makes this one."

They both drank. The spiced rum was amazing, and she hummed in approval as she savored the flavor. It was heavy, spicy but also sweet—*just like Reid*—and it felt warm in her stomach. A pleasant feeling spread to each of her extremities. "Delicious." She smiled at him.

He exhaled as he put down the glass with a heavy clunk, and she wondered if he was feeling the effects of the alcohol as well. "Lila, I really am sorry

I got so angry earlier, and I'm sorry I accused you of being unscrupulous. I acted poorly. You did nothing wrong, and you didn't deserve it."

His apology seemed heartfelt. The beast wasn't all gruff. He might have a heart, after all. "Thank you. This is a weird situation we've found ourselves in. Fate works in mysterious ways."

"I don't believe in fate. It all seems a little too coincidental." He gestured to the last glass. "Shall we drink?"

"Yes, please."

He picked up the last shot, the creamy one. "Last one. This is the cream liqueur. This one is a combination distilled rum and cream. Then Gemma added a little vanilla, cinnamon and a few other delicious spices from around the world. Once again, only Gemma and her guys know the exact recipe."

She held the glass to her nose and sniffed. It smelled sweet. "Down the hatch," she said. When he laughed, she explained. "I know it's not the fanciest toast, but whatever." She savored the flavor. "That was delicious."

When she lowered the glass, she saw that Reid was looking at her, and he was smiling.

"What?" she asked.

"You've got a little..." He reached across the table and swiped his thumb across her top lip. He pulled it away with some of the creamy rum on it, and before bringing his hand back to his side of the table, he paused, and touched it to her mouth. She parted her lips and closed them around his thumb. When she released him, she dragged her tongue along the outer edge of his thumb, tasting the rum on his skin, combined with his own flavor. She wanted more.

He groaned and without saying anything, Reid came around to her side of the table. She was still seated, and he stood behind Lila, towering over her. Resting his palms on the table, one on each side of her own hands, he hovered over her, caging her in. Lila leaned back against him and looked up. The all-too-familiar heat had returned to his eyes. Despite his accusations, he wanted her again. *So goddamn hot and cold.*

He drew the fingers of one hand along her cheek, down her throat, to the crevice of cleavage revealed by the low cut of her dress. Lila again leaned into his touch, unable to do anything else but urge him to keep touching her. His hand slid underneath the neckline of her dress and bra and cupped her breast. He pinched her nipple between two fingers, and she gasped, and it turned into a moan when he smoothed his hand over her.

"Still want to leave?"

Lila drew her bottom lip between her teeth, and closed her eyes, leaning against his chest. She inhaled his cologne, his rum-scented breath, and she moaned. Her laugh was a throaty sound. "I couldn't if I tried. I thought you said we were a one night only thing."

"I was a fool. And we already broke that rule this morning, didn't we?"

His hand left her breast and smoothed down the front of her dress to her thighs, where the material of her skirt had already ridden up. He slid his hand between her thighs, and she responded by spreading them further for him. He hummed in approval. "That's good." His fingers traveled upward to the apex of her thighs, where he found her already wet panties. He stroked her through the soaked satin and her moan filled the small room.

"I don't know what you do to me, Lila," he whispered in her ear, as he slipped his hand underneath her panties and touched her without a barrier. "I know this is a bad idea, but the minute I'm near you, it's all I can do to keep from fucking you."

"Why is this such a bad idea?" She spread her thighs wider, allowing him better access, and she was rewarded when he slid two fingers easily inside her.

"Because nothing that is this fucking sweet can be a good thing."

"Hey, Reid, I figured I'd find you in here—oops!" A male voice behind them interrupted them.

"Fuck," Reid muttered, removing his hand, straightening immediately.

Lila turned her head, and even with Reid blocking her with his body, she could see the other man standing in the doorway.

"Get the fuck out of here, Quin."

"I'm already gone. I'll call you later."

The door closed and they were alone again. But the mood had shifted. For a while, the only sounds were their matched heavy breaths, the pounding of her heart, and her hormones *screaming* to be sated.

"Who was that?"

"My brother. I'm really sorry," he told her, taking a step back from her. Apparently, the moment had passed.

"You're sorry about us being interrupted, or that anything happened in the first place?"

"Both. Damn, Lila—"

"You know, if you're just going to repeat that it was wrong, or a bad idea, or whatever, I'm not interested in hearing it. I'd better leave." Humiliated, she gathered her things as quickly as she could. "Thanks for the tour and the rum." She could still feel the ghost of his touch on her skin. "And whatever that was," she said, gesturing to the table.

"I'll call you a car," Reid said.

"That's not necessary," she said, taking her phone out of her purse and opening a rideshare app. "I get my own rides." She straightened her dress and smoothed down her hair. "See you later, Reid."

Reid was so hot one minute, threatening to rip her clothes off, and then so stern and serious the next. She couldn't read him, and goddamn if that didn't intrigue her.

CHAPTER SIX

LILA TOSSED HER hair over her shoulder as she stepped out of her hired car and onto the sidewalk in the front of the five-star hotel where the Rexford Rum party was located. She looked up, and at the very top, on the roof of the hotel, she could see bright skylights streaking the sky—X marking the spot of the most elite party in Miami. The hotel itself gave off a very you-can't-sit-with-us vibe. And it was one she normally couldn't stand. But this was the job, and she had an invitation to the hottest party in the city in her small, ultra-fashionable purse.

Not to mention that she would undoubtedly see Reid. Almost a week had passed since she'd seen him. He hadn't called like she'd expected him to, nor had she contacted him. If distance was what he'd wanted, then fine. But she was going to be at his party, whether he wanted her there or not. She grinned, thinking about what his reaction might be.

She entered the hotel and at the elevators was met by an attendant who checked her invitation and ID and escorted her to an elevator that would take her to the rooftop bar. She checked her reflection in the mirrored wall of the elevator, touched up her lipstick and fluffed her hair. Despite the Miami humidity, her blowout had held, and when she'd dressed, she'd been inspired by her encounters with Reid, so she picked the sexiest outfit in her suitcase—a black, tight spaghetti-strap cropped camisole, paired with a matching skin-tight, high-waisted skirt. Her favorite red stilettos completed the look. She knew she looked sexy.

The elevator came to a stop with a soft *ding*, and the doors parted in front of her. She was met by another attendant who again checked her ID and invitation and gave her a discreet scan with a metal-detecting wand. The Rexfords had really spared no expense, and took no risks with their security, it seemed. When she'd received the invite from Quin Rexford, she'd known it would be a high-end affair, but she hadn't been prepared for the extent.

The music, courtesy of one of the country's hottest DJs, pumped into the warm night air, but she still managed to hear the dull roar of the Atlantic Ocean against the sandy beach below them. The spotlight beams she'd seen from the street crossed each other high in the sky, and cool blue-and-purple uplighting focused on potted palms and VIP seating.

Looking around, she saw nothing, but the beautiful and glamorous people Miami was known for, with many celebrities and athletes, and their entourages scattered throughout. Lila thought about her blog and even though she had social media followers in the millions across all her platforms, and she'd rubbed shoulders with many rich and famous folks in the past, she wondered how she'd even managed to score an invite to this shindig. Rexford was still run out of their humble distillery, but they apparently knew how to throw a hot party. A passing server held a tray of drinks, and she caught his eyes.

"Cuba Libre, ma'am?" he asked.

Lila blinked in surprise. That one of the featured cocktails was the same that she'd drunk with Reid last week wasn't lost on her. "Yes, please," she told him, taking a glass from the tray. When she sipped, she was hit with notes of lime and a light rum over the cola, and she hummed in appreciation. Just drinking the cocktail brought her back to her time with Reid.

It was Friday, exactly a week since she'd seen him last, and with her time drawing short in Miami, she was starting to kiss goodbye the prospect of partnering with the rum brand. Every time she picked up the phone to call him, to suggest the business partnership between their brands, she chickened out. But was she afraid of his dismissal? His ridicule? His sexual power over her? Lila had no idea.

She drank from her glass again. The rum warmed her pleasantly. A little liquid courage would help her navigate the crowd. Her first stop would be to find her gracious hosts, the Rexfords, and thank them for inviting her.

She decided the best way to start would be to walk the perimeter—do a lap around to see if she could find someone she knew. But she knew nobody in Miami—well, except for mysterious Reid. Many interested men tried to catch her eye. But she ignored them. As she looked around at the faces of the beautiful people, part of her hoped to see Reid among them.

Distracted by the crowd around her, Lila wasn't looking when she collided with another woman, almost spilling her drink on herself. "I'm so sorry about that," she said.

"Don't worry about it," the woman told her. "As long as you didn't spill your drink."

"Thank God, I didn't," Lila said, taking a sip for emphasis. "Spilling something this good would be a sin."

She looked up and saw Gemma Rexford standing in front of her. While Lila had never met Reid's sister in person. They'd been in contact via email, and she recognized her picture from the lock screen of Reid's phone "You like the drink?" she asked.

"Yeah. It's delicious. Apparently, Rexford Rum is quickly becoming one of my favorites."

She laughed. "I'm glad to hear it." She stuck out her hand. "You must be Lila Campbell. I'm Gemma Rexford."

"It's great to finally meet you," Lila said, shaking her hand. "Thanks for the invite to the party."

"We're glad to have you here. I hope you're having a great night."

"I haven't been here long, but it looks like everyone is having a great time."

"I'm really sorry I couldn't make the tour. I trust that Reid took care of you."

He certainly had. Lila felt a flush start on her chest, and she tried to control it before it reached her cheeks.

"He never did tell me how the tour went. Did you enjoy it?"

"I did. I was going to include the distillery in a top ten in Miami list with a small section, but I wrote a full blog featuring the distillery. It's scheduled to go live on my website at midnight, to correspond with pictures and videos from here."

"Thank you so much. We really appreciate it."

This was Lila's chance to lay the groundwork for a partnership. Start small, and they could build a business relationship from there. "I'd love to follow up and do an interview with you. I'm sure my audience would be interested in hearing from the badass master distiller of Rexford Rum."

Gemma laughed. "Oh, I don't know if I'm that badass. I just make rum that I hope people love."

Lila looked around the party. "I think it's safe to say that people do. How about we schedule a time to get together?" She held out hope that the other woman would be free before she left town.

Gemma nodded. "Yeah. Are you free for late lunch tomorrow?"

"I'm in Miami until tomorrow evening. I'd love to get together for lunch."

"Fabulous," Gemma said, clinking her glass against Lila's. "It's a date."

Lila looked around the party "Is Reid here?" she asked, not sure if Gemma knew about the extent of their relationship. "I didn't really get a chance to thank him for the tour."

Gemma's face gave nothing away. "Yeah, he's right behind you."

Lila turned around and froze in place. Reid had been on her mind for the entire week. So much so she thought she'd seen him on the beach, on a scooter tour, in restaurants, behind bushes… He was already ingrained in her memory, tattooed on her skin. As if she could still smell him, hear his laughter in the distance. Lila shook her head. She really had to get a grip on herself.

Her skin prickled and an anticipatory shiver crawled over her, as she was rooted in place. Slowly, Lila turned and once again came face-to-face with Reid Rexford.

Reid stood, dumbfounded, in front of Lila—the saucy redheaded siren who'd consumed his every waking moment since the previous weekend. He hadn't expected her to be among the personalities invited to the party, but he probably should have. Pretending that her presence had no effect on him, Reid stuck out his hand, and put a cordial smile on his face. "Hello, Ms. Campbell. Nice to see you again."

Lila shook his hand. Her hand was warm and soft, and the same current of heat that occurred each time he saw her traveled between them. "Likewise."

"Lila was telling me how much she loves our rum," Gemma said.

He watched as Lila raised her glass to those full, pouty lips. "Yeah, I really do enjoy the taste of Rexford," she told him with a wink. They looked at each other for several beats, and, as the rest of the world fell away, he focused on only Lila. If Gemma noticed the haze of sexual tension between them, she didn't let on.

Realizing it had been some time before either of them spoke, Reid cleared his throat and looked at her drink. "What do you have there?" he asked. Not giving her time to answer, he carried on. "Let me guess, Cuba Libre. One of my favorites."

She nodded. "It's delicious."

Reid was reminded of his sister's presence when she put her hand on his forearm. One look at her, and he knew that she knew something was going on. "Reid, Lila, please excuse me. There are some people over there I need to talk to. Lila, it was wonderful to meet you. I'll see you tomorrow." She pointed a finger at her brother. "Reid, be nice."

"Aren't I always nice?" he asked her, as she walked away, disappearing in the crowd.

And with that, Reid was left alone with the woman who'd completely rocked him the week before. They stood awkwardly in place for several beats. He wondered who would speak first. What would she say? How unbelievable would it be that fate had put them together like this, yet again, in a way neither could have expected? He frowned as she smiled and sipped her drink, giving him a few more seconds before he would have to say anything.

"This is certainly a strange turn of events. Another coincidence?" he asked.

Reid tried to ignore her smile, her luscious curves and the way his body reacted to her.

"Too bad I don't believe in coincidence, right?"

"So, what are you doing here?"

"I was invited."

"You didn't think to mention you'd be coming?"

"If you were really on top of things here, you would think you would have checked the RSVP list."

"Touché."

"But after everything we've been through, you still don't believe that fate can have an influence over our lives? To shape us? To change us?"

"No, the only thing that influences my life is me. I don't put my future in anyone else's hands."

"Oh really?" she asked, leaning in closer. Looking down, he was treated to a view of her ample cleavage. He could still taste the smooth skin of her chest on his tongue. It was the same taste he'd craved all week. Saliva flooded the back of his mouth as he wanted nothing more than to capture the flavor again. "That's a couple of times you've said something like that. You don't trust easily."

He kept his posture rigid, but his fist clenched to stop himself from reaching out to touch her. "I believe that trust has to be earned. And it isn't easy."

"There's something you aren't telling me, isn't there?"

Was there ever. But if the past weekend had taught him anything, it was that Lila tempted him. Around her, he'd already broken most of his rules—he'd found himself revealing far too much to her. No matter how much he wanted to get out of there and spend the rest of the night buried deep inside her, he might be tempted to spill his secrets. And given what she did for a living, peddling in information, he couldn't do that. He was strong, but somehow, she wore him down. That's what she was to him—a temptress, a siren, one that would bring about his downfall if he wasn't careful. He had to end this dalliance and put the necessary distance between them before he did something he regretted. The sooner the better.

The DJ started up again. The familiar notes of a song she knew filled the night air. "Ooh, I love this song," she told him. "Dance with me?"

He shook his head. "No, I don't dance."

"Come on, everybody dances."

"Not me."

"Fine. Suit yourself," she said, turning and heading for the dance floor without him.

She stayed within his sight, and he couldn't take his eyes off her. He watched riveted as Lila swiveled her hips to the music, rolling her body seductively to the beat. She looked over her shoulder and their eyes met, and her lips pursed into a saucy smile. He knew that was her game—he didn't want to dance so she'd at least make him regret it.

Reid's eyes were pinned to Lila as she danced with the crowd. But he knew what she was doing, she was teasing him. Trying to prod him into joining her. He barely noticed when Quin sidled up next to him.

"You're not going to dance with your girl?"

"What makes you think she's my girl?"

"It certainly looked like you two were getting pretty cozy over here. Not to mention what I walked in on at the tasting room last week."

"It was just a conversation," he insisted. "And you walked in on nothing."

"Is that right?"

"That's right." He wouldn't share with his brother that she was a woman he'd already slept with—twice. But he forgot about Quin entirely when his vision focused on the guy who was approaching Lila.

Quin had noticed him, too. "So, you're going to let some other man dance with her then."

Reid's eyebrows narrowed. No, he wasn't. He handed his glass to Quin. "I'll see you later."

Striding across the rooftop to the sunken dance floor, he came upon Lila and the guy who'd tried to insinuate himself into Reid's private show. "May I cut in here?" he asked her.

"Hey, buddy," the guy stepped forward, looked at Reid and backed up quickly. "Sorry, Mr. Rexford, I didn't realize it was you."

"Leave," Reid told him.

"That was rude," Lila told him. "What if I was enjoying his company?"

"Well, I'll apologize for scaring away a kid who ground his pelvis against you without any sort of rhythm. He was making you look bad."

"Is that right? Will you make me look good?"

His eyes swept up and down her body "You already look good. I'll make you feel good."

She drew the tip of her tongue along her upper lip. "I believe that."

It had been years since he'd danced, but it felt so right when he took her hips in his hands and moved in closer. They were chest-to-chest, with no space between them, both of them moving to the music. The song changed and the notes of a Cuban hip-hop song started playing. He shifted his hips against her, swaying with her on the dance floor. Reid turned her in his hands, so that her ass pressed against his crotch. There was no way she missed his already-stiffening cock. Turning her head over her shoulder, she raised an eyebrow at him. He smirked, unembarrassed.

"We move pretty well together, don't we?"

She wasn't just talking about their dance moves, and he knew it. "We certainly do."

The songs changed again, and then again. They danced, pressed together, their bodies moving as one to the beats of the music.

After several songs, Lila stopped, and put her hands on his shoulders, stopping him and leaned in close. "I'm done. My feet hurt," she said in his ear.

"Want to grab a table?" she asked, gesturing to the high-top tables next to the wall closest to the ocean.

"Yeah, sure." So much for staying away. Reid cursed his lack of restraint when it came to the woman.

"I'll get a table and let you buy me a drink."

"It's an open bar," he reminded her.

"Well, you could be a dear and fetch me one then," she told him.

"Cuba Libre?" he asked her.

"I'd love one." She strutted to a nearby table. Her skirt was skin-tight, and showed off her smooth, ample curves. He wanted nothing more than to run his palms over her hips, her breasts, the high curve of her ass. Instead he clenched his fists and shoved them into his pockets as he headed for the bar. He was doomed.

While the bartender mixed their cocktails, Reid watched as Lila secured them a seat at the table. She turned her back to the party, took out her phone, and snapped a picture of herself in front of the crowd, the lights, the glamour that he and his siblings had created. They'd overspent for the party, invited celebrities and personalities that he hadn't dreamed would show up, but all he could see was Lila.

He knew that spending any more time with her would be a mistake, but he just couldn't help himself. After being alone for such a long time, he'd buried himself in his work. He'd stayed guarded. But there was something about the woman that filled his well, gave him a new energy. Who she was, though, and how she made him feel was dangerous, to him and to the business.

"Here you are, Mr. Rexford." The bartender handed him two glasses.

"Thank you."

When he returned, she was staring out into the darkness, toward the sound of the ocean. Her eyes unfocused, and her lips turned down, she looked so pensive and lost in thought that he didn't want to disturb her. In the halo of the lights from the party, she looked so beautiful it made his stomach twist.

Sliding one of the glasses over, he took a seat across from her at the small table. "You okay?"

"Huh? Oh, yeah. I'm fine."

"You looked pretty deep in thought there."

She shook her head, but he wondered if she was hiding something. "I'm just thinking."

"So, what do you think of our little party?"

"Little? Are you kidding? This party is amazing. Look around. This is pretty much the best party I've ever attended. A real who's who of pop culture right now." Her eyes widened. "Which makes me wonder why you're over here talking to little ol' me."

"Maybe I like your company."

"Doesn't seem like it all the time," she pointed out.

"I apologized for that, didn't I?"

"Doesn't mean it isn't well within my rights to give you a hard time about it."

"You got me there. Honestly, the party is a bit much for me. Normally, we do this on a smaller scale. Gemma and Quin handled most of the planning. I just tried to keep them on budget."

"And did they stay on budget?"

He looked around, and her eyes followed his as she took in the spectacle around them. Celebrities, athletes and A-listers laughed and danced, and took photos with Rexford Rum in hand. It was a glamorous party on a beautiful night. Reid laughed. "Does it look like they stayed on budget?" He paused. "But I have to say, they did an awesome job."

"You have a great thing going on here. Rexford is so exclusive, such a premium spirit, though, I don't know if many of my followers even know who you are. But it's going to make a great blog post. People are going to love you guys."

"I just want people to love the rum."

She took a sip and watched him. "They will." She averted her gaze briefly. "Reid, I think we should talk about what happened. I would feel a lot more comfortable if we just addressed what we did." He nodded and waved a hand for her to start talking. "We had a lot of fun that night," she started. "And the next morning. And at the distillery." She laughed. "But I think it's probably best if we leave it at that."

Reid's eyes widened. That wasn't what he'd expected her to say. Part of him had hoped for another night, to finish what they'd started in the distillery. But it was smart for them to part ways amicably. They'd both had a good time, and Lila would give them excellent exposure on her blog. "Yeah, that's a good idea."

"You're a great guy, Reid," she kept going. "It's just that I can't let anything affect my online image. One misstep, and I could just be seen as a party girl. I want to be taken seriously, and that's hard enough for a woman in my field."

Relief came over him, knowing that she was on the same page as him. It would be easier to behave himself. "I completely agree."

"Great. Now that that's settled, you can relax."

"Why are you worried about me relaxing?"

"Because just looking at you, I can see how uptight you are. Look at how rigid you are. If you keep that up, work and stress are going to put you into an early grave."

It bothered him that she had been able to peg him so easily. "You think you know that much about me?"

She nodded. "I do."

"How?"

"Because the night you came on to me at Arlo's,

the night we spent in my hotel room, you were a completely different person. You were loose, fun, charming. But now, even at an incredible party, you're as taut as a violin string. Maybe you're due for another plucking," she surmised with a grin.

"You're terrible."

"I know. It's all part of the personality."

"I think that's enough about me," he said. They'd had the discussion they'd needed to have, but he didn't want to walk away yet. "Tell me about what you do. I never did understand the *influencer culture*," he said, using his fingers to make air quotes around the phrase. He liked Lila, but the whole thing seemed shallow to him. He was a firm believer of living in the moment and didn't think everything needed to be documented and shared online for "likes."

"What do you want to know?"

"How did you get into the business? What is it you do exactly? You're very well-known and apparently have a lot of fans."

She frowned. "I can't tell if you're making fun of me, or not."

He put up his hands. "I'm not making fun, I promise. I'm just a traditional guy. I don't follow social media or celebrities or any of that. I'm more of a private person. I like the quiet life."

She raised an eyebrow and looked around the party. "Really? This doesn't exactly scream the quiet life."

"This is all my brother and sister. I'm not that guy anymore."

"*Anymore?* Was all of this once you?"

He shook his head. He didn't want to get into it, and how he once lived his life.

"There's another story there," she said.

"There are many stories, Lila, but you aren't going to hear them. But we're off track because you distracted me. Tell me what you're all about."

"Where do I start? I've always had a lot of energy, you know? I grew up in a very small town. And I had no intention of staying there. When I turned eighteen, I had big dreams of getting out. But instead, I met the wrong guy, thought I was in love and got married."

"Really?"

"Yeah, it's really embarrassing now. It feels like it was another life from where I am now."

"What happened then?"

"Little did I know that my husband expected me to stay home and cook and clean, until it was time to have babies, and then I could raise children, along with cooking and cleaning. I'd just finished high school, and he told me I'd never have a career, so I'd be dependent on him. He isolated me from my friends and family. I didn't see it at the time, but it was such an unhealthy situation. He was a little older. He was a salesman, and he was good at it. Worked all the time and made a great living. The guy could sell water to a fish. I guess that's how he manipulated me. We looked like the perfect little family. But it was hell." She exhaled, nervously. "I don't know why I'm telling you all of this," she said, shaking her head. "It's been a while since I've talked about it."

"Keep going," he told her. He hated that Lila had been so unhappy. He wanted nothing more than to track down her ex and punch him repeatedly.

"Fine. He was content to keep me at home, but I didn't want that. I wanted to travel, to *finally* leave that town. So, one day, when he was at work, I got the hell out of there. I'd managed to squirrel-away five thousand dollars and I left and never looked back. Then I trained to be a flight attendant."

Reid admired that. "That's great. Then what?"

"I started working, and I got to see and do all the things I'd dreamed about. It was amazing. Along the way I started a blog, began tweeting about my adventures and misadventures, and posting to Instagram. And it just kind of went from there. My videos and posts got a lot of views. I know it sounds easy, but it's a lot of hard work. I started to get sponsors, and ad revenue. It's hell trying to build a dedicated following when you start with nothing."

Reid realized that they had more in common than he would have ever thought. "Tell me about it. My parents worked at the distillery when we were children. They had a small local following, but never intended to have the reach we do now. Some days it feels like marketing and building a brand comes ahead of the actual product."

"So, you know what I'm saying."

"I think I do."

"And that's why your brother invited me here," she said, pulling out her phone. "I take pictures, I write blogs, I show people what a good time they're missing." As if to prove her point, she snapped a photo of the crowd. "I give people extreme FOMO." She stopped when his head tilted at the word she'd used. "*Fear of missing out,*" she explained. "People want to live my life—travel, eat, drink, hang out with celebrities. I get people to do what I do—which in this case is drink your rum."

Before he could ask her about it, she quickly snapped a picture of her glass. Looked at it, frowned, then lifted the glass and held the camera above her to take a picture of herself drinking the rum. She looked at it and smiled. "Perfect," she muttered, and began typing furiously. "Having a wild time at the Rexford Rum party in Miami," she read aloud as she typed. "Hashtag drinks, hashtag Rexford Rum, hashtag Miami, hashtag party-time, hashtag wish you were here." She smiled at him, and then rounded the table and held her camera above them, but tilted downward, and took another picture. She started typing. "Our handsome host, Reid Rexford says hi," she said as she typed. "And post."

"So that's your job?" he asked skeptically. "You take a picture, post it, and sit back to wait for the likes."

"And the shares and comments," she retorted.

"Seems a little shallow," he told her. He hadn't meant for his words to sound as harsh as they did.

"It's all about reach. I'm no different than those fancy traditional marketing firms you hire. In fact, I might be a little more flexible and adaptable to new platforms and technology than those guys. It's all about search engine optimization and cost per click. I get more bang for your buck.

"People see and want my life—that's the product I'm pushing. Brands and events reach out because I have literally millions of followers who want just a small piece of what's perceived to be my amazing life."

Perceived stuck out to him. As much as Lila extolled the wonderful parts of her life, he wondered if it wasn't always as wonderful as it seemed. Maybe the life of a beautiful vagabond wasn't all the glitz and glamor people thought.

"What's the difference between your actual life and what you put out there?"

Her eyes shifted skyward, and then she blew out a shaky breath. "I know I'm lucky, I do have an incredible life," she told him. "I love to travel, meet new people, have new experiences. But sometimes I get tired. I get bored with the same hotel rooms, not making any of those real connections with people. I went to Bonnaroo last year, and all I wanted to do was stay in my hotel room, eat Doritos and watch *The Office* on Netflix. I don't always want to be the social one." Her laugh sounded forced. "Listen to me—poor little girl who has fun for a living."

Hearing her revelation that her life wasn't all fun and glamour, that she trusted him enough to tell him, Reid felt like they were sharing a real moment. "I get that. I'm the most reserved of my siblings. I like the quiet."

"Me too sometimes, but I'm not always allowed to have it."

"Well, why don't you do something else?"

"Why would I? I have everything I want. A fun life, and I get paid to do it. I'm my own boss. I could never be tied to a nine-to-five, Monday-to-Friday gig."

"Except you're on the clock 24/7."

"It sounds to me like you might be, too."

He thought about it, and realized she was right. That was his life. "Not everyone is cut out for it, I guess." He frowned, too, and their eyes connected. For a moment, they shared a knowing solidarity.

"Where do you live?" he asked.

She blinked. "What do you mean?"

He paused. "I'm not sure how else I could ask that question. Where do you go when you aren't globe-trotting? Where's your family?"

Lila pictured the town, and the people she'd come from, and forced the frown from her lips, replacing it with a big, easy smile. "Still in that very small town, and that's also where I escaped from. I don't stop. When I'm tired, I plan some more quiet trips, if I can get a hotel or resort comped, or maybe I'll visit some friends. I've got some stuff in storage in LA, but mostly I live out of my suitcase."

She leaned over the table, coming closer to him. "Can you keep a secret?" she whispered conspiratorially.

He leaned in as well. "My lips are sealed."

"I'm not sure why I'm telling you this. Maybe it was the rum, maybe you make me feel at ease. But here it is. I'm in negotiations with the GO! Channel for my own travel show."

"That's incredible."

"It hasn't been finalized yet, so I'd really appreciate it if you don't tell anyone."

"I know about wanting to keep secrets. Yours dies with me."

"What secrets do you have, Reid?"

He looked down into his drink and didn't say anything for a while. He didn't know what to say, so he deflected. "And what about your family?" he asked, ignoring her question entirely.

She shook her head. "They visit me on the road. Not like I'll ever go back there. My hometown represents oppression, and now I'm free."

"No plans on settling down? Putting down roots?"

"I think eventually I might get a place. Something small. But I don't have to worry about that yet. If I make the deal for my own show, I'll find something in LA. I'll still get to travel but it won't be so much."

Not taking his eyes from her, Reid lifted his glass

and finished his drink. There was more to Lila, with whom he'd had a one-night stand, and then a rare-for-him second round. He liked her, more than he'd liked a woman in a long time. He noticed that she'd also finished her drink. "Another?"

"So, because I missed my train, I was four hours late getting to Prague, I missed the check-in time for the room I'd arranged. I get there, and the innkeeper freaks out at me, saying that he'd given away my room, that it would teach me to plan ahead, and all that. I went to about a dozen other places and found no room anywhere. Here I am, completely alone, with no room in a strange city."

Reid laughed. "What did you do?"

"What any young woman in my predicament would do—I found a pub and got a beer. I fell in with a group of Irish girls, and they offered me a spot on the floor in their small room."

She didn't miss his frown. "Sounds risky."

Lila dismissed him with a wave. "I don't make it a habit to go off with strangers." She caught the way his eyebrows rose. That was exactly what she'd done with him. "But I always open myself up for adventure."

Lila watched as Reid laughed and sipped his drink. She was feeling light-headed, but not from the alcohol—she hadn't had that much—but it was Reid's company. He was funny, smart, but also very serious. "So, what about you?"

"What about me?"

"You have any funny travel stories?"

He shook his head. "Unfortunately, I don't get to travel much."

"Why not?" He clearly had the funds to go on any holiday he wanted.

"I'm so busy with work and everything. I don't feel comfortable leaving the distillery for long periods of time."

"Won't your brother and sister take care of things?"

Reid's eyes shifted over to the bar, where his brother, Quin, downed shots with some players she recognized as starters for the Miami Heat basketball team.

"Yeah," he said slowly. "They're my family and I love them, but they aren't the surest hands I've seen. That's Quin in a nutshell, and Gemma rarely surfaces from the distillery." He shook his head. "I'm not even sure she's ever *seen* a financial statement."

"You're the responsible older brother just trying to hold it all together."

"That's a little dramatic, but some days it feels like that."

"Are you kidding me? You're young, hot, successful. Everyone needs a break every now and then. Don't you ever want to just get away?"

"Sometimes, I might take a weekend away and go to the Everglades or Key West." He sighed. "I'll bet my life sounds boring to you."

She hesitated. The quiet, the solitude, it was what Lila typically avoided at all costs, not wanting to be alone with herself or her own thoughts. She needed the excitement, the buzz around her. But she thought about it. A visit to the Everglades, or a quiet Key West beach, especially one that came with Reid Rexford, sounded nice. She smiled, and shrugging, drained her glass. "I see the appeal. Not sure if it's what I'm looking for, but different strokes, right?"

"Definitely."

A comfortable silence surrounded them, and Lila realized the amount of time that had passed since they'd started talking. "You know, I should be making my rounds," she said. "Earn that invitation your brother sent me."

"Yeah, me too. I should go shake some hands."

"It was nice to see you again. Thanks for the drinks, and the dance. I'm glad I got to see you again tonight. And we got to clear the air a little."

"Me too. It's been fun. It's been a while since I've danced."

She looked up at him and narrowed her eyes. He looked straight ahead; his posture was rigid. "But it's over, right?" she guessed.

"Yeah. Just let the doorman know whenever you're ready to leave. He'll get you a car."

"No, it's fine. I'll just call a cab or walk. My hotel isn't far."

"Yeah, I know exactly where your hotel is," he

reminded her. Of course, he knew. He'd been there. Twice. "But I'm not letting you walk out of here alone," he told her.

"Thanks." They stood. While Lila was disappointed she hadn't set the groundwork for a partnership, she was glad to have had an actual conversation with him and get to know him a little bit better.

"How much longer do you have in Miami?" he asked.

"I fly out tomorrow night," she told him.

He nodded, but he was frowning. "Well, it's been fun."

"It sure was," she agreed. It was too bad that she was leaving soon. She knew she would miss Reid, and for the first time, she wondered if she would be leaving something behind.

Without thinking, she reached out and wrapped her arms around him, and it surprised her when he hugged her back.

His strong arms wrapped around her and the heat from his body made her melt her against him. He was standing so close she could smell the rum on his breath.

She heard a low groan from his chest. "You leave tomorrow night?" he asked, his voice low.

"Yeah," she whispered back. Turning her head put her lips within a fraction of an inch of his jaw. There was only a hairbreadth of space between their bodies, and from the way he looked down at her, there was that spark of desire in his eyes that she couldn't miss and knew he hadn't either.

"You're still staying at the same hotel?"

"I am."

"Why don't I meet you there in an hour?"

CHAPTER SEVEN

TRUE TO HIS WORD, one hour later, Reid was standing outside of Lila's hotel room. He'd been so close to a clean break with her. But instead, when he'd hugged her, the desire he felt had been too much. He'd done one final lap around the party, making sure everything was going smoothly, and avoiding the curious glances of his brother and sister, he quietly left. He knew Quin and Gemma would have questions tomorrow. But as he jogged down the street to Lila's hotel, he didn't give a damn. All he could think about was Lila.

He raised his fist and knocked three times. The force behind the knock told of his urgency.

Lila opened the door. She was still wearing the outfit she'd worn at the party. She smiled and stepped to the side, opening the door wider to let him in.

Once inside, he slammed the door shut and then pounced. He cupped her face in his hands and kissed her. She was so sweet, so hot. Perfect. When he kissed Lila, there was nothing else—no family, no business, no commitments—nothing but her full, delicious lips.

She pulled away first. "Reid," she started, putting her hand on his chest. "I'm so glad you came here. I know we agreed it was best if we didn't do this. What I said earlier—that was the smart, rational Lila speaking, but this is the Lila who wants you so badly she can barely breathe." She smoothed her palms over his chest, and he cursed the material of his shirt for separating them. "There's no reason why we can't have one more night together, is there?"

"I can't think of a goddamn one."

"You sure you aren't missing the party?"

Reid thought briefly of what he might be missing—schmoozing with celebrities, hearing from customers. He knew that the night was an important one for the distillery. If it was a success, it could put them on the map and give them mainstream success. If it failed, it could ruin them. But when he looked down at Lila, it didn't matter. "I'm not missing anything," he told her, roughly pulling her to him. He kissed her.

As he kissed her, her arms wrapped around his neck, her fingers fisting his hair, as she lowered them, running her hands over her shoulders, down his chest. Her fingers were at his buttons, loosening them, undressing him. Reid was harder than he'd ever been in his life, and his need for her was greater than anything he'd ever wanted.

He broke away only long enough to pull her shirt over her head. Her skirt was next. She stood in front of him in only her matching black bra and panties and black stilettos. “Christ,” he muttered against her throat. “You’re the sexiest goddamn thing I’ve ever seen.”

Lila pushed Reid’s shirt from his shoulders. “You’re not so bad yourself,” she told him, moving against his hardened cock, the delicious contact making him flinch. Adrenaline, the need to have her surged through his system, and his entire body clenched. His hands were on her ass. He lifted her and she wrapped her legs around his waist. She fit perfectly against him. He removed one hand from her ass and brought it to her red hair, pushing his fingers through the silky strands, until reaching the back of her head, where he wrapped her hair around his hand and pulled gently, forcing her eyes to his.

Her lips parted with a startled gasp, and his entire body hardened with the image of his dick sliding between them. Her eyes were fiery, and her thighs tightened around his waist, and he could feel her heat against his abdomen. There was no time for any preliminaries—that would come later—right now, he needed to be inside of her.

He closed his eyes and took a deep, calming breath. Lila made him feel like a wild man. He’d never been so out-of-control with a woman. His body was calling the shots, not his mind.

He brought her to the bed and lowered her. He reached for a condom on the nightstand and he made quick work of lowering his pants and covering himself with the latex. He pulled down her panties and stood between her parted thighs.

She reached for him, and when her fingers touched his dick, he thought he might explode. With a growl, he leaned over her and with one hand, he held both of her wrists over her head—pinning her to the bed.

"You okay?" he asked her, his desire-addled brain barely able to form the words.

She nodded. "Yes."

"Good." He used his free hand to guide his dick to her opening and in one hard thrust, he was inside of her.

The cry that tore from Lila's lips filled the hotel room.

Still holding both of her wrists, he pushed in and out of her. Her heat surrounded him, and it was more incredible than he remembered. Long forgotten were all his responsibilities, all his cares and worries. All that existed was Lila and his desire.

His heart was pounding, and his muscles began to tighten. He increased his pace, shifting the bed underneath them. He wouldn't last much longer. But he needed to make sure Lila found her pleasure before he took his own.

With his free hand, he found her clit, and circled the sensitive nubs with the pads of his fingers. Her eyes snapped open, and she gasped. It only took a few seconds before she tightened and spasmed around him, crying out her release.

Reid then let go and let himself succumb to the

pleasure. From the bottom of his curling toes, to the flashes of light he saw behind his closed eyes, he took every amount of bliss from the moment before he collapsed on top of her still-quivering body.

When he awoke the next morning, with the sun in his eyes and his arm slung tightly around Lila's waist, it was after noon, and Reid felt like he'd had the best sleep of his life. Lila's deep, even breaths, accompanied by the rise and fall of her chest told him that she was still sleeping, and he pulled her closer, her red wild curls tickling his nose and cheek. He inhaled deeply. He wasn't sure what had caused him to come to her the night before. He should have stayed at the party. It was his responsibility. But when it came to Lila, for whatever reason, he didn't care about anything else but being with her He'd shirked his responsibilities. Even during his marriage, he hadn't done anything like that. The distillery had always come first.

Lila gave a small whimper and burrowed herself deeper underneath the blanket. Meeting Lila had changed that. It wasn't love, of course, he barely knew her, but Reid was completely in lust with the woman. She was pure temptation. She would be leaving town later that day. And that was how he justified his attraction to her. Theirs was a red-hot affair—but it was temporary.

He heard his cell phone ring, the sound coming from his jacket, which had been left in a pile near the door. He should answer it. But that was when Lila, still asleep, rolled over in his arms to face him. There was no way he could tear himself away from her warm body. The phone quieted, and Reid closed his eyes. But when the phone rang again, he cursed.

"Is that your phone?" Lila murmured, her eyes still closed.

"Yeah," he said. "I'd better getter it."

"Could be an emergency."

Those words hit Reid like a punch to the chest. She was right. It *could* have been an emergency—that something has happened to Gemma, Quin or his father. Maybe something had happened at the distillery. There could have been a fire or mechanical breakdown, there could be batches ruined. Those were the things that plagued his mind on the short walk across the room. How many times had his phone rang and he'd slept through it? How long had he been content to ignore the calls, just as long as he was wrapped up in a woman he barely knew. Reid should know better.

After a walk that took no more than eight steps, but felt like a mile, Reid reached his coat. He pulled out his phone and saw that Quin was calling. He answered. "What's wrong?"

"About time you answered your goddamn phone," his brother admonished him.

"What's up? Is everything okay?"

"We've been fielding phone calls from distributors all morning."

A ball of worry formed in Reid's gut. "About what? What's going on?" he asked, while picturing crisis situations involving ruined shipments, the inability to pay their bills and foreclosure. What had happened while he'd been in bed with Lila.

"We're sold out," Quin told him.

The words didn't make sense at first. "Where?"

"Dude, everywhere. Florida, Georgia and Alabama are dry, and the shelves are emptying as we speak everywhere else. We've got calls from stores LA, New York, Austin, Vegas and a bunch of other cities who want to carry our rum. Gemma's got everyone working this morning, and emergency shipments going out."

"How did this happen? Was it the party?"

"The party helped. But really, I think it was Lila Campbell," he told him.

"Lila?" Just hearing her name was enough for his body to clench in response. He looked over at her, and her eyes were open, watching him. He forced his brain to focus on the business and what Quin was telling him. But that was almost impossible when he could barely hear his brother's words.

"Her blog about the distillery went live last night, and within hours it was picked up by outlets all over the country. Along with her posts and those of the celebrities who attended our party… Reid, we're trending on almost every social media platform—Twitter, Instagram, Snapchat, Facebook. Pictures and videos are being shared everywhere." He could hear the excitement in Quin's voice. "This is insane. We're on the edge, man. This is it. Rexford is going to pop off!"

"Where are you?"

"Gemma and I are here at the distillery, and we've been here since six. We've got her crew in trying to see how quickly we can restock and roll more out."

"Since six?"

"Yeah, as soon as our social media accounts started seeing the action. Then the distributors and stores started calling."

Reid's heart pounded with excitement. Rexford Rum was about to take off, and he'd missed the biggest morning they'd ever had. His siblings were dealing with supply issues, when that was supposed to be his job.

"You left pretty early last night." Quin paused. "Are you with Lila now?"

He didn't want to lie to his brother, so he said nothing. "I'm on my way over there now."

"Bring Lila with you," Quin told him.

"Why?"

"Just do it. There's something I want to discuss with her."

"You can tell me what it is." Reid did not like being left out of the loop when it came to the distillery.

"I will when you get here."

Reid wanted to know what was on his brother's mind, but he knew that the quicker he could get off the phone, the faster he could get to work. “Okay, I’ll be right there.” Without saying goodbye to his brother, Reid disconnected the call, and turned to Lila.

“What’s going on? Is everything okay?”

“Do you have any plans today?”

Lila shook her head. “Just a late lunch with your sister.”

“That’s probably cancelled now. Why don’t you get dressed and come with me?”

“Where?”

“The distillery.”

“Why?”

He watched as Lila got out of bed. His body reacted, wanting to push her down and have her again, but instead he turned away and began gathering his clothes. He had to get to work and put all his energy to solving his current supply problem. “Wouldn’t I love to know.”

CHAPTER EIGHT

LILA WASN'T SURE why Reid had asked her to join him at the Rexford distillery, but she was intrigued. He'd told her that demand for the rum was high thanks to whatever had happened last night. Checking her web site analytics and social media impressions, she knew that internet stars have aligned, and the social media gods had spoken, and Rexford Rum have been struck by lightning. But when it came to social media, posts and reach were not enough. Her blog post on the distillery had been picked up, and it coincided with the posts and pictures from all the celebrities at the party. This was some once-in-a-lifetime exposure for the distillery. And herself. Those kinds of results made her happy—not just for the reach of her own blog, and the increase in ad revenue, but it also gave her something to bring to the GO! Channel. Those stuffy executives couldn't argue with raw data behind her creation of a media sensation.

From her seat in the hard, wooden chair in the distillery, she watched as Gemma's distillers worked feverishly to get product out, while Reid, Quin and Gemma were locked inside Gemma's small office. She was able to see inside, thanks to the large window over her desk. The siblings were engaged in what looked like a serious conversation. Despite their overnight success, they looked stressed. She couldn't count the number of times she watched Reid run his fingers through his hair. His features were tight, serious. She still didn't know why she was there. If only one of them would talk to her.

Lila couldn't sit any longer. She had to do something. So she stood from the uncomfortable chair, stretched her legs, and turned to check out the wall of photos behind her The inscriptions showed the evolution of the Rexford distillery starting with hand-drawn maps from the records of Joseph Rexford, the disgraced bootlegger and alleged pirate, who ran rum from Cuba and the Bahamas to what was now known as Miami Beach. Each photo showed growth, succession through the generations, until she came to the last one—a picture of Reid, Quin and Gemma, the same one she'd seen before on Reid's phone. Smiling, proud in front of their humble distillery. The picture had to have been at least ten-years-old. She could see that Reid had aged gracefully in the past decade. In the photo, he lacked some of the lines at the corners of his eyes and lips. His smile was more carefree, less forced than the ones she'd seen from him in person, and she wondered what had changed.

* * *

"How are we going to meet this demand?" Reid scrubbed his hands over his face. He looked over the production schedules Gemma had shown him, and then the demand projections over the next six months.

"We aren't," Gemma said matter-of-factly, looking as frustrated as he felt. "We can start production ASAP on new batches, so we will have an abundance in a year at the earliest. Unless I can come up with something new, there's no way to speed up the aging process on what we already have while maintaining quality. And I'm not compromising on quality."

"Nor should we. We need a way to keep this momentum, so that by the time the rum we're producing right now is ready, people will still want it." He turned to his brother. "You're the marketing expert. How do we do that?"

"I have something," she offered, opening her locked drawer. "I was going through some old records and journals a little while ago, and I found something." She took out a yellowed sheet of paper and laid it carefully on the desk in front of them.

"What is that?" Reid asked.

"It's a recipe," she told them. "It belonged to our great-grandfather. For an easy-to-make, unaged prohibition-era rum. You know how white and light batches don't need to be aged. That's how they did it back in the day. They made it and then immediately sold it. And it's simple. Simpler than mine, and if I'm right about it, it can most likely be ready, bottled and out the door in just a couple of weeks. If it turns out good, it can keep us going long enough to start production on dark and spiced batches. I just wish there was a way to quick-distill and age those."

Quin nodded. "I like that. We can call it a throwback recipe. Boost the prohibition and rumrunner angle. Give it a good story, tie in the family history. It could work." Reid looked over the orders that had come in that morning so far, and on top of their regular orders, this was the only thing that could help them fill some of the demand for their product. "That's a good plan of attack," Reid agreed, and even though he was glad they had a way out of their current predicament, he was still irritated that he hadn't come up with it. He hadn't even been there while the rest of the employees had worked that morning. He would never let himself get so distracted again. He didn't care what happened, he would never put the family or the business on the back burner again. That was the priority—not rolling around with a gorgeous, charismatic temptress. He looked out through the window and saw Lila. He still didn't know why Quin wanted to see her.

Reid watched her shake her loose hair—those gorgeous red curls—over her shoulder. His fingers itched, wanting to twirl them around his fingers.

"All right we'll get the crews working today." Reid

hadn't even noticed when Gemma had started talking. "Meanwhile, I'm going to try to figure out a way to get the dark and spiced rums out. But I don't know if I can. I'm not making any promises."

"We just need to keep demand high. We need to sustain this spike, and not just fall off again. The new rum could help. But we need to maintain our online popularity. We've got to stay in the public eye. We're in an interesting position right now. Rexford is a hot commodity. But you're right. We can't stay on top forever if we can't get the product into people's hands. So that's why I asked you to bring Lila." Quin stood from the table.

"What does Lila—"

But before he could finish his sentence, Quin had opened the door. "Lila, can you come in here, please?"

"Sure."

She walked into his office, and Quin gestured for her to sit in the chair he'd vacated. Reid still didn't know what his younger brother had in mind, but he could tell from his smirk that he wouldn't like it.

"Lila, thanks for coming in," Quin started. "I wanted to talk to all of you about this. I've got an idea."

"What is it?" Reid and Lila asked at the same time, and their eyes met.

"Here's what I'm thinking," Quin started. "Lila, we want you to be our brand ambassador."

"What?" Again, Reid and Lila spoke at the same

time. He'd had no idea that was where the impromptu meeting Quin had called was leading.

"We'd like to offer you a corporate partnership to represent our brand."

Lila's eyes found his, and she seemed just as surprised as he was. She turned to Quin. "I'm interested. What exactly do you have in mind?"

Lila ignored Reid's stare as Quin detailed what they wanted from her. It was everything she'd wanted from them but had not yet proposed.

"Because of your posts, and the overnight jump in popularity, we have a supply problem," Quin told her.

"Quin," Reid said. "Maybe it's best if we don't talk business with outsiders."

Outsiders. Even though he was right, she was an outsider, hearing him say it hurt. She had no stake in the business. She'd just hooked-up with one of the owners a couple of times. That was it.

But Quin ignored him. "Basically, we want you to do what you've already done. We want you to promote Rexford Rum on all of your platforms, in your blog. Keep the Rexford Rum brand out there so we have time to increase production and distribution. We'll pay you, but also feature you and your brand in our own promotions."

"A corporate partnership would definitely be beneficial for me as well," she told them, leaving out that she was in talks for a television show, and that a corporate partnership with the country's most-wanted liquor brand would make her a hot commodity, as well. “What sort of things do you need me to do?”

“We can discuss specifics later, and we’ll do up the paperwork. I’m just wondering if you’re open to working together.”

“Yeah, I am. Send me the contract and the terms when it’s ready. But I just have to wonder, wouldn’t featuring your rum—when you don’t have enough to meet the demand—just piss people off?”

“Without getting into too many details, we’re hoping to have a new product out soon,” Gemma told her. “We will have rum for sale, just not everything that we have available in the small batches.”

“We want you to focus on that,” Quin explained. “Think prohibition, bootleggers, a real vintage feel.”

“I think you’re both doing a lot of talking about the confidential details of our business,” Reid admonished his siblings. “Lila doesn’t need to know all of our plans.”

“You’re right,” Lila agreed. “But I’m a very trustworthy person, I figured you might agree,” she said with a raised eyebrow. They’d slept together several times. He clearly didn’t trust her. She turned back to Quin.“Let’s work on a contract. But if we can agree to terms, I’m in.” Reid interrupted. “No,” he said, his voice firm.

Lila joined Gemma and Quin in turning to look at Reid with surprise.

“What?” Quin asked him. “Why not?”

“Lila, I know you’re good at what you do. The

numbers prove it. We pay a lot of money to marketing firms. I don't want to pin our distillery's success, and potential failure on a slick, relatively new, fickle marketing plan like social-media exposure. We don't need a social media *influencer* representing our brand." His tone and words were cruel, and they hurt.

What is his problem? As long as she lived, she would never understand Reid Rexford. She wanted to work with the brand, but they needed her as much as she needed them. She knew what happened when people and companies failed to capitalize on their success. They were doomed to fail. But Lila knew she was good at what she did, and she wouldn't put her self-respect on the line to work for a man who didn't respect her or her job.

The room was still. No one spoke until Lila took her phone out of her purse. "That's where your wrong," she said, moving her thumbs quickly over the screen. "Facebook followers," she started, "five million. Twitter: 1.3 million, Snapchat: 870,000, Instagram: 10.9 million. That's organic reach, Reid. Your brother is right. People pay attention to what I have to say. Look at this." She passed her phone over and showed Reid the pictures she'd posted from the party. She'd looked up Rexford Rum's social media accounts. The likes, comments, shares were all more than they'd ever received. "And I'm going to need you to apologize for the tone you just used describing my career before we go any further with this discussion."

Both Quin and Gemma looked to Reid, but he said nothing.

"Goddammit, Reid," Quin said.

"You've seen what I can do," she said, her lips curving upward in an innuendo-laced grin. "But if you don't want to be in business with me, Reid, fine." She looked at Quin and Gemma. "Thanks for the meeting. It was great meeting you." She stood, gathered her phone and purse and headed for the door.

When Lila walked out and slammed the door behind her, Quin turned to Reid and punched him in the arm. "What the fuck was that, man?"

Reid wasn't sure. He knew he would have to give them more of an explanation than that. But what could he say? That he didn't trust himself around her, that when she was around, he could barely focus on anything *but* her? That by leaving the party to be with her last night, it showed that he wanted her beyond everything else. And that terrified him.

He couldn't have her connected to the distillery, he couldn't keep her in his life, even if it meant missing out on the opportunity of what he knew would be a successful campaign. But if he couldn't do his actual work, what was the point?

So, he lied to his siblings. "I didn't think it was a good idea."

"Bullshit," Quin said.

"How do you think that?" Gemma asked. "You saw what she's capable of. Look at this demand. And you just sent away the woman who can keep the buzz going and sell our new batch."

"Stop being so dramatic. We're already successful. Sure, the boost is nice, but it'll still lead to long-term success whether we use Lila, or not."

"Stop being so pigheaded. Is this because you slept with her?"

"How did you know?"

"I saw you guys at the party last night. There was definitely a connection between the two of you. Why were you such a jerk to her?"

He wasn't sure why he'd been so cold to Lila. But he knew that he couldn't have her in his vicinity. Whether it was good for the business or not, he knew it wasn't good for him. And it certainly wouldn't be good for her in the long run.

"You said it yourself," Quin said simply. "We have a great marketing firm, but in the business world, especially some of the older guys have been slow to catch up to recent developments in social media marketing. She's got her finger on the pulse and can reach millions of people, who would consider us to be the rum brand their grandfathers choose. We need to get younger, sexier. We started with the party. This is how we position ourselves, and you basically chased away our shot. I don't care what happened between you guys, go get her," Quin urged him.

"And make sure you apologize," Gemma told him.

Reid knew he wouldn't win, and even though he

was caught between chasing her and letting her walk out the door, he stood. "Fine," he said. "I'll get her." Whether or not she'd want to talk to him, well, that was another story.

Fucking Reid. Lila walked down the hallway. Where did he get off, treating her like that? Well, she knew exactly right where he'd gotten off, she remembered with an eye roll. In her bed. Stopping at the main door, she flipped through her phone to a ride share app to summon a car, but she paused when she heard the even, sure footsteps approach her from behind.

"Lila, wait."

What now? Why had he followed her out the door when she'd made her indignant exit? "What do you want? A second opportunity to disrespect me and the work I do?"

"No." He paused. "I'm sorry about what I said."

"Why did you say it, then? After I explained to you everything I do. How much I told you about it. I thought you understood how much work goes into it."

He sighed and looked away. "I don't know. I panicked, maybe."

"You panicked," she repeated, not understanding him.

"Lila, we were supposed to be a one-night thing. An anonymous thing."

"We blew that out of the water, didn't we?" He said nothing. "We agreed on one night, and you want me gone."

"Yes." Her eyebrows rose. "No, not like that," he stammered. "I like you. But that's where the trouble lies. All I want to do is be near you. And when I see you, all I can think about is taking you to bed. And when Quin suggested you work with us, all I could think about was how dangerous that was."

"Dangerous? Reid, you aren't making any sense."

"I know. It doesn't make any sense to me either. But I know that having you promote us does make sense."

She sighed. If he couldn't be clearer than that, there wasn't a point in her sticking around. "Well, that's too bad. I thought I liked you, Reid. But you're just like the rest. What I do has a real value, and I can be good for your company."

"I know, and that's why I chased you out here."

"Not just because your brother and sister made you?"

He paused for too long, and Lila noticed her car pull up in front of the distillery. "Goodbye, Reid." She patted his chest and dragged her fingers over his nipple, and he flinched at the contact. His reaction made her laugh. She winked. "This time is for good. Congratulations on all your success. I had a lot of fun, and I did want to work with your family." She shrugged. "But you blew it."

Reid didn't move until Lila's car was completely out of sight. Blowing out a heavy, frustrated breath, he pushed his fingers through his hair. That hadn't played out exactly how he'd imagined it would. And he had no one to blame but himself. He'd been cruel to her. And he wasn't even sure why. He'd enjoyed her company and had shown an interest in what she did. But the prospect of having her work with the distillery had caused him to panic, and he'd lashed out.

He walked back to the distillery. He'd hoped his siblings had taken the opportunity to leave and move on to other tasks, but he had no such luck. Gemma and Quin watched him as he wordlessly walked in and took his seat next to Gemma's desk. Their faces showed contempt, anger, disappointment and—he wished he had better news for them—hope that Lila had decided to forgive him.

A heavy silence filled the room until Quin cut through it with a clearing of his throat. "Is she going to do it?" he asked.

"She's gone."

"Goddammit, Reid," Gemma scolded him. "What is wrong with you?"

Not interested in being on the receiving end of an inquisition, Reid wanted to be left alone. He stood. "I'm done. We should get out there and help the crew. We've got bottles to get out."

"Not quite yet," Quin said, stopping him. "*We're* not done. And we're not having this disagreement out there on the floor in front of the workers."

"Yeah, I'm confused about what happened here today," Gemma said. "It looked like you guys were getting along last night. I mean, it's obvious you did."

"We did." He offered nothing else in response.

Quin snorted. Despite how angry he was at Reid, his younger brother loved needling him even more. "If I walked in on what I think I did, the tour probably went better than any other we've had."

Reid flipped him off without saying a word.

Quin put up his hands. "Don't get mad at me."

No one said anything until Gemma spoke again. "So why were you such a jerk to her? This is a good thing for us, and you know it. The fact that you sabotaged it doesn't make any sense. You've always done what's best for the distillery. What's going on?"

He didn't want to respond. But he knew his siblings wouldn't let it go unless he did. He didn't want to get into the real reason he'd dismissed her and let her leave. That she was a temptation. He tried to tell himself that the attraction was physical, but he could feel something more building there. If she was connected to the business, there was no way he could keep his feelings in check. "I told you. I don't think we should be pouring our money into some slick social media campaign. That's not us."

"It's the 21st century, Reid," Quin scolded him. Reid wasn't used to being berated by Quin, and he didn't like it. He'd always been the more practical sibling. "Magazine and television ads don't cut it anymore. It's all about social media, word of mouth, an online presence, *getting clicks*. You need to make this right with her."

"I can't," he conceded. "She's gone." And rightfully so. Reid realized that he didn't deserve Lila's time or presence. He couldn't blame her for walking away after he'd treated her so shabbily. But it was best that parting happened like it did—with her walking away. He couldn't stand to be around her and not have her. The temptation would have been too much to bear.

Gemma's mouth dropped, and he saw the understanding come over her face. "I get it now," she said softly. "This is actually about Carolina, and what she did, isn't it?"

Reid frowned. He wanted to pound his fist on his desk and tell his brother and sister that his ex-wife was the furthest thing from his mind. It'd be a lie, of course. Every business decision he'd made since their divorce was at least partially colored by her betrayal. "This has nothing to do with her," he said, in a feeble attempt to convince them.

Quin shook his head. "I don't know, Reid, I would think that your lack of trust has a lot to do with a woman who betrayed you a couple of years ago."

"Can we just get to work?" Reid asked, wanting to put the issue behind them.

"You're sure that's what you want?"

"That's all I want. The business is my priority. You know that."

"What if the business wasn't your only priority?"

Reid shook his head. The one time he'd dropped the ball and let a woman in, it had almost cost them everything. "It's too late for that. Let's get to work and sell some rum." Reid was ready to roll up his sleeves, do some work to forget about the woman who'd somehow managed to turn him completely inside-out.

CHAPTER NINE

FROM HER VIEW at the table of the beachfront restaurant, Lila watched the ocean crash against the sand. She closed her eyes, sipped her mojito and listened to the roar of the waves hitting the shore.

It was late in the evening, and she watched families pack up their belongings, sun-kissed and smiling from a day at the beach. There were just a few hours before she needed to be at the airport. But Gemma had contacted her after she'd stormed out of the distillery, begging her to meet her for a drink before leaving town. Lila almost said no, still angry at Reid. But she relented. She liked Gemma and it wasn't her fault her brother was an asshole.

Again, she sipped her drink. Before arriving in Miami, she would never have called herself a rum fan, but she was starting to develop a taste for the stuff. It was like an elixir. With every taste, with every smell, she felt Reid. His essence had stayed with her, in her system, and all she could think about was getting her next taste. She was never one to fall quickly for a man, but the physical attraction between them was stronger than she'd ever experienced. It had been a while since she'd been with a man. Maybe she'd just been hornier than she knew.

Ugh. Reid. She didn't have the time or patience to figure out what was going on in his brain. He was hot and cold, night and day, a mystery wrapped in an enigma, and so on.

"Sorry I'm late," Gemma said, coming up behind her. "Traffic was insane. Typical Miami, right?" Lila hadn't spent much time in the city, but she'd been there long enough to know that traffic was a mess. "Have you been waiting long?"

Lila smiled as Gemma Rexford took the seat across from her. She was still wearing the same jeans and tank top that she'd had on at the distillery that afternoon. She looked like she'd been working all day. "Just long enough to get a drink."

"You're probably wondering why I asked you to still meet me. I really appreciate it because I know you have a flight in a few hours."

"I figured I'm just here so you can grovel."

"Yeah, pretty much," Gemma admitted.

"We, Quin and I, really want you to be our representative."

"But not Reid."

Gemma exhaled and smiled. "Reid is stubborn. I don't know what's going on with him, but the way he reacted is so out-of-character. He always does what's best for the business. And that's you, whether he wants to or not. Maybe he's just old-fashioned. I don't know."

Lila flashed back to images of Reid in her mind. In bed, Reid was fiery, impassioned, and nothing like the cold businessman he'd shown her earlier. Old-fashioned, however, wasn't how she'd describe him.

"I really want to apologize for how he acted."

"Reid's a grown man. It's not your place to apologize for him."

"Still, I'd really hate for his attitude to screw up one of the best things that's happened to us. You were a huge part of the boost we've received in the past twenty-four hours."

"So, we're here for you to tell me how great I am?"

"That and we need you. Forget about Reid for a second. We need our customers to embrace this new recipe, until our regular and premium batches are ready for distribution. We want you to work with us. And we'll pay you. Very well." Gemma named a price that made Lila's eyes widen. She received perks from her job, and revenue from ads and endorsements, but nothing close to what Gemma Rexford had just put on the table.

Lila smiled. She wanted to work with Rexford as well. She still needed them for her own reasons. Raising the profile of Rexford would boost her own brand as well. "You know what? I'm probably going to hate myself for this—the way Reid spoke to me, I should already be online canceling your whole brand." She heard Gemma inhale a gasp. "But I'm not. I like the rum, and I like you. And believe it or not, I do want to be associated with you guys." Lila paused. "But I want to make sure Reid suffers at least a little bit," she finished with a smile.

Gemma snorted out a laugh. "You and me, both, girl. I love my brother, but he's just so gruff and serious sometimes. It's been so long since he's taken any sort of break from the distillery. I think he needs a vacation before he snaps."

Reid hadn't revealed too much of himself to her, but she knew what his sister was saying was the truth. Even though he'd been a dick, she couldn't help herself. She had always been a sucker for pain, for men who would break her heart. But she'd turn the tables on him. He'd have to beg for her forgiveness.

She recalled the differences between Reid the lover and Reid the businessman. She knew that she could release his fun, passionate side. If he was forced to, that is. She took out her phone. "I have an idea." She turned on the speakerphone, asked Gemma to dial Reid's number and put the phone down in the center of the table.

A half of a ring went through before Reid's gruff voice came through the speaker. "Hello,"

"Hi Reid."

"Lila." She could hear the tinge of regret in his voice, and she smiled, hoping he felt terrible. "I—"

"Hey Reid, let me talk now. You owe me a massive apology."

"I've already tried to apol—"

"That doesn't sound like an apology to me. But we'll get there. I've been thinking about it. I'm really on the fence here."

"What do you mean?"

"I mean, I might come around," she smiled at Gemma. "For the right price, if you make it up to me, I might consider working with the distillery."

She heard the whoosh of breath come from his end. "That's great, Lila. I'll talk to marketing and get this rolling ASAP."

"Not so fast," she stopped him again. "I haven't agreed yet. You need to hear my terms." She looked up and winked at Gemma, who was hanging on every word, and clearly enjoying her brother's torture.

"What do you want?"

"I've got something I want you to do." She took a sip of her rum. "I need you packed and ready to meet me at the airport in two hours."

CHAPTER TEN

REID GRUMBLED AS he pulled his carry-on through Miami International Airport, thinking about Lila's request. The woman really had him over a barrel on this one. He should be at the distillery, making sure everything was going smoothly with Gemma's newest batch of the prohibition-era experimental rum. But Gemma and Quin had all but packed his bag for him and pushed him out the door to meet her, whether he liked it or not.

His phone pinged. He checked the screen, and saw it was a text from Lila telling him to meet him at a bar near the security line. He picked up his speed, thinking about the woman waiting for him. At least there would be alcohol. For the day he'd had, he could fucking use a drink.

He made it to the bar and easily found her at a table, sipping champagne from a flute while she picked at the high pile of nachos in front of her. He stopped and watched her as she raised the glass to her lips. Her profile was classic—her nose straight, her lips full, her chin rounded. Suddenly he wasn't quite as angry about being summoned to the airport on a Sunday evening, forcing him to take time away from the distillery when they needed him the most.

She must have felt his eyes on her because she turned to look at him. She smirked and waved with a dainty flick of her fingers. Her eyes held no humor, only irritation.

Directed at him.

Steeling himself, Reid prepared to grovel. For good reason. He'd been terrible to Lila—treated her poorly, embarrassed her—and he might not be a gentleman, but he had to make it right.

"Champagne? Celebrating?"

She shrugged and drained the glass, and before answering waved to the nearby server. "Two more. Yeah, I think we should be celebrating."

He took a seat across from her. She was right. He'd been so caught up trying to figure out the logistics getting enough rum out, that he hadn't had a chance to sit back and enjoy the success.

"We've both had a pretty incredible day," she told him. And you're here. I think that means I've won."

"You think you've won?"

She shrugged. "You're here, aren't you?"

"I don't think this hostage situation counts as winning."

"Ooh, a hostage situation? That sounds kind of hot, doesn't it?"

"I didn't realize that was your kink."

She shrugged. "You never asked." The server placed two more champagne flutes on the table.

"What am I doing here?" Reid asked, taking a nacho chip off the pile. "Why am I going to New Orleans?"

"You're here because you showed me such disrespect this afternoon. After I explained to you how much work I do, and how seriously I take it, you still took the opportunity to dismiss me. You really embarrassed me and belittled what I do. So, you're coming on the road with me."

"What?"

"Yeah, I have to be in New Orleans for a few days. You'll live how I do. You'll be my assistant—"

"Oh, come on, now."

Lila held up a finger. "But you'll cut loose, have fun. And learn that hard work doesn't just happen behind a desk. Then we'll come back here, and we'll sign the necessary paperwork to for our partnership, and I'll show you the ideas I already have for getting out the word about your new rum."

Reid's laugh was a short, incredulous guffaw. "You're insane. I can't just walk away from the distillery for three days."

"Why not? Gemma's already been talking to your assistant. Your work's been rerouted. You don't take vacations. Now, you're going to start."

Gemma. He should have figured she was behind this. Lila had him by the short hairs. "Fine. What do I have to do?"

She finished her champagne in one long swallow. "Drink up, take off your shoes and make sure all your liquids are in a sealed bag. It's almost time to board."

Several hours later, Lila was pressed against Reid in the back seat of an economy rideshare car as it pulled to a stop at the curb in front of a budget hotel. It looked fine to her. She probably could have picked a nicer place, but knowing that Reid would be in tow, she thought she'd show him how to slum it a little.

"All right, this is it," she told him, clutching her purse and getting out of the cab.

Reid looked out through the window. "I don't think so."

"Why not? I didn't take you for a snob."

"I'm not a snob. I'm just not interested in bringing bed bugs and roaches back to my own house." He leaned forward and gave the cab driver the name of a higher-end hotel chain.

When they were on the road again, Lila settled back in her seat and crossed her arms.

"Don't pout, Lila. It's a nice hotel."

She knew it was. She'd brought him on her trip to teach him a lesson. To show him how busy and chaotic her life was, and how much work was involved in her job. She wasn't pouting because he'd changed the hotel, she was just mad that already he'd started taking over her trip. And it didn't help that the warmth of his arm against hers radiated throughout her body, as his cologne tingled her nostrils. Everything about the man, even when she was angry at him, turned her on.

"I know it's a nice hotel. But I'd specifically chosen that one to be close to the action of the French Quarter. That's what I'm here for, you know. None of my readers care about the best hotels in the business sector."

"Don't be so dramatic. We can get a ride where we need to go."

"That's not the point." Soon they pulled up in front of the hotel. An upscale chain. If there was one thing she hated, it was chains—a city was best felt through its local establishments, not through corporate ones. "Let me guess," she started. "You get points for staying here?"

Reid's smile was rich. "Of course I do. I'm a diamond member," he said, before exiting the car.

Rolling her eyes and sighing, Lila gathered her purse. The cab driver caught her eye as she handed over her credit card.

"Lady, if you and your man stay this mad at each other, you're going to have a pretty miserable time."

Lila nodded and signed the printout, not bothering to correct his assumption that Reid was *her man.* "You've got that right."

By the time Lila met up with Reid in the hotel lobby, he was already checked in and waiting for her near a bank of elevators. He handed her a room key. "I got us a two-bedroom suite."

"Fine," she said, taking the key card he'd offered. Even though she was angry at Reid—and she'd invited him along out of pettiness—that didn't mean she wasn't looking forward to them sharing a room. A two-bedroom suite would really cut down the intimacy of that, though. She'd had big plans to walk around in her flimsiest pajamas, to tease him, provoke him… Desire tightened her core just thinking about it. But he'd already made the decision for them, relegating them each to their own bedrooms. "Sounds good to me. We should go up there and get settled. I need a shower, and we should get to bed. We have a busy day tomorrow."

In the suite, when the door to Lila's room closed behind her, Reid let out a heavy breath. In the hall of the suite, outside her closed door, he could hear her rustle about, opening drawers, unpacking. Then he heard the faint noise of shower spray. His body tightened and his brain conjured up images of her soft, supple body as streams of water rolled over her soft skin, imagining it was his hands. He clenched his fists to stop himself from knocking on the door. And he looked to his own room and took one step before he stopped and released the handle on his rolling bag. "Aw, fuck it," he muttered to himself, and went to her door.

Hating his lack of control, Reid couldn't help but knock on her door.

"Hold on," she called from deep within the room.

When she opened the door, her wavy red hair was loose but still dry, and she was wearing the fluffy white hotel robe. She looked impatient, still annoyed at him for changing hotels, or for what he'd said to her. Hell, he didn't know. The list of reasons why Lila might be pissed at him wasn't a short one. "What do you want?" she asked.

He didn't say a word, just went to her, cupping her face in his hands as he brought her to him. Her lips parted instantly for him, and he rewarded her with a hard, deep kiss. A surprised sound came from her throat, and her fingers clenched in the material of his shirt, urged him on. She pulled back and they walked further into her room, not separating their mouths.

With nimble fingers, Lila tackled the buttons down the front of his shirt, while he ripped the tie of the robe from her front and pushed the plush material from her shoulders. He barely noticed when it fell to the floor, soon followed by his shirt.

He lifted her and she was feather-light in his arms, and her legs wrapped around his waist. He followed the sound of the running shower and walked her into the bathroom, still not removing his mouth from hers.

She pulled away first. Her breath was heavy, and she gulped in air. "There are condoms in my makeup bag."

He chuckled, setting her on the counter next to the leather tote. "You came prepared."

"Something wrong with that?" she asked, reaching into the box and withdrawing a condom, while he unzipped his pants and pushed them and his boxers down.

"I'm just relieved that now you aren't going to give me a hard time for the box I packed in my own bag." He took the condom from her fingers and under her watchful eye, he took himself in his free hand and rolled the latex over his length.

The shower still ran, and steam began to fill the room. He took a step closer, bringing his rigid cock in contact with her hot, rich center. "Not right here," he told her, wrapping an arm around her waist and pulling her so close she was flush against him, his cock pressed upward between them. She squirmed, creating a delicious feeling up and down his dick. "Keep that up and I won't last to get inside of you. Then where will you be?"

"I'm confident you won't leave me hanging."

"You got that right." Again, he picked her up and walked into the open-stall shower. Scorching hot water poured from the rainfall and the angled shower heads and he gasped, but he soon forgot about the stinging heat when he pinned Lila to the tile wall and pushed deep inside her in one thrust, as his mouth took hers again. No rum he'd ever had could match the rich flavor of Lila's tongue.

He thrust into her, again and again, driving both of them to the heights of pleasure, as her water-slicked body slid against him, awakening new sensations in every nerve ending. She scratched and clawed at his back, and he grimaced at the way her nails dug into his skin, but every small crescent-shaped scar he was left with would be worth it. He felt Lila begin to tense in his grasp, so he tilted her hips, positioning her so that he entered her at the right angle, hitting that sweetest of spots that would take her higher.

Lila's cries tore through the steam and filled the bathroom as she came. Reid pumped a couple more times before his own climax hit him. He groaned into her shoulder, and shuddered, emptying into the condom.

Lila threw her head back lightly against the tiled wall, exposing the smooth skin of her throat. Reid trailed his lips up the sleek line and took her earlobe between his teeth. He wasn't sure how long they stayed like that, but soon Lila began to squirm against him, and he released her.

"Well," she said under the running water. "That was unexpected."

With the postcoital glow wearing off, Reid couldn't believe what he'd done. He faced the hot water, letting it wash over his face "Yeah, I know. Sorry about that."

"You're sorry? Are you married, Reid?"

"You know I'm not."

"You have a girlfriend?"

"Of course not."

"Well, what are you sorry for?"

"It's not that," he insisted, and sighed. "I feel like I've lost control of this conversation."

"It's cute that you thought you ever had it."

"Honestly, hell if I know why I'm apologizing. I can't tell if this trip is off to a great start, or a terrible one."

"You think that was terrible?"

"No, not at all. But I can't lose focus on what I'm doing here."

"And what's that?"

"I'm here to get you to represent my brand."

She turned off the water and faced him. "And that's the only reason?"

Slowly, he ran his eyes up and down her still wet and naked body. She hadn't bothered to cover up. But part of him wished she would. Lila was a woman who could make him forget everything. Every second he was with her, he felt his resolve crumble. This would be a dangerous trip for him. He had to keep the distillery at the forefront of his mind, but he knew it would be the hardest thing he'd ever done in his life.

"Yeah, that's why I'm here."

She smiled. "And that's why you also brought condoms, right? Because this is about business?"

"I brought them in case of a momentary slip-up. Like this," he explained, grabbing a towel from the nearby rack. "And look at us. I was right, wasn't I?"

"Yeah, you were."

She was standing in front of him. Water still beading and rolling down her skin. Again, he was a ball of sexual tension. No matter how hard he tried, his desire grew for her every second he was with her. "You said we had an early morning tomorrow?"

"We do."

Even though he wanted to pick her up in his arms, and bring her to the bed in his room, he didn't. It took all his fortitude to take a step back and put distance between them.

"I guess we'd better get to bed."

The steam in the bathroom had cleared, as had the fog of desire that surrounded them. Lila turned away from him and picked up her towel and wrapped it around her chest. Without saying anything, she left the bathroom. Reid wasn't sure how he would survive the next couple of days, but he knew it wouldn't be easy.

CHAPTER ELEVEN

When Lila exited her room the next morning, Reid had taken over the large table and had turned it into a makeshift office. "I thought you weren't going to be working on this trip."

"I don't remember making that deal. You may have kidnapped me, but that doesn't mean I still don't have a company to run. I need to stay up-to-date on what's going on in production and distribution." He looked up at her. "I should be there, not here messing around with any of this."

Lila bent over and buckled her espadrille sandals, intentionally giving Reid a more than generous look at her ass. When she righted, she caught him staring. "Feel free to leave anytime, Reid. It's not like the door's locked and you're tied to a chair." *Although...* The idea of that held a certain appeal for her. She shook herself free of the image when Reid stood, and she noticed he'd changed into a pair of pants and button-down shirt, like something he would wear to work. He looked like a man who was heading to the office, and not a man who was about to hit the town in New Orleans.

"I'm here to get you to sign on as our brand ambassador."

"And that's all you're here for?"

He didn't answer but closed his laptop and placed it in the hotel safe on top of her own, and she noticed they used the same brand. "You'd better watch out. I might grab yours by mistake."

"You need a fingerprint and three different passwords to access anything on mine," he explained. "So, there's no chance of that happening."

"What? No retinal scan?"

"That comes on the next model."

"What industry secrets do you have on that thing?" she asked with a laugh.

She caught the way he stiffened at her question. "It's confidential."

"Fine," she said, putting her hands up in surrender, moving on, and she wondered what nerve she'd accidentally touched. "Let's get going."

"What's first on the agenda?" he asked, as they left their room and headed for the elevator. "Espresso and beignets at Café du Monde?"

"How'd you know?"

"We're in New Orleans. It's what people do, isn't it?"

Lila snorted, and rolled her eyes. "It's what *everyone* does. A city is best observed through the eyes of a local, not through the touristy areas."

"Why are we going there, then?"

"Because I'm a travel blogger. Of course, I'm going to do the touristy things. I have to get those out of the way. Then I do the things I want to do."

"We all have to do things we don't want to do for work, don't we?"

"That's the nature of work,"

They arrived in the lobby. "Okay what now?" he asked.

"We've got a tour of the French Quarter. Plus, there are some museums, a haunted hike. And whatever other stops strike our fancy. Anything you want to see?"

It surprised Lila when he nodded. "Actually, yeah. There are some spots I wouldn't mind checking out. There are records of Joseph Rexford bootlegging in New Orleans. I'd love to see some of the landmarks he wrote about. There are some prohibition-era speakeasys that are still operating today. If you'd like to go."

"Yeah, and that would be an excellent tie-in to your new rum." She started mentally writing the blog in her head. "Look at us, collaborating already. I'm proud of you, getting into the vacation spirit—even if it is directly related to work."

Reid laughed. "I think we've collaborated before," he said, his eyebrows waggling suggestively. Slowly but surely, Reid was loosening up, turning into the funny, charming man she'd met at Arlo's in Miami.

"Yeah, we have, but that's nothing I can blog about."

* * *

Several hours later, they were strolling side by side in an already crowded French Quarter. They'd stopped at a couple of museums, and the spots that Reid wanted to see, and had enjoyed more food than she would care to admit. But what stood out during the day was how loose Reid had become. Get him away from the distillery, and he was quite a fun guy, and with every touch, smile and glance, she could feel herself falling for him more and more.

With every step, the back of Lila's hand grazed against his, and she felt the sizzle of electricity zap from his skin to hers. It frustrated her that he pretended not to notice, because if he did, he didn't show it.

"What now?" he asked.

"I was thinking about hitting a few food trucks but with how much we've already eaten today, I think that can wait."

They'd already stopped at several food spots, and he rubbed his flat stomach. "So, we eat all day, and your fans eat it up?"

"I'm not posting everything today. I'll spread it out. Swap spots with other bloggers. It's all about creating content. And you never stop creating it."

"That's what your life is? Content?"

"Digital lifespans are short. I've got to plug as much as I can, for as long as I can. The same goes for your rum. If you don't capitalize on the number of people talking about you now—" she shrugged "—you'll lose all interest in your product."

"Well, I guess that means corporate sponsorship is important to you, right? Seeing as how you're hot right now, who's to say how long that'll last? You might as well say yes to us, while you're a hot commodity. If you wait, you might not be any good to us."

She arched an eyebrow, but still it stung. She knew he was right, but she wouldn't give him the satisfaction. "You trying to neg me into submission?"

"Is it working?"

"Not a chance. Would you be satisfied if it did?"

He shook his head. "No. But I think we can negotiate mutually beneficial terms."

"I think we've already been mutually beneficial," she said, poking into his ribs with her elbow.

He was quiet for a moment. "You know, though, that if we agree to this, and we work together, our relationship has to be strictly business. We have to stop whatever it is we have going on, and we'll be just two people who work together."

"I know. I meant what I said to you at the party. It is best if we do that—stay away from each other, but staying away is harder than it should be, isn't it?"

"Yeah," she admitted.

"And seeing as how sex is all we have in common, why do you think I'd agree to anything you guys propose?"

"I'm hoping you'll see reason, and what we can do for each other."

"You're only working so hard on this because your brother and sister are mad at you, right?"

"Well, I agreed to come with you because they were mad at me, but I'm still here because I like a challenge. I want you. And I always get what I want."

"You want me?"

"I want you to rep my rum."

"Is that all you want?"

He stopped walking and they turned to face each other. "That's all we can have. That's all I'm offering." Reid wasn't a good liar, and Lila wasn't convinced. His eyes bored into hers, and she felt the same passion from him that she'd seen when he'd come to her the night before. Even though his body was rigid, and his body language kept him off limits, his eyes, they showed fire, passion. And they were trained solely on her.

He looked down the street at the passing crowds, and when he looked back, it was as if the spell had been broken. He was all business again. "Okay, where to next?" "I think we're done for the day. We can go back to the hotel if you want. I have to write about today and catch up on my interactions."

"Sounds good to me," he said as he started walking.

Lila narrowed her eyes on his back as he remained several steps ahead of her. Maybe this trip would also be a chance for Reid to loosen up. She'd never been one to chase a guy who didn't want her, but she knew Reid wanted her. She'd show him. A little hard work didn't scare her.

CHAPTER TWELVE

IT WAS LATER that evening, and Reid sat at the makeshift desk he'd made at the table, and poured some of the dark Rexford Rum from the bottle he'd bought earlier into a short glass. Already tense and tight from his day with Lila, he'd gone to the hotel minibar for some refreshment, but found only Cain rum—their biggest competitor—and Reid would rather drink used mouthwash than imagine Carolina and her *new family* seeing one cent of profit from him. So he'd left the room again and hit the nearest liquor store to get himself a bottle of Rexford's finest rum.

He grimaced at the bar fridge. He had no idea that Cain had secured a deal with the hotel chain. Quin and Gemma were right, they needed Lila's help to branch out. And he turned back to the laptop in front of him as he scanned the projections the distribution team had sent him. Rexford Rum had gone viral, and they hadn't counted on that. They'd aimed for slow growth and had become a well-known name in high-end circles. Rexford may have been the drink of choice of the elite, but overnight mainstream success was not something they'd planned for. Now they were now scrambling to keep up with demand. Things had never been better for the company but now he was struggling to keep afloat.

If the projections were to be trusted, expanded operations, and a larger facility would be the only way they would be able to keep up in the long-term. But he thought about his office back home, the one where he'd spent his summers working with his grandfather, who'd sneaked teenage Reid cigars and glasses of fine rum. But he was sitting in a hotel suite in New Orleans, and he felt a pang of sadness. He missed the office, the comfort the four walls of the distillery provided him. But there was no time for sentimentality. He had to get some work done, before Lila pulled him off on some other adventure.

He turned back to his open spreadsheets, but his attention kept being drawn to her closed bedroom door, behind which she'd sequestered herself in her room to do her own work.

His eyes blurred under the blue light of his laptop, as his gaze again drifted to Lila's closed door. She'd managed to turn his life completely upside down, as he missed his first day of work in years.

He heard her laugh again, and he pictured her on that king bed that matched the one in his own room. Her underneath him, bringing them both to the heights they'd reached in the shower that morning.

He let go a deep sigh and took another large mouthful of rum, in an attempt to get his body under control, and numb the desire that ate at his gut, before he did something else stupid.

He stared at his laptop, but the numbers on the screen blurred, and his eyes landed on the closed door once more. When it opened, he quickly averted his gaze, so as to not look like he was staring. Lila emerged from the room. She was wearing a flesh-colored tank top—no bra, he noted—and shorts that he had no doubt would ride up over the curve of her ass if she bent over even at the slightest angle. She'd scrubbed off the makeup she didn't need, and her red hair was piled high in a messy knot at the top of her head. She looked incredible, like a bare-bones version of the woman who'd posted vibrant pictures and videos of herself online all day.

He stood up from his desk, the notes, diagrams, charts, reports all but forgotten. "Lila."

Lila smiled at Reid's dumbfounded expression, and she laughed lightly. "Did you forget I was here, or something?"

How could he have forgotten about temptation incarnate in the other room?

"No."

"You're just embarrassed that I caught you staring at my bedroom door?" She took a step closer.

"Absolutely not." He busied himself with straightening the papers.

She looked over her shoulder at the room she'd

just vacated, and when she turned back, a wicked smile and mischievous gleam masked the innocent facade he'd just seen. "Were you wondering what I was doing in there?" she asked.

"I wasn't thinking about you at all," he responded, trying to maintain his stiff, serious composure. "I'm busy working out here."

"Is that right? Why don't I believe you? I think you were out here, trying to work, but instead, you were thinking about what I was doing. Were you wondering if I was naked, wrapped up in my sheets…" She stepped closer and dropped her voice to a whisper. "Were you imagining me *touching myself*?"

He didn't want to admit how accurate she'd been. "No, I was working. And I thought you were doing the same. I was live-chatting with fans. What were you doing?"

But for fantasizing about what was going on behind her closed door. "If you'll excuse me, I have to get back to work."

He felt her eyes travel down his body until her gaze settled on his middle, his stiffening cock, emboldened by her stare, growing, tenting out his pants. *Fucking traitor.*

She laughed. "You sure?" She took a step closer, and it brought her to the table. She sat on it and crossed her legs. And he pictured himself licking a trail up those smooth, delicious thighs.

He frowned at her. "We've discussed this."

"You discussed it." She shrugged. "But I don't follow directions that well. There's no reason we can't have some fun in the meantime."

"If you're going to represent our company—"

"I haven't signed anything yet, Reid," she reminded him.

"I have work to do, if I could just get some peace to do it."

"Nothing that can wait?"

"It shouldn't."

"Sounds important."

"It is."

"Take a break," she said, shoving his chest so he fell into his chair.

"I'm not going to win here, am I?" He found himself lost in the depths of her cleavage as she bent over him, her hands going to his middle.

Lila unbuckled his belt. "Oh, I think you're going to win pretty soon."

With Reid in his chair, Lila put a hand on each of his firm thighs and dropped to the floor. He didn't try to stop her as she loosened the button and zipper of his pants. He was already hard for her. Perfect.

She lowered the elastic of his boxer briefs, and he lifted his hips so she could pull them lower. His cock sprang forth, standing tall and proud. Keeping her eyes on his, she took him in her hand, swirling her palm over the head of his dick, spreading moisture around. His eyes stayed on her, unblinking, but his nostrils flared and a muscle in his jaw ticked. Her touch had the desired effect. She did that to him.

Leaning in, she swept her tongue from the base of his dick to the head and took him into her mouth. She sucked lightly on the head and heard a low growl and a rumble roll through him and into her. She grasped his base in a fist, and dipped her head, taking more of him, not stopping until her lips met her hand.

His breath was heavy, and his hands were on her head. He loosened the bun she'd used to restrain her hair and gripped the loose tendrils in his fist. She increased her speed and pressure as she raised and lowered her head, as his own hold on her hair tightened.

Lila could feel the moisture between her own legs, and she needed to alleviate the pressure, so she squeezed her thighs together and continued her work.

"Lila," he said. "Stop." His voice was low. With a groan, and a firm grip on her hair, he pulled her head back. "I said stop," he told her. He stood and pulled her so she was as well. She thought he would push her away, but instead he turned her around, and with a dramatic movement, he swept the table clear of everything, including his laptop, which crashed to the floor. He didn't even seem to notice, as he bent her over the table.

Now breathless at this turn of events, him completely taking over, she watched out of the corner of her eye when he reached for his wallet and took out a condom. He pulled down her shorts and smacked a hand across her bare ass. She cried out, mostly from the shock, and not the pleasant sting that lingered.

He ran his hand over her ass. His skilled fingers went lower and skirted along the outer lips of her core. Then he delved deeper—pressing the pad of one finger on her clit, and she urged him to go close, to give her the relief she sought. His touch was magical. If he didn't take her soon, she might explode.

Finally, he obliged, and circled her clit with his fingers. She panted under his touch, and he stroked her until she came. When she settled, catching her breath with her cheek against the cool marble of the tabletop, he grabbed her hips and pushed inside her. He was fast, intense, as he pounded his hips against her ass, taking her, fucking her hard.

Reid's fingers dug into her hip and her shoulder. Holding her in place as he took what he wanted from her. She'd come on to him, looking to play with him a little, but he'd quickly turned the tables—and she couldn't have been happier about it.

Feeling another orgasm rise in her, she allowed herself to be completely taken over by him and how he was making her feel. Lila cried out, and as if he'd been waiting for her, he stiffened and hollered out his own release.

They stayed together for a moment, catching their breaths, but then he pushed away. Without speaking, they both straightened their clothes. He picked up his laptop, and she saw that the lid was bent at an unnatural angle and the screen was shattered.

"Might have to get this replaced," he muttered.

"Hopefully you backed up your work."

"I always do," he assured her, bending to pick up the papers, and she did the same.

She picked up one and saw a roughly hand-drawn outline of a distillery. She looked over the rest of the papers that covered the floor. They were scribbles, notes, and hand-drawn charts and diagrams. "What are you working on?" she asked. "Are you expanding? Getting a new distillery?"

Before answering, he took the papers from her. "No. How do you know that?" She raised her eyebrows at his brusque tone, and he noticed. "I didn't. I just guessed from your sketches. What's with the tone?"

"Sorry," he said.

"It's okay. Not really my business." She wouldn't want him snooping in her private matters either. But Reid was so mysterious that she wondered what was behind it. She watched him as he straightened the papers and put them into his bag. "You have some real trust issues, Reid. What happened to you?"

"What are you talking about?"

"What happened to you that you're so secretive, so unable to trust?"

"Nothing."

"Come on," Lila prodded. "I shared all of my painful history with you—my small-town life, my marriage. I know we don't know each other well. But I can see there's something dark brewing within you."

"I don't want to talk about it."

"That's your choice, I guess. You don't trust easily, and I know you don't trust me. I'd just like to know why."

He sighed and sat heavily in his chair. "It's not just you," he told her. "Except for my family, I don't trust anyone." His words were blunt, and she could see the pain on his face.

"Why not?"

He took a deep breath. "Fine. I'm like you, I guess. I too married the wrong person." Lila sat on the edge of the desk, as Reid continued. "We met when we were young. We were in love. We shared everything. She even worked for the distillery. Life was good."

"And then?"

"I didn't know she came with a price. We were at convention, where she met John Cain, the founder of Cain Rum in New York, one of our biggest competitors. I didn't know it at the time, but that was when their affair had commenced."

"She cheated on you?" Lila was shocked. Lila abhorred cheaters. And a woman who would cheat on a man like Reid? The woman must be vile.

Reid laughed. "If that was all she did, it wouldn't have been such a big deal." Bitterness contorted his handsome features. "She took a lot of our recipes and gave them to Cain Rum Distillery."

"What? How did she get away with it?"

"We didn't pursue legal action. I didn't want the

press scrutiny or the spotlight. I screwed up. It was my fault—"

"You were the victim. She stole from you. What she did was corporate espionage."

"It was an embarrassment. Despite what Quin, Gemma and my dad said, and how much they had my back. It was me who was weak. I let it happen. I trusted the wrong person. We rebuilt and moved on. I'm a lot more careful now."

"What happened to Carolina?"

He let out a humorless laugh. "She ended up marrying John Cain."

"Shut up."

"It's true."

"Bitch."

"I try not to think about it. It's best to focus on work and building the best future we can."

"You're right. Getting married was my biggest mistake. But I know I wouldn't have the life I have now without that asshole." She shook her head. "You know, I'm glad you told me about Carolina, but let's not talk about our exes anymore." She stood and reached out for his hand. "Let's just focus on us."

The anger that had transformed his face smoothed, and he smiled up at her. "I like that idea."

Reid held Lila's hand as he led her to his bedroom.

After telling Lila about what had happened during his marriage to Carolina, Reid felt lighter than he had in years. It had been a secret, one known only by the members of his immediate family. He'd expected to be embarrassed, but he wasn't. Telling her his deepest, darkest secret had been easier than he'd expected. She hadn't laughed, she hadn't blamed him for being an idiot. And what surprised him the most was that he trusted Lila.

When they reached the foot of the bed, he stopped, and turned to face her. Cupping her cheeks in his hands, he drew her to him and kissed her. Her lips were full, soft and waiting for him. Her mouth parted, and he took the kiss deeper. He stroked her tongue with his own, entwining, dancing, dueling for who could get the most taste from the other. He needed her again, didn't think he'd ever get enough of her.

He lowered them both to the bed, each pulling at the clothing they'd just straightened only minutes ago.

He reached for a condom from the box he'd left on the nightstand and rolled the latex over his painfully rock-hard dick.

Lining up with her, he pushed inside her, and he was home. Each time with Lila was better than the last. It shocked him how quickly she'd managed to get under his skin. A serious voice in his brain told him that he should be keeping his feelings for her separate from the business. He shouldn't want her. Especially since they would soon be collaborating in business. It was reckless. It was stupid. Somehow, when it came to Lila, he didn't give a damn about anything but being with her. And he had no idea how he would give her up when she signed the papers agreeing to work with them.

Soon, she was pushing back on him, matching his pounding rhythm, her breaths were short, her movements frantic. He knew she was as far-gone as he was. His stomach tightened, and his heartbeat stuttered in his chest.

He looked down at the curve of Lila's body, and he realized that he would do anything for her. She'd managed to awaken long-dormant feelings within him, and he wasn't sure how she'd sneaked in past his barriers and gotten to him. Somewhere along the way, he'd developed feelings for her, and he knew there would be no going back. But he couldn't help that now. He gripped her hips, stilling her as he buried himself deeply within her heat, taking what he wanted, bringing them both to a hard, powerful finish, as their satisfied cries mingled in the quiet of the hotel room.

The waiter removed their dinner plates and replaced them with dishes of chocolate mousse. It was their final night in New Orleans and Reid had insisted they go to dinner. Lila knew she would miss this time alone with Reid. In just a few short days, between exploring the city in the day and making love at night, they'd managed to get so close. But she knew that their time together like this would be short. He'd already made it clear that once she signed on to work with the distillery, they wouldn't have any sort romantic relationship.

"How did you like dinner?" He looked across the table at Lila. They were seated on a balcony and the full moonlight cast a soft white glow over them, while the warm, night air surrounded them.

"Delicious," she said, spooning up some of the mousse. As the creamy, chocolate hit her tongue, she closed her eyes in surrender, and hummed her appreciation. When she opened her eyes, she saw that Reid was watching her, stock still. His fork frozen halfway way to his mouth.

"What?"

"Nothing," he said, and took his own taste of mousse. "Oh, that is good." Watching pleasure cross over his face—whether in bed, or while eating dinner—was something to behold. But his expression grew serious when he put down his spoon and straightened. "I know you made me come on this trip to make me forget about the business, but can we talk about it now?"

"God, you're so boring and predictable, Reid. But I guess it had to come up eventually."

"It did. I need to know if you'll agree to work on our social media campaigns."

Of course, Lila had already agreed to do it, a contract had appeared in her inbox that morning. She looked forward to working with the brand. She wanted to laugh, but Reid face was so serious. And then she remembered that he was only there to get her to sign on. It might feel like they were a couple, but that wasn't reality. She'd extorted him to come on the trip.

"You've seen the offer. It's very fair for the work you'll have to do. Have you looked it over?"

"I have."

"So, you know I've already put—literally—everything on the table, dinner included. Can we just put this to bed already?"

"Well, that sounds like a good idea."

"Lila, what's your answer?"

"I'm going to do it," she told him.

His smile was broad. "That's fantastic."

"I'm going to LA tomorrow," she told him. "I've got a few meetings and I'm going to talk to my agent about your offer."

"You know, that's a huge relief," he told her. "There's a real weight off my shoulders."

He held his glass aloft. "To the beginning of a profitable, professional partnership."

She clinked her glass against his and turned her attention back to her dessert. The Rexford deal would be amazing for her. The exposure, the money, the clout it gave her during her negotiations with the GO! Channel would greatly benefit her. Reid had been quick to remind her of their forthcoming *professional* relationship. That was what he wanted from her. It should be what she wanted, too.

She looked at Reid. He seemed happier than she had ever seen him. It served as a reminder that getting her on board with the distillery was his goal for the trip and nothing else. *Mission accomplished.*

"Lila, I know I was hesitant at first, but I have to say, I've had a great time here with you. Thanks for kidnapping me."

"Anytime. I had a great time, too. It's nice to have some company every now and again. But let's not pretend you didn't spend a lot of the time working remotely."

"It's baby steps," he insisted. "But maybe you're right, I don't always get to enjoy what life has to offer."

"You could have everything you could ever want, but you never leave the office."

"If I don't work, then I can't afford all of the things I have no time to enjoy."

"Why not? You should be able to enjoy the fruits of your success."

"The fruits of my success are continued success. Unlike Quin and Gemma, I can't take my eyes off the prize. Gemma creates an incredible product, and Quin ensures that people see it. But I've got to work behind the scenes to make sure it all comes together."

"So, you work 24/7?"

"Gotta keep my eye on the prize, right?"

"Oh please. I know you guys have been successful for a while. You're doing fine and were doing well before this recent boost."

"You've done your homework."

"I'm a businessperson, too, Reid. I wasn't going

to sign anything until I knew you guys would be good for my own brand. I'm not going to jump into bed blind."

"Like you did with me?" he goaded with a smile.

She rolled her eyes. "I think we were both wearing blinders that first night." She took his hand in hers. "Reid, you can have anything you want. There are so few people in the world who get an experience like this. You're one of the lucky ones."

"I know I am," he said. "But I slipped up once. I took my attention from the distillery and it almost cost us everything."

"You can't hold on to that forever," she told him. "you did nothing wrong."

"It doesn't matter. Still feels like it."

"It's in the past," she told him. "Let's focus on the future and everything we can do for each other."

"I'll drink to that."

CHAPTER THIRTEEN

FINALLY, BACK IN Miami at the distillery, Reid was a ball of tension as he sat at the conference table with Quin and Gemma as they discussed what Reid had missed during his New Orleans trip. During his three days away, he'd stayed up to date on the happenings at the distillery, but Quin had moved forward independently, scouting new locations to set up and expand, which would give them the space they needed, and keep everything under one roof. But Reid disagreed, and he was starting his first day back with an argument with his brother.

"We're not moving operations," he told Quin. "This is where Rexford started. This is where we continue."

"Reid, listen to reason. There's no way we can continue and produce rum to meet the demand in our current distillery. Gemma, tell him."

"I'm with Reid," she said. "I can't imagine not working in this building. It makes us who we are. But I do need more room."

"Well, how about an expansion?" Reid suggested. "We build on and connect with the neighboring buildings that we already own. It keeps everything under one roof, but we stay here."

Gemma nodded. "I like that. Does that work for you, Quin?"

"That could work. But I can't help but feel it'd be a lot easier—and probably cheaper—to find a new place."

Reid knew Quin was probably right, but Reid couldn't imagine leaving the building that was as much a part of the business as he was. "Why don't we get some quotes on what it would cost and we can come back to it later?"

"Fine," Quin relented. "If you're willing to consider an opinion you don't necessarily agree with, you must have had a good time in Louisiana?"

Reid's body tensed. He hadn't seen Lila since they'd parted ways in New Orleans. He'd boarded a flight to Miami as she boarded one to Los Angeles. She'd texted him a couple of times but that was it. He missed her. "It was fine."

"Just fine?" Quin asked, with a smirk that Reid wanted to punch.

"Yes."

"Did you make things right with her?" Gemma asked."

"I believe we came to an understanding," he said vaguely. "She has the paperwork. She's going through it and will get it back to us soon." Gemma smiled. "And you guys had a good time together?"

"I think we did."

"Well," Gemma said. "I'm looking forward to seeing her tomorrow. I really like her."

"What do you mean? Tomorrow?"

"She'll be back in Miami."

"How do you know that?"

"She told me on the phone last night."

"You talk to her on the phone?"

"Yeah, we've been in touch."

"Then why are you asking me if she's signing the contracts? Why am I on the hook for being the one unable to convince her to work for us?"

"Because you're the one with the obvious attraction to her. And we don't generally discuss work when there are far more interesting things to talk about," she told him with a wink. "What's that supposed to mean?" "Oh, nothing," Gemma said, standing from the table. "If you'll excuse me, I've got to head down to the distillery. Just do me a favor, Reid."

"What's that?"

"Make sure you call Lila tomorrow."

"And why should I do that?"

"Because when I look at you—I can tell you're relaxed, refreshed, you're smiling. I think she's good for you."

CHAPTER FOURTEEN

BACK IN MIAMI, Lila sat on the bed in her hotel room and looked over the offer from Go! Channel production team. They'd been thoroughly impressed by her social media reach and by her screen test, so they gave the green light to develop her show. She still couldn't believe their offer. The papers in front of her represented everything she wanted, but there was something about the deal that didn't sit right with her. In her career, she'd always done what she wanted. And as she reviewed the proposed itinerary that the travel channel had given her, the things she could and couldn't do, she started to feel the control slip away from her. She craved the security that came from the network deal, but at what price to the life she wanted to live? She'd already lived one lifetime under the thumbs of her parents, and then her husband. Did she really want to do it again?

She had planned to stay in LA for a couple more days, but after seeing what the television execs wanted her to do, she panicked. She needed to get away. And she booked the next flight across the country to Miami. She hadn't had a *home* in about five years—she'd spent her time traveling. But there was something that drew her to Miami, and she knew that *something* was Reid.

While she'd been in contact with Gemma, she hadn't called Reid. Why would he want to see her? He'd gotten what he wanted and had made it clear they would only have a professional relationship from here out.

Her phone rang. When she picked it up, she tried to quell the rush of excitement that went through her when she saw Reid's name on her screen. *Well, speak of the devil.*

"Reid Rexford," she purred in greeting. "I didn't think I'd be hearing from you so soon. Did you really miss me that much?"

"I heard you were back in town."

"Yeah, just a short stopover."

"How short?"

"It's up in the air."

He chuckled and the sound warmed her. "How do you live like that?"

"Easily. There's no pressure to do things I don't want to do," she told him, thinking of the things the GO! Channel asked of her. "So, what's up? Why are you calling me?"

A beat of silence was followed by a chuckle. "Okay, Lila," he said, and she tried not to shiver at the way he said her name. Clearly, he had more control than either of them thought. “I was wondering if you had any plans for dinner.”

“I don’t. But I’d like to.”

“All right. Why don’t I send a car for you at seven? We can have dinner here.”

“Sounds good to me.” She smiled. The prospect of seeing Reid again thrilled her. “I’ll be ready. I just have one question, though.”

“What is it?”

“Is this a professional dinner, where we discuss our collaboration, or something else?”

“It can be whatever you want it to be.”

“Good answer. See you then.”

So much for a professional dinner, Lila thought as Reid wrapped his arms around her waist.

She had barely stepped into his foyer when he was on her, his lips pressing against hers. He was frantic, but no more than she was. Their discarded clothing littered the floor as they made their way into the house. They got as far as the kitchen, wearing only their underwear, and Lila knew they wouldn’t make it any further than that.

She didn’t have a chance to look around, take in the view of the backyard, or even check out what he’d cooked, food which was simmering on the stovetop. But that was fine. She could get the tour later.

Reid lifted her onto the countertop, and ran his hands down her body, while she busied herself with his. She reached down and squeezed his length through the material of his boxers, and he groaned in response, letting her touch him for only a moment before he pushed her hand away and dropped his own between her thighs.

Touching her, he found her wet, needy. The minute his fingers met her clit, a bolt of electricity shot through her. Reid was different than any other man that she'd been with. Just his touch was enough to set her ablaze.

He stroked her and her heart rate increased, as he slipped past the satin barrier of her panties and slid a finger inside of her. She could feel herself tighten around his finger and she gripped him even harder when he inserted another. He moved his hand back and forth, plunging his fingers in and out of her, circling her clit with the master's touch of his thumb. He was driving her crazy, as she was splayed on the countertop, trapped between the wall behind her and the hard muscles of his chest. Her breathing increased, and she clenched her hands into tight, little fists, finding it difficult to hold on.

It had only been a couple of days since she'd been with him in New Orleans, but even that had been far too long. She needed him again. Now!

"Reid," she gasped. "Condoms. In my purse," she told him, apparently unable to form complete sentences.

"Aren't you eager?" he teased, slowly the speed of his touches, lazily drawing out her pleasure.

"Reid, now. Please," she pleaded.

"You don't have to ask me again," he told her, pulling his hand away from her and bringing his fingers to his mouth, licking his digits free of her juices. She was so far gone, that just the sight of the pleasure he took from it, almost pushed her over the edge. She squeezed her eyes shut, to get her hormones under control, but it was useless.

When she opened her eyes again, she watched, riveted, as Reid rolled the latex over himself, and took position again between her spread thighs. He roughly grabbed her hips in his large, strong hands and entered her. Her eyes fluttered shut in relief, but she opened them again, not wanting to miss the look on Reid's face as he pushed into her over and over.

The look that came over him was rough, serious, as he possessed her, rearing back, almost pulling his entire length from her, before slamming back into her again. He squeezed her hips in a tight grip as he filled her, possessing her so fully, as he held her in place, thrusting his hips against her with a force that made her head crash against the wall cupboard door. Immediately, he put a hand at the back of her head, cushioning the blows, but not slowing his pace.

Lila felt her orgasm grow again. His movements grew more strained and she knew that he was close, as well. He pulled her close, and hit her just right, and soon, her orgasm erupted with force, and bliss overcame her, as he continued pumping his hips. "Reid," she yelled out, barely recognizing her own voice, as she exploded. But her cries were muted by his lips, as he entered her one more time, before he stiffened and came with his own thick groan.

Waking up in Reid's bed the next morning, Lila felt warm, firm chest at her back. A strong arm was draped over her middle and it took her several seconds to remember where she was. But when she inhaled Reid's spicy cologne and the unmistakable scent of their lovemaking, it all came rushing back to her.

She turned in his arms, and he kept his eyes closed, still sleeping. His face was soft, but day-old stubble peppered his chin. Her fingers itching to touch it, she reached out and felt the rough bristles under her fingertips. His eyes opened slowly and when they focused on her, he smiled.

"Morning."

"Sorry to wake you."

His eyes shifted downward, at their naked bodies pressed together, and his smile turned devilish. "I'm glad you did." Between them, his cock hardened, and she felt him grow against her belly.

"Well, hello down there," she said, and he flexed his hips against her.

He laughed and cupped her cheek, coming close to kiss her, but she drew back, and covered her mouth with the back of her hand. "Watch out," she warned him. "Morning breath."

He moved her hand and leaned in, kissing her

anyway, before he pulled back and grimaced. "Yeah, you're right."

Lila laughed. "Jerk."

Reid laughed and kissed her again, taking his time, his tongue brushing against hers. "I'm kidding. You're good," he assured her, before kissing her again to prove his point.

She moaned into his mouth, and he rolled her over onto her back, holding himself over her with his strong forearms. She ran her fingernails up the soft dark hair and wrapped her arms around his neck. She pulled Reid closer, and they kissed more before he pulled away. "Aw, damn," he muttered against her skin, his lips skimming down her throat.

"What's wrong?"

"We used all of my condoms last night."

The bubble of desire popped. "Are you serious? For such a responsible guy, you don't keep your place stocked with the necessities?"

"Sorry for my poor planning. But that doesn't mean we can't improvise."

Lila spread her legs, and flexed her hips upward, allowing his midsection to rest more fully on top of hers. "What do you have in mind?"

He quirked an eyebrow upward. "This," he said, before disappearing below the thin blanket that covered them.

Reid kissed, licked, nibbled his way across her chest, stopping to circle one tight nipple with his lips. He sucked and swished his tongue across the bud.

He cupped the other breast with his large hands and pinched the nipple between his fingers, making her cry out. Her back arched off the bed as he worked, played over her breasts, plucking at strings of desire that settled in her center. "Reid," she gasped, not understanding how it was possible that he could have such an effect on her, as he played with her breasts. "I can't wait anymore."

He released one rosy bud from his rounded lips with a light pop, and he grinned. "You got it, sweetheart." He ventured lower, dipping his tongue into her belly button, before he found his destination. He threw off the blanket, left her exposed to the chilly air of his room and maneuvered her legs so that they draped over his back, thighs on his shoulders.

From his position, he looked up at her, a playful smile perched on wicked lips, amusement putting a glisten in his eyes. This was a different Reid—not the hard, serious, callous jerk, with a tongue that could cut. No, he was having fun—he was playful, funny, cute, even. *With an even more wicked tongue.* His mouth descended upon her flesh again, his tongue snaking between her folds, and hit the spot she needed him to. He closed his lips around the bud and applied pressure, giving her the same attention he'd given her nipples. Stroking, pinching, licking, feasting.

While one hand fisted the cotton bedsheet, her other gripped the back of his head. Wanting him to get closer and relieve the delicious pressure. The feeling was almost too much for her, and she whined, pushing her hips closer to his mouth. He pulled back momentarily and flipped over so that he was on his back, and he pulled her to him, so that she straddled his head between her thighs, he held her so closely, that she wasn't sure how he was able to breathe down there. He nipped her clit with his lips just right and she let out a wild yell. She began to move her hips, riding his face, surely cutting off his air supply. And yet he still didn't stop. She swayed and shook her hair behind her shoulders as she chased her own pleasure. *If he dies, he dies,* she reasoned, not caring about anything how he made her feel. Every muscle in her body tensed, as he ate from her, and she barely noticed the hand he snaked across her ass, and the finger he pressed into the crevice.

Her breath went short and her orgasm powered through her and she continued to ride him, as he held on to her, guiding her climax. When her body quieted from the rapturous pleasure, she rolled over in a heap on the bed. Her heart was pounding, and she tried to regain her breath. Reid lay by her side, his chest rising and falling rapidly.

"You okay?" she asked him, putting a hand on his sweat-glistened chest.

"Yeah," he said in between breaths. "I thought I might black out there for a moment," he added with a laugh.

"Sorry I almost killed you."

"It was worth it. It would have been a good way to go."

She smiled, and then rolled over onto him so that she straddled his hips. "Well, don't go anywhere yet," she told him, grabbing his length. "It's your turn now."

CHAPTER FIFTEEN

On Monday morning, Reid walked into the distillery with a smile on his face, whistling as made the way to his office. He'd had a spectacular weekend with Lila. She'd gotten under his skin, and no matter how much he scratched that itch there was no relief like being inside her. He may have resisted her at first, but he'd found himself wanting to be with her. It was a need at this point. And he'd almost skipped work to stay with her in his bed.

"Well, aren't you in a good mood this morning," he heard Quin say, coming up behind him. "What's put the jump in your step?"

"I'm in a good mood," he told him. "Is that allowed?"

"It's allowed. It's just not very common, coming from you." His little brother narrowed his eyes at him. "What were you up to this weekend?"

"If you have to know, I was with Lila."

"Oh really? Just discussing business, right?" he asked with a wink.

"We did a little, but really, I barely thought about work at all."

"The woman deserves an award for keeping your mind off the office."

Reid rolled his eyes. Quin could use his imagination if he wanted. Reid wouldn't provide any more details about Lila. "Can I help you with something? Or do you not have enough of your own work to do?"

"I stopped by to tell you that Gemma wants to see both of us in the distillery."

Reid checked his phone and didn't see a message from her.

"She texted me this morning," Quin explained. "And you weren't anywhere to be found so I told her I'd let you know."

"Thanks."

Side by side they made their way down to the distillery where Gemma was waiting for them.

"So, Lila, huh?" Quin asked.

"Yeah, I guess so. You have anything to say about it?"

"Not at all. Good for you, man," he said. "I really like her. And you guys are so different, it seems like a great fit. Do you see a future there?"

"You're getting way ahead of this," Reid told him. "It's nothing serious. We're just hanging out. She's got her work, I've got mine. Especially if she's partnering with us. We're having fun for the time being because it won't last forever." There was no way that two people as different as he and Lila would ever be able to work romantically in the real world.

"Why not?" Quin asked.

Reid was about to give him reasons he'd given himself—their differences, work, propriety, blah, blah, blah—but he didn't. The more he thought about the reasons, the less sense they made.

Reid walked into the distillery alongside Quin. Gemma was standing next to the large copper fermenters with several of her employees, directing them. Reid was proud of the way she ran her distillery. She was a fierce, talented leader with a firm but gentle hand, all wrapped up in a small package.

"About time you guys got here," she told Reid and Quin.

"What did you want?"

"I've got some news," she told them. "Let's talk in my office."

They followed her to the small, cluttered office in the distillery, and Reid and Quin took seats on the battered couch next to her desk. "What have you got?" Reid asked.

Gemma handed over a notebook, and when he flipped through the pages, he found diagrams, notes, recipes, random scribbles. "What am I looking at, Gem?"

"It's very preliminary at the moment. But I may have come up with a way to quick-distill and quickly age our rum."

"Are you serious?"

"I'm not sure. But here's what might work," she said before going into an in-depth discussion of the science behind distilling. Reid was impressed. She had come up with a way to speed up the aging process, taking what would typically be at least a five-year process for their dark and spiced rums and turning it into a six-month one. But he had reservations.

"Will the quality suffer?" Quin asked.

"That's the beauty of it," she told them. "I won't know for sure until we get some test batches done. But I don't think it will. I've played with something before, but nothing on a grand scale like this."

"So along with the prohibition recipe, you'll be quick-aging all other batches. What about space or equipment?" Reid asked.

"I already ordered the special equipment we'll need. If this works, we'll need to expand, so the sooner we get to converting our current properties, or buying new ones, the better."

"That really puts some pressure on us. We haven't planned on expanding this quickly. I guess you'd better get started and we'll handle the facilities," Quin told her. "This is a lot," Reid said. "It's risky. I hope it's worth it."

"It will be."

"I'm not one to take a risk."

"We all have to be on board here," Quin reminded them. "It's how we do this. Either we waste the opportunity we've been given with this newfound popularity, or we let it ride on expansion and a procedure that's completely new to us."

"All in favor of *new to us*?" Gemma asked, raising her hand. Quin did also.

"Guys, we have to be careful here," Reid maintained.

"Raise your hand, Reid," Quin warned him. "We're doing this."

"Fine," Reid relented. "We'll do this your way." He raised his hand and he hoped to God the decision wouldn't ruin them.

No matter how hard she tried, Lila couldn't will herself to get out of bed, not as long as she could smell Reid on the bedsheets, still see the indent of his head on the pillow next to her. She'd slept so soundly in his bed, against his chest with his arms wrapped tightly around her that it had felt like only minutes had passed when his alarm sounded that morning and he'd gone to work. They'd spent the night wrapped up in each other. They ran so hot and cold—between goading each other and tearing each other's clothes off. Teasing him provided her with just as much a rush as sex with him. Maybe it was all part of the same emotion.

She pushed herself up from Reid's bed and looked around his room—so masculine, neat, and ordered. Just like the man himself.

She picked up the shirt he'd discarded the night

before and held it to her nose, taking in his scent before throwing it into his clothes hamper.

She hadn't gotten a good look at the place last night. When she'd showed up, they'd immediately taken things to the bedroom. Not that she had any complaints, of course. Her stroll to the kitchen took her past a couple more immaculate bedrooms, a living room, a dining room, and his office.

Knowing that Reid didn't trust easily, it meant a lot to her that he let her stay there without him. In such a short time, they'd come a long way.

Her phone rang and she saw it was a call from her agent in LA.

"Lila, where are you?" he asked, skipping the traditional greetings.

"I'm in Miami," she told him. "Why?"

"You were supposed to stay in LA for the contract negotiations."

Lila sighed, and despite the great opportunity that a television network provided her, she increasingly felt doubt about signing the contract. "I had to take care of something in Miami first," she told him.

"That rum thing?" he asked, indifferent. Lila knew he didn't care about it because she'd lined it up without him, excluding him from ten percent of her paycheck. "That's not your future. This internet fame you have—you're a flash in the pan, girl. You have to strike while the iron is hot," he said, mixing metaphors in a way that bugged her every time.

He was right. She had to take advantage of every

lucrative opportunity that came her way. Even if it meant doing something she didn't really want to do—like sign her name, image, brand over to a corporation. "Can I do a video chat with them?" She still had things to take care of with the distillery. And whether she admitted it to herself not, that was the deal she wanted to sign.

"No, we'll need you back in LA as soon as possible."

"Okay," Lila agreed with a frown. Sure, it was just a matter of hopping a flight, but part of her felt like she would be cutting off an important piece of her life. Her independence, her freedom.

And Reid.

With another trip across the country on the horizon, Lila wanted to soak up as much of Miami as she could. But Reid's home was the only place she wanted to be. She lay next to his pool and sprayed more sunblock over her skin.

Reaching behind her back, she smoothed in the spray as best she could.

"Want me to get that for you?" The deep baritone that set her panties ablaze came from somewhere behind her. She turned her head and saw Reid walk out onto the pool deck with an easy gait. He was smiling and looked relaxed with the first couple of buttons of his shirt unbuttoned and his sleeves rolled halfway up his corded, tanned forearms.

He sat next to her, took the bottle from her hands

and sprayed the sunscreen on her back and shoulders before spreading it over her skin. Looking over her shoulder, she saw that he looked like he was surprisingly in a good mood. "Look, he *does* smile," she teased. He swatted her ass and she giggled and rolled over. "What's gotten into you?"

"God, a guy can't smile once in a while without getting the third degree? I had a good day. It might be too soon to say, but we think we might have solved our supply problem for good. Gemma's working on it now with her crew."

"Oh, that's great. What is it?" Reid paused. "Trade secrets?" she asked.

Again, he hesitated. "Gemma may have come up with a way to quick-distill and age the rum."

"Oh really?"

"Yeah, it's highly experimental. But, besides the prohibition-era recipe it's pretty much our only option to get all our product on the shelves and to the people who want it. Hopefully it'll work out. Otherwise, it could be a bust."

"I think that if Gemma believes she can do it, she will."

"Me too. Any word from your agent?"

"Yeah, I have to head back to Los Angeles tomorrow. Negotiations for the GO! Channel," she said with a sigh.

"You don't sound very happy."

"I know. He isn't happy I left LA so quickly."

"You couldn't stay away, though, huh?" His smile was cocky as he lay back in the chair.

"That's right."

"Why exactly aren't you happy about the TV deal?"

"I don't know. I should be happier. This is everything I wanted."

"But?" he prompted.

"I don't know. Something just doesn't feel right about it. My agent and everyone else on the team tells me it's the right thing to do, that it's a good deal. But it feels like they're just going to strip me of my independence and put restrictions on what I want to do."

"Don't sign anything if it doesn't feel right. If you're going to do it, do it right. Go into negotiations and kick their asses. Get what you want."

"What if they say no?"

He shrugged. "Then you tried. But you've got to take that risk, right? But if this is what you want, fight for it," he told her. He sounded serious. Lila watched him for a moment from behind her sunglasses. He stared off into the distance, as if he was deep in thought about something.

"Are you talking about my contract, or us?"

"I'm talking about everything. A very smart woman taught me that life should be fun. Not all serious work stuff," he said, pouncing on her and rolling back over so she sprawled on his chest.

“Sounds like a smart woman,” she said, kissing the underside of his jaw. “In the meantime, I have something more fun we can do.”

CHAPTER SIXTEEN

REID SAT IN HIS OFFICE, working on the next step of their expansion. The team had worked quickly and based on the price quotes and time estimations they received from several contractors, they'd decided to go ahead with expanding the current distillery into the adjacent properties, which they also owned. He was glad that they would be staying in the building. It was part of what tied them to their past. Reid couldn't imagine going to work every day in another building—nor would he. He would take the old, worn, hurricane-and-sun-battered exterior over any flashy new designs. The old distillery was just as much a part of the business as he and his siblings were.

He signed off on an invoice for their contractor and scanned over the orders for the new equipment Gemma would need to quick-distill her recipes. He still wasn't completely on board with the idea. If it failed, it would cost them a lot of resources—*a lot* of money. And there was the risk that the quality would suffer. That was what didn't sit well with him. Rexford Rum had a reputation to uphold. It was a huge risk, but if there was anything that Lila had taught him, it was that he should take more risks, live a little. Have some fun.

Lila. A smile formed on his lips as he thought of her. In such a short time, she had transformed his entire life. He never thought he would get close to another woman, but she had managed to break through each of the walls he'd erected around himself.

The door to his office opened and he looked up. His smile turned down, as in walked the woman who'd caused him to build them those walls.

His jaw became tight and clenched. "What are you doing here?" he asked Carolina without standing.

"Is that how you greet your ex-wife?"

"It's the politest way I could muster," he told her.

She ignored him. "I'm in Miami with some girlfriends. I thought I'd pay you a visit, and I knew I'd find you here." She looked around his simple office with disdain. "The place looks exactly the same."

"I'll ask again, why are you here?"

"I wanted to see you."

"Why, old man Cain can't keep you satisfied?" Reid smiled at the anger in her eyes.

"He keeps me plenty satisfied. Thank you for your concern. But I've seen pictures of you around the internet with that little blogger of yours."

"Lila is none of your concern. I've had enough of this tête-à-tête. You should leave."

"I just wanted to stop by and congratulate you,

Quin and Gemma. I've been hearing a lot of buzz about Rexford Rum."

"Get out," he told her, not wanting to discuss rum, or anything else with the woman who'd almost ruined him.

"Word on the street has it that Gemma is up to something here. She's placed orders for some very specialized equipment. Just makes everyone wonder what she's up to. Seeing as how you're the hot commodity right now, and I know how long Gemma ages her stuff. I don't have any idea how you're going to fill the demand your popularity has created. You haven't got enough stock, have you?"

He wasn't about to confirm or deny anything she thought. "You're lucky I don't pick you up and bodily remove you from my building," he warned her.

"You would never do such a thing, Reid. I know you. I also know you guys aren't as slick as you pretend to be. Whatever you're planning down here, and I think I know exactly what it is, just give up, because you're going to lose."

"What do you think we're doing?"

"Those five-to-ten-year batches that Gemma is so proud of, there's no way they're ready to hit shelves. My theory is that Gemma's found a way to quick-distill rum." Reid kept his face impassive, not letting on the anger or surprise he felt at finding out their little secret wasn't so secret. "I know Gemma is smart, but that's pretty good."

"Is that what you think? Where did you hear that?"

She shrugged. "A little bird told me. Don't think that the master distiller at Cain Rum isn't currently working on a way to do the same."

"Carolina, I could stay here and chat all day, but I've really got to go. I have actual work to do. Like you would know anything about that."

"So, it sounds like nothing's changed for you, then. Work, work, work. That's too bad."

"Did I say that *I* had to go? I clearly meant you. Leave before I call the police."

"Fine, you're no fun. Good luck, Reid."

Carolina turned and with a swivel in her hips that he'd once found appealing, she sashayed out of his office, and hopefully out of his life for the last time.

In the silence of his office, Reid stewed over his ex-wife's visit. How had word gotten out what they were doing? They'd kept it in house. The only people who knew were him, his brother and sister, Gemma's workers in the distillery…

And Lila.

"Fuck," Reid muttered. Had Lila sold him out? She was the only person on the outside he'd told about the expansion and their new production plans. And she was alone in his house. Following a hunch, he turned to his laptop and typed the names *Lila Campbell* and *Carolina Cain.* The results were what he'd suspected and yet hoped to never see.

There were pictures of Lila and Carolina attending the same Cain party. The women were all smiles as photographers captured them deep in conversation, smiling for the cameras, their arms around each other. Reid slammed his laptop shut. He'd trusted Lila, let her in, told her things. Is this why she was here? Why she'd stayed close and gotten under his skin?

He pushed back from his desk. Lila was at his house right now. He had to go there and get to the bottom of this.

When Reid came into the house, Lila could tell something was wrong. He said nothing, and she followed him to the study, where he stalked to the wet bar and poured himself a glass of the ten-year-aged dark rum that she knew he preferred.

"You okay?" she asked.

He didn't say anything for a moment, as he watched her over the rim of his glass. His eyes were full of fire, but it wasn't from passion, how she'd grown accustomed to having him watch her. There was anger there. He lowered the glass. "No," he said finally.

"What's up?"

"What do you know about Carolina Cain?"

She thought for a moment. "Carolina? Carolina Cain?" She flashed back to several Cain rum parties and events she'd attended, and the tall, slim, glamorous woman she'd met. "I can't believe I never connected it before. Carolina is your ex-wife?"

"As if you didn't know."

"What's that supposed to mean?"

"You didn't think to mention you were at any of their parties?"

"I go to a lot of parties, Reid. I greet the hosts. I know Carolina by name, and that's it."

He didn't seem to hear her. "I told you. I told you everything. About me, Carolina, about the distillery, and the whole time, you're playing me for a fucking idiot."

"Whoa," she said, putting up a hand, cutting him off. "What are you accusing me of?"

"You sold me out."

"To who?"

"Carolina."

"I met the woman two or three times in my life, and I haven't seen her since I went to their Labor Day party in the Hamptons last year."

"Then how did she know all about our plans at the distillery? Why was Gemma ordering new equipment even on her radar?"

"I don't know. Are you accusing me of leaking your secrets? You barely tell *me* anything about the distillery. Do you think I have such little integrity?"

"I know that Carolina and Cain Rum will pay any price to take us out."

Lila figured it out, and the realization hit her like a ton of bricks. "You never trusted me."

"I trusted you enough to tell you about our plans,

to leave you alone in my house. And this happens. Christ!"

"No, you didn't trust me. You gave me a basic run-down of what you were doing. Then you changed the topic to sex—like you always do when we're having a deep or intense conversation. And then you think I did what, exactly? Went right to Carolina and told her everything while she cut me a check?"

"It wouldn't be the first time something like that happened."

"I know she screwed you over. But I'm not her. And the fact that you don't trust me, after everything we've been through? That you think I can do that?"

"No. I don't know. I barely know you. But I do know what Carolina is. And she's capable of charming the devil. This is why I didn't want you working for us. I wanted to keep you separate from the business. But I couldn't. That's why I knew this was a bad idea."

"You want to keep me in a separate box? That's not good enough for me, Reid. I don't want to be involved in one part of your life. I want all of you."

"Clearly, I can't give you that."

"You know, you're a lot more fun when you're away from work."

"Is that right? Because not all of us have the luxury of traveling and eating and taking in festivals for income. I have responsibilities. I'm not like you. You don't even have a home."

She shook her head in disbelief. "You're just getting all your shots in now? You think I don't have any responsibilities?"

"That's not what I meant."

"Yes, it is. You still don't take me seriously, do you? You think I'm breezing through life. I tried to show you how hard I work, how my life isn't all a party."

"You can agree that our lives are very different."

"Yeah, because you close yourself off to joy, and love, and everything else but your fucking office and bottles of rum. You're going to work yourself to death." Lila took a deep breath. "I should leave."

"Where are you going?"

"I don't know. The airport, I guess, seeing as how I don't have a home or anything."

"Lila, don't, wait."

"What?"

"Don't go. Let's talk."

"You've already said enough. But what I need to know is this—did you say all those things, try to hurt my feelings in order to push me away?

"Are you going to take the chance, and welcome me into your life, or are you going to keep me separate? Because I don't do half measures, Reid. I don't settle down, especially not with someone who won't make me a priority. Hell, you won't make anything but your work a priority. You're *too* settled down, if you ask me."

He turned away from her, not bothering to answer all of her questions. "I don't have anything to give you, Lila. I'm needed at the distillery and keeping it running smoothly is what I do. It's my family, my name."

Reid wouldn't look at her, and she didn't believe he meant the hurtful words he'd said. She hadn't known him long, but she knew him well enough to read his face, his actions. But she wouldn't chase a man who didn't want her. Her head bobbed. "Okay. You've made your decision, I guess. I should go."

"Should we get together to nullify the contract we signed?"

"If you want to get out of it, we can arrange it. But I don't think we need to cut professional ties. Just whatever this—" she motioned between the two of them "—was."

"Okay."

"I'll just contact Quin for anything I might need," she told him.

"I'll let him know."

They were both quiet, and Lila knew the conversation was over. This was it. "I'll go get my things."

CHAPTER SEVENTEEN

LILA STOOD IN front of the camera, and with a shake of her head, tossed her hair over her shoulders. The microphone buried between her breasts was invisible to anyone who looked at her, but it felt as foreign as she did in front of the green screen in the studio. She should be outside, using her phone's camera, speaking to her audience, not to the besuited men in the room who looked as bored as she was.

"Okay, from the top, Lila," the cameraman said in an indifferent tone.

"Hey, it's Lila Campbell and I'm coming to you live from—" she looked over her shoulder at the screen that would project an image later "—where am I again?"

"Spring break in Cozumel," one of the suits told her without looking up from his phone.

"Spring break? It's summer."

"This commercial will launch in March, during spring break. We're going to send you there."

"You know I'm in my thirties, right? Spring break isn't exactly my thing."

"Well, you look twenty-one in TV years. Should we remind you that this is what you're being paid for."

"From the top again," the director said.

She looked over at herself in the monitor and saw that they'd projected a video of raucous spring breakers behind her. But she stared at herself. Her hair and makeup done within an inch of her life, the wardrobe that she would have never picked for herself, and she frowned.

Lila took a deep breath and turned on her brightest smile, reminding herself that she was living every online influencer's dream—a deal with a television network, worldwide exposure. She tamped down her frustration and looked back into the camera lens.

"Hey guys, it's Lila Campbell..."

Later, she was seated at a table in the conference room above the studio. Across from her sat her three studio executives from the GO! Channel.

"Ms. Campbell," the woman started. "We loved your reel from this morning. We're so excited about this partnership."

"Thank you. It was definitely a different experience for me. But I'm used to being a little more hands-on when it comes to my content."

The male exec in the middle waved off her concern. "We'll get you out in the field soon. But you'll find we record a lot of segments here in the studio.

It's cheaper, easier and safer than some of the exotic locales you may be used to."

"That sounds pretty inauthentic. Why would a travel channel operate like that—"

"Ms. Campbell, here is your updated contract." The third executive slid the papers across the table. "I'm sure you'll see the contract is in order and contains the provisions we discussed previously."

Lila nodded. She and James had negotiated an excellent contract for her. GO! Channel was going to pay her handsomely. But it was the heavily detailed itinerary that bothered her the most. Even with the segments that would be produced in-house, it was loaded with stops, and some left her in a town for only a day at a time—some places for a few hours. Also included was something new she hadn't seen before—a list of brands she could use and advertise on her personal blog.

"Excuse me," she spoke over the executives who had barely let her say two words since she sat down with them. "This list of products and brands—"

"Yes, they're affiliated with the network and our advertisers."

"Rexford Rum isn't here."

"No," one of the suits said, checking his own notes. "Our network has a deal with Cain rum."

"I needed a provision to still work with Rexford, since I have a promotion deal with them." She and Reid may have fought, but she still had a professional responsibility to them. She wouldn't renege on that.

The executives exchanged looks. "You'll have to terminate that. It doesn't align with our advertisers."

She looked at her agent. "Why wasn't I consulted on this before the contract was drafted? That was on my list of provisions. Did you think I wouldn't notice?"

"We were hoping it wouldn't matter. Do we have to remind you that this is a television deal?"

She'd heard enough. With the pressure that came along with the channel, she felt herself snap. She could do it. She didn't want it. If she wanted success, she would do it on her own. Not everything was about money and stability. "You know that cable TV is basically obsolete, right?"

"Lila—" James warned.

"No, I'm not going to sell out, sell my soul, and turn on people who have been good to me." Reid might have been a dick, but she was still a professional, and wouldn't renege on their contract. She put down the contact and slid it back to the executives. "I'm not signing this."

"You're a blogger, and you should be counting yourself lucky that we're even talking to you," the woman executive said.

"You know what? I'm done. Thank you for your time and consideration, but I think I'm better off remaining independent."

"Lila, wait—" her agent called to her.

She stopped and turned, felt herself become light, and free. "James, you're fired."

CHAPTER EIGHTEEN

IT WAS THE first day Reid had called in sick since he'd taken over the distillery. He'd even gone to work with walking pneumonia, fractured ribs, that bout of flu that kept him quarantined in his office. But as he sat on his couch, he tried to summon the strength to sit up. He failed. He wasn't physically sick, he reasoned, but tell that to the painful hollow beneath his breastbone. He missed Lila. There was no way around it. He sipped the rum from the crystal glass beside him. He'd done it to himself.

Knowing he would regret it, he pulled up her Instagram account—her pictures were fun, colorful, and he could see the passion in them. His thumb slipped and he accidentally double-tapped, liking one of her old photos. "Shit." But his eyes were glued to the picture, one from Belize, where she wore an emerald-colored bikini on a beautiful beach. His heart throbbed. He regretted what had happened between them, but there was nothing he could do about it now. It was best to keep her separate from his personal life. She was a good brand ambassador. There was no room for a romantic relationship. It was what they'd both wanted from the start. He should have listened to reason and stayed away from her. If he had, he wouldn't be in this situation.

"I thought we'd find you here," he heard Gemma say. He raised his head and saw her and Quin walking toward him. They each took a seat on a lounger flanking him, boxing him in. "I heard you called in sick. Feeling okay?"

"No, I'm sick," he told her, pointedly taking a drink from his glass.

"You're hardly ever sick," she reminded him. "And even if you were, it's never kept you from work."

"That's how we know I'm *really* sick," he told her.

Quin ripped his phone from his hand. "Looks like *lovesick* to me, big brother."

"Give that back," Reid demanded, reaching to grab it from his brother's hand, but he was too slow as Quin tossed the phone over him to Gemma.

"You're stalking her social media now?" Gemma asked. "What happened? I thought you guys had a good thing going."

"We did. Until I fucked it up."

"What did you do?"

"I said some things to her. Cruel."

"Why?"

He shrugged. "I don't know. I think I did it to drive her away."

"Reid Rexford caught in deep introspection?" Quin teased.

"Shut up."

"What did driving her away accomplish?" Gemma asked. "Besides make you miserable."

He shook his head. "Check out the pictures. *I'm* miserable and she's having a ball."

"No, she isn't," Gemma said. "I might not know her as intimately as you do, but I know she really cares for you."

"I thought Carolina did, too."

"Holy shit," Quin whispered. "That's what this is about? What Carolina did to you?"

"You know she isn't like Carolina. You can tell that right away," Gemma said.

"I fell too deep, too fast for Lila. She was too close. I had to end it, to protect the distillery."

"That's bullshit and you know it," Gemma said. "You drove her away because you're afraid. You're afraid of being burned again."

Reid didn't answer. He couldn't because Gemma had nailed it. "Can I have my phone back?"

She handed it back to him without a fight. "Figure out your life, Reid, or you'll end up miserable and alone." She took a deep breath. "But that's not why we're here."

The grave look on her face got Reid's attention. "What's going on?"

"After Carolina's visit, I asked my crew if anyone had leaked anything to our competitors. I found out one of them has been feeding information to Cain Rum."

"What?" There was a sinking feeling in Reid's stomach.

"He came to me this morning. He's remorseful. They paid him to tell them what we're doing. I fired him. It sucks."

Reid put his head in his hands. He'd blamed Lila. He had pushed her away because he jumped to conclusions, and automatically believed the worst when he thought she'd betrayed him.

"Are you okay, Reid?" Quin asked him.

"No. I blamed Lila for the leak."

"How could you?" Gemma whispered. "I didn't know that was why she left. You've got to call her and apologize."

"I can't. She won't talk to me. Nor should she."

In her hotel room in San Francisco, Lila checked her planner. Her day was completely filled. But at least it was her own schedule, not some television network telling her where to go and what to do there. Even though she'd wanted a little downtime, she'd packed her day with activities. She forced herself to stay busy. If she didn't, it might lead to too much thinking. And she knew the subject of those thoughts would be Reid.

She picked up the package that had been delivered to the hotel. It proudly bore the Rexford logo. She opened it and saw the promotional materials that she would start wearing and giving away. She picked up a cropped tank top. She wasn't sure why, but she brought it to her nose. It didn't smell like Reid. It just smelled like cotton and cardboard. She sighed and went to lie on her bed. She had it bad.

She rolled over and looked at her phone. It was time to check her notifications. She spent time every day moderating her feeds, responding to comments and messages. Instagram had hundreds of likes, but one stuck out to her. @RRexford. Reid. He'd liked one of her photos from a year ago. Someone was internet-stalking.

She smiled. So, he'd been creeping her feed. She brought up his contact information and debated whether or not she should dial. Before she could stop herself, she did. One ring went through. Two rings. She toyed with the idea of hanging up, but she couldn't. There was no going back now. Even if he didn't answer, he would still see her name on his caller ID.

"Hello?" he answered.

"Hi, Reid."

"How are you?"

"I'm good. And yourself?"

"I can't complain. I'm in San Francisco. So that's always good."

"Nice city."

Their conversation was so strained, so formal that it made her heart ache.

"What can I do for you, Lila?"

I miss you. What could she say? "I received that promotional package from you guys. Everything looks fine."

"Great. And the payment went through fine?"

"Yeah it did."

"That's good."

She could hear him take a deep breath.

"Lila, I need to say something."

She almost gasped with anticipation of what Reid might have to say.

"I owe you an apology. We found out who was behind the leak. I know it wasn't you. And I shouldn't have blamed you."

That's it? She appreciated the apology, but she'd wanted to hear more. That he wanted her to come back. He wanted to try again. But those words never came.

"And if you have any other concerns, don't be afraid to contact Quin. You have his number, right?"

Her eyes squeezed shut. "Yeah," she said, feeling her eyes water and her throat tighten. "Listen, I'm really busy at the moment. Why don't we talk later?" She managed to squeak out the words.

She heard his sigh on the other end. "Okay. Take care, Lila."

"You too, Reid."

CHAPTER NINETEEN

THE MAIN STAGE held little interest for Lila, as she made her way through the throngs of festival-goers. She was tired, wanted to go home. *Home.* That was a thought she'd never had before. But where was home, exactly? The only place she could think of was Miami.

"You ready?" one of the organizers asked her.

She had set up a booth at the music festival event to distribute the Rexford gear she'd been sent. "All set," she muttered. She should be interacting, creating posts, going live from the festival. But she was tired and not feeling it. She gave herself a shake to relax. Her phone buzzed in her pocket. She considered ignoring it, but she pulled it out. It was a text from Reid—the first she'd heard from him in more than a month.

All it said was French toast truck.

She looked up from the screen and took in her surroundings. The food truck area was nearby. Not caring that the organizer was calling after her, or that he was ready to start, Lila took off in the direction of the smell of the food, not sure what she was looking for, but hoping against hope that she would see Reid when she got there.

Lila wasn't disappointed.

When she stopped in front of the food truck, the scent of maple syrup and butter tickling her nostrils, all she could focus on was Reid. He looked casual, in khaki-colored linen pants and a button-down shirt. He'd grown a short, dark beard since she'd last seen him, and his hair was mussed, as if he'd pushed his fingers through it more than once in the ninety-degree heat.

"What are you doing here?" she asked.

"I came hoping to find you, not that I was certain you'd want to see me."

She looked around at the crowd. "You thought you'd find me among thousands of people?"

"It was a bit of long shot, I know, but I thought I'd try my luck drawing you to the food."

She laughed. "I guess you know me after all."

"Can I get you some French toast?"

She nodded. "Share an order?"

"Sure. Why don't you find somewhere for us to sit?"

The few tables were all full, so she walked a short distance and found a mostly flat section of grass where they could sit. When he joined her, they picked at their food.

"Drop the crap, Reid. Why are you here?"

"I really wanted to see you. In fact, that's all I've wanted to do since you left my house that day when I was a huge asshole to you. I missed you."

"I missed you, too."

"And I wasn't fair to you. You were right, I didn't trust you. But it wasn't because you gave me a reason not to. It was my own inability to let someone get close. I got scared and found a reason to push you away."

Lila nodded. Reid had been terrible, but she couldn't put the blame fully on Reid. She'd run, too. The move to Los Angeles had been the easy option, not staying to work it out. "I'm pretty sure I was the one who ran. Like, literally. I moved across the country."

He shook his head. "I wouldn't even listen to you. I should have known you weren't responsible for the leak."

"We can discuss this in circles all day, and I'll miss Childish Gambino's set. So why don't we say what we want. What do you want?"

"I want you," he said simply. He took a swallow of his beer, and Lila marveled at the scene. Reid Rexford, the buttoned-down businessman, always in control of his life, his appearance always impeccable, sitting cross-legged with her in a field, in rumpled clothes, drinking from a beer can, eating a piece of French toast on a paper plate. "And I'm so used to getting what I want. I don't know if you noticed this, but I might be just a little bit spoiled."

She faked a gasp. "You?" she asked, clutching her chest.

He laughed, but the sound was hollow. "When I realized you weren't coming back, I was miserable. I tried to bury myself in the business, but that didn't work. Nothing let me forget about you. Especially since I've been following your social media accounts. I wouldn't let myself forget about you. Especially since it you looked like you'd moved on. You're out here having a blast. It just reminds me that I'm not as fun and carefree as you. I like the quiet. What I held onto the most was that we couldn't be together if we were working together. I know I was just making excuse."

"Reid, you're plenty fun. Think of all the fun we had together."

He looked around. "We did have fun. But it's not like this. Your life is so much bigger than mine." He shook his head, laughing. "Can you make me stop talking?"

"No, I'm liking this. Talk some more."

"I know you have a life in LA now, and God, I don't even know what I'm asking you, or how we can make this work, but I don't care. I want you in my life."

She leaned forward and kissed him. She tasted the maple syrup and butter on his lips. "I want you in my life, too." She looked around. "I know my life is more chaotic than yours. You're more settled, I'm a little wild. I'm carefree, you're serious. The balance is what makes us good together."

"I know you're living out here now, but we can make the distance work. If you want, I can take leave from the distillery and travel with you."

"You'd take leave from the distillery?"

He nodded. "I know Quin and Gemma have everything under control. I can stay away for short periods of time. You taught me that." He blew out a breath. "And you showed me that I can love again. I love you, Lila, and I'll do anything to keep you in my life."

She couldn't believe the words he was saying. "I don't want you to think that you can just come here and say some nice things, and all is forgiven."

"I don't expect that," he told her. "I'm just grateful you're willing to listen to me."

"I love you, too, Reid."

Reid dropped his food and drew Lila into an embrace. His mouth found hers and they kissed, and she poured every bit of love and emotion she could muster into him. She couldn't believe they'd been given a second chance.

"I don't want you to walk away from the distillery," she told him when she broke away. "That place is everything to you."

"It isn't anymore," he assured her. "You are. Why don't we get out of here?"

"I would, but I have a whole box of Rexford swag to give away."

"Just leave the boxes open on the ground, and let people take what they want."

“Are you suggesting I bail on work?” she teased.

“Lila,” he said against her lips, kissing her lightly. “When are you going to learn that there is more to life than just work?”

* * * * *

PURE TEMPTATION

REBECCA HUNTER

MILLS & BOON

To Megan and Maneesha, who entertained the topics of free climbing, adrenaline sports and cautionary tales on an Inspiration Point hike, and to the group of climbers I accosted while on a walk in the Berkeley Hills, especially Alicia, who answered all my probing questions. Thanks to Kim Ryan, former hotshot and current hotshot wife, for detailed clarifications—all mistakes are my own, of course—and thanks to both Stacy Finz and Kira for yet another round of insightful beta comments. Can you tell that it truly takes a village to build a book? I'm so lucky to have mine.

CHAPTER ONE

Tap, tap.

The knock on the front door of the cabin came in the open window, cutting through the sounds of the shower just as Daxon Miles was turning it off. He scrubbed his face and searched the ultramodern bathroom for a clock, but all he saw was tile, glass, and the wooden box filled with hibiscus-scented soaps and shampoos he had passed over earlier. How long had he stood under the shower, letting the water run over his body? After a long plane ride, it was surprising just how satisfying something as simple as hot water felt.

Tap, tap.

"Just a minute," he called.

Daxon grabbed a towel and scrubbed the water from his hair, then wrapped it around his waist. The towel was just long enough to secure, though not by a wide margin. He would have thought that a super-exclusive resort like this would lean toward overindulgent for everything, including towel length, but like the rest of the bathroom, minimalism seemed to be the guiding principle. He stepped out through the glass door, his body drinking in the humid Hawaiian heat.

"It's your *personal healing coach*."

The sentence wafted through the window, hitting him hard in the middle of his chest. Daxon froze midstride. What the hell? It wasn't the sarcasm dripping from those last three words that had his heart jumping in his chest. It was the voice.

Her voice. The sound of it flooded him with the same liquid heat he had fought off six months ago.

Impossible. It couldn't be her…could it? No, it couldn't. The hot shower, the beautiful beachside location, the Kalani Resort itself with its wish-fulfillment promise must have lulled him into a fantasy world where *she* was here, too. But that couldn't be right.

The doctor's strict orders to put his well-known focus on chilling out must be messing with his head. Why else would his mind have wandered to Kendall Clark? Back to those days in his suite in a different resort, the lush breeze blowing the curtains, when she was his physical therapist and he was trying not to be yet another douchey client with a hard-on. But her hands had felt soft and good in a way no physical therapist's should—or had. And he had spent too much time wondering if the rest of her body was just as soft. Oh, how he had wanted to take her to bed on his final night there when they'd kissed, spend the whole night exploring her…except it didn't happen. Which must be why he was hearing her voice, six months later, on the other side of the world.

"Be right there," he called, pushing those memories away.

His focus here at the Kalani was getting himself back in top shape for the Moonlight Buttress free solo that'd be filmed live in two weeks. No ropes, no safety measures to fall back on. And absolutely no distractions. Which meant no thinking about Kendall Clark.

Daxon headed out of the bathroom, into the main room of his private cabin. Halfway across the floor, it occurred to him to grab a hold of his towel to keep it in place—because he didn't need his junk hanging out. He made his way to the door, took a deep breath and turned the handle.

"Listen, I lost track of—" Daxon stopped mid-sentence, mouth gaping as he swung the door open and he caught sight of the woman standing in front of him.

Kendall Clark.

Was it really her? She seemed very real in the little entryway, cheeks flushed, her big brown eyes round, framed by the longest lashes—just like he remembered. He stared at those eyes, blinking, a little dazed. Her gaze swooped down, over his bare chest, then up again to his mouth, and his whole body prickled with awareness. His ultimate distraction was standing right in front of him…wasn't she?

He lifted a hand to reach for her, to make sure she was real. Halfway there, he thought better of it, so he rested that hand on the doorframe, trying to jump-start his stalled thoughts.

What the hell was going on right now? Was all this Hawaiian heat having some sort of rock-to-the-head effect? Because what he was seeing was Kendall, dressed in a red Kalani Wellness polo shirt and shorts that exposed miles of her lean, tanned legs. The same legs he had ached to touch for one, tantalizing week. Her long hair was back in a ponytail, the way she'd worn it in Costa Rica when she had knelt down… Shit. Not what he should be thinking about.

Daxon blinked a couple times, but Kendall was still there, staring at him. She was holding a tablet and looking all business. Or at least, she had been a few moments ago. Now she was gaping at him, too.

Her eyes narrowed. "Is this your way of saying hello?"

What? He gave himself a little shake and furrowed his brow. As her gaze traveled down his body, instinctively he looked down, too, and—fuck.

His hand was resting on the doorframe, which meant it was no longer holding his towel up. His brain hadn't even registered that he dropped it, but clearly, his dick had been a lot quicker to believe that she was real.

"Shit," he muttered. Daxon grabbed his towel off the floor and wrapped it around his waist again, but that did nothing to hide his growing hard-on.

Slick, Dax. Really subtle.

He straightened up and met her eyes again. "You might not believe this, but that was an accident."

She gestured to his cock. "And that is, too?"

"In a manner of speaking, yes." Daxon rubbed the back of his neck—with his free hand this time.

Then he found himself just staring at her again, his brain still malfunctioning, trying to process the fact that Kendall was really here. She stared back for a bit, and then a burst of laughter came from her sexy mouth. He blew out a breath and smiled. This was ridiculous. Thank God she didn't look too pissed. Maybe he wasn't the first asshole to drop his towel for her, though he really hoped this wasn't one of her occupational hazards.

Finally, she caught her breath and gave him a look that suggested something between amusement and exasperation. "Classy."

"That's me. Come on in," he said before his mind could fall into another gutter.

He stepped aside, and Kendall wandered into the main room of his cabin. A zing of raw attraction ran through him as she passed by, and Daxon paused in the hall and ran a hand through his hair, trying to get a handle on the situation. He had come to the Kalani to fully heal, away from public eyes, and *she* was his physical therapist? Either this was the world's most improbable coincidence…or something else was going on. Daxon was betting everything on the latter, and he needed to figure out what that *something* was.

He watched her as she wandered over to peek at the view of the ocean through the French doors. She looked…different. What was it? Her hair was lighter, streaked with hints of blond. The taper of her waist, the curve of her hips, those fit legs—her body was just as distracting as before. Her skin tone was a little darker, from all the Hawaiian sun no doubt, but there was something else.

"You look good," he said, following her in. "More…relaxed."

That's what it was. There was an ease to her that he hadn't seen the last time.

Kendall turned. "Thanks, I think. You look very… relaxed, too." She gestured to his current state of undress. "Well, most of you."

There was a hint of a smile on her lips, a good sign. But after that full-frontal greeting, he needed to tone this the fuck down.

"I'll put on some clothes. In case you've seen enough of me for the day."

She waved him off. "Nothing I haven't seen before."

Daxon frowned. She had thrown out that comment in the most casual tone, like getting a peek at him naked was just another part of her day, somewhere between taping up an injured wrist and paperwork. Not that she was supposed to be jumping with joy at seeing his dick, unsolicited, but, well, wasn't she at least a little…impressed?

"I'll be out in a minute," he grumbled over his

shoulder. But as he turned away, he caught her gaze wandering lower, like she was checking him out. Or at least he thought he saw it. Maybe that was his ego talking, but a guy could hope.

Daxon headed for the bedroom and shut himself in the large walk-in closet. He rested his forehead against the door and let out a quiet groan. *Focus.* Kendall Clark, the star of far too many of his fantasies, was sitting on the couch, a dozen steps away from his bedroom, and he still had the lingering remains of a hard-on. Time to get this situation under control.

Goal number one: fully heal his injured calf so he could face off with Moonlight Buttress on schedule. Goal number two: keep his overeager cock down and safely covered. Because Kendall didn't strike him as the kind of woman who enjoyed a flasher. Even if she may have been checking him out.

He grabbed a pair of shorts and T-shirt and slipped them on. He ran his hand through his wet hair a couple times and hung his towel on a hook, then rested his hand on the door handle.

Apparently his brain had started working again because he was almost sure he knew who had set this up. Calvin. His business partner and producer's last words before he got on the plane to Hawaii sank in. *I arranged a special wish for you, one I know you'll love.* The asshole had set this up, probably assuming that Daxon had, in fact, slept with her back in Costa Rica and wouldn't mind a repeat. Dax had guessed Calvin's wish for him would be misguided, but this was an epic miss. Because spending hours a day with hot-as-hell Kendall Clark was the polar opposite of relaxation. More like excruciatingly tense. Hard in every way.

Kendall Clark didn't do hesitant, fumbling girlishness. Definitely not around high-profile men in general, and especially not around Daxon Miles in particular. So as soon as Daxon left the room, Kendall plopped down on the sofa and took deep breaths, trying to get her runaway pulse under control. Because despite all the rehearsals in front of her bathroom mirror, that greeting didn't go anything like the one she'd planned.

In the entryway, as her eyes had wandered south, a rush of tempting heat had spread through her, shutting off all reasonable thought. Then the memories of Costa Rica flooded back. Seven long days of trying to ignore all those perfect, taut muscles. That sharp pull of sexual interest that came anyway each time she touched him, each time she felt him move under her hands. As she tried like hell to focus on her job.

She could sense it all starting again: the client crush she never should have had, the one she had tried so hard to resist, was taking hold. And she definitely didn't do celebrity client crushes.

Plus, Daxon Miles made her nervous. Kendall had assumed his love of danger was all an act, a show he put on for his bazillions of YouTube followers. Who the hell in his right mind would actually want to dive off cliffs just for fun? But after a week in Costa Rica with him, she was forced to admit that, number one, he truly did love these stunts, and number two, he wasn't crazy. Okay, number three, he was hot as sin, but she wasn't counting that realization.

She might have even written him off. It wasn't like she'd never had a hot, ultra-fit client before. But the conversation she'd had with him back then about the difference between high risk and high consequence—the one that stretched long beyond working hours—had her questioning all her safe choices. The things he had said that last night in Costa Rica had stayed with her, bubbling inside when she was debating whether or not to accept a job at the Kalani Resort and move to Hawaii. With enough preparation, Daxon really was up for just about anything, and she…well, over the past six months, she was trying harder to be. But ignoring her risk-averse nature certainly didn't come easily.

When Sheila Alleyne, the Kalani's mysterious "wish maker," had contacted her about this assignment, she'd said Daxon Miles had specially requested her. Though each guest at the resort was entitled to a "wish"—a special request to be fulfilled during their stay—she had never heard of a personal request like this. Wishes were usually more along the lines of a personal chef or a paragliding instructor, and Sheila and the staff took care of it. Kendall had tried hard not to waste her time contemplating questions like

How the hell did he know I was here? or *Do I just ignore the scorching-hot kiss that happened in Costa Rica while my hands are on his thighs?* Instead, she'd focused on the reason she hoped he'd requested her: because she was a damn good physical therapist. Thorough, methodical and careful.

But for a guy who had personally asked for her, Daxon had seemed awfully surprised to see her at his door. Then again, her first clue that she wasn't getting the full story was in Sheila's words: *he also wished for you as a personal healing coach.* The Daxon Miles she knew would never use words like that. The man wasn't really the type to wish for help with anything. And what the hell did that title mean? The only service she was giving him this week was physical therapy.

Her last assignment with him in Costa Rica had been her most memorable as a travelling physical therapist for many reasons… Daxon being one of them. Kendall had started to think her memories had mixed with fantasy, overexaggerating his appeal. But no. When he opened the door earlier, tousled wet hair, strong jaw and piercing grey-green eyes, she remembered why she had turned him down that last night. Daxon Miles was trouble. Shirtless, his hard, lean muscles flexed in stark relief. Up close, the raw sexuality of his body was almost irresistible. Another wave of heat rippled through her. Trouble. Especially for her, who seemed to have been born with an extra-large caution gene.

Daxon entered the room again, and the scent of him—freshly showered and very male—wafted in the air. She shivered as he brushed by her. Definitely trouble.

He took a seat at a safe distance on the couch and leaned forward, resting his forearms on his thighs. All the surprise from their greeting was gone, and in its place, he was giving her that smile. The one that said he knew exactly what effect he had on women. He had been melting panties with it for years between all the skydives and cliff dives and free climbs, if the tabloids were to be believed. She should know better, but that look was pulling her in.

"I promise I won't flash you again," he said, eyes glittering. "Unless you ask for it."

"You know, most people start conversations with 'hello' or 'how have you been?'"

His smile spread wider. "Do you really think I'm aiming to be like most people?"

Everyone with internet access knew the answer to that.

"Let's just get this started." Kendall opened her tablet and found the bullet points for the introduction. "Welcome to the Kalani," she said, reading straight from the notes, in her best professional voice. "I want to make sure your stay is everything you want it to be."

Kendall almost rolled her eyes. *Everything you want it to be.* Yeah, that definitely had sexy overtones.

She scanned the rest of the key talking points

Sheila had given her for the meeting. The wording of the resort's welcome was carefully chosen so as to flatter—and not to bruise any egos. God forbid. But she got the feeling that the whole *Fantasy Island* appeal of the Kalani Resort would take this conversation in the wrong direction. Time to go off-script.

"What are you doing here, Daxon?"

He blinked at her in surprise, then frowned. "Taking a break, healing my calf. *Relaxing.*" He said that last word with plenty of sarcasm. "Lying low before my next filming. My producer's the cautious type, and he thinks this is the best option."

"I see," she said slowly. "He's the one who booked your stay here, right?"

Daxon nodded.

"So you don't want to be here?"

He hesitated, rubbing his jaw. "I do." His gaze was laser-sharp, and she squirmed under his scrutiny. It felt like he was planning, calculating, waiting for the right moment to…what? Drop his towel? No, he already did that. But the pull she had felt six months ago was just as strong now, like they were picking up right where they left off that last night.

In the hallway of a luxury hotel in Costa Rica, lit by the setting sun, oh, Lord, what a kiss they'd had. The whole world had been his soft mouth and his hard body, moving against hers. The feel of it was still so easy to recall, the physical memories, dreamy and ethereal. His big calloused hand cupping her jaw. Hungry strokes of his tongue as their hips fit together. Gasping for breath as he came in for more. And the hunger in his eyes as she broke the kiss off, long after it had gotten out of hand. The memory was still vivid. Very vivid. But she could think about that later…after she got through this first session.

"Let's get started," she said again. She scrolled through his files on her tablet until she found the one she was looking for: the doctor's report she'd reviewed a few days before. "You tore your calf a few weeks ago, Grade 1, and it still hasn't fully healed." She looked up at Daxon. "The doctor thinks the slow healing is a combination of not enough physical rest and possibly stress."

Daxon shrugged. "I doubt it's stress. I have the best job in the world. Cliff diving last season, rock climbing this season and a bunch of other adventures planned for the future."

"But a free solo climb has absolutely no margin for error. One missed foothold, one loose rock, one bee sting—if anything goes wrong, you could die."

He nodded solemnly, and for a moment she thought she was getting her point through to him, but then he smiled. "That's why people love to watch it."

His raspy voice strummed something inside her, but Kendall was trying hard not to be swayed by it, or his enthusiasm. He made it all sound so natural, so…sane. "You're talking about the rush of all this, but you have to understand that at some level this is stressful, both physically and mentally, even if it's fun. You jumped out of an airplane with no parachute a few months ago, for God's sake."

Daxon flashed her a cheeky grin. "Did you watch?"

This man was incorrigible.

"Maybe," she hedged. "Just to make sure you got to the ground safely."

Daxon waved off the comment. "I trusted my partner enough to put my life in his hands. Besides, Calvin wouldn't have shown the footage if I didn't make it."

"Good point," said Kendall.

He winked at her mischievously. "Which is why my free climb of Moonlight Buttress is going to have a live broadcasting element. Everyone will be watching, wondering if I'll make it. One slip of my fingers and…" He lifted his hands in surrender, adding, "It ups the stakes."

"Aaaand now we have the answer to where your added stress level is coming from."

Daxon's smile turned cocky.

"Not a chance. I thrive on the pressure. And I perform best that way, too." He lifted his eyebrows as that last sentence left his lips. "Just in case you're wondering."

It was the kind of thing a guy said right before he headed into bedroom talk. She could tell Daxon's mind went there for a moment by the way his eyes glittered with heat. And despite the fact that it was one step away from a bad pick-up line, that tempting heat traveled right through her body. *Don't get distracted.*

"I'm sure your performances are…fine," she said evenly. His eyes narrowed at that last word. "But that's still stress, and it has to come out somehow. In your case, it could be taking on physical manifestations."

"Like tension, which means the slow healing of my calf muscles?"

"Exactly."

"I see," said Daxon.

He actually looked serious, like he was really considering what she was saying. He was quiet, staring out the open French doors at the ocean, but she got the feeling he wasn't seeing it.

And for just a moment, she wondered what it was like to be Daxon Miles. He probably didn't even let himself think about his own vulnerabilities two weeks before a free solo climb. He'd have to have shut all his doubts out long ago, build a wall so they didn't creep in. Kendall knew exactly how people like this worked. She'd grown up with a man like this in her very own home.

She studied Daxon for an extra beat. "Can we rewind back to when you answered the door a bit ago?"

"Sure."

"What would you have done if someone else had been standing outside your door, someone you didn't know?"

Daxon laughed. "Well, for starters, I wouldn't have dropped my towel."

Yeah, right. Her face must have said exactly that because he tilted his head to the side, his brow wrinkling.

"Truthfully, I probably would have sent someone else away today. I'd also probably dodge them a few times this week, just for a little space." His mouth turned up, sliding back into his signature grin. "But I'm definitely not going to dodge you."

Damn. One-on-one with this man for seven days? He was already distracting her after fifteen minutes. It was time for a new plan, a better one. The plan she had decided on before she knocked on the door—*resist his charm*—wasn't going to hold up for long. At this point, she wasn't sure if she even wanted to avoid this particular brand of trouble anymore…

"My turn for a question," he said. "At dinner that night in Costa Rica, you said you were traveling to Hawaii for your next assignment. Is that when you got this job?"

Kendall shook her head slowly. She was a little thrown off by the fact that he actually remembered a detail like that from their conversation. But she shouldn't be. There was an intensity to him when they were alone, like every ounce of his attention was on her.

"That assignment never panned out," she said. "But I couldn't get Hawaii out of my mind."

He looked out the window, and she did, too.

Across the patio and his private pool, through the palm trees, the ocean spread out in front of them, a sparkling blanket of blue.

"I understand why," said Daxon softly.

"Costa Rica was gorgeous, too," she said. "That night at dinner, I got the feeling you loved it there, like you were considering staying. What's stopping you?"

Daxon's forehead wrinkled as he seemed to consider his answer. "I don't have any desire to stop traveling, to stop exploring new places, but I wouldn't mind a little beach house somewhere to come back to."

"You could still get one."

He tilted his head, studying her. "My turn again. And tell the truth."

Kendall crossed her arms, trying to resist the twitch at the corners of her mouth. "Ask away."

"I want to go back to that hallway in Costa Rica. That kiss was…" His voice trailed off, and his smile turned hungry. "You can fill in that last word yourself. But something made you stop. What was it?"

Of course he wanted to discuss that. Though she supposed it was better to get this topic out of the way from the start.

"The obvious. You hired me." She shrugged, as if that kiss hadn't been a big deal. As if she hadn't replayed it in her mind too many times.

"But the job was over," he said. "And I'm not into mixing work with pleasure, either. The idea of you feeling obligated in some way to have sex is a boner-killer for me."

She shook her head. "Thank you for that TMI moment."

Daxon's laugh was so real, so deep and easy and infectious, and Kendall found herself smiling, too. His laughter waned, leaving a glint of determination in his eyes.

"Do the same rules apply between us now?" His voice was low and sexy, making this question even more torturous.

Lord, he was tempting. Could there possibly be a way to explore this attraction and still keep her principles firmly in place? Kendall sighed. "I haven't decided."

"If we chose to explore…mutual pleasure this week, could it in any way interfere with your career? In theory, of course."

The word *pleasure* rolled off his beautiful lips, echoing through her. More physical memories came back. The hard, defined muscles of Daxon's biceps moving, flexing beneath her hands as he slid his tongue over hers. She shook her head again. "Not that I'm aware of. Though it's not exactly the reputation I'm cultivating here."

"Noted," he said, and he sounded a little more serious. At least he seemed to understand that part. "I can keep my mouth shut."

"Noted," she said, giving him what she hoped was a dry smile. "I'll take it under consideration."

His signature grin curved seductively at the corners of his mouth, like he was considering it, too. In detail.

His sharp gaze was on her again. His hand stopped halfway down his jaw. There was heat in his eyes along with something that looked an awful lot like resolve. He was deciding something, and she was almost sure it was about her.

He rose from the couch and stretched, his T-shirt lifting, exposing the sculpted abs and dark trail of hair that led into his shorts. Was she gawking at him again? Kendall swallowed and met his eyes.

He flashed her a smile, a mix of amusement and challenge. "Well, if stress is why my muscles aren't relaxing, I think we should start right away with my welcome massage."

Kendall's face flushed as she leveled her gaze on him. "This isn't the kind of massage that has a happy ending."

When Daxon's smile broadened, still hot and even more determined, she knew she was in so much trouble. "If anyone's getting a happy ending today, it's you."

CHAPTER TWO

Was that last comment a little too much? Maybe, but Daxon had made a decision, and once he put his mind to something, he couldn't let up. His brain had kicked back into gear, and he had decided to pursue the most obvious route, the perfect relaxation plan, one they'd both enjoy. He had never had much success at reducing his intensity level, but he could switch his focus.

His attraction to Kendall was a little dizzying, but that was likely just because he had resisted it—of course, her appeal had intensified when she walked away after a hot-as-hell kiss. His mind had filled in all the details that his body had missed out on that night. Solution: instead of spending another week trying *not* to picture Kendall Clark underneath him, they could have a little fun, get this thing between them out of their systems.

Besides, he needed a really good distraction, something to take his mind off the fact that he'd rather be in Zion National Park right now, preparing to climb Moonlight Buttress. Thinking about that had driven him crazy today. Thinking about sex with Kendall was a stellar alternative, and he had one glorious week to divert himself with it. But she looked far from convinced, which meant he had to get this next part right: keep her laughing and figure out her hesitations and limits. Make it clear from the beginning that getting naked with him meant plenty of fun for her, too. *And no more flashing your hard-on, buddy.*

Daxon gave her a playful wink. “Satisfaction guaranteed.”

She cracked a little grin. Slowly, it grew wider until her whole face lit up in a beautiful, thousand-watt smile. “You’re relentless.”

“That’s my strength,” he said. “For better or for worse.”

It felt so good to see her again. A whole week with Kendall stretched in front of him, and his smile just wouldn’t quit. She stood, smoothing her tiny shorts over her long legs. Daxon loved any challenge, and this one involved a hot woman whom he’d thought about too much…in the shower, most often. His mind was going in a dozen different directions right now, but it was time to focus and let her do her job.

He rubbed his hands together, quirked an eyebrow at her and nodded to the massage table. “You can go first if you want.”

She rolled her eyes. “Climb up, champ. I want to check out your leg.” She walked over to the table and spread a towel over one half, and he climbed on. “I’m going to start by feeling around and moving your leg to get a sense of what’s going on. Let me know how it feels.”

He nodded.

Kendall moved to his left side, her attention focused completely on his leg, which meant he was free to watch her work. And not stare down her shirt, since he was pretty sure that would fall under obnoxious client behavior. He respected that. After a few unsolicited kisses by women when he was in front of the camera, he understood that there were many reasons why it could put her in a tricky position. So seeing her off duty was the—

“Ooooh,” he groaned as her fingers gently kneaded the top of his calf. “Right there.”

“Does it hurt?” She moved her hands farther down and to the sides, testing.

Daxon shook his head. “Just a little tight.”

She moved to the base of the table and picked up his foot, flexing it gently.

“Still okay?”

“Yeah,” he said. “Rarely hurts anymore. I’m just trying not to push it too hard this week. Which means mandatory R&R for me.” Daxon sighed. Some people just weren’t built to relax, and he was one of them. This week he’d work on his core and hand strength while going easy on his legs—that was the best he could do.

She put down his foot and rested her hands on the

table. "I don't see anything worrisome at this point, but I agree that three weeks is a bit long for a Class 1 tear to heal. Though if you're still the same person as you were in Costa Rica, I'd guess the reason for the slow recovery is that you're still pushing yourself too hard."

"Which is what my 'personal healing coach' is supposed to help with?"

Kendall laughed. "Who came up with that title?"

Daxon shook his head. "That would be Calvin. Definitely his sense of humor."

"Calvin, your producer?" She frowned a little. "Does he think we…?" Her sentence drifted off as she gestured between the two of them.

He paused, considering his answer carefully. "I think he assumes I sleep with a lot of women." Kendall's frown grew deeper. "Shitty, I know. Still, assuming we slept together is not enough for him to arrange this."

Her expression softened. "Then why did he specifically request me?"

Daxon shrugged. "Probably because I actually followed what you said I should do back in Costa Rica."

"And you don't follow orders?"

He heard the hint of sarcasm in her voice, but he ignored it. "I'm not being a dick about this, just honest. I need someone who takes lots of things into consideration, including working within my business obligations." He paused. "I've been told I'm frustrating to work with."

"I see."

"You're a great physical therapist, Kendall," he said softly. "And I'm not just saying that to get into your pants. Though I wouldn't say no if that's an option."

"Thanks, Daxon," she said, then, with a smirk, added, "for the professional compliment, of course."

The compliment was the unfiltered truth. In Costa Rica, Kendall went beyond the physical aspects of healing and actually listened when he said he couldn't make a particular accommodation.

She was also hot, of course, but there were plenty of hot women in the world and only one Moonlight Buttress to free solo. Not that he was celibate these days, but it had been a while…which probably wasn't a good thing since Kendall was about to put her hands on him again.

This would likely turn into the world's most torturous PT session. Daxon tried to clear his mind of the lusty haze that was still lingering. He—or Calvin, actually—had pushed her into this setup. If he wanted to propose after-hours fun, Dax needed to figure out how to give her a real choice, the freedom to opt in or opt out. Hopefully it wouldn't be the latter, but this would only work if she was all in.

"Look, I've made it clear that I find you incredibly attractive, and maybe you're feeling this vibe, too." He lifted one eyebrow, and he got a wry smile from her in return. "But I respect that you probably don't want to fool around on the clock."

She gave a little nod, which hopefully meant he was on the right track. Now for the solution.

"I have an idea for you to think about," he continued, keeping his gaze steady on her eyes, not letting it wander down to her mouth, no matter how tempting it was. "I'm not looking for an answer right now, just something to consider. You check out my leg and do your job, and I won't come on to you." She gave a little snort, but he pushed on. "When you're finished, you walk out my cabin door. Then you have a choice—you can keep walking, or you can turn around and come back in for that happy ending I'm dying to give you. Off duty."

She lifted her gaze to his, and her eyes were filled with heat. She licked her lips, and his eyes went straight there, fixating on her tongue. A bolt of heavy lust ran through him. Fuck, he had to keep this decent. He forced his gaze back up, and a smile quirked at the corners of her mouth.

"Just think about it," he whispered.

The body was a truly miraculous instrument, intricate connections of nerves and muscles and ligaments and bones. They all worked together to do the simple movements humans took for granted... until the system broke down. Then the different parts came into painful relief.

Kendall had seen the toll this breakdown could

take on someone, how it could crush a person. Her father had come so close to that breaking point during one awful fire season, when the worst came so close to happening. Being a hotshot firefighter came with a ticking clock, and both her parents knew that when they started. In the intimate game with nature's forces, nature always won. The night the tree limb fell and crushed her father's arm, ending his hotshot career, was a reminder neither she nor her mother would ever forget. Her dad got out alive, thanks to his team, and after a long, painful recovery period—thanks to both his physical therapist and Kendall's mother—he had moved on. Still, all these years later, her father missed it, some days wistfully, other days fiercely. Kendall tried not to get hung up on the question she had asked too many times: Why the hell did he still want to run toward danger instead of away from it?

All this had unfolded when she was in her tweens, and she had decided to become a physical therapist.

Her family history had probably made her a better one, or at the very least, a more dedicated one. Each client was a new path into the intricate art of movement. Each client meant learning the ways that a person could heal.

Her fingers brushed the dusting of hair on Daxon's thighs. His body was truly a wonder. She moved her hands up and down his leg, over all that golden skin, those well-defined muscles. She was trying hard not to get distracted by his off-duty idea, but every time her fingers moved up to his thighs, he sucked in a breath, reminding her of where this could go. Later.

Concentrate.

She had seen her fair share of men in amazing shape as a traveling physical therapist, athletes with bodies fine-tuned for sports. This was different. The switch had flipped that night in Costa Rica, and she couldn't figure out how to flip it back. She was no longer studying Daxon's body the way she would study a work of art. She was thinking about what it could do. What his muscular thighs would feel like pressed against hers. How it would feel to run her hands over those biceps as he lowered himself over her with each heavy thrust.

She glanced up at Daxon. His eyes were fixed on her, hot and intense. Holy hell. His hands gripped the sides of the massage table, his knuckles white. Still, he said nothing. Kendall smiled. She had to admit the man had impressive focusing skills. Much better than hers, clearly. Still, it was amusing to see him all worked up like this.

She quirked her eyebrow at him. "Not your best day for relaxing?"

He gave her a wry smile. "It's not a strength of mine, even on a good day."

"I think if you spend this week with a little stretching, massage and low-strain exercise for your legs, you'll be fine," she said, rocking back onto her heels, putting a little distance between them. "The real challenge is to go easy on your calf during the rest of the day. Try to stay off your feet as much as possible."

"I'll think of something."

She narrowed her eyes, and he put up his hands in surrender, laughing. "I wasn't coming on to you. Just a guy and his 'personal healing coach'—" He put air quotes around those last words "—having a conversation."

"Can we stop with the job title? It sounds like I'm part of some sort of cult fitness retreat."

He chuckled. "I already told you you're an amazing physical therapist," he said. "But the truth is I don't want you as a coach. And in the interest of keeping my word, I'll stop before I tell you what I want instead."

She bit her lip as Daxon's proposition came back. Off-hours fun. Low risk and high reward, if their kiss back in Costa Rica was any indication.

Kendall ended the session and packed her bags, taking her time, enjoying the heat of Daxon's intense gaze on her. She scrolled through the tablet, reviewing and adding to his schedule for the next day. She ticked off sailing, snorkeling, and a few more of the Kalani's features that were well suited for a guy with an itch for adventure and a body that wasn't currently cooperating. After all, he wasn't the resort's first guest in this situation.

"Here's a map of the Kalani, and I'll take you on a tour tomorrow afternoon," she said, handing it to him. "You can also use this tablet to book appointments or activities, order food—anything you need."

He scrolled through his options. "Can I book as many sessions with you as I want?"

"Don't push it." She tried to hold back her smile, but Daxon seemed to catch it anyway.

His mouth quirked up. "Thank you for doing this."

"My pleasure," she said, giving him the same playful wink he'd given her earlier. Before he could respond, she turned and walked toward the door.

Daxon followed. He didn't say anything, but she got his message just fine. *Remember how hot it was between us? I'd love to take it further this time.* Or maybe that was her own voice.

She paused at the door, then turned around. "I'll see you soon."

"I hope so." His gaze dipped to her lips, then back to her eyes. He opened his mouth, as if to say something more, then closed it with a little frown. Lord, she wanted to kiss that mouth, so she turned around, opened the door and walked out, shutting it with a click.

Then she came to a full stop on the wooden porch. *Whoa.*

Kendall took a deep breath. In front of her, Mauna Kea, the enormous volcano, rose up in the middle of the island. She was surrounded by miles of untouched hills and beaches, and the only other people anywhere near the place were high-profile guests, equally interested in privacy. A perfect place for escape and fun. Behind her, just on the other side of the door, was the hot, ultra-fit, six-foot-something man who had fueled her sexiest fantasies for the last six months—and that was only after a kiss. The man just had to breathe next to her and she was turned on. Escape and fun? Definitely.

Back in Costa Rica, Daxon had been hard enough to resist. Her employer at the time hadn't forbidden any intimate relations with clients…and she'd heard stories. But until that assignment, Kendall had never once been tempted to cross the line. Daxon didn't make on-the-job advances, but for one aching week, she found herself wondering what it would be like if he had.

Today she was getting a chance to reconsider that night in Costa Rica when she had walked away. She had taken this job as Daxon's physical therapist knowing full well that spending time with him would be intense. All she had to do was walk back in the door.

Kendall took a deep breath. Another breath. Another. Not helping. The anticipation of kissing Daxon again, all that intense energy focused—

The door creaked open behind her. She spun around and stood face-to-face with Daxon.

He blinked at her, lust written all over his face. Then he rubbed the back of his neck and gave her a sheepish smile. "Just checking the weather."

"Liar."

"I *was* checking the weather." He glanced up at

the cloudless sky. Then he stretched out his hand, palm up. “No rain. I *also* might have been checking to see if you had left. In addition.”

“Just thinking through my options.” Kendall crossed her arms, going for her best casual pose.

“Sure,” he said lightly. “Let me know if you want any help thinking through those options. Or trying some of them out.”

She raised an eyebrow. “Are you offering to drop your towel again?”

“I’m never going to live that one down, am I?”

“Probably not.”

“You know where to find me.” He started to close the door.

It was time. Kendall put her hand on the door. “Wait.”

The door swung open again, and he was grinning. She stood, facing him, staring into those glittering green eyes. God, those eyes. They were filled with the same kinds of *more* that she had spent a week resisting last time: more games, more sexy, more fun. And right now, that was exactly the kind of *more* she needed.

“Made up your mind?” he asked, his voice soft, low.

She nodded.

“You’re coming in?”

She nodded again. “Otherwise, I’ll spend another six months wondering what I missed.”

CHAPTER THREE

DAXON STEPPED ASIDE, leaving just enough room for her to pass through. Kendall's eyes narrowed, like she saw exactly what he was doing. She stopped in front of him, her body brushing up against his.

"I can play this game, too, you know," she whispered.

Then her hand was on his chest, and she looked up at him with wide brown eyes. He tried to read her expression, but he was sidetracked by her lips, so plush and inviting. His body was on high alert, memories mingling with the immediate sensation of her fingers on him. Her mouth was so close, and he was aching to kiss her. *Just a little more patience.* Last time this ended with him watching her walk away. This time felt…right. But he wanted her to lead.

So he waited as long as he could, which wasn't long. It was too tempting not to brush his fingers over her skin. Spending the last hour resisting her wasn't doing him any favors now. Daxon slipped his hand around her waist, bringing their bodies together, and walked them into the cabin, one slow step at a time. He kicked the door closed and rested his hand on it, leaning over her, breathing in the scent of her hair.

"Will you let your hair down?"

She blinked, a little surprised, it seemed, then nodded and slipped the fastener out. Shiny, sun-streaked chestnut-brown waves cascaded over her shoulders. Daxon groaned as his cock gave an urgent throb. She rested her hands around his neck, coaxing him closer.

He found the shell of her earlobe with his lips. "I got it wrong back in Costa Rica. Tell me how to get it right this time."

Kendall arched against him, their bodies flush. "You didn't get it wrong. I just wasn't ready."

"Are you ready now?" Thinking was getting more and more difficult.

"Mmm."

Oh, that sound out of her mouth… *Focus.* "Is that a yes?"

She tilted her head up and smiled at him. "That's a *hell yes.*"

Then finally, *finally* he was pressing his mouth against hers, and she sighed, like she had been waiting for this just as much as he had. She kissed him, her lips brushing against his in achingly slow caresses. Months of pent-up desire flooded through him as he met each stroke, each invitation. He threaded his fingers through all that soft, beautiful hair, grabbing on, pulling her closer. He took a gulp of air and then dived in for more. He had forgotten just how good she tasted, like endless sunshine and warmth. Each hungry stroke of her tongue fueled another jolt of pleasure to his system.

His muscles tensed as her hands traveled down, farther, until she found the hem of his T-shirt and slipped her hands underneath. Goddamn, this was better than he had remembered. Everything else faded, and what was left was Kendall. He pressed up against her, her body trapped between his and the door, his cock hard and straining inside his boxers. Her teeth raked over his bottom lip, and she hooked her leg around him, starting a slow, sensual grind that made his eyes roll back. He could come like this, fully clothed and panting in this little hallway, just from finally kissing Kendall, feeling her body against his again.

Aaaaand…no. That wasn't where this was going.

Daxon slowed the kiss, reining himself in, loosening his grip on her hair. She pulled her hands from under his shirt and settled them on his hips. He rested his forehead against hers.

"Fuck, sweets. This is really hot, and you haven't even taken off your clothes."

"Yet," she added, smiling. "You haven't, either."

"You haven't seen enough of me today?"

One of her hands moved lower, down between his legs, and she stroked his rock-hard cock. Pleasure rippled through him.

"I've changed my mind," she whispered. "I'd like a closer view."

The image from Costa Rica of Kendall kneeling between his legs came back, his own fantasies layered on, and he groaned. He had to stop thinking about that for now. If this was his only chance to touch her, to enjoy her, to taste her, he wanted to get it right.

"We'll see about that," he said with a wink. "Right now, I want to get you on that table."

Now Kendall remembered exactly why she had walked out of Daxon's room in Costa Rica. She had played back that kiss so many times in her mind, but somehow she had forgotten important details. The way his breath hitched when she touched his bare skin. The hunger in each brush of his lips. The way she lost herself as the tidal wave of want took over, building, threatening to crash through her body. She wanted more of this man, his hard muscles, the weight of him against her, his thick cock that was pressing against her, his mouth everywhere. She wanted *more*.

It had been almost impossible to walk away last time, but when she came up for air, she'd known she had to. Because drowning in a kiss with Daxon Miles had suddenly felt like a different kind of risk, one that had nothing to do with her job. One she knew was dangerous.

And yet here she was again, aching for more. During their sessions, her hands had traveled up and down his legs many times. She wanted to explore further. She wanted to learn his body, how it worked, how his muscles flexed when she touched him, what he sounded like when he came. This was a man with a preternatural ability to focus. What would it be like to feel him let go of all that control and lose himself in pleasure?

She just had to make sure this stayed uncomplicated. People had uncomplicated sex all the time, so why shouldn't this new, more adventurous version of her do it, too?

Kendall laced her fingers with his. "Let's try the bedroom instead. I think it'll be a little more comfortable."

"Maybe we can try the table later," he said. "But I'm happy to start anywhere, sweets, as long as I get to put my mouth on you."

Damn, he sounded so sincere, like he was aching to go down on her. No wonder women tripped over one another for this man.

"Right this way, champ." She led the way to the bedroom, her heart jumping in her chest. After months of watching his videos, just to make sure his previous injury had healed, of course—okay, and possibly using him as fodder for a late-night date with her vibrator because she never planned to see him again—after six months of *not real*, this was about to get very real.

A warm breeze blew through the open windows

of the light, airy room. The bed was enormous, covered with a fluffy duvet and a stack of pillows. A tray of hibiscus flowers lay on the long, narrow bench in front of the windows. He turned to her, tucking her hair behind her ear. The echoes of waves and the brush of palm leaves mixed with the sounds of turned-on male, so close. His hand lingered on her neck.

"I want to undress you."

"Sounds a little impractical."

He laughed. "Sounds sexy to me. As long as you don't mind me staring at you like a hungry dog."

Well, if he wanted to. She might as well get the whole Daxon Miles experience, from start to finish.

"Oooh, hungry dog," she said. "Very sexy."

He tickled her sides, and she yelped and wriggled. His laugh grew huskier.

"You like to tease me?" he said, his hands gentling, urging her to face him. "Just so you know, it only makes me harder for you."

When she turned around, his smile was so full of heat, and it sent a shiver of desire through her. Her eyes met his, and his smile faded. What would this incredible man feel like inside her, thrusting, working her hard? God, she wanted to know.

Slowly he slipped his hands under her shirt and lifted it up, his palms skimming her sides. She raised her arms, and he pulled the shirt over her head, tossing it on the floor. His warm hands rested on her arms, and he ran them up and down a few times, as if he were learning her in the same way that she was learning him back on the table. He traced the outline of her bra, around the curve of her breasts.

She'd always had mixed feelings about her chest size. Her body was a comfortable one to live in, fit, strong, and as a physical therapist, she was reminded daily not to take any of these pieces for granted. But she had been an early bloomer, and having large breasts at an younger age had made her self-conscious long after she should have outgrown it. She still had to fight her instinct to cover them. But with Daxon's eyes hot, his mouth parted as he gazed at her breasts, she didn't want to hide. Not when he was looking at her like she was the only thing on earth he wanted right now.

He traced the straps up to her shoulders, then moved down, exploring her nipples through the silky material. Pulses of heat spread through her, and she drew in a quiet gasp. He slipped his hands around her and unhooked her bra, eased the straps over her shoulders and tossed it on top of her shirt. He ran his fingers down her chest, and she covered his hands with hers. There was so much pleasure in this slow exploration. His eyes fluttered closed, and he leaned forward to kiss her neck, holding her breasts in his palms, kneading, learning them. Then, with a soft bite on her neck, he let go and knelt down in front of her.

"I love getting you naked," he said, reaching between his legs to adjust himself. His voice was getting lower, rougher. "I've wanted to do this for so long."

She spent so much time concentrating on other people's bodies and movements that it was strange to have the roles reversed. But definitely not a bad kind of strange.

He urged her to turn around, so she did, but she could still feel his gaze on her, hot and heavy. His hands moved from her hips, lower. He cupped her rear.

"You have one fine behind, Kendall." The rumble of his voice was making her giddy.

She peered over her shoulder, down at him. "You do, too, you know."

He looked up at her and cracked a cocky smile. "I'm glad you noticed."

"At the risk of inflating your ego, I admit that I've peeked at your ass more than once," she said, laughing.

"I've watched yours, too. Many times." Amusement threaded through the desire in his voice.

Would she ever tell him that she had stood at her dresser that very morning, choosing her outfit and, in the end, selected her shortest pair of jersey shorts, the ones that hugged her ass and showed off her legs, just for this meeting? Maybe. He slipped his fingers under the waistband of her shorts and pulled them down, revealing the scrap of her thong and a lot of her ass.

"Fuck," he whispered. "Just touching you like this makes me want to come."

His hands returned to her ass and his teeth grazed one side as he tugged down her panties. He paused, and she waited, not breathing. Then he got to his feet again. He brushed her hair over her shoulder and pressed his body up against hers, and he nibbled the shell of her ear. “On the bed, sweets.”

She climbed up, and he followed her, tugging off his shirt as he settled between her legs. Then he made his way up her body, holding himself over her, his muscles flexing. She pressed her hands against his biceps, feeling the way they moved. When he leaned down to kiss, it was sweet, almost tender. Then he moved to her neck, her chest and, oh, her breasts. His lips closed around one nipple, and he swirled his tongue and dragged his teeth until she squirmed and ground against him. Watching him suck her breast added another erotic layer, and her mouth hung open in anticipation as he moved to the other. New jolts of pleasure shot through her. How close would she get to an orgasm, just like this?

But he moved lower before she found out, his lips on her belly. Her hips. The inside of her legs. She moaned as he came closer, his tongue hungry against her skin. Finally, he pressed his mouth against her clit. The spark was electric, sending shuddering waves of pleasure through her body, bringing her so close to the edge. He was kissing her everywhere, drinking her with endless thirst, his tongue exploring, repeating the strokes she responded to. Learning. When she moaned, he groaned, too, and came in for more.

Oh, *more*. Daxon's mouth was its own category of more. He slipped two fingers inside her and thrust, in and out, driving her mad as he worshipped her with his mouth. It happened so fast. Kendall arched her back and came, crying out, shuddering as Daxon took his last hungry licks of her, drawing out her pleasure.

She sucked in gulps of air as she came back down. The quiet sound of the ocean blew through the windows. Daxon crawled up her body and lay by her side. He propped his head on one hand, his other hand resting on her stomach.

"I've been thinking about doing that for so long," he whispered.

Kendall was trying to get her thoughts together, though her entire body protested. But when his cock pressed against her thigh, her mind skidded back to her earlier question: What would he feel like inside her? She took a couple more breaths and turned to Daxon. "Want to try something else?"

His eyes darkened with desire, but he shook his head. "Some other day, if you want. But I meant what I said earlier. Today is all about your happy ending."

She closed her eyes and let the mix of languid pleasure and the heat from Daxon's body lull her into a rare moment of peace. Was this his plan to get her to come back another time? If so, it was working.

CHAPTER FOUR

"DAXON MILES WISHED for you specifically?" Alana asked with a burst of laughter. "Based on your past experience together? Sounds like fun."

"Not *that* kind of experience." Kendall chuckled. "But definitely fun. And potentially overwhelming, considering his reputation. Plus, he's even hotter in person."

The words slipped out of Kendall's mouth before she could check her tone, almost definitely revealing her current state of client lusting.

"Just about everyone who walks into this place has an ego and a reputation," said Alana. "If they're hot, too, why not?" She waggled her eyebrows, like it was no big deal. Maybe it wasn't.

Alana, one of the Kalani's chefs, had a few years' experience granting the wishes that made this resort so famous. Visitors' wishes weren't sexual per se, but the whole *Fantasy Island* appeal of the resort set the tone for indulgence of all kinds. Kendall looked over at her friend, with her long purple hair and blunt, irreverent style. If anyone could help her navigate hang-up-free casual sex in this place, it was Alana.

Kendall leaned back on her elbows, sinking into the warm sand, and looked out at the ocean, sparkling in the morning sun. Even after six months in Hawaii, she still hadn't gotten used to this warm and welcoming beach, so different from the ice-cold water and whipping winds of Northern California. But it was time she started to get the hang of the laid-back Hawaiian vibe…and maybe Daxon could help with that.

"Can I ask you a personal question?" she asked. "You don't have to answer it."

Alana leaned back on one elbow, facing Kendall, and a smile curved on her lips. "Now I'm intrigued."

"You ever sleep with a guest?"

"Of course. Sheila must have told you there's no policy against client-employee relations here." Then she gave Kendall a conspiratorial wink. "Come on. You can ask me something better than that. Like the best location or more than one at a time."

A splash of a wave washed over Kendall's feet, and she flicked some water onto Alana's bare legs. "I mean someone you're working with."

"Only if I think it's really going to be worth potential complications."

The day before had definitely felt worth it, especially when she was lying on his bed.

"My turn for a question," said Alana, rolling onto

her side. "Did you sleep with Daxon the last time you worked with him?"

"Nope. Not at all," said Kendall quickly.

Not at all? What kind of wacky answer was that?

A tiny hint of a smile tugged at the corners of Alana's mouth. "I'm guessing it wasn't for lack of interest. But if he didn't talk you into bed the last time, I'm trusting you'll be able to hold out for a week. If that's what you want."

"It's too late for holding out," said Kendall, "though I guess it depends on how broadly you define sleeping together."

Alana drew a little heart with cupid's arrow in the wet sand between them. "I hope that definition includes your orgasm."

"Of course it does," she said with a smirk. "Daxon Miles seems to take pride in mastering *all* of his performances."

"So I'm not seeing the problem." Alana added a "D + K" to her sand art project. "The guests at the Kalani are used to being the masters of their own domains, and they come here looking for something they still haven't found. Sometimes it's explicitly what they ask for, and sometimes it's not. As long as it involves two willing partners, there's nothing wrong with that."

"Willing isn't the problem." Kendall dug her toes deeper into the cool, wet sand, waiting for the next wave to wash it away. She had certainly been willing the day before on his bed. It was just so easy to get carried away when he was close, and she didn't know where that would lead.

"We're just talking about sex, right? What happened to the new, adventurous version of you?" asked Alana, gesturing to the long, sandy beach that stretched out on both sides.

"You're not going to talk me out of this, are you?"

Alana shook her head. "I think you should go for it. Besides, you said Daxon Miles is here because of a torn calf. He's a man who thrives on physical thrills, and if he's not performing some crazy stunt, all that energy has to go somewhere..."

Yes, it certainly did. Why not be the one who enjoyed his reputed endurance performances in bed? Now that she'd seen what else his mouth could do, well, Daxon was the perfect—

Alana nudged her. "Hey, lady, stop daydreaming about hot extreme sportsmen. The real thing is approaching."

Kendall snapped out of her thoughts and looked down the beach. And there was Daxon Miles, tanned, shirtless, his abs flexing with each step as he... jogged? With his injured calf? Slowly, she shook her head. What the hell was he thinking?

"I can't believe you requested Kendall Clark," Daxon muttered into the phone as he closed the door to his cabin.

"You're welcome," said Calvin brightly. Cheers

erupted from some sort of sporting event in the background of the call.

"You stalked her and figured out where she was working now?"

"So you didn't have to."

The path from his cabin curved through flowering bushes that wafted their sweet scent. A woman walked by in a bikini, all smiles. The boardwalk crossed a stream and headed into the sand, where the cabins stretched out along the beach…if they could be called cabins. More like small luxury residences. In one direction, the island's highest volcano rose up to a barren, treeless peak, and in the other, the endless blue-green ocean rippled and sparkled in the sunlight. Both tempting, both off-limits for anything remotely interesting. So instead, he was heading to the beach for an easy morning run, the best antidote for the stir-crazy he was already feeling, less than a day after arrival.

"You'll thank me," said Calvin, optimism oozing from his voice. "Just do whatever it takes to be ready for filming in two weeks. The Kalani has every service you could need."

"And which kind of services are you recommending?" This was sounding a lot like *go get laid.*

"The kind that gets you back on the face of Moonlight Buttress for your free solo," he said, his voice turning serious. "I mean it, Daxon. Do whatever it takes. We've built up a lot of hype around this climb, and I don't think I need to tell you that we have a lot riding on it. You are the Pure Adrenaline brand, and people want to see you, shirtless, at the top of your game, in front of the camera. And with the Moonlight Buttress free solo and then the El Capitan free solo, you're giving viewers a peek into the next level of crazy."

"Nice way to put it," Daxon grumbled.

When the Pure Adrenaline YouTube channel began, it had been all about having fun. Daxon had been the young upstart, back when their videos were all about taking each climb or dive or jump to the next level by filming it live. As viewership multiplied and sponsorships exploded, so did the offers for all-expenses-paid trips, endorsement opportunities and other ways to make money. During his mother's hardest years, back before they knew what was wrong, he had been grateful for the money. After years of worrying about her, scrambling to make ends meet, he had taken those opportunities that fell into his lap so he could finally carry the financial burden for her. But none of it would last if the videos didn't keep coming.

Which was why Calvin had come up with a strategy to make Pure Adrenaline into a more permanent business. Instead of putting up videos sporadically, whenever Daxon was ready to film, this new series on his explorations of elite free-climb spots was on a regular streaming schedule to encourage regular viewership. Daxon had already done a set of training videos on smaller routes, and the viewership bump had been impressive. A lot was riding on his ability to deliver a stellar performance on Moonlight Buttress…and then El Capitan. The latter was the ultimate free solo climb, and only one person had ever done it and survived. When Daxon succeeded on live camera, he'd be a legend—a living one. In between the two major climbs, Calvin had worked out a plan for merchandising, guest appearances on television and other publicity boosts. At the other end of all these plans was the hope that he could leverage his Pure Adrenaline image to be less reliant on his next live video. A long-term plan, as Calvin put it. Daxon still wasn't sure about any of it, but he trusted his friend's business instincts. That's what had gotten them this far.

"This is an opportunity to make our business venture last, and it's all resting on your image as a high-risk adventurer. People either want to be you or fuck you," Calvin said with a derisive laugh. "But that attention depends on you in front of the camera. So find a way to redirect that adrenaline impulse for the week."

Earlier that morning, he'd used the tablet Kendall had left for him to scroll through the Kalani's recreational offerings—private dolphin sightings? Just the thought of spending an entire week on enforced relaxation was making him restless. Which was why he was going to focus the entire week on having fun with Kendall. Hopefully naked, at least some of the time. That thought cheered him up a bit.

"Is this the point where you say I need a girlfriend?"

"Nah. I think you're right on that one," said Calvin. "No one looking for a future together wants to watch you dangle from a sheer rock face, over and over again."

Daxon had made this point to Calvin many times, and apparently, it was finally sinking in. Any relationships he had attempted ended not long after the woman understood that extreme adventures were his lifestyle, now and in the future. Plus he couldn't afford to be distracted by someone on the ground. He never said that last part aloud to a woman, but they all seemed to get the message anyway.

"But there are other options for fun of the less serious variety," Calvin continued, chuckling. "Both men and women have come back from this place positively rejuvenated."

"Kendall would probably kick you in the balls if she heard that, even if that's not why you requested her," Daxon grumbled. "Plus, rejuvenated is quite a promise to a guy who's not getting any younger."

He hung up his phone as he wandered along the boardwalk, past more cabins and through a lush tangle of palms and what looked like ferns, until the pathway split. In one direction, arrowed signs pointed him toward Reception, the pool, the spa and various other facilities. In the other direction, a lone sign pointed him toward the beach. He sighed and headed that way.

Daxon glanced at his watch. It was 7:28 a.m., and he was already itching to do something. He had completed a round of pull-ups on the fingerboard he had installed in the bedroom doorway, and he'd do another round when he got back. Then Kendall would show up for his physical therapy session and make everything feel better.

The boardwalk ended, opening up onto the sand. A smattering of palms guided the way to the shore, and everything else in front of him was sand and ocean. No people, no cameras, nothing except him and the elements and his goddamn injured calf.

But it hadn't bothered him at all when he woke up this morning, not sore or stiff, maybe thanks to the massage Kendall had given him yesterday. All attraction aside, she was really good at what she did.

Daxon walked across the soft sand, letting his leg muscles stretch with each stride. The resort was located on a rather remote part of the North Shore, far from other developments, so there was nothing else in sight, just the stretch of beach and greenery that disappeared in the gentle curve of the Hawaiian shoreline. He could probably run for thirty minutes in one direction and thirty minutes back without much strain.

Daxon reached the shore and stopped, facing the ocean, taking the time to stretch on the empty beach. What the hell was everyone else at this place doing? Sleeping? Fucking? Soon this area would be filled with rich, sunburned mainlanders, but for now, at least he was alone.

He used to spend long stretches of time on his own when he first got into adrenaline sports. No one around, just him and the natural world as he climbed a peak or jumped out of a plane and fell toward the ground. And he had liked it that way. Now, for this new venture, everything he did was monitored by a camera crew, with three takes to get better angles and Calvin's direction for maximum viewer appeal.

But right now, it was time to ease some of the tension, both mind and body. Daxon started off at a leisurely pace, nothing like the clip he'd take if he were in top form. If Kendall were here, she'd probably tell him that running was a stupid risk. Maybe it was, but it was also key to keeping him sane in paradise. And she would never know the difference.

The ocean breeze was a warm caress against his skin, a welcome change from the dry heat of southern Utah. He had spent a number of hot days and cold nights in Zion National Park, just hiking around, getting the feel of the place after the summer tourists had scattered. Moonlight Buttress was an old friend, one of his earliest challenges in his home state and off-camera, so he was more than ready for his second free solo of it. Free, with no partner, with no harness. Just the mountain and him. And his camera crew this time, of course.

He had done plenty of practice climbs with ropes, choreographing his route while harnessed in. He wouldn't think twice about this plan if it weren't for the injury. And Moonlight Buttress was calling to him, louder every day. The wide canyons of Zion that stretched out below him, the red rock face rising up on either side, the chalk on his fingers, when the only sounds were the quiet wind and the scrape of rubber soles on the rock.

Pulling the earbuds out of his pocket, he selected one of the focus tracks on his audio app, then slipped his phone into his shorts pocket. Each track was thirty minutes, serving as a perfect timer for his run.

The music began and he was there, at the base, tracing his path up the mountain, seeing it, feeling the rock with his fingertips. The route drew and redrew itself as he moved, one foot at a time, one crevice at a time, one hand at a time as he made his way up. He thought through all possible routes as he ran, focusing on each challenge as it came, problem-solving it in different ways, just to be certain. Daxon saw the mountain, not the sand and the ocean in front of him. The first track ended, and he turned back down the empty beach, back toward the resort, and focused on the last stretch of mountain terrain, factoring in the sun and his thirst and the tingle in his muscles, craving energy.

And then…there she was.

Daxon might have missed Kendall entirely if the audio track hadn't ended. He had seen two figures, but he hadn't really registered them. Now all he could do was stare. His steps slowed as he approached her, and he felt a strange twist in the pit of his stomach.

What the hell was that? It felt almost like…loneliness? Nah. More likely hunger.

But damn, Kendall looked hot. She was lounging on the beach in shorts and a T-shirt, her feet in the water, and another woman was next to her, with purple hair and a string bikini. And they were both looking at him. The other woman's smile sparkled with amusement, but there was no trace of humor on Kendall's face. She sat up, brushing the sand off her hands. Half of his body, the lower half, was thrilled to see her. The upper half had a little more sense than that. He could guess what would come out of her mouth before she even said it.

"What the hell, Daxon?"

That wasn't quite the tone he was hoping for.

"Good morning, Kendall," he tried, flashing her his camera-ready smile. "Lovely to see you, too."

Purple Hair chuckled, but Kendall didn't look pleased.

"I'm supposed to help you, and you're actively countering my efforts." It wasn't a question.

He slowed to a stop in front of her. "That's not what I'm doing. I just needed to get out and go for a run. To clear my head."

Kendall stood up and put her hands on her hips. His gaze traveled down as she moved, to her hips, then farther to her bare, toned legs…but this really wasn't the time to get distracted. He rubbed the back of his neck and looked up again. Her eyebrows were raised, and she was frowning. "You didn't hear when

I told you to take it easy on your calf yesterday? Or you just ignored me?"

That wasn't really a question either, but he ran his hand through his hair and attempted to answer it anyway. "I *was* taking it easy. I could have done this run in half the time."

Kendall rolled her eyes. "Bullshit. You know exactly what I would've said if you had floated the idea of going out on a jog while your calf is recovering. So now you're ignoring my professional opinion after we…"

She let the sentence drift off and looked away as the weight of her accusation sank in. *Shit.* That wasn't a connection he had consciously made, but he could see why it would really sting from her perspective.

He stared down at the sand, trying to think, but his eyes caught something in the sand next to Kendall's friend. A heart and an arrow and… D + K? Daxon covered his mouth to hide his smile. Had they been discussing him? God, he hoped so.

Purple Hair caught where his gaze was and quickly brushed it away, then stood up. "Time for me to stop eavesdropping. I'll catch you later."

"Later, Alana," said Kendall, not looking in her friend's direction. She kept her glare steady on Daxon, and the last of his smile faded. She shook her head. "I'm feeling like an idiot right now."

Daxon grimaced. "Why? I'm the idiot who went running, not you."

“And I’m the physical therapist that got distracted by all this—” She gestured up and down his body.

His shirtless state had been in deference to the climate, but he couldn’t deny he liked hearing that Kendall was enjoying the view…

She shook her head. “Daxon, I don’t think this is going to work.”

Whoa. His thoughts screeched to a halt.

“What’s not going to work?” he asked carefully.

“Me as your physical therapist,” she said. “I can arrange to get you someone else, someone good.”

“No.” His answer came out louder than he meant it to, but the idea that he wouldn’t see Kendall…well, the thought was like a kick in the stomach, and he wasn’t about to sort out why. He took a deep breath and softened his tone. “Please don’t back out. I don’t want anyone else.”

She gave him a sidelong glance. “That’s just because you haven’t gotten your happy ending yet.”

“No. That’s not why.” *Shit, shit, shit.* This run was shaping up to be the worst idea he had had in a long time. He tried to stanch the feeling of panic that was rising up in him. He couldn’t let her leave. “If you want the after-hours part of this to stop, that’s your call. But please don’t quit. I’ll do exactly what you say. I promise.”

They were standing close together, and Daxon had no idea who had stepped forward or when it had happened. All he knew was that Kendall looked upset. He was dying to close that last distance, to comfort her in ways he had no business doing right now. Her hair was back in a ponytail again, and her cheeks were flushed. In her eyes, behind everything else, he could see the stubborn wall of determination. If he promised to do exactly what she said, she'd hold him to his promise, no exceptions. And she seemed to be considering it. She raised her eyebrows skeptically. "Exactly as I say?"

He nodded.

"Like—" her expression brightened "—if I said dive in the ocean right now with your clothes on, you'd do it?" She gestured out into the turquoise water.

He blinked at her. "These running shoes are specially made for me, and they're the only pair I brought."

She gave him a look of impatience. "That wasn't a serious req—"

"Never mind. Hold my phone."

"What?"

He unzipped his pocket, picked up her hand, and placed his phone in it, along with his earbuds. His fingers brushed the soft skin of her palm, reminding him just how much he wanted to touch her. Definitely time to cool off in the ocean.

So he turned and walked straight in, special shoes and all.

CHAPTER FIVE

KENDALL WAS NOT going to stare at this perfect specimen of a man, mostly naked, entering the water. She was not going to gape as the muscles of his shoulders flexed and moved with each step. Nope, she wasn't.

Okay, maybe for just a moment. Purely from a kinesiology perspective, of course.

A few drops of sweat ran down his tanned back, following the intricate ridges of his muscles. His torso was long and lean, and his dark hair curled a little around his neck. She had shamelessly lusted after him while watching his videos, but that body in real life? Holy hell. He waded in until the water was up to his waist, then lifted his arms over his head and dived. He stayed under for a while, his underwater image moving with each stroke he took, those overpriced orange shoes glowing in the blue-green sea.

Finally, Daxon emerged again. He turned, shaking out his hair, and smiled at her. It was a beautiful smile, a smile that held pure joy, the same smile millions of viewers had seen when he was in the middle of doing something he loved. But right now, that smile was aimed directly at Kendall. Her insides fluttered dangerously.

"I'll do exactly what you say, Kendall," he called, swimming back toward her.

He stood up, emerging like some sort of sea god, and walked through the shallow water, back to shore. His body glistened in the morning sun. He stopped in front of her, closer now. His hair dripped on her shirt and then on her nose. He wiped it away with the pad of his thumb.

"Please don't quit," he whispered softly. "We'll do this exactly the way you want. You decide. Just tell me you'll stay."

Kendall was dying to reach out and touch him, to trace the paths of water running down his chest. Maybe even lick them. But before she got carried away—again—the work relationship part of this had to be cleared up.

"If you go back with your calf in worse shape than when you started, what kind of a physical therapist does that make me?" she asked.

He looked down at her, and all traces of playfulness were gone. "I see your point."

"This isn't worth my professional reputation, Dax."

He leaned down, and his lips brushed against her ear, but he didn't touch her. More ocean water dripped from his hair, onto her cheek, and ran down her neck. "I'll behave," he whispered. "And I'll make it worth it. I promise."

Kendall closed her eyes and let herself take in everything at that moment. The shush of waves breaking on the shore, the warm, salty wind, the cool sand under her feet, the sun heating her back, and Daxon, his wet body so close, short-circuiting most of her rational thoughts. The truth was she didn't want to walk away, but she would if she needed to. Even if it would be harder to walk away the longer she spent with him, she knew in her heart she'd do it.

So she leveled a steady gaze at him. "Okay, Dax. We'll give this a try. But the moment you break that promise, I'm out. Both as a PT and anything after-hours."

He nodded, and his intense green eyes were serious, drawing her in. It was just the two of them on a gorgeous morning, standing on the edge of the ocean, all alone. For a moment, she wasn't with Daxon Miles, Pure Adrenaline YouTube phenomenon. They were two people on a precipice. Something was unfolding, something strong and complicated and so, so tempting.

Then he straightened up and gave her another nod. He took his phone out of her hand and looked at the screen.

"It's a little past eight thirty now," he said. "I've got thirty minutes before you show up at my door for PT, so I'm going to hop in the shower and get changed in plenty of time. Just to make sure there's no more towel-dropping."

* * *

Waves of warmth radiated through Daxon's muscles. Kendall's hands on his leg were heaven. This was the ultimate distraction, and he struggled not to groan. If he did, she might mistake it for sexual, and he was trying his hardest not to take things in that direction, despite the fact that the sexiest woman in the world had her hands all over him. And, fuck, it was exactly what he needed.

Lying here in this luxury cabin, with Kendall's hands on his skin, was also easing that knot in his stomach, the one that had formed on the beach. It had stayed with him as he'd waited for her to show up for his morning appointment, wondering if she'd have second thoughts about coming back. But she was here, and her fingers were working their magic.

Daxon gritted his teeth to stop whatever sound was about to come out of his mouth, and Kendall pulled back, softening her touch.

"Too intense?" she asked.

He shook his head. "Not at all. Just sparing you the wild animal noises that are probably going to come out. It feels so goddamn good."

She started moving her fingers again, kneading into his muscles. "I thought you had a physical therapist back in Utah."

"I did," he said. "Not as good as you."

Kendall laughed. "I'm going to assume that comment is about my PT services."

"Trust me, it is," he said with a sigh.

She began the stretching exercises, flexing his foot, changing positions. She had been right about the run, of course; his calf was a little tighter. But what else was he supposed to do with the restlessness that came back when he tried to relax? Without an outlet for all this energy, it was like he was eighteen again, sleeping in the back of his truck, always on the move, always looking for the next rush. But he had to figure out something else, because the idea of her quitting sure as hell hadn't sat well. Daxon frowned.

He really had to leave this place in top shape. Over the last weeks, as the Moonlight Buttress climb grew closer and he hadn't bounced back from his torn calf, more tension had been building. Every free solo was a high-consequence pursuit, and over half of the very best climbers had faced that consequence. Just about every season, an elite climber fell to their death. Sometimes two. That was the reality of the sport, a factor he accepted in exchange for the freedom that came from climbing impossible mountains. But he wouldn't attempt the climb if he wasn't confident he'd live through it.

Still…

Doing Moonlight Buttress again would be full-on intense. Amazing. But the next climb was El Capitan in Yosemite, a mountain face that was much taller, made of unforgiving granite, and it featured a couple spots that were near impossible. Meeting the El Cap challenge would be an accomplishment of a lifetime, a personal achievement that would last beyond the popularity of a YouTube channel. And if Calvin was right, the payoff would be long-term for Pure Adrenaline, too. It would be a huge financial jump, the kind of money that sponsorships and merchandising and everything else Calvin had planned would bring, the kind that would support his mother when her body no longer cooperated. It would make up for all those years he wasn't there for her.

Kendall flexed his foot, gently stretching his calf. Man, that felt good. Then, before he could ask himself why, an image of Kendall watching from the base of Moonlight Buttress as he climbed flashed through his mind. He already knew what Kendall thought about Pure Adrenaline, and as a PT, that probably came with the territory to some degree. But the idea of her watching from the base was both thrilling and disconcerting...which was exactly why relationships didn't work—not just for the woman but also for him. Because a relationship would mean he'd have to consider how she felt about the climb, too.

Why was he even thinking about that?

Probably because that scene on the beach with Kendall had driven home just how much he was looking forward to seeing her. And when she made the point about her professional reputation, he'd felt like a real asshole. He hadn't even considered what it would say about her as a PT if he hurt himself further. Daxon cringed.

"Tell me about your Moonlight Buttress plans,"

said Kendall. "Free solo, so you're going up without equipment."

"Just me and the mountain. I've done it once before."

"Were you climbing when you tore your calf?"

"Yeah. The move I tried was risky, but it was better than falling." Daxon thought he caught a hint of a frown. He didn't take the possibility of death lightly, if that's what she was thinking.

"What happens if you get into trouble this time?" She started to work her hands up his leg now, and he was trying like hell to keep his mind on the conversation.

"It's up to me to practice every single move enough to make sure there's no trouble."

He had given this answer countless times to the media, but unlike the others, Kendall didn't look suitably impressed. In fact, she was definitely frowning now. She was quiet for a while, lifting his leg, stretching it, searching for points of tension. Finally, she lowered his leg back onto the table and then turned to him. Her hand was still resting on his thigh, though she didn't seem to notice it. Daxon certainly did.

"Why?"

He raised his eyebrows. "Why practice?"

"I mean why are you doing this at all?" Her brow was furrowed, as if she already knew the answer and didn't like it. "I get the adrenaline rush thing. When I was younger, I used to stand at the top of the ten-meter platform at the Stanford pool and look down, thinking, *there's nothing like this in the world.* But climbing a cliff face without a rope isn't just that."

Daxon raised his eyebrows. "I thought diving had the highest death rates of any sport."

"I didn't actually jump."

He smiled a little. "That's the difference. I'd jump any day."

He propped himself up on his elbow and looked into her eyes. The outer rims were dark, and there were streaks of yellow that grew brighter toward the center. Beautiful and unlike any eyes he had seen before. "You don't think I know what I'm doing?"

She blinked, staring down at him, the lines still creasing her forehead. Then she opened her mouth, like she was about to speak, but she closed it. Finally, she started to laugh. "We're not going to get anywhere in this discussion, are we?"

"If you're going to try to talk me out of the climbs, then probably not," he said, smiling. "The filming is already scheduled. But I'm happy to discuss whatever else is on your mind."

"What do your girlfriends say about Pure Adrenaline?"

He shook his head. "This lifestyle doesn't leave a lot of room for girlfriends. You can probably imagine why."

Her hand was still on his thigh, and his dick didn't seem to care that it was unintentional.

He cleared his throat. "If you're finished, you

should probably stop touching me so I can keep my promise not to come on to you."

Kendall's brow wrinkled in confusion for a moment, and then she pulled her hand away.

"Sorry," she muttered, a flush creeping up her neck.

Daxon sat up and waved off her apology. "Let's sit out on the lanai and go through what I should or shouldn't be doing here this week."

One of the many appeals of the Kalani was that he never had to leave the cabin if he didn't want to. He and Kendall could spend a meal in the privacy of his own lanai, without any interference from the rest of the world. Off duty.

"I'll order us some lunch, too," he added. "I looked at my schedule, and we have a few hours to kill until you're showing me around the Kalani. We can take a dip in this pool I have all to myself."

He gestured out the door to the private rectangular pool. Her eyes widened a little, bright and glittering, but she shook her head. "I can't. I have an appointment with another client. In fact, he is scheduled..." She glanced down at her watch. "In thirty minutes."

Daxon didn't move, but a grumble somehow still escaped. Another client? *He*—as in, a male client? Holy fuck, he really was a self-centered prick, because this whole time, in his mind, Daxon had assumed that her week was all about him. But of course it wasn't. Other clients could book regular times for her services. Including other *male* clients.

"Something wrong?" Kendall was eyeing him, her expression somewhere between skeptical and amused. Daxon massaged some of the tightness out of his jaw.

"It's nothing," he said roughly, though he knew he sounded petulant and sulky.

But she seemed to know the reason behind the change in the course of this conversation without him saying it. "Did you think being your PT meant my week was dedicated to you and only you?" She had the nerve to smile. "Sorry, Dax. I do have some regular clients I had scheduled before I got this assignment."

Regular clients? Every single week? This really wasn't what he wanted to think about right now. He just grunted in response, trying to cut off the discussion before he said something stupid.

She crossed her arms, and the skeptical look on her face suggested he hadn't quite convinced her yet.

"Fine," he said. "It's not my favorite thought that you would be touching some other guy today. But I know that's stupid and childish and maybe even probably crossing the line. But there it is."

Kendall tilted her head, like she was thinking about what he said…and all of the things he didn't say but that might have slipped through in that confession. *Well, fuck it all.* He had said it, and she could do with it what she wanted.

But she smiled. It was a beautiful smile, so full of laughter and warmth. "Do you have a crush on me?"

Did he? Daxon sighed. This wasn't just about sex so… "Maybe." The corners of his mouth tugged up. "Yes."

"Just checking."

A crush. His smile grew. The great thing about a crush was that it was fleeting. Which meant it would fizzle by the time he left the Kalani.

"So help me out here." He waggled his eyebrows. "Spend more off-hours time with me, tomorrow if you can't today. I promise I'll make it worth your while."

Kendall hesitated. "Um, I'll think about it."

"You'll think about it?" Christ, this woman was killing him.

"I'm your PT, not your babysitter," she said.

"Don't worry. I'm not into the babysitter thing," he said with a straight face. "But I could get into naughty schoolgirl."

Kendall buried her face in her hands, her shoulders shaking with laughter. "Didn't you promise me you weren't going to flirt with me on the clock?"

Oh, right. "Shit. Sorry. Let's get back to the real issue," he said. "Are you going to let me take you on an outing tomorrow? Or the next day?"

"Maybe," she said, her sexy mouth curving up again. He was getting closer.

"You're free to stop by this evening, off duty, and let me know your decision."

"Thanks," she said. "Generous offer."

He had toyed with her, and now she was enjoying toying with him. Time to take it a step further.

"Just think what I'll do to entertain myself while you're off with another man."

Kendall snorted. "The internet is full of wonders, isn't it?"

Daxon let his gaze wander down her body. "I have many ideas," he said softly.

Her cheeks flushed, and pleasure danced on her face. "As long as it doesn't involve any strain on your calf I'm all for it."

"I hope you don't regret saying that later," he said with a lusty laugh. "I've got a dirty mind and too much time on my hands."

"Now I'm curious."

"That's definitely off-duty material," he said, smirking. "Looks like you'll have to come back."

She laughed and then turned for the door. "Bye, Dax. See you later."

And she walked right out without telling him when off-the-clock *later* would be.

CHAPTER SIX

THE LATE-AFTERNOON sun glittered on everything, reflecting off the blue-green water and the white sand beach. It was a beautiful day, the kind Kendall had imagined when she left everything behind in Northern California. The warmth surrounding her as she walked barefoot through the shallow waves, on her afternoon walk with Alana.

"So he asked you on a mystery date." Alana lifted her sunglasses and gave Kendall a look, the kind that said *right on*. "Not really following why you'd say no to this."

"It's not a date. And it's complicated," said Kendall, shading her eyes from the sun. "Though I'm not on the clock, which was my first concern. I'm not *that* kind of professional."

Alana grinned. "But the paid escort game sounds rather fun."

Kendall gave her friend a little shove, and Alana kicked a splash of water her way in return. She opened her mouth to respond when her phone buzzed in her pocket. She pulled it out and looked at the screen. *Home.* Her heart jumped, and an ominous shiver ran through her. Her mother was calling in the middle of the day. Something must be wrong. Kendall frowned and blew out her breath. *Chill out.* Not every unexpected call had to be a tragedy. She'd thought moving across the ocean would make her less jumpy about her father's health, but apparently that part of her psyche was immune to the mellow Hawaiian vibe.

"Sorry. I have to take this," she said to Alana.

Alana waved her off as Kendall waded deeper into the water and accepted the call.

"Mom? Is everything okay?"

"Everything's fine, honey." The lightness in her mother's voice sent a rush of relief through her. After years of anxiety that wore on her family, fire season after fire season, Kendall had learned to read her mother's voice well. "Am I catching you at a bad time?"

"No. This is fine." She tried to shake the last of her worry.

"I thought quitting the traveling PT job and moving to Hawaii was supposed to be relaxing."

"I'm relaxed…most of the time." Or as relaxed as she'd probably ever be. Her father was sure she'd outgrow her goal of becoming a physical therapist after the fear of his career-ending injury had faded, but her mother understood all too well that the mark that night had made was permanent. Who wouldn't err on the cautious side after almost losing her father? Okay, maybe Kendall had leaned just a little too far in that direction, but now she was spreading her wings…safely. "It's just that you usually call in the morning, and I wondered if…" Her voice trailed off. "Never mind."

"You wondered if something had happened to your father?" Her mother's voice was more serious. "He's fine. No emergency."

Kendall hung her head. "Sorry," she mumbled. She let out another breath, then injected a little more cheer into her voice. "How are you?"

"We both took the day off, so your dad's out surfing, and I'm about to sit down on the deck with a book."

"Sounds great," said Kendall, keeping her tone light, but the unease came back. Why did her parents take the day off? Her mother had to be calling for some reason.

"You're still worried, aren't you?" said her mother gently. "Honestly, nothing's wrong. We just got back from your dad's appointment, and I promised I'd call right after."

Her father had begun to feel the long-term effects of smoke inhalation—yet another occupational hazard.

"How's his breathing?"

"No worse than it was on his last visit."

The words settled in, relief spreading through her muscles. Thank God. She didn't spend all her days worrying about her father's health, but these unexpected calls still triggered the same feelings they did when she was a kid, when she and her mother would jump every time the phone rang during fire season. It was the kind of thing she thought would dull after a while, but it didn't. Even years after her father retired from hotshot duty.

"That's great news," she said. "Can I call you tonight, talk to both of you?"

"Of course." Her mother sighed. "You don't have to worry so much about us."

"Old habits die hard, Mom. You know that."

Her mother laughed. "I guess I do. Love you."

"Love you, too."

Kendall shoved her phone back into her pocket and wandered back over to Alana, who was currently inspecting a shell on the beach. Her friend looked up at her.

"Isn't it the parents that are supposed to worry about their kids? How did you get it backward?"

"I've been practicing since I was a kid." Kendall's smile faded. "I don't know how my mom survived all those years of forest fire seasons. She said it's harder to be a hotshot's wife than it is to be a hotshot."

"Your dad must have been worth it."

"She'd say so, but there were some hellish times, too." When the tree limb that crushed his arm fell, her father had been knocked unconscious. For one terrible day, they hadn't known if he would ever wake up. That day had almost broken her mother, and it was the last thing Kendall wanted to think about right now.

"Don't most relationships have a few hellish times?" Alana gave her a pointed look.

"Maybe, but marrying a hotshot set her up for more than her share."

But Alana waved off her comment. "Makes the fun times all the better. You don't want to miss a single one of those."

Kendall chuckled. "You're bringing this back to Daxon, aren't you? You think I should get naked with him."

"I certainly do. As soon as possible."

Daxon clung to the hangboard, mounted on the wall of the lanai, holding up the weight of his body with only his first three fingers. The timer beeped, so he shook out his hand, then started another set of pull-ups. Ten…then twenty. This was his last interval. Thirty-five, thirty-six, thirty-seven…just a few more.

Forty-two, forty-three, forty-four… His hands were aching, and each pull-up was slower, but he couldn't stop now. If he was going to make it up Moonlight Buttress, his shoulders, his arms, his hands, his fingers—everything needed to be in top shape. It was his fifth set of pull-ups today, and he was almost done. Three more. Two. One. He let go and his arms fell to his side as his feet found the ground. Daxon leaned back against the wall and wiped the sweat from his forehead. The warm breeze blew off the ocean as he flexed his hands, in and out, stretching out the soreness.

Done. Now it was time for his reward. The lanai formed a U shape, and inside the U, his private swimming pool was glassy-smooth and ocean blue. It wasn't made for laps, just big enough and the right temperature for a quick dip, which would be followed by the oldest relaxation technique known to man.

Daxon set his phone on the side of the pool, stripped and dived in. He stayed under for a few strokes, the rush of the water cooling him off. He emerged for a breath and swam over to the side, where there was a ledge so he could sit chest-deep in the water. The sun shone down on him, reflecting everywhere. Beautiful, but it would be so much better if Kendall were here.

He imagined her swimming up to him. She'd sit next to him on the ledge, work her hands up his leg, much like she did in PT, with that crease between her eyebrows when she was concentrating. But instead of stopping mid-thigh, she'd keep moving higher. Then, just before her hands reached his cock, she'd look at him, her lips parted with just a hint of a smile.

"You want the deluxe treatment today?" she'd ask with a little laugh.

"Hell, yes," he'd say.

And now he was hard. He'd need to climb out of the pool…soon. He wrapped his hand around his cock and squeezed.

Kendall's words from the bedroom came back.

Your turn now. Her voice had been husky with pleasure, pleasure he had given her. Daxon gritted his teeth and moved his hand up and down. Next she'd run her hand up his cock, exploring his length before she reached for the strings of her bikini. Then, slowly, she'd—

His phone dinged, jolting him out of his fantasies. He glanced at his phone, lying on the pool deck. Another ding. Who the hell was calling him? Kendall had his number, and that call would be worth answering. Daxon reached for his phone.

The Kalani concierge.

Daxon sighed and answered it.

"Mr. Miles, I hope I'm not catching you at a bad time," said the woman. "You told me to call when I had an update about your requests."

"Perfect timing," he deadpanned.

"Great. Just wanted to let you know that I located the exact convertible model you requested in red. Would you like me to have it delivered to the Kalani tomorrow morning?"

Kendall hadn't given him an answer about the outing. Should he plan it anyway? Better than the opposite—she agreed to go and he wasn't ready.

"Yes, please reserve the car for a few days," said Daxon. "And I'll send you the other items I'd like to have picked up."

"Very good, sir."

Daxon hung up and set down his phone. His dick had mellowed out a bit, and a little more of his reason flooded in. As far as distractions went, Kendall was a very effective one. Daxon frowned. He sounded like an asshole when he called her a distraction, even in his own head. She was funny and sexy, and being with her was so much more than just passing the time.

There was this niggling thought in the back of his mind that it might not be very easy to just shut off these days with Kendall when he left the island. But he had to, and he would. Climbing demanded every ounce of his concentration, which meant shutting everything else—and everyone else—off. He had never had a problem blocking out everything once he got on the mountain. Whatever happened this week wouldn't change that.

"You're not getting dressed for this?" Kendall's gaze raked down Daxon's bare torso, then snapped back up to his face.

Daxon bit back a grin and flashed an innocent smile. "What? This?" He gestured to his chest and his abs.

Kendall rolled her eyes. "Put a shirt on, Dax."

"Whatever you want, sweets."

He hadn't really planned to take his private Kalani tour shirtless, but he was loving this habit of answering the door in various stages of undress. Did it count as a come-on? Naaah.

Daxon grabbed the shirt he'd left on the table by the door and pulled it over his head. Then he tugged on a baseball cap and picked up his sunglasses. "Better?"

"Come on, champ. Let's do the tour."

The path to Daxon's cabin opened onto a private road, lined with tall palm trees and flowering bushes. From his glance at the map of the resort when he first arrived, he knew the resort spread out for miles along the northeast shore of the island. Much of the property was untouched coast. The buildings were clustered on a narrow peninsula, lined with white sand beaches, and the guest cabins of various sizes were tucked away just inside the trees, dotting both shores. On the stretch of land between these strings of cabins were the bar, the tennis courts and other resort offerings for guests who were feeling social. The head of the peninsula was mostly undeveloped, with a few trails, an ocean-side restaurant and an unmarked building that looked like a private residence.

"I assume you got a glimpse of some of the facilities when you came in," said Kendall as they walked past the trail to the large pool. "As you've seen, guest cabins have pools that overlook the ocean, and the main pool is for guests looking for something larger."

The stone-lined path led to an area built up an incline, with different levels of pools, connected by waterfalls, one leading to the next. At the base was the largest. One side was rectangular and well-suited for lap swimming, while the other seemed to be shallower, curved with seating along the edges. More splashes of waterfalls fell along the rocky incline, and the pool was surrounded by leafy plants and palms. Nicely done for people who liked to sit around. Daxon didn't.

They wandered on, past the tennis courts and the spa, as Kendall continued to list the luxury services the Kalani offered and how to access them. Daxon wasn't paying close attention to what she said. In fact, he was almost sure he wasn't going to use any of this during his stay. He was more at home out in the wilderness, and what the resort had to offer him—discretion while his calf healed—had nothing to do with the facilities. He supposed it would've been the nicest thing to decline Kendall's tour, but the truth was that he wanted to spend a little more time with her. Climbing was a social activity, despite the list of very individual skills it required, and he was used to being around other people, doing what he loved. Now he was alone and practically on house arrest, granted it was pretty much the best location for it. But he wanted to talk to someone. No, not just *someone*. He wanted to talk to Kendall.

"Inside that building is the gym, in case you want to do...whatever it is you do that doesn't involve your calf."

He cracked a little smile. "Is that a hint that I should work out a little more?"

Kendall smirked. "Are you fishing for a compliment?"

"From you? Always."

"You look just fine the way you are," she said

evenly. The word *fine* came out the same way it had when she had called his performance *fine* in his cabin yesterday. But this time she said it with a little grin.

He laughed. "Thanks for that lukewarm praise. But I won't be using the gym this week. I brought everything I need to keep up my strength."

The truth was that he didn't need much in the way of equipment. Climbing favored lean muscle strength, not bulk, which made pull-ups on his fingerboard his top activity, not lifting weights.

They passed the last of the cabins, but the road continued a ways, up a slope and into a lush tangle of green, and then forked. Kendall chose the road to the left.

"What's up that way?" he asked, nodding to the right.

"There's a waterfront restaurant up there, the fine dining option, if you're interested in that."

Daxon shook his head. Growing up without money, he and his mother never once ate anything fancier than In-N-Out Burger. Though he had more than enough money now, he still avoided any place that might require a button-down shirt. Did he even own a tie? Not likely. If he did, it was long forgotten at the back of his closet at home.

"The rest is hiking trails and lookouts except for that area." Kendall pointed up to the hillside, where a gate peeked out over the foliage. Probably leading to the unmarked building from the map. "That's where Byron Keahi lives."

"The owner?" Daxon knew just the basics about him: ultra-successful businessman with Hawaiian roots. "I read the *New York Chronicle* article about him. Interesting guy."

"Probably." She shrugged. "I almost never see him around the resort, though he surfs early every morning when he's here. Actually, I think he bought this land because of its waves."

"He doesn't hang around the bar?" He'd read that Keahi was known for enjoying all of life's pleasures. Often.

"He meets with a few guests and works the jobs around here every now and then, but he definitely keeps a low profile."

Good. Because the idea of Byron Keahi flirting with Kendall wasn't sitting well with him.

"So no staff Christmas dinners at the boss's house?"

Kendall shook her head. "Nope. But a good Christmas bonus more than makes up for it."

The road took them to the shore and turned, heading along the stretch between the beach and the forest, toward the tip of the peninsula. They were high above the ocean and still climbing, high enough to see the curl of each wave, rolling around the point and breaking in long-running tubes toward shore.

Kendall stopped at the turnoff to a trail that zigzagged down to the beach, weaving through the rocky hillside. He stopped next to her, close enough to settle his hand on her waist or against the small of her back. He was dying to touch her.

But he couldn't, so he just leaned closer. "If we continued heading uphill, where would the path take us?"

"If you keep left on the trail, you get to one of my favorite places. Maybe I'll show it to you one day."

"As my reward for behaving?"

She gave a little snort. "Your life is already full of rewards, Dax."

It was true, so why did he still have this hole inside him, this need he couldn't seem to fill in any lasting way? There were moments of real satisfaction, like right now, standing here with Kendall. But mostly they came when he was doing something physical, something that took every bit of his concentration, every ounce of his focus. The satisfaction used to last longer, but lately it faded too quickly. And it was a selfish kind of satisfaction, which Kendall had gently pointed out to him six months ago.

"Remember that conversation we had back in Costa Rica?" he asked.

"The one about high risk versus high consequence?"

He nodded. It began at the end of a PT session and continued so naturally and easily into dinner, unfolding as the evening darkened in that beachside restaurant. Hell, he'd wanted her badly that night. He had replayed that conversation in so many different ways, but right now, he was thinking about the part where she had pointed out some gaping holes in his ideas.

"You know, that conversation was one of the reasons I took the job at the Kalani," she said softly.

His eyebrows shot up. There had been an intensity between them that night, and he was pretty sure she wouldn't have forgotten it. But he hadn't been sure if the night had stuck with her in the same way it had with him. Maybe it had.

"I loved visiting new places as a traveling PT, but I didn't love the impermanence of it. There was always this idea in the back of my mind that someday I'd move somewhere new, stay there." She looked out at the ocean, like she was debating how much to say. Then she turned to him again. "At dinner that night, you told me that I was mixing up risk and consequence, and you were right. I had never differentiated the two. I used high risk as a reason for not trying things, things that I wanted, when I really should have been looking at consequence. The risk of moving, that my life would change drastically, that I would be far away from my parents if anything happened—those risks could be high. But the consequence was low. I could get on a flight and go see them at any point. And I could probably even get my old job back."

"And the move turned out fine?"

"Better than fine." She smiled. "What made you think of that night?"

There was the fact that he wanted to kiss her just

as badly then as he did right now, but that probably wasn't the connection she was looking for at the moment.

Daxon ran a hand through his hair. "I just wanted to say that you were right that day, too. That my assessment of risk and consequence was based on how things affected me. But the decisions *don't* just affect me."

Kendall laughed. "Sounds a little harsh now, out of context."

He shook his head. "Just honest. And understandable, considering what you and your mom went through when your dad was in the middle of fire season, choosing to go back, again and again."

She smiled a little. "I wasn't sure how closely you were listening that evening. Especially when I caught you looking down the front of my dress."

He chuckled. "I was multitasking."

Then his smile faded. He wanted her to know that he hadn't forgotten a word she'd said that day about what it was like to watch someone she loved choose a high-consequence profession. Nor had he forgotten the reservations she voiced that came from having clients who were injured in high-consequence situations. But in the end, her drive to help these people was stronger than her personal opinion. No, he had not forgotten any of that.

"I talked with my mother after that conversation," he said quietly. "I wanted to hear what she thought about what you said."

Kendall nodded, but she said nothing.

"She said it was hard sometimes, watching me do the things I did. But she trusted me to make the right decisions." He rubbed the back of his neck. "I was hoping she'd give me a definite answer, but she pushed it back on me. I hope I'm making the right choices for her."

"Everyone hopes that, right?"

Kendall was looking up at him, her big brown eyes pulling him in. He felt the shift between them, the tension, the awareness. Her long dark lashes fluttered, like they had just before she kissed him.

"Are we on the clock right now?" he whispered.

Her eyes sparkled with humor. "I'm afraid so."

"Just checking."

Damn, she was tempting. And she looked like she might give in. But he had promised not to make the first move, so he held back.

"It's a beautiful view from here," he said softly, keeping his gaze focused on her deep brown eyes. He smoothed her hair off her face. "Come visit me tonight. Please."

Slowly, her mouth curved up into a smile. "I'll think about it."

CHAPTER SEVEN

KENDALL HAD TAKEN the safe route for as long as she could remember. She had chosen San Francisco State University, closest to home, instead of the school with the best kinesiology program. She had taken the summer internship at San Francisco General instead of the internship with the WNBA. Even the traveling physical therapy job had been a compromise. She had chosen it instead of a position on the location of a movie set because of the lack of job security. At the time, Kendall had thought of each one of these decisions as logical, as strategic, as better financially, especially considering her dad's health limited his work possibilities these days. But deep down, she knew why she made all of these decisions: fear.

The evening breeze was warm as she walked down the path through the trees toward Daxon's cabin. Every decision she made was run through some sort of internal risk-assessment monitor that played in the background of her mind. Boyfriends, travel plans, airplane rides and of course, her move to Hawaii, which she had come so close to backing out of.

That evening, as she stared in the mirror, tracing her mouth with lip gloss, she had tried to calculate the risks and consequences of this evening visit. The risk of liking Daxon a little too much, the consequence. What exactly were the hidden risks of a really hot man who was amazing at…well, just about everything? It was impossible to weigh them when her mind kept wandering back to the kiss in his hallway the day before. Pulling back from the kiss, his thumbs brushing against her skin, rough, calloused, she had looked up into his eyes, and she had seen something she wanted.

So here she was, on this beautiful Hawaiian night, heading to Daxon's cabin to proposition him. The ticking clock of his stay was why she'd finally decided to come. She knew that no matter what it felt like between them, he was leaving to climb a mountain without ropes, and he had decided that this was worth the consequence of death. Every free solo climb could end his life, and she would never, for one minute, forget that. That was enough to keep this casual. At least that was her thinking as she headed out of her little rental cabin, down the hill and over to the guest lodgings.

The walkway turned off to Daxon's place, and Kendall approached the front patio, slowing with every step. The Kalani was a truly beautiful resort, every building exuding the kind of exclusive luxury it was known for. Modern, simple, sustainably built with reclaimed mango wood beams.

Kendall stopped in front of Daxon's door and smoothed the wrinkles of her spaghetti-strap hibiscus-print dress. She had paired it with her cowboy boots in a sort of mainland-meets-Hawaii effort, but now she was having second thoughts. Too cute? Too revealing? Her breasts weren't really made for a strapless bra, but if things went the way she hoped they would, the bra wouldn't stay on for long. Her heart was jumping in her throat, fluttering, her breath coming quicker.

She swallowed and tapped on his door. Nothing. She tried again, louder. Still nothing. *Damn.* She had spent her afternoon debating whether or not she should come, and he wasn't home? She wasn't giving up this easily. Maybe she could break in and wait for him. Naked on his bed? No, too cliché. She could do better than that. She turned, leaning against the door, and blew out a breath.

But just as her back touched the wood, the door opened from behind her, hitting the heels of one cowboy boot and pushing her forward. She stumbled across the porch, grabbing the support beam in front of her, clutching it.

"Fuck." Daxon's low mutter came from behind her, followed by a rush of footsteps. Then his hands were on her waist—large, warm hands. Slowly, Kendall let go of the beam and turned around. In front of her was a stunned Daxon Miles dressed in a pair of board shorts and nothing else. His washboard abs and his broad, muscular shoulders were on full display, but this time, she was sure he wasn't just showing off. He blinked, as if she were the last person he ever expected to see at his doorstep.

"Kendall?" he whispered as he searched her face, his forehead lined with concern. "Are you hurt?"

She shook her head, but he didn't look convinced. He lifted his hands to her forehead, which was probably bright red at this point, then touched her cheeks. His fingers tested her bare shoulders, then worked their way down her arms, gently probing.

"Where did I hit you?"

"Just my boot," she said, the corners of her mouth tugging up. "Good thing I came prepared. Most people around here wear sandals."

He was so close, his body warm, his muscles flexing as he touched her, lines of worry across his forehead. Each brush of his fingers sent a delicious shiver through her. His hair was wet, she noticed for the first time, the water dripping onto his shoulders and sliding down his bronzed skin in trails. It looked like he had come straight from the shower to the door, without bothering to towel off.

He touched one of her palms, then the other, and she flinched. Daxon frowned and lifted her hand, inspecting it. He found a little splinter—she hadn't noticed it in the rush of his nearness—and pulled it out.

Kendall sighed. "The perils of reclaimed wood. Thanks."

He smiled a little but continued his inspection. His hands skimmed her body and wrapped around her back, testing, until finally he seemed satisfied.

"I'm sorry." He stroked her cheek.

"I'm fine, really. You just surprised me, that's all."

Slowly he nodded, and then he broke out into a grin. "You're here."

His smile was infectious, and the corners of her mouth turned up. "I'm definitely here."

One arm was still around her, his thumb gently stroking her back, and he was looking at her like he was about to kiss her. Like he was dying to but holding himself back.

"You want to come in?"

"I walked all the way over here in my dress, after hours," she said with a little smile. "I suppose I'll come in."

Daxon started to laugh, a low rumble that shook his shoulders and crinkled at the corners of his eyes. But he didn't move. He looked at her, his eyes searching. His hand moved to her waist, sliding up and down her sides. Finally his mouth turned up into his signature grin, tinged with teasing and humor and desire. "Well, by all means, let's go inside."

The sunset colored the white walls shades of pinks and oranges and purples, and the evening breeze blew through the open room, warm, bringing the scents and the sounds of the ocean closer. Kendall had never been inside one of the guest cabins in the evening. The pool on the lanai sparkled in the evening light.

It was as if they had been transported, not here at the Kalani but somewhere else, just the two of them.

"It's lovely here tonight," she said, walking into the large room.

"Lovelier now that you're here." He rested his hand on her hip. "I can say that now that we're after hours, right?"

Kendall chuckled. "You can get a lot dirtier than that."

His hand traveled lower, down around her ass, his thumb still stroking, reminding her of how close he was. It was almost as if he didn't want to stop touching her, as if waiting the whole day had made him just as hungry as it had made her. And there was satisfaction in that idea, that this driven, highly focused man wanted *her*.

"I hope the rest of your day went well," she said, looking up at him.

"I would've preferred to spend it with you, but you were busy with another guy," Daxon grumbled.

"We don't always get exactly what we want, do we?"

"No, we sure don't," he said, chuckling. "But every once in a while, we do."

Kendall laughed. "Looking forward to your happy ending tonight, champ?"

"I already got what I want. You're here in my cabin," he said softly. Then his familiar grin took over again. "Though I suppose a guy can want more than one thing."

Lord, this man knew exactly what to say. She had imagined what sex with Daxon would be like so many times since Costa Rica, but she hadn't imagined this part, where he'd talk to her, touch her. In her experience, pre-sex time was usually fumbling and awkward conversation. She had never imagined that she would feel so…comfortable with him.

He lowered his head, bringing his mouth to hers. Their lips brushed once, twice. His hands were strong, firm around her, but his kiss was achingly slow, as if he were savoring it. She parted her mouth, meeting each stroke of his tongue. Shivers of pleasure ran through her, heating her up, turning her insides molten hot. She ground her hips against his, trying to get closer. It was happening again, that same thing that had happened in the hallway, as kissing Daxon took over. She was too short, couldn't reach enough of him, couldn't touch enough of his taut, firm muscles. She put her hands on his shoulders and tried to pull him down, closer. Daxon chuckled, kissing her neck.

"I've got you, sweetheart," he whispered. His hands traveled over her ass, finding her bare thighs, and he lifted her, the bottom half of her dress bunched up around her hips. She wrapped her legs around him and wedged his cock between her thighs. He was so deliciously full and hard, and she shamelessly rubbed herself against him. He came in for another kiss, this one hungrier than the last, each stroke of his tongue mimicking the thrust of his hips. His biceps flexed against her, holding her up.

"Your calf," she said breathlessly. "Don't hurt it."

Daxon stopped, slowly blinking down at her. "My calf?"

She nodded. "I just don't want you to strain it. It's already frustrating enough…"

He was looking at her, wide-eyed with wonder. "You're thinking about my calf?" His laugh was rough and full of humor. "I was kind of hoping your mind was elsewhere."

"Actually, it was, which is how I ended up here," she said, squeezing the muscles of his arms, which were currently holding her up. "I shouldn't forget. This climb is everything to you, and I'm your physical therapist, even if I'm off duty." She smiled. "I'm supposed to heal, not injure you further."

But he didn't put her down. He just looked at her, waiting, like he was still a little stunned.

"Sorry to ruin the mood," she added.

"Not at all." He shifted his weight to balance her on one arm and slipped his other hand behind her neck, caressing her with his thumb. His gaze swept over her face. "The mood is perfect."

She was still thinking about his calf. Despite the hunger in her kiss, the way she moved against his body, sighing, moaning, she was thinking about his injury. His first reaction was that he wasn't anywhere near giving her a performance she couldn't forget.

But then the concern in her voice hit him, along with this realization: never once had a woman stopped to worry about *him* in the middle of sex. It wasn't like he had been harboring unspoken complaints about it, but at this moment, it occurred to him that all along, he was just expected to…perform.

Well, that's what he got for living relationship-free.

The irony of it all was that for once, he hadn't been thinking about performance. He hadn't been thinking about anything except kissing Kendall, about those full lips and her soft skin and her sweet body moving up and down against his, with only a thin layer of panties and his board shorts between them. All he was thinking about was how goddamn good it felt to get lost in her.

He had been moments away from dropping his pants and sinking into the sweet, wet heat of her right there, in the middle of the living room. He probably would have done it if she hadn't stopped him, and frankly, with her legs wrapped around his waist, grinding against him, he doubted Kendall would protest. But she was right. He should put her down and get himself together.

This was a woman he wanted to take his time with. And he wasn't just topping his performance reputation, making sure he exceeded expectations. This wasn't a personal challenge. He could slow the hell down and make sure they were right together.

Daxon let her slip down onto the floor, keeping

his hands on her hips, making sure she was stable on her feet. Then he bent down for a languid kiss, full of promises.

He found her hand and squeezed it. "Let's go out on the lanai."

She tilted her head up for another kiss and then turned toward the French doors, giving his hand a tug.

"Give me one minute," he said, letting go.

She nodded, and he took off for the bathroom to find his stash of condoms. When he walked back out onto the lanai, he found Kendall on the couch facing the pool, one sexy leg crossed over the other, cowboy boots and short dress giving the whole scene a fantasy fuck vibe. Except she was so very real. He sat down next to her, and she smiled. Damn, that smile. It was beautiful, and it was for him. *He* was making her happy right now, and he hadn't even taken off his shorts. It had been a long time since he had thought about pleasing a woman outside of the bedroom, so long he had forgotten he had ever even wanted to.

"You look so sexy, Kendall," he whispered. "Relaxed."

"I have almost as much trouble relaxing as you do. Almost." It felt so good to see her at ease with him. He could stare at her all night.

"Then we know what we're aiming for." He motioned with his hand. "Come over here, cowgirl."

CHAPTER EIGHT

KENDALL GOT UP on her knees and climbed onto Daxon's lap, straddling him. She pulled off her dress and dropped it on the sofa, leaving her in panties, a bra and cowboy boots. Then she ran her fingers over his shoulders, feeling his muscles twitch. His big hands rested on her waist and moved lower, around her ass, pressing against her thighs.

"Hey there," he said, pulling her closer. "What's a nice girl like you doing in a place like this?"

"Slumming it. Clearly." She smiled up at him. "I have terrible taste in luxury resorts."

His laugh rumbled in his chest. "And men."

"The worst."

"Thanks for coming." He leaned in and kissed her on the base of her neck, right where her pulse was kicking and jumping. "If you had seen me ten years ago, you probably wouldn't have given me the time of day." His hands began to move up and down her sides, the calluses rough against her skin. "I was the kind of dude with a big truck and a fondness for old

'80s music. Actually, those parts haven't changed. I'm just no longer living in that truck."

He said that all with a laugh, but she detected some seriousness in his voice. Like he was opening up a more private part of his life, just a little bit. His hands moved lower, over her panties, palming her ass. It felt so good to be touched by him, so easy to be with him, just like this, half-dressed and straddling his lap.

"You never can tell what a girl might like," she said after a while. Her voice was starting to sound breathless.

He chuckled. "I can think of a few things that I'm pretty sure you'd like."

"Of course." Kendall smiled. "Even with a mullet, you'd probably still know how to please the ladies."

Daxon pulled back and gave her a mock-offended look. "Hey, I didn't say I had a mullet. A guy can like '80s music without the hair."

"Sure."

He'd probably look great, either way. She slid her hands into his hair. It was soft and thick, and he let out a sigh each time she moved her fingers against his scalp. His hands were exploring, too, skimming over her skin, caressing. His eyes were heavy with desire, and the way he was touching her felt very… intimate.

"Besides, living out of my truck while I'm out looking for the next adrenaline rush doesn't leave room for lots of styling."

"Too late. I can't unthink it now," she said, messing up the top until his hair stuck up in all directions. "Business in the front, party in the back."

He tickled her sides, and she squirmed on his lap, pressing herself hard on his erection. The intensity in Daxon's gaze grew stronger, so she did it again. She felt so lucky to be here right now, but she didn't want him to misunderstand. This wasn't about getting naked with Daxon Miles, Pure Adrenaline star. The chemistry between them had been electric from the start, but it was all the touching and laughing, the comfortable intimacy together, that had her beyond turned on.

"Still thinking about my hair?"

Kendall laughed. "Not quite as much."

It was on the tip of her tongue to say how good this felt, just laughing with him, but luckily, her brain caught up with her. This was Daxon Miles, who would leave in a few days on his quest to climb up another mountain with no ropes. She had to keep this light.

So she distracted him the best way she knew how. She reached behind her back and unfastened her bra. And, *surprise, surprise*, it worked. Daxon's gaze wandered down her body as she arched toward him, his eyes on the cups as she slid them down, slowly revealing the tops of her breasts.

"Fuck, Kendall. Your tits make me so hard," he muttered. "And the cowboy boots are really doing it for me."

Her nipples were sensitive, always had been, and when his thumbs brushed over them, a shiver ran through her body. He did it again, a little harder, rougher. She moved up and down on his lap, getting more of that delicious friction against his erection. God, yes.

Their height difference wasn't nearly as pronounced when she sat on his lap, so they were almost eye to eye. She closed her eyes and opened her lips. His mouth was so hungry, so eager, soft and warm as he opened for her. He met each stroke of her tongue, but it felt like he was holding back, letting her lead. She threaded her hands behind his neck, tilting her head a little, exploring. She got the sense that he usually just took charge, but today, he didn't. It was as if he was saying, *learn more of me, look closer*. His palms moved up her thighs, over her ass, feeling her. He was learning more of her, too.

"You're a good kisser," she said when she broke away. "Really good."

Daxon chuckled. "I'm just really into kissing you."

"Smooth talker, too."

"You hoping I can back it up?"

"Of course." Her cheeks flushed.

"Are you asking me to pull it out?"

"Okay, yes," she said with a little laugh. "I've been a bit curious since you flashed me." She held up her thumb and finger a centimeter apart. "Just a little bit."

He chuckled. "Then feel free to explore. Just a little bit."

"Purely as a professional, of course," she said, her hands moving down his chest. "I mean, your body does some amazing things."

Her heart was pounding hard. She was teasing him, but there was true admiration behind it, too. After years as a physical therapist, she knew intimately the kind of dedication it took to do the things he did.

Her fingers moved down the ridges of his abs, down his stomach. His breath was coming quicker as her fingers trailed lower, lower, to the waistband of his shorts.

A hiss escaped his lips. "That feels good."

"Can I take off your shorts?" She smiled up at him. "Still just professional interest, of course."

"Of course," he echoed, but he made no effort to help.

Kendall drew the tie of his board shorts, and his cock popped out of the opening right away. She blinked a little in surprise but kept unlacing, her fingers brushing against his skin.

"You look skeptical." Daxon's voice was full of humor, but there was a rough undercurrent of need in this voice.

She wanted to tease him, but she couldn't. Not while that intensity burned in his eyes.

"Just admiring," she said. "I never get a chance to look like this."

He gave a hum of satisfaction, so she ventured closer. She ran her hands up his legs, his rough, coarse hair under her fingers. He stilled as she moved higher, higher. He was so hard, all the ridges and colors in stark relief. She had spent the last couple days working on the perfectly formed muscles of his legs, wondering what it would feel like to explore the rest of him. And now she was. She started at the bottom, brushing her fingers against his balls. How sensitive were they? She cupped them, and he sucked in a gasp.

"Are you sure you're doing okay up there?"

"I'm sure," he said, his voice strained. "I'll tell you if it gets too much."

He said the last words through gritted teeth, and something told her he saw this as a challenge of endurance and will, like everything else he did. Which would make this even more fun. How far could she push Daxon Miles, professional adrenaline junkie, his endurance well-known? What were his limits?

She moved her other hand to his cock, testing its feel, its thickness, tracing the veins. His stomach muscles were tense and his thighs, tight, but he held still, all that intense energy coiled, waiting. Kendall took her time. She moved her hand higher, higher, along the smooth skin, up to the head. Drops of precum leaked out the tip, and she had the urge to lick…so she scooted off his lap and did it. Leaning forward, she swirled her tongue around the head, tasting, feeling him with her mouth. He let out a loud groan. Kendall backed up a little, inspecting his entire length.

Daxon was big. The kind of *holy shit* big that legitimized some of the more far-fetched rumors about him. It would take a hell of a lot of blood to keep that thing hard, which meant his other head probably wasn't getting much. She looked up at him, his mouth parted and his eyes heavy-lidded. His arms were spread along the back of the couch, his incredible wingspan on display, muscles flexed, knuckles white as he gripped the pillows.

Her hand closed around his cock, squeezing a little. Then she bent forward and put her mouth on the tip again. She sucked experimentally and then took more, testing him.

His body shuddered, and he muttered a curse. "Yes, sweets. Just like that," he rasped, his big hand coming down to stroke her head. "This is so fucking amazing, Kendall."

She sucked again, hollowing out her cheeks as she pulled out, and another shudder ran through his body. His hands moved through her hair, and at first she thought he was going to guide her, to show her what he liked, but he didn't.

"I want to see your mouth," he whispered.

His last words were mixed with another groan as she took him in, deeper this time. His head hit the back of her throat. She did it a few times, relishing the way Daxon trembled under her fingers, and a surge of energy ran through her. There was so much power in giving him pleasure, so much freedom.

She did it a couple more times, in and out, before he pushed her shoulders gently back. “Enough.” His voice was tight in his throat, as if he were one breath away from snapping. Kendall leaned forward, wanting to be the one to make him snap, but he chuckled and held her in place.

“Not a chance, sweetheart,” he said. “Not this time. There’s no way in hell I am going to come in your mouth if there’s a possibility I can come inside you.”

Daxon had spent a week in Costa Rica with Kendall kneeling in front of him every day, working on his calf muscle, and he had tried like hell to think of anything but the fact that her mouth was so close to his dick. Each one of those images, memory and fantasy, layered on to the real thing right in front of him. Kendall was kneeling on the ground, staring at his cock, her lips still so close to his head. And that alone was going to make him come if he wasn’t careful.

“You finding what you’re looking for?”

She smiled. “And more.”

A chuckle rumbled from his chest. “Glad to hear it. And I hope you don’t mind a little dirty talk.”

“I love it.” Her smile was wide and genuine, and his heart thudded harder.

He motioned for her to climb up on him, and she did, losing her panties on the way to his lap.

"Because I have a feeling the words are just going to come out," he said, tugging her closer.

He traced a line down her body with his hand, slipping it between them, finding her pussy.

"You're wet," he murmured. "So fucking wet. And I am so goddamn lucky."

"I was just thinking the same thing."

He reached beside him and grabbed a condom that was on the couch. "Put it on me. Please."

She leaned back a little and tore off the wrapper, then placed the condom on his glistening tip, rolling it down carefully. He stared at her hands, his mouth hanging open. Holy hell, he wanted her.

Slowly, her gaze wandered up and met his, and a hard jolt of lust hit him. Daxon let out a groan. "I want you to ride it, sweets. Make us both feel so good."

"I did wear my cowboy boots tonight," she said in an exaggerated Texas accent.

He tipped his head back and laughed. She was the most fun woman he had met in…well, pretty much ever. He brought his lips to her neck, breathing in a little of that sweet scent he had resisted all day long. "Did I mention I really, really like you?"

She shook her head slowly.

He kissed the spot right below her ear. "Just want you to remember that."

Then she raised herself up on her knees, positioned his cock at her entrance, and began to sink down. Holy hell, he wasn't going to survive this. The loveliest woman in the world also happened to have the tightest pussy, which was currently milking his tip, threatening to overpower even his self-control. Or maybe it wasn't the tightness of her pussy or the soft jiggle of her tits that was driving him crazy. Maybe it was just her. But he couldn't process what that meant, and he needed to devote most of his brainpower to not coming right now.

Kendall had her hands on his shoulders, and she was lowering herself, inch by inch, onto him. Her head was tipped back, and her hair fell down her back, tangled and free. She looked like a goddess of sex, sacrificing on the throne of his cock. Yeah, he liked that idea a whole hell of a lot. But even that thought dimmed, along with every other one, as her tight, warm channel squeezed his cock.

"I'll make sure it's good for you," he said, his heart bursting in his chest. "I promise. But take it slow right now."

Lower, lower, she sank onto his aching cock, filling the night air with groans and sighs. His breaths were coming so quickly that Daxon no longer knew which gasps were his. She moved up and down in little movements, stretching to fit him. He held on to her hips, trying hard not to grasp her too tightly, letting her take her time until his entire cock was inside her, all the way to the base. Her breath was shaky, and she wove her hands into his hair and kissed him hungrily. It was as if they were reinventing sex, finding a whole new kind of pleasure.

"This feels so good," she whispered, pulling back, wonder in her eyes.

Daxon chuckled. "It does, and we haven't even started."

She pressed her lips to his for another kiss, slower, luxurious this time.

"Are you ready, sweets?" he whispered when she pulled away.

Kendall nodded. She lifted herself slowly and then sank all the way back down. His fingers flexed against her soft hips as he tried to hold on to this moment, make it last. Thank fuck she had shown up at his door tonight, so lovely and a little nervous. And right now, with his arms around her, buried inside her, it was magical. She slid up his cock again, and he brought her down on him, tilting his hips. She let out a loud cry, hoarse and so hot. He didn't give a shit if the neighboring cabins could hear them. All he could think about was this incredible woman, pleasuring herself with him.

They found a rhythm, up and down, his hips bucking to meet hers. Her eyes met his, half-lidded, and a fresh wave of desire ran through him. He was getting way too close, so he reached a hand between them and found her clit, pressing against it each time he thrust. She was so slippery and wet, his fingers gliding.

"Kendall," he muttered. "Do you feel how much I want you?"

As the last words left his mouth, her orgasm started, clenching his cock, setting him off. His hips bucked, and his cock erupted in hard jolts. Her cries sent more waves of ecstasy through him, warmer, lulling him into bliss. The rush of pleasure turned into languid satisfaction as her body draped over his, her cheek on his shoulder. He buried his face in her hair and took long, steady drags of her scent, letting it fill him.

"Wow," she said against his skin.

The waves crashed on the beach, and the wind blew her hair over her forehead. He brushed it out of her face, tucking it behind her ear. Then he wrapped his arms around her and squeezed her against him.

"Yeah. Wow," he said, kissing her on the top of her head.

What he wanted to say was that she was amazing. That his heart was thumping in his chest, and he never wanted to let her go. That for the first time in a long, long while he felt…content. When she moved to get up, he had the strongest urge to pull her closer. But she had come here just for sex, not more.

"Wait, sweets. I'm not letting you go yet." He took another surreptitious inhale of her scent. "What's your schedule tomorrow?" he whispered into her ear. "Any other clients?"

She shook her head.

"Can I take you somewhere after my morning PT session?"

"Um..."

Daxon's cock was still in her, making it hard to focus, but he pushed on. "I'll make it the best day of your life."

She didn't answer right away, and the longer she was quiet, the more his heart pounded. Finally, she smiled and looked up into his eyes. "Okay, best day of my life. Just to make sure it doesn't involve you doing any life-threatening stunts that might injure your calf."

"Me?" He gave her a mock-innocent look. "Never."

For the first time in years, that hadn't even crossed his mind. All he could think about was that he had less than twelve hours to perfect his plans for a day that would blow her away.

He pulled her close again, breathing in the coconut scent of her shampoo, mingling with the scent of her. He liked this woman. All sorts of ideas were running through his head, ways he could impress her, make her laugh, satisfy her, hold her...and make her want him more. Except their clock was ticking. Loudly. In a few days, there wouldn't be a "more."

So he focused on tomorrow. There was a location he and Calvin had discussed in a planning meeting, right here on the Big Island, and an idea that may or may not fall under the category of crazy stunts. Kendall would either love it or hate it. But if Daxon was going for the best day of her life, it was time to go big. The philosophy "the bigger the risk, the bigger the reward" had been the guiding principle that had gotten him to where he was today. If it worked for his career, it might work on one particular woman… hopefully.

CHAPTER NINE

KENDALL WATCHED DAXON from across the lobby of the Kalani. He was talking to the woman at the concierge desk. It was too far to hear what she said, but the low, soft tones of her voice drifted on the warm breeze of the open-air lobby. The low-cut dress, the flower behind her ear, the seductive smile…ugh. Daxon wasn't encouraging her, and still it was painful to watch. Anyone who signed up to be his girlfriend would have to be okay with this kind of ogling.

Plus a lot of other challenges. And a lot of fun. Hypothetically speaking, of course.

This was the point where Kendall had to be very, very careful. She was a worrier, both by nature and by circumstance, and after twenty-eight years, she had been around herself enough to know that wasn't going to change. After she'd left his cabin the night before, she had had a dream where Daxon was scaling the mountain face with no ropes. When he turned to wave to her, smiling that easy smile of his, he lost his grip and plunged toward earth. She had awoken with a start right before he hit the ground. Morbid and completely on par for her worst-case-scenario brain.

Just one sexy night together poked at her deepest fears. Soon, he would leave the Kalani and go back to putting his life on the line—not just in her nightmares but for real. Which meant the consequences could be real, too. After too many years of watching her father head back to the most dangerous jobs, over and over, she knew that itch to take risks wouldn't go away. Which meant the days at the Kalani were going to be a true test of her new, adventurous approach to living in the moment, not worrying about the future. She was going to enjoy the hell out of this day with Daxon, no matter what.

Because the more time she spent with him, the more she was sure that if she didn't try, she'd spend the rest of her life regretting it. There were so many things about Daxon that surprised her. He was much more considerate than she had expected. Not that she thought he would be an asshole, but for a person who did so many reckless stunts, who treated his own life so carelessly, she had expected him to be a little more self-centered. Instead, he was unselfish, particularly in bed. And on his moonlit lanai. And maybe in other places today…wherever they were going.

Daxon finished what he was saying to the concierge and turned around. Kendall could see the moment he caught sight of her. His eyes raked down her body, and then he gave her a slow smile like she was still naked. She glanced down, just to make sure, but she did indeed have clothes on. Of course she did. But that look he gave her… He crossed the room, and when he came close, he reached out, as if he was going to wrap his arms around her. His gaze dipped to her lips, his mouth parted, and she was almost sure he was thinking about kissing her. Right here, in the middle of the lobby. But then his hand fell to his side again.

"Hey," he said. "I was just arranging a few last-minute things."

"Are you going to tell me where we're going?"

"Hmm…" He pretended to give that idea some thought. "Nah. But if you guess correctly, I'll tell you."

Kendall raised an eyebrow. "Are we climbing Mauna Loa?"

He shook his head. "Not a chance with my calf."

"Hiking to one of the waterfalls?"

He shook his head again. "Same. I'd rather save it for a time when I don't have to hold back."

"Surfing?"

"Sounds fun. Maybe next time." He waggled his eyebrows. "You're getting closer."

Kendall wrinkled her brow. "Boogie boarding?"

Daxon cringed. "Isn't that the B-level version of surfing?"

"Says the guy who's never tried it, right?"

He didn't look convinced. "Fine, you're right. It

sounds like fun. Then maybe we can try water aerobics in the shallow end of the pool?"

"I'm sure I can arrange that if you want," she said, smiling sweetly. "I'm done guessing. Let's just go."

They walked out of the open-air lobby and into the sun. The entranceway to the Kalani was full of palms and bright, blooming flowers, and the driveway was made of large stones, just a little darker than the sand. In the middle of the drive, a red convertible was parked, shiny and inviting.

"You like it?"

She swallowed the thump of excitement in her throat and tried to sound bored. "It's okay."

His hands slipped around her waist, and he tickled her until she burst out into laughter.

"All right, it looks like a lot of fun," she said between gasps.

He beamed at her. "I thought so, too."

Was there a hint of pride in his voice? She was getting the feeling that he really did want to please her. A lot. Which was probably just his competitive spirit at work. But a convertible sports car did look like a fun way to drive around the island.

"You know how to get where we're going?" she asked.

"Of course I do," he said. "Do you really think I'd go into an adventure unprepared?"

"Probably not."

He winked at her. "The right answer is *hell, no*."

Daxon slipped on his sunglasses, walked over to

the passenger-side door and opened it for her. She had never really seen the point of this chivalrous gesture, since she could easily open a door for herself. But with Daxon watching as she hesitated, his smile faltering a little, she was starting to understand his message: *I'm paying attention to every detail.* Which she was *not* going to overthink. Not even a little bit.

The seat was warm from the morning sun, shining down, filling the air with the kind of sultry heat that made everything nicer…and sexier. It was one of the things she loved most about living here. Back in Northern California, it was as if the thermostat never was cranked quite right. Foggy and cool in the summer, winter alternating between warm sun and rain, and just when the spring seemed to get it perfect, the fog would roll in again, cutting through the bliss of warmth. But here in Hawaii, even the rain didn't interfere with the lazy heat. Maybe someday she'd get tired of the perpetual good weather, but that day wasn't coming anytime soon.

Daxon climbed into the driver's seat, his long, muscular legs on display. If she wasn't careful, she'd spend the whole day gawking at him.

"Did you bring your bathing suit?" he asked, catching her mid-ogle.

Kendall pulled the collar of her T-shirt over to reveal a strap. "That was my only clue about our destination."

"Unless you can think of a way to coax more hints

out of me." He lifted his sunglasses, his gray-green eyes sparkling. "Ready for the best day of your life?"

She laughed. "Impress me, Daxon."

"I will." He lowered his sunglasses and started the car.

The resort's long driveway wound through more palms and bushes before they came to the main road and turned, heading south. The landscape of the north end of the island was drier, and when left alone, without fancy resort plantings, a lot of it was barren, with long stretches of grassy fields that barely covered the lava beds. But they were headed south, toward the greener, rainier side, with the kind of tropical hillsides she had expected when she first came.

From the moment they turned onto the highway, Daxon peppered her with questions. He wanted to know everything about her—growing up just outside San Francisco, her adventures as a physical therapist, and all her memories from when her father would disappear for weeks into wildfire territory.

"How did your mother feel about it?" he asked as he turned off the main road, heading for what was supposed to be the best smoothie place on the island, according to the hand-painted signs on the side of the road.

"It was really hard on her. But complicated. She was a hotshot, too, before they had me, so she understood why he wanted to be there, on the front lines of the fires."

Her mother's experience also gave her mother a well-honed sense of when to worry. There were days of silence, where her father's absence took up all the air in the house, all the space at the dinner table, suffocating them both. Then, when he finally called, the relief came first. Meals were filled with bright bursts of a week's worth of conversation, finally freed, now that her father was safe. But there were nights, not long after, when that relief turned to anger, usually when she caught sight of her mother's expression, worn and weary. Why did her father keep going back when he knew how much they worried?

Kendall didn't reveal all these details, but she could tell she had said enough that Daxon understood. When they pulled over by the smoothie place, under the shade of the palm trees that lined the parking lot, he turned off the engine but stayed in his seat.

"You didn't tell me all of this when we were in Costa Rica," he said.

She shrugged. "It's not a secret. But we were talking in general terms, not about my situation. I didn't think it was relevant."

He was quiet for a moment, and then he nodded. "But it's relevant to me."

The little smoothie shack was on the edge of a farm, with a grove of banana trees where guests could wander and spiky pineapple bushes sprouting out of the ground. They walked around the grounds, sipping smoothies, as he asked more questions about San Francisco State University, about her traveling physical therapy job, about boyfriends and friends. Then they climbed back into the car, and as they headed back to the main road, she thought it was fair to turn the inquiry tables on Daxon.

She knew the basics about his past—just about everyone did: growing up with only his mother, adventurous from a young age, never much for school. He entertained her with stories about his travels while filming, trying local foods and local activities all over the world, and she got the sense that he played down the more dangerous parts of these stories.

"How many people would you say do what you do, climbing the faces of mountains without ropes?" she asked.

"Expert-level free soloists? Not sure. Probably under fifty."

"How many died this year?"

There was a long pause. "One."

"How about last year?"

"One."

And he was going to follow up his Moonlight Buttress ascent with El Capitan, the most dangerous climb of them all. Didn't he see that these crazy stunts would probably lead to his death? One glance at him told her he knew exactly what she was thinking, and he didn't agree. Kendall opened her mouth to argue, then closed it. Not her battle. And she wasn't going to let it ruin her day, either.

They continued south, past Hilo, past the active volcanoes. Kendall looked out the window at the lush, green hills that rose up on one side. The dormant volcanos were steep, green and treeless, and the road cut into the side of them, winding around each cone. There was nothing in sight but the sea and the grass and an occasional cow grazing on the mountainside. It was gorgeous, but where were they going? For most of the ride, she had assumed that they'd go to the active volcano, but they had passed that turnoff miles ago. They had also passed the Black Sand Beach, another attraction in the area. What else was there?

"You're still not going to tell me where we're going?"

"You haven't guessed yet?" he said, glancing over at her with a little smile. "We don't have far to go before we start heading north, up the other side of the island."

"Exactly. So whatever it is must be coming soon."

Daxon pointed to a sign in the distance. "That's where we're going."

It read South Point, 12 Miles, with an arrow pointing to a turnoff on the left. The southernmost point in the US?

This was the destination Daxon had chosen for the best day of her life? It was…a little underwhelming.

"You've never been there, have you?" he asked, turning down the narrow road.

Kendall shook her head slowly. She hadn't even considered visiting this spot.

"Good. I checked with Alana," said Daxon.

Her eyebrows shot up. “You talked to Alana about this?” she asked, motioning between them.

He looked a little guilty, but not nearly guilty enough. “It, um, depends upon what part of this—” he motioned between them like she had “—you’re referring to. I would’ve just asked you but you were busy with a client.”

There was a hint of mocking in his tone.

Kendall let out a breath and steered the conversation back on track. “Well, Alana was right. I’ve never been here.”

The grin was back on his face. “I was hoping so. There’s something here that I thought might be fun to watch.”

Daxon Miles, the man who threw himself out of an airplane with no parachute, thought it would be fun to watch…the southernmost edge the United States, where it met the ocean? Was she missing something?

Daxon reached over and squeezed her leg. “I hope you love it. It’s either that or you hate me for bringing you here, which will make for a very long car ride back.”

Okay, now she was really curious.

They drove for miles, past houses and little stores until finally they reached the ocean. Daxon pulled into a dusty area and parked the car. He took off his sunglasses, and he opened his mouth to speak but hesitated. Shaking his head, he removed her seat belt, then his, shifting in the seat to face her. He leaned forward, putting his hand on her thigh.

He brushed his lips against hers, so achingly slow. Her pulse jumped, and she reached for him, pressing her hands against the soft stubble of his jaw. He opened his mouth and kissed her, his teeth tugging at her bottom lip as his hand slid farther up her thigh. She tilted her head and stroked his tongue with hers. Her whole body ached for this man…and they were in the middle of a parking lot.

He backed up, and she swallowed. "Did we come all this way for a nice make-out spot? It would have been easier just to stay back at the Kalani."

The corners of his mouth tugged up into a hint of a smile. "It's not what we came for. But I wanted to kiss you before we get out, just in case you get mad at me for this."

Kendall threw up her arms in resignation. "What the hell are you taking me to do, Dax?"

"The southernmost point also happens to be a popular cliff diving spot," he said with a mischievous smile. "I thought it might be fun to watch."

He pointed to the edge of the cliff. Now that he mentioned it, there were groups of people in bathing suits standing awfully close to the edge. Right around a platform of some kind.

"Or we could jump," she deadpanned, narrowing her eyes at him.

Daxon just shrugged. "Only if you want, but not on my account. I can always come back another time, but you probably won't. Not without someone to nudge you a little."

She stared at him, stunned. He was taking her to watch cliff diving, thinking it might look like enough fun to join in? Jesus.

"What do you think?" he asked, assessing her closely.

"I'm thinking that you're crazy if you think I might jump off that cliff in the name of adventure."

Daxon laughed.

"What?"

"I was prepared for much worse." Then he leaned forward and kissed her again. "I'm not going to pressure you at all. Seriously. I brought drinks and a pad we can sit on. I figured it would be fun to just watch."

"In our bathing suits?"

"Yep."

"Okay," she said slowly.

Daxon grabbed bags out of the trunk of the car, and they headed toward the water. The day was clear, and the blue ocean sparkled in front of her. The coast was different on this side of the island, the water deeper, and the cliffs riding high above it. She walked along the black rock, watching the people near the platform, letting Daxon lead the way. He stopped a little farther down, at a spot where they could watch the others without hanging over the edge, and laid out a large pad to sit on.

"Just out of curiosity, how high up is this spot?" she asked as she plopped down.

"About ten meters." His voice was casual, but she caught a glimpse of a grin that told her just how carefully he had planned this out.

Her heart stuttered. He hadn't chosen something truly crazy, a jump that she might barely survive from. Instead, he chose the height of the platform at every Olympic diving well. The height she had contemplated at the age of thirteen—and then backed down from, while all the rest of her friends jumped. Daxon knew this was the height she'd chickened out from before. He had been listening to her, really listening, and he had taken a risk, designing today around a thrill that was just outside of her comfort zone. She wasn't sure if she loved him or hated him for it—and Daxon probably knew that.

Kendall teetered on that brink, back and forth. Then, finally, she did the only thing she could do—she buried her face in her hands and laughed. The wind was blowing gently and the sound of the waves crashed around them, and she just let go. "You are trouble, Daxon Miles," she said.

His mouth quirked up into a cocky smile. "The best kind of trouble, hopefully."

"Yet to be determined."

He could do this all day long. Just sit here with Kendall's long, tanned legs resting across his, the ocean at his side, watching as groups of people climbed out of their cars, peeked over the edge of the cliff, debated, backed away or, finally, jumped.

Daxon meant what he had said. He had absolutely no intention of pressuring her. That wasn't the point of this trip, though if she did jump, he was betting that it would transform a beautiful day into an amazing one. But in truth, he had chosen this destination with something completely different in mind.

He had wanted to show Kendall a new way to see her experiences. That first day at the Kalani, she had asked him questions he hadn't fully answered. Why climb a mountain without ropes? Why jump out of an airplane with no parachute? Behind those questions and every other one like it was one basic question: Why risk his life for these experiences? After being asked variations of this for years, Daxon had realized that this wasn't *his* question. He was asking something completely different: What made him feel alive?

He respected that jumping out of airplanes wasn't everyone's thing. Some people pushed themselves to stand up in front of an audience and tell jokes, hoping that everyone would laugh. Before she got sick, his mother's job as an emergency room nurse had made her come alive. Kendall was looking for the same thing, too: an experience that transcended time, moments when the mind and the body and the world around were all one. Moments like this were worth years and years of a life without them.

He'd heard hints about her aversion to risks back in Costa Rica, and after their conversation in the car today, he understood it much better. He hadn't said much when she talked about her father's absences, just listened, but Daxon supposed this day was the closest he had to an answer as to why a person might choose work that involved danger.

Not that this trip was conceived that way. When he first suggested a day together, he was thinking about sex. On the beach, maybe in the convertible with the top down—lots of fantasies ran through his head, some more than once. But, as usual, he had to take the challenge to the next level. It was then that the little snippet of conversation had come back to him, where she was standing on top of the diving platform, so curious, so ready to jump, so afraid. He knew that feeling. He had lived with it inside, explored it, leaned into it. He had learned more about it—and himself—doing stunts like skydiving, where the real risks weren't high but the fear factor was. Then, once he had understood fear, learned how to work with it, he had moved on to adventures where the consequences were higher. He had learned to trust himself, to harness that fear and turn it into learning what he needed to stay in the moment.

But he hadn't forgotten that messy mixture of fear, temptation and exhilaration, that feeling of standing on top of that ten-meter platform, ready to jump for the first time.

This day's success had nothing to do with whether or not Kendall jumped. Together, they were watching others in that moment, the thoughts written on their faces. While they talked to each other, touched each other, skin on skin. These new explorations were so fresh and alive as they studied each person looking over the edge. This, right now, was what he searched for: the moments when what he said and thought and did were all perfectly aligned. And for once, he was experiencing this fully dressed and sitting down.

Daxon was hoping like hell that she was feeling it, too. That when she leaned over to kiss him after he made her laugh, it was because that was exactly what she wanted to do right then.

"Check out that kid over there," said Kendall. She nodded to the far platform where a group was gathered. "He can't be more than thirteen or fourteen. You think he's going to jump?"

The small wooden platform stuck out a few feet beyond the rocky cliff with a rickety-looking railing. Next to it, a long metal ladder extended the entire ten meters down to the water. The kid was wiry and determined-looking, dressed in board shorts and bare feet, and he was gripping the railing of the platform hard as he peered over the edge. Behind him were two kids, a little older, maybe brothers, who were egging him on.

"He's definitely going to jump," said Daxon, chuckling. "Those guys behind him are making sure of it."

The teens behind the boy said something Daxon didn't catch, and the kid straightened up. He turned to the others, smiled, and then, with a whoop of glee, he jumped. Kendall leaned forward, watching him descend, flailing, until he hit the water. The other kids came to the edge, watching, cheering as the boy emerged from the surface. He swam over to the ladder and called his own taunts back up to the others.

"Now I really can't claim that this is too risky," said Kendall with a smirk. "If a thirteen-year-old kid can do it, it can't be that bad, right?"

Daxon laughed. "You sure you want to use a teenage boy as a risk-assessment gauge? Speaking as a former member of that group, we do a lot of stupid things."

She smiled. "And have a lot of fun along the way."

Daxon ran his hand along her cheek and then tugged softly on her ponytail. "It is a relatively low-consequence thrill, especially on a calm day like today. I think the only way to know whether or not to jump is to ask yourself, will this be fun? Will the thrill of it be worthwhile enough to fight the fear?"

Kendall looked at him. "You're really not going to talk me into this, are you?"

"Nope." He leaned over and kissed her. "But if you decide to jump, I'll go first. I'll be there at the bottom for you."

She was quiet a while, and they watched as the second guy stood at the ledge, the third throwing out comments, half encouragement, half insult. The guy walked forward, calling down to the kid at the bottom, wringing his hands, all nerves and pride, and then he jumped, too. Finally, the last kid looked around as the other two called to him.

"He wants witnesses," said Daxon as the kid looked their way. "Someone to be in this moment with him."

Daxon pumped his fist in the air, cheering the guy on. He stepped forward, standing on the edge, backed up, and with a resigned shrug he jumped off the cliff. When he came up for air, the three boys gathered at the bottom, laughing, giving each other high fives.

"I want to check it out," said Kendall.

"You sure?"

"Just a peek. I still might change my mind."

"No pressure. But just in case, let's strip." Daxon waggled his eyebrows salaciously. She pinched his side, but a smile tugged at the corners of her mouth. Making Kendall smile was becoming his new favorite pastime. The rush he got when her lips curved up and her eyes crinkled at the corners as she looked at him—that rush was addictive, different from anything he had felt in a long, long time. If ever.

He reached inside one of the bags, searching around. "The biggest risk in this jump is probably smacking your feet or cutting them on the barnacles on the way up the ladder, so I brought some water shoes for us, just in case." He pulled out a pair and handed them to Kendall. "That was the reason I contacted Alana in the first place, by the way—to get your shoe size."

But Kendall didn't take the shoes. Instead, she got that look in her eyes like she did the night she came over, like she was about to have her way with him. She shifted onto her knees and climbed onto his lap, straddling him. She was warm from the sun, and her lips still tasted of pineapple and mango as she brushed her mouth against his. Relief rushed through him, relief at kissing her again. Her tongue stroked his in slow, deep moves, like she was showing him what she wanted from him right now. And fuck, he wanted it, too. He slipped his hands onto her hips and helped her ride, pulling her against his cock. Hell, this woman drove him crazy.

The sound of teenage voices broke into their kiss, and Kendall pulled away.

"Damn." Daxon gave her one last squeeze. "I should buy you water shoes more often."

"What can I say? I'm easy to please."

Yeah, right. "Or maybe you're trying to distract me from the jump? Because I'm not against this kind of distraction."

She shook her head. "No distracting. I'm doing it. I just needed a little fortification first."

Daxon set aside his sunglasses and pulled off his shirt, then watched as she stripped down to her swimsuit and tugged on her booties. But watching her was getting him even more worked up, and they were in public. He stood up and offered Kendall a hand, and when she took it, he pulled her close, into his arms.

"I'm almost sure this won't strain your calf. It's almost healed."

He nodded his head slowly. "It feels great. My calf will be fine."

She slipped her hands onto his waist so naturally, as if they were meant to be together like this.

"I'll be there for you, sweets," he murmured into her ear. "You're safe with me."

She stilled in his arms, and for a moment, he wondered if he had said the wrong thing. But when he pulled back, she was smiling. "Let's do it."

They walked along the rocky cliff, over toward the platform where the boys had jumped. The three kids had climbed up the ladder and headed back to a spot farther along the warm black rocks, their cheering and needling still loud, adrenaline-filled.

Kendall walked to the edge of the platform and hung on to the railing as she peeked over the edge. "Holy shit. That's a long way down."

"You sure you want to do this?"

She nodded decisively. "Just working myself up to it."

He smoothed a hand over her cheek and kissed her. "Okay. I'll go first and wait for you at the bottom. Just remember to keep your arms close to your sides and go in straight so you don't smack anything."

"I still remember all the warnings from years ago."

Daxon laughed. "I'm sure you do."

"You've jumped from higher than this, haven't you?"

"Still gives me the same thrill." Even more right

now, when Kendall was next to him. "If you change your mind, just let me know and I'll come back up. But otherwise, I'll wait for you at the bottom for as long as you need me to. Take your time."

He leaned over, cupping her neck with his hand for one more kiss, hard and fast. Her eyes were closed when he backed away, and she sighed. His heart thudded harder in his chest as the thrill of her nearness amped the thrill of the height. This, right here, was the ultimate rush. He took one more breath, soaking in this moment, and then turned to the Pacific Ocean, wide open in front of him, glittering in the afternoon sun. *Best day ever.* The thought filled him as he curled his toes over the edge of the platform for grip and threw himself out into the endless blue sea.

CHAPTER TEN

Holy shit. She really was doing this. Kendall was going to jump from a height that looked crazy-high. Though logically, she knew it wasn't life-threatening, her body was still in panic mode. She so, so wanted to do this, but could she actually make herself take that last step off the cliff?

That day years ago on the ten-meter platform wasn't the only time she had considered jumping off the high dive. She had talked herself into similar situations—and then out of them—at least a dozen times before. This time, she was finally following through because Daxon Miles was waiting for her at the bottom. He was probably the most famous risk-taker in the world, and yet she trusted him right now. She trusted he wouldn't bring her here if she couldn't handle it.

Daxon hit the water with a yell and a splash, then disappeared into the darkness. She held her breath, waiting, until he emerged with another shout of glee.

"It's amazing," he yelled up to her. "Best jump ever."

His words pumped another rush of adrenaline through her, as she watched him swim over to the ladder on the side of the cliff. She was standing at the southern tip of Hawaii, ready to jump off into nothing. If she chickened out now, she would regret it for the rest of her life.

"Ready?" she called down to him.

"Ready when you are, beautiful."

Kendall drew in a deep breath and let it out. She wasn't backing down. If she died now, she would die a happy woman, in the middle of the best day of her life. Stepping off the ledge was the hardest part, and the more she stalled, the harder it would be. Deep breath. One more. Kendall shut off her thoughts and pushed off the edge, plunging toward the water.

Words, yelps and squeals came out of her mouth in a tangled cry as the water rushed toward her, too fast. Her heart pounded in her chest and her whole body tingled as she tried desperately to keep her arms by her side, but it was hard to think when she felt so free.

She hit the water with a startling crash, the impact almost knocking the wind out of her. The ocean swallowed her in one quick gulp, and she went down, down, into the dark water. So far down…

Her brain kicked back into gear. She needed to breathe. Which meant she needed to swim like hell for the surface. Her survival instincts took over, and she kicked, but her booties made it hard. Almost there. Finally, finally, she popped out and gasped for air. Her heart thumped as she stared out into the endless blue ocean, sucking in breaths.

Lying back in the cool water, the rush of adrenaline pumped through her. Holy hell. She had done it. She actually jumped.

Kendall didn't register the splash of Daxon's strokes until he was right behind her. His hands came to her waist, lifting her. "You okay, sweets? It took a while for you to come up."

He sounded shaky, worried. She turned around, and he was right there, so close. Another surge of excitement rushed through her.

"It was incredible," she said. "I'm so glad I did it."

She leaned forward and kissed him, a giddy, fumbling kiss full of water and joy. The worry in his expression eased a little, and he smiled, kissing her back, harder. "Fuck. I think I'm the one who came closest to a heart attack today."

He moved closer, their bodies brushing as they treaded water. He touched her cheek, her arms, her waist, like he was checking to make sure she was okay. She treaded water, trying not to kick him, as she stared into the deep pools of his eyes. Maybe it was all the adrenaline pumping through her, but right now, there was nothing else in the world but Daxon, staring right back, his eyes filled with smoldering licks of flames. Finally, he whispered, "Let's get out and find somewhere more private."

Oh, Lord, she wanted that right now. She glanced over at the long ladder up the cliff.

"Right after we climb back up those ten meters."

Kendall's body was still a rubbery mess. As it turned out, climbing ten meters worth of rickety metal ladder was more frightening than jumping, especially if you kept glancing down to see how high the fall would be. If Daxon hadn't been right behind her, talking her through it, she'd probably still be at the bottom of that ladder, treading water until the Coast Guard arrived. But she wasn't. Instead, she was standing on the empty Green Sand Beach, and Daxon was next to her, spreading out a blanket. He ran a hand through his salty, windblown hair, his biceps flexing, but that didn't do anything to tame it. He was all suntan and messy hair and laid-back, sexy male. He was beautiful.

"I read that this was one of the less visited beaches on the island," he said. "Of course, that was publicized on the internet, so I'm not sure how accurate that is, but it's nice so far."

The empty beach was nestled into a sea-etched cove, surrounded by cliffs. The middle of it sloped down gradually, as if nature had designed its own rocky amphitheater for a perfect view of the ocean. They were sitting in the only shaded, semi-secluded spot, where the cliff jutted out. The sand was coarse, more yellow than green, and the water was a bright, shimmering turquoise.

"I'd like to come back to that spot where we jumped sometime," he added, scanning the coastline. "Scope it out for a free climb, right over the water."

"I'm impressed, Dax," she said, rolling onto her side. "All of this is amazing. The drive, the jump, the beach..."

She was expecting a snappy comeback, but his smile was soft. He took off his sunglasses and looked into her eyes. "The best day of your life, remember?"

The words echoed deep inside, shaking her at her core. It was getting harder and harder not to let this mean anything more. But thinking about anything beyond this week was a reminder that Daxon Miles, an incredible man who created this amazing day just for her, could very well die on the mountainside in a few weeks. He would risk everything in the stupid pursuit of man versus the elements, for everyone to watch, livestreamed. In the end, everyone knew how these battles went. Nature always won. It was only a matter of time, and nature had all the time in the world. Daxon Miles didn't.

Which meant she needed to be enjoying the hell out of their day together instead of wasting it worrying.

Kendall got up on her knees, facing him, and rested her hand on his cheek. His body was a warm, welcoming wall of muscles. She leaned over so her mouth was close to his, and his gaze wandered over her face, to her lips.

"Thank you," she whispered. "For all of this."

Then she closed that last distance, pressing her lips against his. His mouth was warm and hungry as he opened it to hers. Kissing Daxon was its own language, each stroke of his tongue a new word, each sigh or moan the punctuation. He strung kisses together into sentences, fresh, like no other one before it. Kendall immersed herself in his dialect of wants and responses while she showed him her own.

This kiss on an empty beach, with the ocean breeze blowing over her skin, this one was all new. The hunger and the desire were there, the undercurrent to everything they did together. It would probably always be that way, even if they kept doing this for hundreds of years. But she felt something else, something like the ache of loneliness, exposed. His? Hers? Maybe both of theirs. He took the kiss deeper, following her lead, unleashing more of that hunger he had been holding back all day. He growled as her tongue swept against his, her heart thumping harder. Then he pulled back, resting his forehead on hers.

"This is supposed to be the best beach for skinny-dipping on the island. Just in case you're interested."

Kendall smiled. "Is this best day mine or yours?"

"The two aren't mutually exclusive."

She pulled back a little, studying him, and raised

an eyebrow. “I think you’re making up the skinny-dipping thing.”

“Okay, maybe it’s not known as that *officially*,” he conceded, his eyes alive with mischief. “But *I* certainly think it makes the best beach to get naked.”

She gave him a little shove, and he tumbled to the side. Lazily, she turned and stretched out her legs in front of her, staring out at the ocean, trying hard not to stare at Daxon. He pulled off his shirt, and his sculpted muscles flexed underneath sun-kissed skin. Okay, maybe just a little glance. Oh, *Lord*, he was incredible. And probably showing off again.

He scooted back onto the blanket and reached for the cooler bag he had pulled from the trunk of the car.

“I had the resort pack up a few things for us. All healthy, of course,” he said, his gray-green eyes crinkling at the corners. His smile for her right now was so different from the one she had watched too many times in his videos. It was relaxed. Intimate. After taking out little dishes of nuts and fruits and a couple canteens of drinks, he unwrapped a baguette sandwich and handed it to her, then unwrapped one for himself.

“Where do you live?” he asked, taking a bite of his sandwich. “You just appear at my place every morning, so either you’re getting up at the crack of dawn to drive in, or you’re not that far.”

“The Kalani has cabins for staff, visiting or long-term. It's one of the perks, since it's so expensive to move to the island."

"By the beach?"

"Yep." She glanced over at him. "You probably passed the area when you went for your illicit run."

"Which I promised I won't do again." Daxon chuckled. "I've followed every single one of your directions. I'll do whatever you ask."

He gave her a sexy, mock-serious look. On anyone else, it would have come off as ridiculous, but Daxon managed it with exactly the right amount of confidence and humor.

"Whatever I ask?" She mimicked his sexy overtones in his question.

"Oh, yeah." His smile was so lazy and sensual.

What if she asked him not to free climb Moonlight Buttress? The question popped into her mind before she could quash it. Kendall wasn't even tempted to voice this unwanted jolt of reality, so far out of bounds of this playful discussion. The thought was another cliff, but when she crashed into the bottom of this one, Daxon wouldn't be waiting.

Plus, she had no right to bring this up, to push him. He was free to make his own choices, just like everyone else. The warm wind blew strands of hair in her face, despite the tight ponytail she had fastened. She closed her eyes and pushed her worries out of her mind. Instead, she found a different question, one she had been thinking about ever since the Costa Rica trip.

"I read about how you started the Pure Adrenaline videos," she said. "About wanting to experience life in the moment. I think you even quoted Sartre."

Daxon groaned. "I'll never live that interview down. God, what a pompous ass I come off as."

She gave him a skeptical glance. "You did call your stunts existentially enlightening."

He laughed. "Aaah, you memorized my words."

"You *would* see it that way." She took another bite of her sandwich.

"Absolutely." Daxon's smile faded. "Seriously, that guy was out to make me look like a fool, but it's my fault I took the bait. He kept pushing me about why anyone in their right mind—his words—would want to do high-risk stunts."

"So you're not after existential enlightenment?"

"I detect some judgment in that question," he said, humor dancing in his voice. "Go ahead, judge away. I wouldn't expect anything less from the person who's supposed to help me recover from my injuries."

Kendall frowned. Was she judging him? The truth was that she actually admired him. He had pushed himself to take risks, and even after years of raising the stakes in each Pure Adrenaline episode, he still hadn't yet reached his breaking point.

"I'm not being judgmental, really," she said. "I want to understand. Why do you take these risks, over and over again?"

"I do love the thrill of it, of course," he said. "That

existential awakening thing isn't complete bullshit, even if it sounds like it."

For a moment, Daxon's smile faltered. "But I didn't need the Pure Adrenaline show to do all that. I would've been happy rock climbing and sky diving and living out of my truck for years, with no one watching."

He took a bite out of the baguette and stared down at the sand. He had put his sunglasses back on, and she wished that he would take them off so she could look in his eyes when he said this. But he didn't.

"What changed?" she asked.

He swallowed, his Adam's apple bobbing in his throat. "My mother got sick."

Oh.

"I'm sorry," she said softly. Kendall wasn't sure what she had been expecting him to say, but this definitely wasn't it.

Daxon gave a little nod, but he didn't say anything. She had basically cyber stalked this guy, read all the articles she could find on him, but she had never seen even a hint of this part of his story. In fact, it occurred to her that she knew nothing about his family. Did he have siblings? Where did his father fit in? She had been so caught up in the excitement of sex and fun that she hadn't thought to ask.

She wasn't sure if they were done with this topic, but after a while, Daxon continued.

"It took me a while to notice she was sick. I had dropped out of college, and I was just driving around to different locations, hanging out with other people doing the same thing. I'd come by her house from time to time, do my laundry, hang out with her for a few days and then leave again. I was getting some sponsorships, making enough money to eat and buy gas, but not much more." Daxon sighed. "Even she didn't know what was wrong for a while, either. She was just tired in the beginning. I guess no one really thinks of Parkinson's at that age."

Oh. Kendall had worked with some Parkinson's patients back in school, so she had an idea of what that could mean. And just how hard it could be on families.

"How's she doing these days?" she asked.

"Surprisingly well, though some days are better than others. It's hard to tell how fast the illness will progress. And the medications seem to work well for her, which isn't always the case."

Kendall was trying to digest this story. She tried to picture a younger Daxon, living out of his truck and looking for the next big thrill. His mother's illness could have made him reconsider high-risk stunts, but apparently he didn't. Instead, he started filming them.

Daxon looked at her, his expression serious. "We had to face the fact that there would be a time when she would no longer be able to work, maybe soon. And then what? Disability doesn't get you far. With my dad long out of the picture, well, I needed to figure something out. I'm a college dropout with a shaky work history, and I really don't like to follow orders. I liked to push myself, test the limits. Not many people's ideal job candidate."

"Depends on what kind of job you're looking for." Kendall gave him a salacious wink. "I think Las Vegas is always looking for hot, fit men pushing limits with their endless endurance."

Daxon chuckled. "I never considered that angle."

She smiled. "And so you got creative."

"And so *Calvin* got creative," he said wryly. "He came up with the idea, he filmed it and got everyone in the community to boost it. I owe him a lot, though he has certainly made out well in all of this, too."

"And now you have money," said Kendall. "And the world is graced with videos of Daxon Miles doing half-naked stunts."

He leaned over her and tickled her side. "Which you watched."

She shrieked and scooted away. "I sure did."

He scooped her up by her waist and put her down on her back, underneath him. He rested on his elbows, his bare torso pressed against her. His muscles flexed under his weight, seductively. Was he distracting her now, steering them away from the more serious territory they had treaded into?

Daxon leaned down and brushed his mouth over hers. "Pure Adrenaline has been a wild ride, and I'm incredibly grateful for it. Calvin has a great plan for making it more sustainable, long term…"

He pulled off his sunglasses and set them aside,

then stared down at her. His eyes were so serious now. What kind of future was he planning? One with fewer risks, with lower consequences?

"We're going to use my free solo of Moonlight Buttress to make the El Capitan climb bigger, far beyond YouTube."

The words shattered that crystal of hope into shards, tearing at her in new places inside. Of course he wasn't going to stop doing high-consequence stunts. No matter what happened between them this week, she knew how this worked long term. Her parents had fought about her father's job for years, but he didn't stop until his arm was crushed…and he was lucky that he got out of it alive. She had known all this when she said yes to this whole slippery slope of intimacy with Daxon.

Stop worrying and just enjoy the goddamn day.

Daxon looked lost in his own thoughts, too, but then he lowered his head for a warm kiss. "Fuck. I really like this position."

She untangled her hands from his hair. "It's hot. I think we need a swim to cool off."

His eyes widened, hazy with lust, as she wriggled out from under him and stood up, brushing off the sand. They had a few more days for sex, but this was probably her only chance to skinny-dip with him. Kendall tugged off her tank top and shimmied out of her shorts, dropping them on the blanket next to Daxon. Next, she slipped the straps of her swimsuit off, and her breasts bounced out. She didn't have to look to know he was watching her as she pulled it down her thighs. She bent over, giving Daxon a show, then headed for the water.

"You coming?" she called over her shoulder.

After a moment, his voice came, rough and full of humor. "Hell, yes."

So she took off, her feet digging into the sand. The water was clear, the bottom sandy, so she ran in, splashing everywhere. It got deep quickly, so she dived under the cool water, closing her eyes. Hawaii was amazing. After living her life next to the foggy, frigid Northern California beaches, the warmth was a pleasure she couldn't get enough of.

Kendall took another long stroke underwater and then came up for air. She found the bottom with her feet and turned around. Daxon was heading straight for her. He was a powerful swimmer, because of course he was. Mastering some stunt had probably required him to hone his skills from good to impressive. Was there anything this man wasn't good at?

He caught up to her and stood, his body against hers. His hands came to her waist, and he pulled her against him, trapping his cock between them.

"I thought it would take a lot more convincing before you skinny-dipped," he said, his mouth next to her ear. His lips closed around her earlobe.

Kendall laughed. "I'm not the famous YouTube phenomenon. No one cares if I'm caught naked on camera. You should be worrying about yourself."

"Calvin would have a heart attack if he knew I was doing this." He pressed his lips against her neck. "But right now, I don't care."

Her heart stuttered in her chest as his words sank in. The water was shoulder-deep, and she wrapped her legs around him, the waves lapping between them.

She brushed her lips against his. "You taste good."

Her body slid against his, and his hands moved down, one on her back and the other on her ass, holding her against him. The water was warm, but his body was warmer. Every time the water slipped between them, she pressed herself against him again, trying to get closer. Their kisses were slow and deep as the thrill of the jump and the pull of their nearness turned into something more intense. Her breaths and his groans all mingled with the sounds of the water. It was incredible just to touch, just to feel every part of him. It was just the two of them, so light, so free, unattached to anything that existed on land.

A larger wave hit them from the side, splashing everywhere, and she pulled away, laughing, but he guided her back against him. He took his cock in his hand and lined it up, and she wrapped her legs around his waist. Slowly, he pushed in. Oh, Lord, the feeling of him inside her was like nothing else. She couldn't get close enough to him, the water winding between their bodies, keeping her away from that sweet friction of his skin against hers.

His hands were on her hips, and his cock was filling her in slow thrusts, the water setting the pace. He smiled at her, his gray-green eyes sparkling like the ocean around them, full of warmth and wonder. The sun beat its languid heat down on her shoulders as he slid in and out of her. This was heaven. It was a whole new kind of sex, not goal-oriented. Each thrust, each tightening of her legs around his hips, wasn't just one step toward an orgasm. It was simply an exquisitely pleasurable moment. And another. And another. Floating in the warm water with Daxon's body pressed against hers, his cock slowly moving inside her, turning her insides into liquid the way only he seemed to be able to do: each of these moments was worth the risk of whatever came in the future.

The intensity in his eyes was growing, and he opened his mouth, like he was about to say something, something serious and beautiful. Something she wasn't sure she could keep in perspective right now, with her heart so full and free. So she pulled him close and whispered in his ear, "I think I'm done swimming now."

He nodded against her but didn't let her go. Kissing the top of her head, he turned and started toward the shore. The water got shallower, revealing her ass. She was left clinging to him, naked and still with his cock inside her, so she unwrapped her legs. He gave her a playful smack on her rear before easing her back into the water. Laughing, she turned around, and he placed his hands on her hips, keeping her close as they start walking toward shore.

"I can't believe we're still alone on this beach," she said over her shoulder. "How long do you think that will last?"

He grinned. "We're about to find out. What are your feelings about getting caught?"

Kendall's heart kicked up another notch. She had never considered herself an exhibitionist, but today was all about risk, wasn't it?

"I don't know," she said, biting her lip. "I guess I'm willing to see where this takes us."

Daxon laughed. "I'm pretty sure I know where this will take us, with or without spectators."

His body brushed against her as she came out of the water and walked across the beach, to the sliver of shade underneath the rocks. The soft blanket lay, waiting. Was this whole scenario going exactly as planned, the way that he seemed to plan so carefully for everything else? Or were there parts of today that were just as much a wonder to him as they were to her?

He came to a stop in front of the blanket, and she pressed her body against his for a slow, deep kiss. His skin was wet and salty from the ocean, and her fingers glided over his muscles, warm and hard and so satisfying.

She kissed his jaw, then his lips, opening for more. His tongue swept over hers, and he rocked his hips with the same thrust. If the water was about languid pleasure, this was about hunger and satisfaction. His cock was hard against her belly, and his groans were deep, resonating inside her. She dug her fingers into the muscles of his arms, testing the resistance, and he let out a deep growl as he thrust his hips hard.

"We've got to lie down, sweets," he grumbled. "I'm losing my mind here. I need to lick your pussy." She shuddered at the erotic image of watching him pleasure her.

Kendall looked up into his eyes and smiled. "I love being what you desire, hearing all the things you want to do to me."

His eyes narrowed, sparkling with mischief, and he tickled her sides, sending her into a fit of laughter. "Good. Because it's about to get a hell of a lot dirtier."

They tumbled onto the blanket, a tangle of legs and arms, clumsy and yet unbearably sexy. She lay back as he propped himself over her, his hard muscles straining. He bent down and brushed his lips over hers, kissing her neck.

"I want to lick and suck and devour your body," he rasped, moving lower. "I want you to come so long and hard and good that you never forget what it's like when we're together."

She gasped in a shaky breath as his words hit her. He didn't want her to forget him. Ever. But before that thought could gain momentum, his mouth descended on her breast, just as his fingers brushed between her legs and all rational thought left her.

"*Oh God*, Dax," she cried as his teeth raked over her nipple.

He shifted lower, kissing a trail down her belly. "You can say that as much as you want."

He rested his hands on her thighs and looked up and down her body with that intense stare he had. "I want to get you all worked up and make you feel good. But I'm not gonna let you come. I'm going to make you wait until my cock is deep inside you." His words were like a tuning fork vibrating in her body, pitch-perfect, resonating deep inside. "Tell me now if you want the condom."

"No, no condom."

He swore, or at least she thought he did, because nothing fully registered after that. His mouth descended onto her clit, coaxing it, sucking it, *enjoying it*, like he was enjoying this just as much as she was. The building pleasure was dizzying, lighting her body on fire, turning into that molten liquid of need and want, pushing her quickly to the edge of an orgasm. Then just as her legs began to shake, he pulled back, looking down at her with a wolfish smile.

"You want my cock?"

"Yes, Dax."

"How much?"

She gave an impatient groan. "You're not playing fair."

He was making her ask for it, maybe even beg for it, and he didn't look one bit sorry. Instead, he reached between her legs, running his hand up her thigh for another burst of pleasure, coating his fingers with her wetness. Then he gave his cock a couple sharp tugs. "Don't worry, sweets," he said through gritted teeth. "I am going to give us both what we want."

He lined his blunt head with her, and in one slow, insistent thrust, he pushed into her, filling her.

"You feel so good," she whimpered as he stretched her, rubbing against her G-spot, making her body sing. The pleasure was overwhelming, and she wrapped her legs around him, pulling him closer. Her mind registered a car engine in the distance, but she was too far gone in the haze of need to care. She dug her nails into the tight muscles of his back as his hips thrust against hers. She met each thrust, begging for *harder, more*.

"You gonna come with me, beautiful?" He bit out the words in a sandpaper-rough voice. "Is your pussy going to beg my cock for more? You want me to fill you up, over and over?"

"Yes," she cried. "Please, yes."

The orgasm came fast and hard, red-hot pleasure crashing through her body in wave after wave, spurred on by Daxon's deep, guttural moan.

"Kendall," he bit out, his voice heavy with satisfaction, as he buried his face in her neck. Breathless gasps slowed into dreamy kisses…

A car door slammed. Daxon pulled away. "I'd love to stay here like this for the rest of the day. But I'm pretty sure we're about to be discovered, naked, with my cock in you." He nodded up the slope.

Right. She shifted out from under him, despite every protest from her body. She grabbed a towel out of one of the bags and wrapped it around her. When she glanced back at Daxon, he hadn't moved. He was still lying naked on the blanket, watching her.

"You gonna do something about that?" She gestured to his half-hard, fully exposed cock. Voices traveled down the slope. Soon they'd be in sight.

"Am I making you nervous?"

Kendall threw him his shorts. "I should have known you'd have an exhibitionist streak."

He shook his head as he leisurely put a foot into his board shorts, like he had all the time in the world. "Not particularly. But I definitely have a test-Kendall's-limits streak."

The convertible's top was down, and the wind was blowing everywhere as they headed north along the winding highway on the island's eastern coast, making conversation a challenge. But Kendall had insisted on the open-air drive, and hopefully that meant she was just making the most of the experience.

The quiet between them left Daxon with his thoughts. He had said some intense things back on the beach. Like telling her that he loved being the best at everything, especially when it came to her. *I want you to come so long and hard and good that you never forget what it's like when we're together.*

This was supposed to be a fling, but the silver lining in the dark cloud of a restless week of recovery was turning into something else. Something he wasn't in any position to think further about…unless she was willing to wait out the next six months of training and travel and guest appearances.

Yes, waiting would be shitty for both of them, but they could work that out, couldn't they?

His ideas about the future had always been about exploring, pushing himself further. Before today, he hadn't consciously considered a future with Kendall—with anyone—and yet the moment this thought crossed his mind, the images came, fully formed, as if they had been lurking in his brain all this time, just waiting to be acknowledged. The images weren't all horizontal, though most of them eventually involved sex at some point. But there were others, too, like sitting on a beach with her, much like they had today, but on the banks of Lake Powell. They'd take the trailer he lived out of at climbing sites and go off on their own, just the two of them, with no one else around. And he could visit her in Hawaii, maybe buy a place here? In that scenario, Kendall was leaning back against him on an outdoor sofa…yeah, that one definitely ended horizontally.

He glanced over at her, in the passenger seat next to him, her chin propped on her hand, staring out at the ocean. Damn. Riding along the beautiful coastline, just the two of them, felt so right. The whole day did. He wanted a thousand more days just like this.

But how the hell did he fit that into reality, where he was getting on the plane soon to prepare for his live free solo climb up Moonlight Buttress? Kendall had made it clear that this kind of high-consequence adventure was pretty much her worst nightmare. Which meant any talk beyond this week brought them to an impasse. What the hell was he supposed to do next?

The sun was setting as they reached the north end of the island, and Mauna Kea glowed in oranges and reds. Kendall pointed to a drive along the Kalani's entrance, and he turned in. The string of wooden, no-frills cabins didn't have the same high-end vibe as the one he was staying in. But they looked welcoming, at least from the outside. Lush green trees cast long shadows on the narrow road, and the little groups of cabins were mostly unlit.

Kendall pointed to a cabin tucked back from the road, closer to the beach, and he pulled up on the sandy shoulder.

"It's dark here," he said, looking around.

Kendall shrugged. "I didn't leave the front porch light on. I thought we'd be back earlier."

It looked peaceful enough, but that wasn't a guarantee. How often did she come home alone? Had she taken self-defense courses? Did she carry Mace? The risk of attack was probably low, but the consequence was high. He frowned. His rationale about risks versus consequences sounded a lot more reasonable when it was about his free climbs. It didn't sit nearly as well with him when applied to Kendall's safety.

None of these safety questions were any of his business anyway. Kendall had a life here in Hawaii, and she'd go on living it just the same way she had before he'd come. The thought unsettled him, but what could he do about it? Unless he came up with a brilliant solution, in a few days, he would leave, going back to Zion to prepare for the big climb. And Kendall would go back to walking on the beach with Alana and physical therapy appointments with her clients. Her male clients. Daxon clenched his teeth.

They still had time. That's what he should be focusing on, not all the things that wouldn't change. Where was that live-for-the-moment wisdom he had spouted in that interview years earlier?

He climbed out of the car and followed her up the path to her cabin, his hand on the small of her back. She turned to him, silent in the darkness. The sounds of the trees and the waves whispered in the background, but all he was thinking about was Kendall. Her hair was mussed and her cheeks were pink from the sun. She looked happy. And so lovely.

"So…" She smiled a little at him. "Here we are."

"Here we are," Daxon whispered, smoothing the salty strands of hair out of her face.

She didn't look away, and neither did he, just stared, letting his gaze wander down to her mouth. He thought about how red her lips were, how good it felt to spend time just kissing her, feeling her. The longer they stayed in this silent purgatory of desire, the more the intensity built inside him.

Finally, he leaned forward and kissed her, brushing his lips against hers. The hunger for her should have gone by now after a full day of touching and kissing and laughing and sex, but it hadn't. He was ready for more, ready to lie down beside her, to take his time. He could—

"I'm tempted to ask you in, but part of me thinks it's not a good idea."

The words cut into his little fantasy. "Why not?"

He waited for an answer, but she didn't speak. She just shook her head slowly, and there was a hint of sadness in her smile. He opened his mouth to protest, but the look on her face stopped him. He was supposed to be giving her the best day of her life, and that probably included listening when she said stop.

"Maybe tomorrow night instead?"

Her smile widened. "Maybe."

He kissed her one more time, slowly, reminding her of all the reasons she should say yes. Then he sighed and pulled away before he took it too far.

"Best day ever," she whispered. "Thank you."

Then she turned around and walked inside, giving him one last smile over her shoulder before shutting the door behind her. Daxon stared at the cabin, blinking, still not ready to walk away. He turned and sat down on her front step. His heart was still pumping from the kiss, and his head was full of memories from the day. At the cliffs, at the beach, in the water…shit.

He had to figure this out, to get this right. Unfortunately, he still didn't know what *right* meant for Kendall and him.

CHAPTER ELEVEN

KENDALL STOOD OUTSIDE Daxon's door, her knuckles just inches from the wood, waiting. Why was she hesitating? After the trip to South Point, the days had flowed quickly, with his stretches and massages mixing with the rest of her clients', but their nights were always together. It wasn't like anything had changed, not really. But this was his last full day at the Kalani. She would be his physical therapist for one more morning, and she'd spend one final night with him before he went back to being Daxon Miles, YouTube phenomenon. Before he left to free solo Moonlight Buttress.

After their excursion together, the idea of letting him go was getting harder. He felt so close, so real. *They* felt real together. Kendall shook her head. This week was supposed to be an exercise in living in the moment, not ruining her joy with worries about the future. She had promised herself a fun fling, and that's what this was…right?

In their first conversation about risks and consequences back in Costa Rica, she had been quick to point out that his risk assessment was about him, not others. But now, as she stood outside his door, she understood another layer of this complicated puzzle. People were much better at assessing practical risks, risks that could be measured in statistics, such as how likely it was to die when fighting fires for almost twenty years. But what about those that were less clear, emotional risks? Like the risk that she wouldn't be able to move on easily after he left? The risk that he'd leave a big, gaping hole in the newfound happiness of her life in Hawaii?

Still, every concern was full of unknowns. She had spent so much time worrying about her father getting trapped during fire season that a crushed arm hadn't even crossed her mind. Had it crossed her father's when he had chosen his path?

Kendall massaged her forehead. *Focus on this last day together.* She could spend the next week or ten overanalyzing. Until then, she just had to shut this off. And if she didn't do it soon, Daxon would probably open the door on her again, and this time she wasn't wearing cowboy boots.

Kendall straightened up and knocked, and the knob turned almost immediately. Had he been watching her out the little side window as she angsted over him? Nope, not going to think about that either.

Daxon opened the door, one large hand leaning against the doorframe. Her heartbeat kicked up another notch when she saw him, all ripped muscles and golden tan in a T-shirt and shorts. She had touched him so many times over the last five days, both professionally and personally, that she wasn't expecting for her heart to thump so hard when he stood in the hallway.

The memories from the past week before were clear. The sleek muscles of his forearms, the bulges of his tight biceps against his shirtsleeves. She took in his full lips, his gray-green eyes. He looked like he was drinking her in, too.

Kendall gave herself a little shake, coming to her senses. She was at work.

"Ready for your last day of personal healing coach treatment?" she asked, raising his eyebrow.

Daxon's laugh was an easy rumble. "Not making sexy jokes is killing me."

"The world is a darker place for it," she said drily, but she couldn't stop from grinning, too.

He motioned for her to come into the living room, and she sat on the couch, opening up her tablet. He sat down next to her, not quite touching.

She bit her lip. "I want to start creating a care plan for after you leave."

He nodded, looking a little more serious.

"I don't want you to get hurt again," she added softly.

Daxon sighed. "Believe it or not, I'm getting cautious as I get older. Calvin warned me that I was aging out of the adrenaline sports world."

Kendall frowned. “He’s worried your body might break down on you, so he’s planning to fit in as many things as possible before that happens?”

“That doesn’t make him sound like a very good friend, does it?” His voice was getting tighter.

“He sounds like a great business strategist. But you’re the one who has to live with the consequences. Then again, it doesn’t sound like you’re too worried about it, either.”

He paused, then let out his breath. “Point taken.”

Daxon looked out through the French doors, at the deep blue ocean in the distance, his expression serious. Then he turned to her, looking at her straight in the eye.

“So what’s your recommendation, Kendall?”

The truth was on the tip of her tongue. She wanted to tell him to quit, to back out of the climb, to stay away from any other extreme activities. Lord, she wanted to, and the tightness in his jaw made her suspect that Daxon knew this. Maybe that’s why he had asked. She was trying like hell to remain objective. He was a client, and she had to give him professional advice. So she swallowed back her emotions and gave him an answer that could pass as objective.

“You’re great at doing exercises on your own, stretching, and you should definitely keep that up. Otherwise, I think you’re fine to resume your normal training. It’s the best way to tell whether or not that calf will give you problems when you’re in the middle of a climb.” She took a deep breath, searching for the right way to say this last part, to express her worries while keeping it impersonal. "But I'd still feel better if you waited a little longer. And if it does give you trouble, I think it goes without saying that I'd advise postponing the climb."

Had she kept the ache out of her voice? God, she hoped so.

Daxon had that intense look, like he was reading every single nuance in what she had said and what she hadn't said. He nodded his head slowly.

"I'm willing to consider that." He swallowed. "Would you consider a traveling physical therapist job?"

Kendall's heart leaped in her chest. She shook her head before she could be tempted to give any other answer.

"Not even for a special case?"

Absolutely not. She wasn't going to follow Daxon around, playing nurse while he took more risks. She didn't want this to end, but nothing good could come from that road. Even seeing him again would be so hard. She had already misjudged the consequences of this week, misjudged how much she loved being around him after just a few days. What would it be like if they spent more time together?

So she schooled her expression into a casual smile and shook her head again. "Not even for a superhot adrenaline junkie."

"That's what I thought," he said. "I just wanted to make sure."

His words weren't a surprise, but something in his voice gave her pause. It sounded a lot like determination. She drew in a shaky breath. When Daxon Miles made up his mind, he was relentless. What was he making up his mind about now?

This man had an enormous capacity to harness his attention and focus on it to get what he wanted. She had experienced the power of this during the week. Hell, she had enjoyed it. This week, she had been a very willing participant. But what if he used his powers to get something she was no longer sure she could handle? Something that part of her wanted badly but the other part knew she shouldn't have? It would gut her—that's what would happen.

But this was physical therapy, the time she had promised herself she would not get personal...or more personal than it already was.

So she ignored his determined stare and put her thoughts aside. When she looked up, Daxon was smiling at her.

"You ready for some healing?" she said with a wink.

He laughed. "With you? Always."

He climbed onto the physical therapy table and lounged back onto his elbows. Some clients were quiet, and some were talkers—Kendall could go either way—but today, she needed a distraction.

"Explain to me how the next week will go, leading up to the climb," she said, trying not to think too hard about the hard muscles under her fingers, muscles she had intimate knowledge of. She bit her lip and tuned them out.

"Nothing like a week at this resort, that's for sure," he said with a chuckle. "I'll be living out of my trailer at the base of the mountain while Calvin and a few other crew members and I work out all the specifics."

"I thought the days living out of your truck were over," she said, moving her hands higher. "You have more than enough money to upgrade your accommodations."

From the tension in his jaw, she wondered if he was having trouble focusing, too.

"Money isn't the issue. It's proximity. I need to be close, and Zion hasn't built luxury accommodations next to Moonlight Buttress. Yet. I can't imagine why."

She laughed. "I see. So you get there and then what? Climb it a few times off-camera first?"

"Most of the preparation is long over. At this point, I spend a lot of time visualizing each move, each hold. I'll film a couple live promo trailers, and the crowds will start coming a few days before, which means we need to have our area well staked out beforehand."

"What do you think about the crowds?"

He hesitated, then shrugged. "I'm used to it. I just tune it out. And when I start climbing, there's nothing else. Just me and the mountain."

The sound of the waves floated through the windows as she finished with his leg, lost in thought. She could feel Daxon's gaze on her, and finally, she met it.

"You've been a perfect PT client this week, doing exactly what I told you to."

Daxon smirked. "And then some."

She gave him an amused snort. "Just keep doing these exercises. I'd say take it easy, but we both know that's a stretch."

"Plus, my favorite relaxation method will be gone."

"I'm sure you and your hand will think of something."

"I'm getting good at coming up with ideas," he said, his eyes brimming with lust.

"I'm not sure what to say about that." The laughter bubbled inside her. Lord, this man made her laugh. "We're on the clock, during a physical therapy session."

He made an effort to look scandalized, but it quickly dissolved into a smile. Then his smile faded. "Kendall, I've been thinking…"

She froze. His voice was quiet and serious, and he was looking at her like he was about to suggest something big, something she wasn't prepared for, that didn't belong in a physical therapy session.

"Wait, Daxon," she said. "Not now."

He opened his mouth, like he was going to protest, then he closed it and nodded.

"When?"

"Later."

He frowned but didn't say anything. She would come later. It wouldn't be easy, but staying away from him wouldn't change anything. It would be painful when they said goodbye, no matter what she decided. There was no reason to start that struggle early.

CHAPTER TWELVE

DAXON THOUGHT ABOUT Kendall all day. He thought about her as he did his pull-ups on his fingerboard, he thought about her as he did another set of push-ups on the hanging rings that he had installed on the lanai, and he thought about her as he climbed into his private pool and stared out at the ocean. There were times that morning she had been quiet during his physical therapy session, as if she were just as lost in thought as he was. Something had shifted in her at the end of that spectacular day at South Point, but he still wasn't sure of the direction of her shift.

Either way, he was never one to back down from a challenge. Hell, he thrived on it, testing his limits, seeing how far he could push himself. But this challenge wasn't a mountain, an impersonal object that didn't care whether or not he succeeded. This was a woman, with her own wants, needs and reservations. Whose heart could break, and he would have to live with himself if he broke it. He would never be able to rehearse his approach the same way he rehearsed his climbs, putting every move into a well-choreographed routine, a road map for successful execution. No matter how much he planned, this wasn't something he could master.

The more he thought about this last evening together, the more he realized how unprepared he was for what she might say. Despite carefully hoarding every bit of knowledge about her over this past week, he was only beginning to learn what pleased her and what she cared about, what she wanted. He was so hungry for more, more, more. Every part of him ached for more of her.

But that wasn't the biggest stumbling block. He was no stranger to the drive to satisfy his own wants, anticipating the adrenaline rush that came with it. He had ignored it before, turned it off to focus on the next climb, the next challenge. This was different. He didn't just want more from her; he wanted to *give* her more. Except…what would make her happy was for him to *not* do what he did. For him not to be the man who free soloed Moonlight Buttress in a week. For him not to cause her the kind of anguish that her father's risks had caused her.

He knew all this. It was a puzzle with pieces that didn't belong together, and yet later that night, he still walked along the resort's path with a packed dinner in his hand, heading for her cabin. Because despite the fact that their hurdles seemed insurmountable, he wasn't backing down from the challenge. He had done impossible things before. This was infinitely more complicated, and yet even the hint of a payoff sounded infinitely more satisfying.

He had visualized what he wanted: Kendall lying over him in the narrow bed of his trailer in the middle of the night, running his hands over her bare skin. And when he woke up the next day for the climb, she would be right there with him.

It was a selfish vision. He knew it, he knew that was the crux of their problem, and yet he wanted it. There had to be a possibility that looked something like this…right? After the next six months of publicity plans, after the El Capitan climb, after Calvin's vision for the future of Pure Adrenaline was secure, he could make adjustments, maybe lay off the stunts that had highest consequence. That idea had run through his mind since his injury in Costa Rica, for his mother's sake. Now he had even more reason to consider it.

But he had months before he could change course. Right now, he had less than a day to convince her that maybe she could hang on in the meantime. His focus needed to be on tonight. He had decided what he'd say and do, and as with any other challenge, he would redraw his route as he made progress.

Kendall's cabin was lit up, glowing from the inside, but she didn't answer when he knocked. He followed the little trail around to the lanai and found her on a chaise lounge with a tub of ice cream in her lap.

Health-conscious Kendall was eating straight from a half gallon tub of mint chocolate chip ice cream. Daxon suspected this was a sign of some sort, but he had no idea whether it was a good one.

She turned as he scraped through the large flat leaves of some tropical plant in his path, and he had no idea how to interpret the uneasy look she gave him.

So he flashed her a smile. “Isn’t it a little early to be hitting the hard stuff?”

The uneasy look faded. “You can grab a spoon from the kitchen. You know you want some.”

“I brought some addition to that dinner.” He set the bag next to the ice cream tub and eased into the lounge chair next to her.

She peeked into the bag, then blinked up at him, a little dazed. “Burritos?”

“Alana tipped me off.” It wasn’t the most luxurious meal, but her friend had said that good burritos were one of the things Kendall missed most about Northern California. So Daxon had gone with the recommendation. From Kendall’s expression, he had chosen right.

“Thank you.” She was looking at him, almost guarded, but possibly hopeful. Then a smile curved at her lips. “I still had a good hour of agonizing to go before I came over.”

“Figured I’d save us both some time.” He gave her a playful wink. “There are so many better ways to spend the evening.”

She rolled her eyes. “Of course there are. But I just can’t seem to help myself.”

“That’s just you being you. I wouldn’t want to change that.”

The words just came, but after he spoke them, he was pretty sure he had just stumbled onto what was probably the most profound thing he had said all week. At the most inconvenient time, he was falling in love with a woman who was wary of who he was, and yet, at this moment, it felt perfect. It must be love, because otherwise, it didn’t make a hell of a lot of sense.

She watched him through those dark, impossibly long lashes, like she was drinking him in one last time, getting her fill. Daxon frowned. That’s not the direction he wanted to go. He searched for a way to divert to a better route.

“You want to eat?”

She shook her head.

“Not in the mood for burritos tonight?”

“Not yet.”

She stood up and held out her hand, nodding to the door. *Oh.*

He followed her inside. It was a much smaller version of his cabin, in the same style that mixed modern with the island. But instead of the sleek, impersonal furniture he had found in his living room, Kendall’s place was filled with all the details that made it a home. Photographs of her parents hung on the wall, books were neatly arranged on the shelves, and her bright green couch looked comfortable and inviting.

But she wasn't giving him a tour right now. She took his hand and led him straight to her bedroom. The kelly-green duvet covered the bed neatly. Was green her favorite color? There was so much he didn't know about her. Everything in the room was in its place, because of course it was. Kendall was a careful woman with careful boundaries. She worked to keep her life that way, and he was trampling all over it. He still wasn't sure if this was exactly why they fit together or exactly why he should stay away.

But he could worry about that later. Right now she didn't seem to want to talk. She was silent as she turned to face him, her expression warm and serious. She said nothing as she pulled off her shirt, and she said nothing as she unfastened her bra, letting her beautiful breasts free. And yet with each move, he could hear her, loud and clear.

One last time.

She was giving this message off in waves, and despite the fact that he vehemently disagreed, he knew arguing wasn't the right path. Instead, he told her with his body, with his gaze.

Don't worry, sweets. I'll give you what you want. And more. So much more.

She stripped off her shorts and her panties, and then she stood in front of him, solemn.

I'll give you this, she was saying in the silence of the room. *This is what we have together.*

And, fuck, how he wanted it. He wanted that and so much more. So he took off his own clothes, stripping himself bare, and he stood in front of her, naked. His cock had responded to her long ago, and he hadn't bothered to fight it. But standing here, naked in front of her, he was starting to wish that he had. Sex was where this was unquestionably headed, but at this moment, as she watched him, her brown eyes tinged with sadness, sex felt like a distraction.

Daxon took a step forward and rested a hand on her cheek. It was the wrong time to say all the things he had planned to say to her, so instead, he pressed his mouth against hers. He kissed her, trying hard to resist the urge to memorize this feeling. This wasn't the end. It wasn't the last time, even if she was thinking that. It couldn't be…could it? When they had kissed in Costa Rica, thinking it was the only time, they had still managed to find their way back to each other. Or rather, Calvin had managed it. So much had happened since she had walked into his cabin at the Kalani. After all that, they'd reunite again… wouldn't they?

Slowly, he sucked her lower lip into his mouth, scraping his teeth against it, letting her know how much he wanted her. The intensity of this physical attraction was the one thing they both agreed on without hesitation. But it was also the way he could show her this was more.

I want this, he said with each stroke of his tongue, *and not just for tonight.*

He could feel the moment Kendall put aside all of her hesitations and let herself go. She matched each stroke of his tongue with hers, pressing her body against his. The night was warm, and her skin was soft and hot, and kissing her was so goddamn intoxicating. Her hands closed around his shoulders as she tried to lessen the height distance between them, so he lifted her. His cock wedged between her legs, and they both groaned. He turned and laid her on the bed, collapsing against her as their bodies tangled together, laughter and moans filling him with a deep happiness. Daxon's heart was pounding—anticipation, desire and joy all wrapped up into one long adrenaline rush he'd never find anywhere else. They kissed some more, and he cupped her breasts, sucked on them, teasing her. He was trying so hard to resist the dizzying abyss of pleasure, but the feeling was too strong. So he gave in, holding himself over her, resting on his elbows, staring down at her. Slowly, she lifted her gaze and met his. For a moment, she looked so lost, but after a blink, that look was gone.

"On your back," she said. She gave his shoulder a little shove, her eyes twinkling with mischief.

Kendall on top? Yeah, that was more than fine with him. He'd give her anything she wanted… almost anything. Daxon pushed that last thought away. Instead, he tipped onto his back, holding her close, taking her with him. She sat up and arranged herself, wiggling her hips, dragging her pussy against his cock. He let out a quiet groan. Fuck, she was already so wet.

"You wanna ride, sweets?" He flexed his hips and moved his hands down, around her ass. "Use me. Ride my cock, take whatever you want. It's yours."

She smile down at him, her eyes half-lidded with pleasure. Kendall shimmied backward and reached between them, wrapping her fingers around his dick. She gave it an exploratory tug, and his eyes rolled back in his head. She sat back and smiled, like she was admiring it right now.

"I could spend days playing with it. I think I'm a little obsessed with your cock, Daxon." She let out a little huff of laughter. "Don't let it go to your head."

"It's all yours," he rasped. "I won't come until you come first."

"Satisfaction guaranteed, right?"

It was his promise from the first day, but that version of them seemed so far away.

She took her hand away and shifted forward to press herself over his cock again. He was already seeing stars, but damn if he'd give in to that urge to come before she was ready, so he focused on her, naked, moving over him, finding her pleasure. He reached up to palm her beautiful breasts, pinching her nipples, enjoying her sighs and moans.

"Are we using condoms?" she asked, her voice breathless.

"Your call."

She smiled a little. "Then I think we'll go for a careless end to a spectacularly careless week."

Her words grated on him, so light and final, but tonight was her show. They could discuss the future later.

"Then fuck me, sweets," he said. "Let go."

She took his cock in her hand again and positioned it, rising over him. In one slow movement, she eased down onto him, slick and hot and so goddamn tight. Daxon clenched his teeth, resisting the urge to hold on to her hips and buck his way into oblivion. She moved slowly up and down, taking him deeper and deeper, until she'd settled, his cock buried inside her. She paused, gazing at him seriously. Was she hoping for the same things he was?

Then she began to move, and that thought faded. He slipped his hands around her waist and held on, letting her set the pace, meeting her with a flex of his hips. She was clenching around him, and he could feel that she was close, so soon. She closed her eyes and tipped her head back, like a goddess riding her way to the heavens. But he was a selfish prick, because he didn't want her riding to the heavens. He wanted her riding to him.

"Open your eyes, Kendall," he rasped, holding back his thrust.

She let out a frustrated moan and glared down at him.

"That's right, sweets. I want you looking at me when you come."

He punctuated that sentence with a hard thrust of his hips, and she found her release. She cried out, saying his name, over and over. Daxon couldn't wait any longer. He let go, jackknifing forward as the pleasure shot through him, holding her tight against him.

"Kendall," he whispered in her ear. "My Kendall."

They ate burritos in the darkness of her lanai, the ocean and the wind whispering around them. Daxon had pulled his shorts on again, leaving his ripped abs for Kendall to admire as he lay back in the chaise lounge, taking his last bite. She was shamelessly staring because...well, he didn't seem to care, so why should she? This was their last night, and she was getting her last gulp of Daxon Miles.

Plus, she was trying not to think too hard about what had happened between them in her bedroom.

My Kendall.

It was almost as if she had imagined it. But no. He had said it with a reverence that her brain wouldn't have invented. Neither of them had spoken as they lay on the bed, their bodies slick and pressed together.

Daxon set aside the paper wrap that had held the burrito. He parted his legs and then motioned for Kendall to come sit with him.

She settled between his legs and eased back against the hard planes of his chest. He wrapped his arms around her, pulling her closer, and she rested her head against his shoulder. In front of them, the dark ocean shimmered with the last reflections of the sun. His lips pressed into her hair.

If staring at Daxon was a fun pastime, lying with him in the darkness of the night was a whole different class of pleasure. His fingers wandered under her tank top, brushing over her bare skin, radiating warmth through her body. A calm had settled through her, but it was laced with that same undercurrent of attraction that never seemed to fade around him. That was just how it was between them, she supposed. And she had one last night to enjoy it.

"What's on your mind?" she asked.

He kissed the top of her head again. "Transcendent moments."

Right. The topic of his infamous interview.

"You thinking about your climb?" she asked, trying to keep the disappointment out of her voice.

"Not even a little bit."

Oh. Her stubborn heart gave a new jolt.

"Are you?" he asked after a while.

She bit her lip. "Maybe." Now she was.

His hand stilled against her, and his breath in her ear stopped. "I wanted to talk to you about an idea."

His voice was casual, but she could feel tension coming off him. She was almost sure whatever he wanted to say had the power to either make this moment perfect or splinter this peaceful night apart.

Kendall bit her lip. "What is it?"

“I don’t want this to end.”

She swallowed, waiting, trying to hold back the swell of hope inside her. She had asked so many what-ifs since she tossed herself off that cliff, but each scenario ended in disappointment. Had he thought of a path she hadn’t?

“I was thinking how much I’d love it if you came to Utah with me.”

The sentence deflated every bit of hope that she had let fizz inside her just moments ago.

But Daxon took her silence as a prompt to press forward. “Maybe, if you have a few vacation days, you could come stay with me. I know living out of a trailer isn’t quite Kalani standards, but Zion is incred—”

“The trailer’s not the problem, and you know it,” she whispered, cutting him off before he indulged in that idea for one more second. If Daxon thought that she was going to follow him around while he scaled mountains without ropes, maybe he really was crazy.

Kendall shifted to sit up, but Daxon’s arms were tight around her. He heaved out a sigh and let her go. She turned to face him. A frown tugged down at the corners of his mouth, as if she were the one who was disappointing him. Kendall couldn’t believe how angry she suddenly was. It was as if she had saved up all her feelings about his recklessness all week, just for this moment.

She drew in a shaky breath. “You want me to

watch while you risk your life, just for another stunt? For another adrenaline rush?"

Daxon's jaw tightened. "You don't have to watch the climb. I just want you there with me. We could spend some time together there, and maybe you'd understand this part of me."

"But—"

"I won't be doing this forever," he said. "After the El Cap climb, I can rethink what I want to do. We can think through what comes next for us. Together."

There was no hint of Daxon's usual playfulness, that easygoing side of him that he showed the world. What was left was the person who always lurked underneath, serious and determined.

"You knew who I was from the beginning. That's the reason why Calvin sent me to the Kalani in the first place," he said, his voice harder. "So that I could do this climb."

She was so frustrated she could scream. Yes, this was true, and she had reminded herself of this at each step. But hadn't everything shifted since he arrived? She wasn't just his physical therapist anymore, and he was no longer here solely to heal his calf. Or at least she had hoped this was true, but apparently, in the end, it still came down to his goddamn stunts.

Daxon probably meant what he said about finding something that worked, but she had seen a version of this scenario play out between her parents, and she knew that quitting was complicated. How many times did her father talk about taking a less dangerous job only to hop back on a plane the next fire season because they needed the money…or his buddies needed him…or whatever excuse he found? How many fights had she listened to? Enough to know that for someone who loved the rush, quitting was highly unlikely. Her father had waited until his body began to fail. Any failure on Daxon's part would have the ultimate consequence.

All Kendall could think about right now was that one misstep meant he would die. And he was willing to accept the consequence of falling from a sheer wall of stone. They'd never have a chance to really be together. She didn't need to say any of these things aloud, because she was almost sure he knew exactly what she was thinking.

Daxon blew out a breath. "Did you think this would end any other way than me doing these climbs?"

Kendall closed her eyes. Yes, she had hoped. Against all better judgment, all past experience, the hope had formed during the week that there was a way this could end well.

"Where does it stop?" she whispered. "Do you just keep doing these stunts until you die?"

"Either of us could get hit by a car tomorrow, too," he said, scowling. "That doesn't mean we should stop ourselves from living today."

"It's not the same," she said quickly. Was it? Maybe

there was some truth in what he said, but the scale of risk wasn't even close.

His gaze softened a little. "The next six months will be intense, and, yes, I'll be doing a lot of the kind of high-consequence climbing that scares you. But after that, we can take Pure Adrenaline in a new direction. I'm just asking you to hang on until then."

Until after he free soloed two mountains, including the elusive El Cap, the mountain face where experienced climbers died, even with ropes? And he'd climb them without any safety net?

"You're not willing to try?" he added, his voice quiet.

The words hurt. Kendall massaged her temples.

"Let's just say that I accept this crazy premise, that I can stomach knowing you're doing these two insane climbs. What happens next?" She had lived this life as a kid, watching her father run right back into the fire zone, over and over, even after he promised to quit. It was getting harder and harder to keep her voice calm. "That drive to do things like this doesn't just go away. I've seen this firsthand."

His mouth was a hard line, grim and determined. "We could find a compromise if we both want this to work. I know we could."

Right now, he probably believed he'd truly meet her halfway, but when it came to actually quitting, it wouldn't be that simple. Where would all of that energy go? Would it churn inside, curdling into resentment and restlessness? Then the next time that siren song of a new adventure called, he'd find a way to talk her into it.

Kendall swallowed, knowing she had one last card to play. Goddamn him for making her play it, for bringing her to the point where she was desperate enough to ask for it. It wasn't fair of her—it was straight-up manipulative—but this was his *life* on the line. If she didn't ask him and he did die, she'd never forgive herself for not trying.

So she took a deep breath and said it. "You promised to follow exactly what I said. What if I ask you not to do this climb?"

Daxon's expression went hard as stone. He didn't move, but now there was anger in his eyes. "You can't really mean that."

"But that's the problem. I really do."

Maybe he could never forgive her for pushing him like this, or maybe at some point, he would understand just how desperately scared she would have to be to ask it. But even as his cold glare broke her heart, she didn't want to take it back.

He stared at her through a few more fuming breaths. "Are you saying that as my physical therapist, or is that a personal request?"

"Of course it's personal," she whispered. "I know you're going to do this climb and the next one. It's who you are, and I hate that I want to change that. Part of me even wants you to do all these amazing things."

Some of the anger faded from his expression, and in its place, she saw hurt.

Kendall swallowed back the lump in her throat and continued. "But I also know myself. This is my breaking point. I can't let myself fall in love with someone who lets himself be one loose handhold away from death, over and over again."

How many nights had she woken up in the middle of the night, thinking about her father, stuck on a ridge, surrounded by flames on all sides? Enough to know that this feeling didn't get better with time.

How could she even consider a relationship with Daxon, who seemed to love the challenge of high-consequence adventures even more than her father did? This wasn't a rift; it was a chasm, deep and wide, and no amount of discussion was going to bridge it. She had to cut this off now, because she couldn't handle going down that road again.

Kendall had no idea how long they stared at each other, waging silent warfare. And then, suddenly, it ended, or at least Daxon stepped out of it. His eyes softened, and he took a long breath. "I'm going to figure this out. I know you don't believe it, but I will."

Kendall didn't speak. He could do all the figuring out he wanted by himself, but it still didn't change the fact that he was going to go climb a mountain with no ropes. That he chose a path that had led other top climbers to their deaths.

Daxon wrapped his hands around her waist, silently calling her back to him. This was the very last time she would lie with him. This amazing man who was so full of laughter and energy and life might not be alive in a few weeks. Or maybe it would be the El Cap climb that would be his downfall. She had to live with that. But this was their last night, her last chance, so she eased back onto his chest, closed her eyes, and tried like hell to concentrate on the moment she was in. It was a resounding failure.

Kendall must have dozed off because there was no trace of sunlight when Daxon whispered in her ear, asking if he could stay the night. When they lay in her bed for the last time, she curled up next to him, breathing in his scent, memorizing it. His heart thumped wildly in his chest, and his breaths were uneven. She drank in every detail, getting her fill one more time.

He woke her in the middle of the night, hard, his big body flush behind hers, his arm wrapped around her, pulling her against him. His muscles strained as he held her, thrusting, his breath heavy in her ear. She came twice before he followed her, his lips in her hair, whispering things she couldn't hear.

He awoke early. The sun was just peeking over the horizon when he leaned down to kiss her, fully clothed.

"I won't come to say goodbye before I leave for the airport," he said softly. "I'd rather end like this."

She nodded.

"Goodbye, Daxon," she whispered, not wanting to see his expression. But she made herself look at him one more time. "I hope you get everything you're looking for up on that mountain."

He blinked down at her, his gaze searching. But there was nothing to search for anymore.

So she closed her eyes and let him go.

CHAPTER THIRTEEN

KENDALL SAT ON the floor of her tiny living room, staring at the blank screen of her television. The last week since Daxon had left had been miserable, and today was sinking into new depths. She was not going to watch his climb. She was not going to torture herself, analyzing every step he took, watching for each little slip of his foot, looking for signs of fatigue.

But not watching was just as nerve-racking as watching. Daxon could have, at this point, already fallen to his death, and she wouldn't know. As it turned out, it mattered a hell of a lot whether he was alive somewhere else in the world, even if they were never going to see each other again.

Kendall couldn't shake the restlessness that had been building in her, and it wasn't just fueled by fear. What if Daxon did make it to the top of the mountain? Part of her wanted to see his mastery of this mountain, share it with him. Not watching felt…a bit lonely.

God, she missed him, his deep, easy laugh, the intense attention that he had given to her while they were together. During his stay at the Kalani, the world of his next Pure Adrenaline stunt had been on hold, and oh, what a glorious week it had been. That cliff jumping day was the best of her life. Honestly, the entire week had been.

Damn you, Daxon Miles. It wasn't supposed to be this way. Maybe she should just go ahead and watch instead of spending the next few hours staring at the blank screen, making herself miserable.

A knock on the sliding glass door startled her out of her agonizing.

"Kendall?"

Alana's head appeared through the sliding door. Her friend's gaze slid to the dark TV screen, where Kendall had been staring. Alana quirked up an eyebrow. "Busy?"

Kendall shrugged. "Come join the *not-watching* party."

Alana slid opened the door and stepped in, plopping a bag down next to Kendall. "Sounds fun. I brought refreshments."

She headed for the kitchen, and Kendall peeked inside the bag. A bottle of vodka, a jug of orange juice and a box of doughnuts. Hmm…temporary relief from her current mood?

Alana returned from the kitchen with plates, glasses and napkins. "I figured you could use a little breakfast."

"I'm feeling more than a little pathetic, so I guess day drinking over this guy won't be any worse. Or at least I'll have more fun with it."

"That's the spirit," said Alana, opening the doughnut box.

Kendall groaned as she looked inside. "Oh, yes. Guava."

"I couldn't remember if that was your favorite. Or was it lilikoi? I got both," said Alana, reaching for the vodka. She poured generous shots into each tumbler and topped them off with a few splashes of orange juice. Then she grabbed an old-fashioned doughnut out of the box and held it up. "Cheers."

Kendall tapped hers against Alana's. "Breakfast of champions."

She took a big bite of her doughnut and washed it down with a swig from her glass, wrinkling her nose. The last time she had drank vodka was in college. And even then, it hadn't been in the morning.

Alana took a bite of her doughnut and they sat, staring at the blank screen. "Pretty fun, this not-watching party," said Alana. "Want to know what would be even more fun?"

"A watching party?"

"Yep." Alana smiled brightly.

"Fine." Kendall grumbled. Not watching wasn't really working for her anyway.

She grabbed the remote next to her and flipped on the screen, navigating to the YouTube app. She clicked on Daxon's channel, and there he was, shirtless and beautiful, halfway up Moonlight Buttress. With no ropes. She took a long drink of her screwdriver.

"He's still alive. Cheers to that," said Alana, raising her glass.

Kendall clinked her glass with Alana's and took another gulp.

"Damn, he's hot," said Alana.

She waved off the comment. "I know, I know."

"What? It had to be said."

Yes, he was hot, but she wasn't thinking about how he looked. She was remembering what it felt like to lie on the lounge chair, her back against his hard chest, his arms around her. Or lying in her bed, half-asleep, the scent of him everywhere.

"He's incredible," she muttered.

"Plus he's good in bed and ultra-attentive to you."

"When he's not climbing up a sheer mountain face with no ropes, and it's only in preparation for an even riskier climb."

"There's plenty of time for good sex before that climb."

"This is ridiculous," said Kendall. "No amount of sex is worth watching him willingly take these risks. It's just too much. I watched what living like that did to my mother. I'm not going to do that, too."

"But your parents are still together, aren't they?"

"Yes. That's part of why it's so painful. My mom

loves him so much, so she put herself through that, over and over."

"But your mom's no pushover. I've met her," said Alana, with a smirk. "Wasn't she a firefighter a long time ago, too?"

"She was. She quit when she got pregnant with me. Too risky."

"But your dad didn't quit?"

"Not until his arm was crushed. Not until it became personal."

Alana's expression softened. "I see."

Daxon's progress up the mountain was slow, methodical and confident. He had clearly rehearsed this route many times, because he seemed to know exactly where he was going. His muscles flexed as he dipped his fingers into the chalk pouch by his side and then found his grip to climb the next few inches of rock. It was incredible. Of course millions of subscribers tuned in each time, captivated.

Watching him move, his broad back and shoulder muscles as chiseled as the mountain face, bunching, rippling, his focus solely on the rock in front of him, this was about so much more than money and fame. His comments about existential awakening hadn't just been bullshit. As he moved along the face of the mountain, it was as if a part of him came alive. He was at peace, wearing that same look he'd had that day on the beach. Watching it was both beautiful and incredibly depressing. She had asked him to give this up, this part of him. That twist in her stomach came back, the one that had started during their last night together, when she couldn't decide if she was mad at Daxon for taking this risk or angry with herself for asking him to quit. Was this how her mother had felt about her father, too?

Kendall bit her lip and watched the man in front of her. There was a good chance he would die at a young age, like most free solo climbers, unless he wanted to stop. But he didn't want to. That was his path, and she had to respect that. She just didn't want to watch it play out…except here she was, glued to his YouTube channel, despite everything.

Muscles coiling, toes digging into rock, springing up, sideways, fingers catching on ledges with each full-body extension, he rose, concentrating on every move. He paused, and Kendall stiffened, holding her breath. But then he smiled. Hanging by one hand, shaking out the other, he smiled that cocky smile at the camera, the one that said, *I've got it all under control.* Daxon Miles was in his element, working—

And then it happened.

Just as Daxon shifted his weight, the rock loosened under his foot, and it slipped. As he scrambled for a foothold, she saw it. Fear. It flashed across his face. She had watched his Pure Adrenaline videos embarrassingly often, and never once had she seen fear. He knew it, too; he must have, because he stopped and looked away. Something had gone wrong, but this was a live broadcast, and there was nowhere to go. The camera panned back, waiting. How long would she and the rest of the crew just watch?

"Help him," Kendall whispered.

Alana had grabbed her hand somewhere in the last few seconds. Kendall didn't remember it happening, but now she was squeezing it hard. She could see Daxon's shoulders rising and falling. Were these his last breaths?

The simmering regret boiled over, flooding her thoughts. She should have gone with him. Just spent a few more days together. And she had given it up because she was afraid he would die in one of these stunts.

Except the truth was that despite all her fears, she had never really believed that he could die *today.* In her heart, she had believed he had more time. But what if there was no future? What if she had just spent the last week worrying about him from across the Pacific when she could have been worrying about him while she lay next to him? Or under him…

"I should be there right now," she whispered.

Alana shook her head decidedly. "You absolutely should not. If something goes wrong, you shouldn't be there."

Kendall frowned. "Maybe. But what about all those other moments before the climb? I gave up days with him. I chose to give up what could be my very last chance with him."

Alana nodded slowly.

Tears welled in Kendall's eyes, and she fought to hold them back. "If he falls, it won't hurt any less. Staying back doesn't make me care less. But it does make me regret the time I missed."

"You're falling in love with him," she said softly.

"It's ridiculous," said Kendall with a sniff. "I've only spent two weeks with the man, and they were six months apart."

"But those were two very intense weeks, one of which included plenty of spectacular sex, right? If you convert all those hours together to dating time, that's probably months."

"Still." Kendall glanced at the screen. Daxon was still there, in the same position. She took another drink of her screwdriver, but it wasn't helping the jumble of worries and hopes that was stirring in her mind.

The camera zoomed in slowly, and Kendall and Alana fell silent, their gazes fixed on the TV. Then Daxon started to move, slowly at first, then gaining speed. He found his rhythm, climbing with the same confidence she had seen so many times in his videos. Kendall let out a shuddering sigh. If he made it up the mountain, she was going to…do something. She didn't know exactly what, but she had to let him know that she had made a mistake. That she shouldn't have shut him out, because as it turned out, even a few more days of being with him was more important than her fears. But there was no reason to plan her apology yet. He still had a long way to go before he reached the top. Then, if he made it, she'd figure this out. In the meantime, she was going to need another drink.

Daxon Miles had never once been afraid when he filmed a Pure Adrenaline episode. He prepared everything he did meticulously, and if he felt even a twinge of fear, it was a good indication that he needed more preparation. He choreographed every last move so that when the camera rolled, all he was thinking about was the moment he was living in. It was why Calvin had suggested the video series in the first place and probably the reason behind their runaway success: because when Daxon was in the middle of a stunt, anyone who watched could see that he was on top of the world.

Until today. His foothold slipped. It was the kind of thing that could happen during climbs, the kind of thing he was prepared for, and he had been in more perilous situations before. He had walked himself through this scenario so many times and trained his brain to move on, to focus on his next move. Instead his mind went somewhere new, somewhere that had hit him hard in the gut and twisted into fear, a climber's worst enemy. Instead he thought of Kendall. He had seen her face etched with worry and sadness when he left her cabin.

He never thought about worst-case scenarios on the mountain. Despite the fact that death could be one slip of the foot away, he blocked it out, both as a matter of self-preservation and because embedded in the decision to take the risk was the acceptance of this possibility.

But when his foot slipped, he saw the whole thing through Kendall's eyes. Which was exactly what he shouldn't do, exactly what put him in the most danger. Lin, the camerawoman, was filming his every move, but this time, he couldn't smile at the camera. He turned away and stared at the rock under his hands. He couldn't go back in time and stay in Kendall's cabin instead of walking away. He couldn't change the path he was on. Not yet. But when he got to the top, he could do something about it. What the hell that something was, he didn't know. But he'd figure that out once he wasn't scaring the shit out of Kendall, if she was watching. And his entire team. And himself, if he were completely honest. Because every second he stalled made falling to his death more likely.

It took all of Daxon's mental strength to turn his focus back to the mountain in front of him, and those years of training were powerful. One hand, one heel hook, one toe jam, one extension, a high foot, a weight shift, exactly the way he had done it a dozen times before, until finally he was close. Just three more moves. Two. One. And then he was at the summit. Lin climbed over the last ledge, and Calvin was there, waiting for him. Daxon knew he was supposed to say something to his viewers, but he had no idea what it was. Calvin, probably sensing this, motioned for Lin to pan to him.

"That was incredible," he said, his own face lit up with joy. "Thank you to the over one million viewers who are watching this live, across the world."

Daxon listened as Calvin went through their plans for the next six months, as they prepared for the El Cap free solo. He was supposed to be happy about this. The sponsorships, the ad revenue, the worldwide brand expansion—everything that Calvin had so carefully planned was making a leap forward today. Pure Adrenaline was taking off on a whole new level.

This should've been the ultimate adrenaline rush, his moment of triumph. But instead, it was as if he had fallen into a big empty hole of uncertainty. He didn't care if a million or even a hundred million strangers were watching him right now. There was only one person that he was thinking about, and he was worried that *she* might be watching. Because if she was, he had just scared the hell out of her. Enough so that she'd never want to speak to him again.

Calvin glanced over at him, his mouth in a flat line. Then he turned back to the camera and smiled. "Lin, let's get a look at the views."

When she had stepped away, his friend furrowed his brow, his eyes serious. "You okay, Dax?"

"That slip really threw me off," he muttered.

"I bought you a couple minutes to get your shit together." Calvin tilted his head a little, staring at him. "You've done worse. Are you sure you're feeling okay?"

Slowly, Daxon shook his head. "I'm not sure what the hell I'm feeling."

It seemed an awful lot like regret. He had just successfully pulled off his best climb, but it felt like he had made the biggest mistake of his life.

Before Calvin could pry anymore, Lin turned, heading right back toward them.

Calvin swung his arm around Daxon's shoulder and whispered, "Two more minutes of being the man who just fucking free soloed Moonlight Buttress. Two minutes of being the Daxon Miles who smiles at the camera, the guy everyone tuned in for. Then you can go back to looking like your dog just died."

So Daxon took a deep breath and did it. He stood up and pasted on his camera-ready smile. As Lin came over, he flexed his muscles, just the way he was supposed to. Then he tried to slip away, but Calvin held him in place, and Lin stopped in front of him. There was no escape.

"Daxon, you've just completed the first live free solo climb of Moonlight Buttress in history. What do you want to say to everyone who joined us this afternoon to watch?"

Daxon stared into the camera, but he still couldn't think of a single thing he wanted to say to a million strangers. Even the easy platitudes weren't coming. He needed to talk to Kendall. The silence hung heavily in the air, and Lin was frowning at him. Daxon felt the smile on his face fade. There was only one thing to say, and it definitely wasn't what Calvin and Lin had in mind. As he opened his mouth, he was fully aware that this could be the stupidest thing he had ever done. Still, he did it.

"What I have to say is for one person, and she knows who she is. I'm so, so sorry. I messed up. You deserve someone who listens when you say you've reached your limit." Lin's jaw had dropped, but Daxon didn't stop. "For the rest of you out there, thank you for showing up today and every time before this. This has been Calvin's and Lin's and my dream for a while, and it wouldn't have happened without you." He swallowed and glanced over at Calvin, who wasn't bothering to hide his wary expression. But Daxon looked back into the camera and cleared his throat. "But as of today, I am officially backing out of the free solo El Capitan climb. Back in the middle of the mountain, my foothold gave out, and I'm taking that as a sign that this is no longer what I should be doing."

Lin's mouth was still hanging open, and Daxon wasn't ready to hazard a glance toward Calvin. When his friend finally spoke, his voice was filled with false cheer.

"We'll update you soon on the future of Pure Adrenaline. And thanks to everyone out there who is watching."

CHAPTER FOURTEEN

DAXON KNOCKED ON Kendall's door for the third time. Her windows were open, and he could have sworn he heard a noise from inside when he walked up the path. Kendall hadn't answered any of his attempts to get in touch. After a flurry of desperate emails, Alana had given in and told him that today was Kendall's day off. Which meant she should be here… which had led to the conclusion that she was inside but wasn't answering the door.

Had she seen the video that would forever live in Pure Adrenaline infamy? It would probably be used in future marketing classes around the world as an example of how to lose your sponsorships in less than a minute, flat. But Daxon didn't care. He'd figure that out later, after talking to Kendall. He had tried to pry the answer out of Alana, but she was tight-lipped about almost everything he had asked. She was clearly a good friend to Kendall, so she got props for that, but in this situation, he would have preferred a slightly looser moral code.

Daxon knocked again. “Kendall?”

He was trying not to make a scene, but he had flown in from Utah the day before in preparation, and he knew she didn’t have another day off for almost a week. If he had to, he’d wait, but right now, he was feeling impatient as hell.

“Kendall? Please can we talk?” He glanced around. Most of the neighbors’ windows were open, too, so none of what he said would be a secret. Not that he cared, but this was where she worked. He wanted to respect that…though he wasn’t above a little leveraging. Not at this point.

“I know I messed up badly, sweets. But please give me a chance to talk this through. Just talk. I promise I won’t…” He glanced around, wondering how far to take this in public. “I won’t use other methods of convincing.”

No sounds came from inside, no footsteps, nothing to hang his hopes on. Shit. Daxon swiped a hand over his forehead. Climbing through the open window was tempting…and probably a little crazy. Yeah, that definitely crossed the line, especially since she hadn’t answered his calls this morning. But he could wait her out.

Daxon turned around and sat on the doorstep, running his hand through his hair. He hung his head, trying to summon his patience for the long day ahead of him. She had to leave the place at some point, didn’t she? Did this count as stalking? Shit, if he had to ask himself that question, he was really not in a good place.

Not so long ago, he had sat on this very step after the best day of his entire life, his body filled with giddy hope, grasping at future possibilities. He had managed to quash all of that the moment he left the Kalani to do the thing Kendall wanted absolutely no part of. He knew this conversation would require a hell of a lot of groveling, but he had assumed that she would at least—

"Aaah, the famous Daxon Miles."

Daxon looked up, taking in the flurry of purple hair.

"Alana." He sighed, greeting her with a tilt of his chin.

"I would've come over earlier, but I was waiting to see how much pleading you were willing to do on Kendall's doorstep."

"Glad to provide you with some entertainment." He ran his hand through his hair.

Alana gave him an amused smile. "I just came out to tell you that she went for a run."

Daxon took a deep breath as a mixture of relief and hope coursed through him. Kendall wasn't inside, ignoring him. God, he was a desperate man if that little comment gave him hope. But at this point he didn't care. He just wanted to work out things with Kendall.

"How long ago did she leave?"

Alana shrugged. "Maybe five minutes before you

showed up. She might have heard you if you started calling for her a little earlier. You're pretty loud." She smiled at him like she was enjoying this. His ever-optimistic brain took Alana's smile as yet another reason to hope.

But damn, he had just missed seeing Kendall. He was definitely not going to take *that* as a sign. Hell, no. He was going to find her. The Kalani's peninsula wasn't big, and he was in great shape. He could cover a lot of territory on foot over the next hour and then turn back for her cabin if he didn't find her. But this talk would probably go best if they were somewhere private. And that sure as hell wasn't her doorstep.

Daxon stood up, envisioning the layout of the resort's grounds. "Did you see which way she went?"

"That direction." Alana pointed toward the tip of the peninsula.

It was good news. In that direction, there were only a few trails: one up to the restaurant area, one private trail to Byron Keahi's house, which he could rule out, and one more to the surfing beach where she took him on his first tour of the resort…on the path to the waterfall. Kendall's favorite spot. She told him how to get there on the tour of the Kalani, and he was pretty sure he remembered… *Yes.* That's where he'd try first.

He flashed Alana a smile. "Thanks."

"Don't hurt her," she said, all the mischief fading from her expression. "If you're going after her, you better do it right this time."

"I want to do it right, too," he said softly. Badly. Fuck, he *had* to get this right.

Daxon took a few steps and then glanced down at what he was wearing. The button-down shirt and leather shoes weren't the best choices for running, so he stopped by the red convertible he had rented and tugged off everything but his shorts, throwing them into the trunk. He pulled out a T-shirt and his new pair of running shoes, since his last ones were, in fact, ruined. The challenge was on.

Daxon headed for the resort's main road. As long as she hadn't cut out onto the beach, he'd pass her if she was heading back. The road wound past the pool and the tennis courts, beyond the guest cabins and into the undeveloped tip of the island, where it forked. Damn, he hoped he was choosing the right path. His heart was thumping in his chest, but he wasn't tired. Kendall was close, and he'd finally, finally see her again. Daxon widened his stride as hope burst through him again.

He turned off to the left, up the hill and through the lush forest to the path along the hillside that overlooked the beach. He ran past the spot where he had stood with Kendall, so eager to kiss her that day, and continued to where the path left the beach, veering into the forest. He climbed farther, and then he came to a stop. Another fork. Shit. He laced his hands behind his head, his breaths coming fast, impatience driving his pulse higher. What the hell was he supposed to do now?

"Kendall," he called, his voice tense.

Then he quieted his breath and listened. No answer...but was that a splash of water in the distance? The waterfall. He started for the trail where the sound seemed to be coming from. Thank God. He was getting closer.

Daxon ran toward the waterfall, speeding up. Like everything else he did, he had planned this day meticulously, but this wasn't going according to plan. He had been aching to talk to her for days. He had things he needed to say to her in person. But what if he had miscalculated? What if she returned to her cabin while he was running through the forest? What if she took one look at the red convertible parked outside her cabin and left again? Uncertainty was building inside, churning in his gut. He was heading down a path without a map, and still, he pushed forward.

Finally, the forest trail opened, and there, on a rock beside the river, Daxon saw her. Kendall was facing away from him, leaning back on her arms, dressed in a tank top and running shorts, showing off miles of tanned skin. She had taken her shoes off, and her feet dangled into the stream. Above her, the waterfall cascaded, splashing over the rocks.

Daxon slowed to a stop, drinking her in. He missed her. He missed laughing with her and touching her. He missed her soft, warm body, her breath teasing his skin. Kendall looked relaxed, lost in thought. Goddamn. He was about to disturb her peace, and he hoped like hell she'd think it was worth it. He knew he didn't deserve a second chance with her, but he was a selfish bastard, and he wasn't giving up. But this time was different. This time, he was willing to listen.

So he took a deep breath and started for her.

"Kendall?"

Slowly, she turned around, her eyes wide, so beautiful and full of hope. At that moment, everything he had planned to say disappeared, and he was left with a single thought: *please, please, let me be the one to keep that look on her face.*

What made a risk worth taking? Was the tipping point when the want inside became stronger than the fear? Because Kendall's rising want for Daxon since he had left was spilling over, and now that he had appeared, she was ready to do just about anything to keep him here.

It was this feeling that had kept her from calling him, despite his very public message for her. Hearing that he was backing out of the El Cap climb was an enormous relief, but it didn't solve the more fundamental issue between them: Daxon loved risk, and she didn't know if she could live with that. Right now, she was willing to, but what happened when this almost desperate need to see him dulled? What happened when that itch to push the limits came back? It would, eventually, and they needed a way to deal with this. When he made it to the top of Moonlight Buttress, she promised herself she'd figure out how to deal with this, but so far, she hadn't come up with answers.

And now Daxon had just…shown up. He had found her at her favorite spot, looking so serious and determined, setting her heart into overdrive. A rush of hope and happiness was filling her, leaking out, despite her best efforts. Where was her well-honed sense of wariness when she needed it? Trying to be rational about Daxon was a losing battle.

He walked over and sat down on a rock, so close, facing her. He lifted his hand, like he was reaching for her, but then it dropped. Instead he rested his forearms on his thighs and looked at her. He was so gorgeous, those gray-green eyes stormy, worried and hopeful. But he looked tired, too, and it had been a couple days since he had last shaved. Was he struggling to sleep at night, too?

Lord, she'd missed him.

But she couldn't forget that the last time he'd sat next to her and proposed a future together, it included two free solos. And despite his heartfelt declaration after his climb, she still didn't know what their middle ground looked like. But she had promised herself she wouldn't ask him to quit again.

Daxon ran his hands through his hair and gave her a tentative smile. "So this is your favorite spot?"

She nodded. He looked around at the waterfall and the river that passed by on its way out into the ocean. The trees shaded most of the area, but the early-morning sun filtered through to where they were sitting. There was a rock face beside the waterfall, possibly climbable, but he didn't seem to notice.

"It's beautiful." He was quiet for a long time, hanging his head, as if he was gathering words slowly and carefully. His shoulders rose and fell, his muscles showing through the thin material of his T-shirt. Those muscles were the difference between life and death back on the face of Moonlight Buttress. She wanted to kiss them, worship them, give them her deepest appreciation for the strength that had kept him alive so that they could sit here together at this moment.

"I watched your climb," she said softly.

He blinked up at her, his eyes sad. "Did you?"

The last time she had admitted watching his show, Daxon had given her his signature cocky smile. This time he looked almost pained.

"Well, some of it," she continued, pushing herself to be honest. "I spent the first half staring at the blank TV screen, wondering if you had fallen."

The stricken look on his face almost made her feel sorry for him. Almost.

"I am so sorry, Kendall," he said. His expression was grave. "I didn't really understand this through your eyes until I was up there. Until it was too late."

Kendall swallowed and nodded.

"I should have," he continued. "That day when you jumped from the cliff, you were underwater for so long, long enough for my panic to set in. You came up all smiling and happy, but I couldn't shake that feeling of you being under the water, possibly drowning. The panic didn't just go away. When I was up there on the mountain, there was a moment when I wondered if you were feeling the same thing, magnified. The idea that I made you go through that, not just for seconds but for the hours of that climb—I can't do that anymore."

She shook her head. "You can't quit for me. I saw the way you looked at me when I told you not to climb that last day. Even if you don't resent it now, you will in the future."

He ran a hand through his hair and sighed. "I've been thinking about that a lot. It's possible that I'll feel that way, even if I don't think it will happen now. But is that really enough to stop us? It's also possible that I'll have a heart attack tomorrow. Maybe you will. We can't predict all the things that could go wrong, and that's the reason you and I should push on. If something does happen to you, if you leave me—anything—the happiness of being with you, even for a little while, is worth all the heartbreak I'd feel."

Kendall swallowed the lump in her throat. She wanted this so badly. Should she take the risk and believe in them?

"I'm falling in love with you," he said, his voice rough. "I'm not sure how we'll work everything out.

All I know is that I'm willing to listen and make compromises so that I don't hurt you like that again."

Kendall's heart was so full it was bursting. "I'm willing to compromise, too."

She turned to face him and rested her hand on his cheek. The bristly scruff on his jaw felt different, but his lips were the same as she pressed her mouth against his. Then she met his gaze. "There was a moment when you slipped, and then you stopped and looked away from the camera."

Daxon pulled back, cringing. "You saw that part?"

She nodded and kissed him again. "All I could think about was that if you fell, I would have spent the rest of my life regretting that I gave up my last chance to see you. I regretted that I turned down your offer to come. Even though I was mad that you asked, that was nothing compared to the way that I felt when I thought you might fall."

"I promise I won't do that again," he said quickly. Then he blinked at her, his eyes wide. "Will you give us a chance to do this right? Try to work something out?"

"I want that," she said. "So much."

When Daxon reached for her this time, there was no hesitation. He lifted her onto his lap so she straddled him, and he wrapped his arms around her, pulling her against him. She pressed her face into his neck, and his skin tasted of salt and of him. She found his mouth, hungry, waiting for her. The kiss was slow, filled with longing and regret and something else. Was it love? Whatever it was, she felt it deep inside.

"Calvin must be angry as hell at you," she whispered.

Daxon shrugged. "He was at first, but now he has a bunch of other ideas, ways we could still keep the Pure Adrenaline brand alive. He even had this crazy idea that we should start something called Adrenaline Vacations, where I scout out low-consequence thrills, make a video and set up a vacation tour. I would do the promo video and maybe make a guest appearance, but the rest of it we'd hire out. I thought it was a pretty good idea, but I didn't want to say yes to anything until I talk to you first."

It was almost too much to take in. His words from the top of Moonlight Buttress weren't just adrenaline-fueled promises. He was making real changes.

"I don't want you to give up climbing," she said. "It's just these climbs with no ropes, or the jumping out of airplanes with no parachute—that kind of danger level."

He nodded. "I've been thinking I'll try some deep-water soloing."

She wrinkled her brow. "Sounds a lot like free soloing."

"But without the high stakes," he said, pulling her closer. "It's free soloing over deep water—like that cliff jumping area we visited. It means all of the joy of free soloing and much less worry for you. Hawaii has a lot of potential deep-water soloing sites to explore. More cliffs you can jump from, too." His soft chuckle sent a flutter of desire through her. "I'm willing to listen to your limits. I know we can work this out, Kendall."

For the first time, she truly let herself believe it.

She kissed him again. "Are we falling in love?"

A smile spread across Daxon's face as he nodded. "This is only the beginning, sweets."

He rested his big warm hands on her thighs. It wasn't a come-on, though it seemed impossible to be near him without an undercurrent of sex flowing between them. They were simply there on a rock next to the river, his skin on hers, the sounds of their breathing and the sounds of the water all coming together to make something more than the sum of these parts. She rested her hand on the back of his neck and played with the overgrown locks that curled at the ends, sun-bleached and carefree.

He smiled a lazy smile at her, like they had all the time in the world. "Do you like it here at the Kalani, making people's wishes come true?"

Kendall laughed. "I'm not usually at the front lines of the wish fulfillment business. I'm more like support staff."

"Pretty much the best working conditions I've ever seen," he said, giving her a tight squeeze. "Besides the face of a mountain, of course."

"Of course."

"You want to stay here, don't you?" His hands

had come to a stop on her thighs, the pressure of them almost possessive, and he had that intense look, like there was nothing more important in the world than her.

She nodded. "This is my dream job, and I just started it."

"I could get a place close by." He waggled his eyebrows and lowered his voice. "So I can focus on exploring the island's best attraction more intimately."

She gave a snort of laughter. "That's the line you're giving me? You're going to need to up your game, champ."

Daxon tickled her until she scooted away. "I'm working on it, sweets. And I'm going to devote as much time as I need to pleasing you."

Kendall shifted back onto his lap. It felt so good to hold him close again…and it would feel even better to be naked together. "So what have you been doing since the climb?"

He shrugged. "Packing up, putting my trailer in storage, looking at my Photoshop porn of you…"

She raised an eyebrow.

"Kidding." His eyes glittered with amusement. He was teasing her, but she could play that game, too.

"By the way, did you know there's a whole catalog of erotic fan fiction starring you?" she said, biting her lip trying not to laugh.

He blinked. Clearly the answer was no. But he recovered quickly. "Did you read it?"

"Hell, yes."

She couldn't suppress her laughter anymore, and neither could he. She buried her face in his neck, breathing him in, letting the rush of pure joy run through her.

"I could do this forever, Kendall," he whispered into her hair. "Just you and me."

* * * * *

COMING SOON!

We really hope you enjoyed reading this book. If you're looking for more romance, be sure to head to the shops when new books are available on

Thursday 26th June

To see which titles are coming soon, please visit

millsandboon.co.uk/nextmonth